A Spring for Spears

The Wolf Song Saga

Book One

Katie Cross

Derek Alan Siddoway

DEDICATION

To Evee:
Don't be afraid to run ahead of the pack.
—Derek

To my readers.
May Astrid's world inspire you as much as Bianca's.
—Katie

Vocabulary List

Bannu: A Skolvarg term of endearment or affection.

Berzar: Member of the Thyrling King's personal guard.

Druzar: Thyrling word for a warrior or guard.

Fylga: Spirit body; Manifestation of the soul in the spirit realm.

Grimstens: Mountain range to the north.

Jaegar: The Thyrling nobility.

Kerys: A kingdom on the coast to the west of Ochland

Lake Vyla: A large lake with no outlet situated between the Stallofells and Little Stallofells. Marks the northern border of Ochland.

Nistlefolk: Race of fae who are trading partners with the Skolvarg.

Ochland: The country south of the Wolfmoors and Thyrden, separated by the Stallofells mountain range.

Omegr: Outcast, lesser, non-contributor.

Shine: Curse word.

The Slidrfalls: A series of impassable waterfalls and cliffs splitting the upper and lower Auroran River

Stallofells: The mountain range to the south of the Wolfmoors, inhabited by a race of giants called Stallogres.

Thyrden: The western kingdom of the Thyrlings ruled by King Oskar.

Tyrvik: The capital of Thyrden

Ulfsark: Skolvarg warriors who ride the giant Amarok wolves.

Vigard: Name of all the land.

Wolfmoors: The plains and rolling hills where the Skolvarg live.

Wolfwood: The giant forest to the east of the Wolfmoors where the Skolvarg winter. Also a home of the Nistlefolk.

The Seasons (also known as the Greater Spirits)

Spirit of Winter: Margu - Blue
Spirit of Spring: Radi - Green
Spirit of Summer: Vaesta - Yellow
Spirit of Autumn: Anike - Red

ONE

A spear whistled past Astrid's ear, glancing so close to the fragile skin that the breeze stirred her hair.

Before her opponent, Torva, could recover, Astrid ducked into a roll and sprang back to her feet, just inside Torva's spear defenses. Torva sneered. Her freckles scrunched together, red hair spiraled around her face in frizzy strands half-soaked with sweat.

Astrid tsked.

Torva shouted and attacked again.

Quick as a lynx, Astrid clamped a hand around the incoming spear, twisted it out of Torva's grip, and earned a blow to the chin in the process. Torva lumbered to the side in a poor attempt to get her feet under her again, while Astrid staggered back, jerking the spear from Torva's paw-like hands. She shook her head to clear the pain radiating through her jaw. Her fingers tightened around Torva's now-claimed spear.

Take that, bully, she thought.

They circled each other for several moments, chests heaving, eyes locked. Astrid wiped away strands of hair that had fallen out of her braid.

She smirked. "Sloppy, sloppy, Torva," she sang. "You let me get your spear."

Astrid twirled the stolen spear around her back, then snapped it into guard in front of her.

"I'll step on you, runt," Torva snarled. "Then you'll break in half like the little thing you are. You're not even a whole Skolvarg. You're half-sized."

Around the sparring ring, other warriors snickered or rolled their eyes. Torva's rage-scrunched face looked like an ogre's. She advanced with a stomp, cracked her thick knuckles, and rolled her shoulders. There had to be Stallogre blood somewhere in her lineage. Astrid had always been small, but not short enough to throw off her comprehension of an opponent's size.

"Stop dancing around and fight me like a real Skolvarg," Torva hissed.

"I *am* fighting like a Skolvarg," Astrid snapped. She backed away, spear held low, a wary gaze on Torva's advancing form. "You're the one lumbering around like an ogre."

Torva's face turned red as she bellowed and charged. The speed of Torva's assault startled Astrid—she didn't know Torva could move that fast. Astrid swung the shaft of the spear around at the last moment.

Being Torva's spear, the ogre-like girl wouldn't want to snap it in half. Torva would be forced to lessen the intensity of the attack at the last moment to protect her own gear. But Astrid miscalculated Torva's desire for blood—she charged with full strength anyway. Astrid managed to lift the spear. It struck Torva on the shoulder, but glanced off. Torva wrapped her arms around Astrid and drove her hard into the ground.

All the air fled Astrid's chest. Caught between Astrid and Torva's descending bulk, the spear shaft cracked. A rock jabbed into Astrid's ribs, slicing skin under her shirt. She gasped from pain and lack of air.

Torva shoved herself to her feet, looming over Astrid like one of the giant, grizzled gray bears that followed the streams in the spring.

This time, Torva smirked.

"Not so quick after all, *Astrid.*" Torva always drawled the vowels in an annoying, brutish way. "You'd think someone as little as you would at least be quick. Then again, you've always been a disappointment."

Astrid gasped through frozen lungs, wheezing out an incomprehensible retort. Torva rolled her eyes, then nudged Astrid not-so-gently in the ribs with her foot.

"Try again, *omegr.*"

Shock rippled through Astrid. *Omegr* was the highest insult possible in their Skolvarg tribe. Rage fueled her recovery. She forced her lungs to take the air back in.

"I said," Astrid wheezed, "you fight like an ogre."

Astrid's foot slammed into Torva's thigh. Torva dropped to one knee, but her sturdy bones only bought Astrid a few seconds. Just enough to snatch the top half of the spear off the ground and spring back to her feet before Torva had her balance again.

Astrid fought off a grimace. Her ribs ached. One of them might be broken. As a Skolvarg, she healed faster than other folk, but it would still hurt like shine for a few hours anyway. Her breath came in shallow gulps.

Torva staggered as she gained her feet and picked up a discarded shield from earlier in the fight. The rounded edges looked more like a buckler, except for points on the bottom and both sides. She advanced slowly, wiping the back of her mouth with a meaty hand. Astrid took a step back for each step forward.

"At least I hear the Wolf Song, Astrid. Do you?" Torva laughed a grating sound, like wood pieces groaning together. "Of course you don't. I'm not a tiny, pathetic freak like you.

The wolves want me, not you. You'll never be an Ulfsark. A sheep doesn't run with the wolves."

Astrid's control slipped away. Just like that— quick as the snap of two fingers—and Torva gained control over the fight. Because the *one* thing Astrid couldn't defend herself on was the truth. The ragged, undeniable truth.

She didn't hear the Wolf Song.

Instead of ignoring the taunt the way she usually did, Astrid let her rage come forward. She didn't send it back, didn't deal with it later. She felt it *now*. It flowed to the front of her mind like a rush of fire.

Blood boiling, Astrid charged.

Torva absorbed Astrid's ramming shoulder with her shield, the way Astrid knew she would. The pain sent hot spikes all the way down her spine and through her already sensitive ribs. Astrid pushed through it, because Torva would have expected her to abandon the charge. She didn't. She pressed on.

Torva grunted as she stepped back, gained footing again. Astrid shoved, using all her fury to propel her. Torva stumbled once, twice, then dug her toes into the ground and planted herself. Astrid's advance halted. Torva caught Astrid low with the shield, and heaved, sending Astrid flying overhead.

Astrid landed hard on the cold, spring earth. The half-spear clattered to the ground next to her. She panted as she tried to pull her thoughts together. The pain left her too scattered. Her shoulder ached. Her ribs blossomed with agony at every breath. Her body settled into something that tasted like misery.

Meanwhile, the chants and jeers of the other Skolvarg had settled into a low hum. Torva flashed a gaping, toothy grin and beckoned with a curl of her fingers for more. Astrid tensed in anticipation of leaping back to her feet. Her body refused to respond. Somehow. Somehow she'd find the fight in her again.

A commanding voice rang across the circle.

"*Enough!*"

Two younger Skolvarg grabbed Astrid and heaved her off the ground. Despite the pain rocketing through her ribs, she struggled against them until a woman appeared in front of her.

Huntress Vanna.

Dressed in fighting leathers, and with her hands resting on her hips, Huntress Vanna left no room for question. The fight was over. She wouldn't scold either of them—sometimes things got heated in the sparring ring—but her blatant disapproval didn't make Astrid feel any better. Nor did the sidelong glances from the rest of the Skolvarg, all aimed at her. Whether this fight began because Astrid defended two younger girls or not didn't matter. Torva had played the trump card of Astrid's failure to hear the Wolf Song and none of them would forget it. Maybe Torva was right.

Maybe she didn't belong here.

The hands gripping her arms relaxed. Astrid shook the two young girls off. "Let me go."

The girls faded back. Astrid turned around to face Huntress Vanna. Heat flooded Astrid's shoulder from the failed charge. Her nostrils flared as she tried to breathe through the spasms of pain that followed. Her right side felt like a single massive bruise from the rock, and her elbow hurt from being thrown.

"Grasp hands and leave the ill feelings here," Vanna commanded, then eyed both of them. Her gaze lingered a breath longer on Astrid.

Astrid hesitated, then stuck out her hand first. With a scowl, Torva accepted, and they broke touch the second they could. Astrid shuffled back, gaze dropped. Embarrassment burned hot in her throat.

"Are we settled?" Vanna murmured. The creak of her

leather as she folded her arms across her chest was the only sound in the field.

Torva nodded. "Yes, Huntress."

"Yes, Huntress," Astrid said.

"Go clean yourselves up."

Astrid curled her hands into fists as Torva stomped away, her half-grown wolf, Syndr, trotting at her side. The two of them together sent a deep stab of jealousy through Astrid. She kept her gaze even, her face flat. Still, she couldn't stop watching. Torva's words echoed through her mind like an empty cavern. *You'll never be an Ulfsark. I hear the Wolf Song. Do you?*

No, Astrid thought helplessly, *and I don't know why.*

When the field fell empty, and the dying light of day a kiss on the horizon, Vanna turned to Astrid. For some reason, the Huntress had stayed behind. She hadn't told Astrid to wait, either, but the implication was heavy enough to keep Astrid rooted to the spot.

"I had thought name-calling above you," Vanna drawled. "Ogre? Even if it's true, it's not all that original."

Astrid motioned to what had once been a ring of Skolvarg, now little more than an emptying field.

"It was in the ring."

"That doesn't make it advisable."

"So Torva can call me a runt? An omegr."

Vanna frowned. "I didn't say I approved of that either."

"But you didn't stay behind to scold Torva."

"Because she didn't stay behind. You did. Now, what does that mean?"

A building protest died on Astrid's lips. Vanna had always been harder on her. Called on her more. Pushed her harder. Was it her skill in the ring? No, other Skolvarg were more talented than her, even if Astrid had proven herself in the fights as best she could. Short stature and lean frame notwithstanding.

Other Skolvarg were mightier than her, yet Vanna didn't pull *them* aside for name-calling.

"Nothing yet?" Vanna asked, head canted slightly to the side. Her dark hair fell to a braid on her right shoulder. She lifted an eyebrow, which softened her piercing eyes. Vanna didn't need to say the words *Wolf Song* for Astrid to know exactly what she meant.

Shame burned deep when Astrid licked her lips.

"No."

Vanna arched a second delicate, curved eyebrow. As usual, she gave no response. Just a light bob of her head—not even a full nod—and turned to leave. Vanna had always been graceful. Her fine-boned face and gentle hands were deceiving. She didn't look like she'd be hard to win against, yet Vanna always surprised Astrid.

Vanna stopped and said over her shoulder, "What would your parents say about that taunting?"

Astrid's reply stuttered to a stop. She clamped her mouth shut, at a loss. Her parents had been dead for years. She'd like to pretend she didn't know what her fierce mother and quiet father would say, but she did.

"They'd say to fight with weapons, not words," Astrid muttered.

Vanna's brow rose in question, then dropped again. "Exactly. Torva may have started it, but I expected better from you, that's all."

"I always show up," Astrid cried. "I train harder than anyone. Torva and I fought because she was tormenting the younger girls with her spear. How is that right?"

"She will be dealt with."

"You expect more from me than the rest. Is it because I'm

small? Because I haven't heard the Wolf Song from one of our wolf pups so we can bond and I can be an Ulfsark too?"

"Yes," Vanna said simply.

The daughter of Hildr the Pack Leader, unable to even find an Amarok wolf willing to bond with her. Astrid shook her head at the utter disparity. It didn't make sense, not in any case.

The absence of the Wolf Song was never supposed to happen for someone like her, the daughter of a famous Ulfsark. As far as Astrid knew, it had never happened to anyone in her family who desired it, until her.

Vanna focused her gaze on the camp not far away. Fires winked at the edge of the Wolfwood and the bough of the pines darkened with the lowering sun. The Huntress gave no further explanation before she walked away. Astrid hissed in pain again.

Several moments of long thought later, Astrid grabbed the remnants of Torva's spear. She jammed it into the ground over and over until her injuries forced her to stop. Once her frustration settled, she dropped to her knees with a grunt. Her shoulder and ribs still burned in the aftermath but not as bad. She'd be fine in a few days.

Losing to Torva wasn't the worst thing to happen. It had happened before. It would probably happen again. Astrid was no match for Torva's brawny size. Still, losing left a metallic taste in her mouth. Almost as bad as the taste of Vanna admitting that she was harder on Astrid because she couldn't hear the Wolf Song. What rankled Astrid the most was that Torva walked away from this fight *with a wolf.*

That hulking bully had a bond with an Amarok wolf and Astrid didn't.

It wasn't right.

Astrid gazed into the settling darkness, the same taunting question circling in her mind:

What is wrong with me?

Two

Astrid's frustration carried her to the outskirts of the Skolvarg camp, where the eaves of the Wolfwood forest gave way to the open, rolling hills of the west. Now that spring had come, her Skolvarg tribe would venture farther into the wide spaces called the Wolfmoors.

The Wolfmoors were infamous for fierce predators and unpredictable weather. Such a vast expanse of hilly plains stretched all the way south to the mountains known as the Stallofells, which were weeks away when riding one of their giant Amarok wolves. The Wolfmoors ran west to the kingdom of Thyrden, east to the Wolfwood, and north into even wilder forests and mountains where the Skolvarg did not go.

If you didn't know where you were going, it didn't take much to get lost.

As the clutch of winter ebbed, the Skolvarg tribes moved back into the Wolfmoors to hunt the bountiful game and prepare for trading season in the fall. The call to the hunt would be issued soon now that spring began her return.

The shift in season thrilled every Skolvarg—it was born

into their bones. The Amarok wolves and their riders, together known as the Ulfsark, led each hunt. Very few animals escaped a fully-grown wolf the size of a horse, especially when paired with the hunting prowess of a Skolvarg.

For a Skolvarg with no wolf like Astrid . . . well, the hunting season wasn't quite as exciting.

Astrid stopped walking a long bowshot from camp. She sat on a rock jutting out of the ground, part of a low-rolling hill that led down to the yurts. Her knees stuck in the air as she braced her forearms on top.

Finally, her body relaxed.

The aftermath of the fight melted away. Astrid turned her mind from it by thinking of the younger girls that had hidden out of sight while the fight unfolded. Very young. Ten, if that, to Torva and Astrid's nineteen years. No doubt they'd enjoyed seeing Torva livid as a raging bull, nearly defeated.

Nearly.

Her mind skipped over the golden sunlight that shone from the edge of the sky. It rested on top of just-green grasses that poked through last year's yellowed carpet.

Frightening or not, the Wolfmoors had their own beauty. An admiration for their wild state, their unapologetic ferocity, caused a shiver. Verdant grass meandered out of last year's golden turf in elegant strands, already longer than a person's finger, in spite of the early season.

Deer and giant elk, just coming out of winter's gauntness, spotted the plains even this close to the camps, though they would be quick to flee if they caught sight or scent of an Amarok wolf approaching. Through the years, the males used their sweeping antlers to carve a sort of tunnel system through the hedges and oak brambles clinging to the bottoms of the valleys and dales. Poisonous flowers and barbs longer than her hand lined the hedges.

Commotion stirred in the camp below. She glanced down.

A pack of wolf-mounted Ulfsark loped in from a hunt or patrol. Far enough away to be unrecognized individually, she watched the wolves and their riders pad back into camp. They brought several carcasses with them.

There were only six Ulfsarks in her tribe, but each of their Amarok displayed a variety of hues. The leading wolf, an all-black male, was followed by a tan female. Two light grays, a reddish-and-cream-colored, and a white wolf brought up the rear.

All were easily the size of the horses used for farming and warring by Thyrden and the other kingdoms south of the Stallofells. Astrid had only seen a horse once in her life, but the skittish creature darting around on its thin, twig-like legs hadn't impressed her.

Why would anyone want to ride on something so fragile? Especially into a battle. It seemed safer and more effective to just remain on the ground.

When a pack of Ulfsark descended on an enemy, now that was a different matter.

Fierce pride for the Ulfsark, immediately followed by a familiar longing, gripped Astrid as the wolves and Skolvarg passed by below. Shaking her head, she shoved away the disappointment of losing to Torva and focused on her next task.

Telling her uncle.

Careful to avoid anyone else, Astrid skirted the edge of the yurts that made up the wide camp circle. Eventually, she reached the hut belonging to her and her uncle, Rolf. The shadow of an enormous gray Amarok, head between his paws fast asleep, greeted her at the yurt's entrance.

Atka.

Atka had been her mother's wolf, one of the largest and

fiercest Amarok wolves in his day. Big enough to take down a bull moose all by himself. These days, Atka didn't do much but sleep. He rose only to pad off alone and hunt for himself. He'd been that way since Astrid's mother, Hildr, his Skolvarg rider, had died of a sickness six years earlier.

Sighing, Astrid crouched down and laid a hand between his ears, which perked up. Atka didn't open his eyes. She gently scratched behind his ears, her mind drifting back to the days when she could run underneath his legs and climb him like a furry gray tree.

Those days were long gone now.

As a grown woman, she wasn't able to climb on Atka and ride the wolf as her mother had done. The sacred bond Atka had shared with her mother prohibited anyone else from riding him to hunt or battle. Atka might be calm and docile, but anyone trying to claim the wolf for their own would risk their life. Such was the life of an Amarok wolf who outlived their Skolvarg.

"Niece," called a voice. "You're back?"

Astrid startled out of her thoughts. Atka's ears perked up. Her uncle grabbed her hand, pulled her to her feet, and wrapped her in a hug.

"I didn't expect you back from the ring yet."

"Let's just say it didn't go the way I wanted," she mumbled.

"Tell me."

Like always, he listened quietly, expression neutral. Astrid had participated in six Wolf Songs since she'd reached twelve. The Wolf Song came every springtime, with the new pups. Teenaged Skolvarg would hear the Wolf Song in a dream and be chosen by the Amarok wolf pups. With that bonding, they became an Ulfsark—a fighting pair.

"You must learn to control that temper of yours," Rolf said. He sat down next to Astrid and put an arm around her. Astrid leaned over and rested her head on Rolf's shoulder.

"I will."

"I know."

His flimsy shirt carried a soil-like scent. Rolf always smelled like mud in the spring, when he scrounged for early blooming herbs. All year, he carried roots and flowers in pouches around his waist.

"This year, I have a good feeling you'll hear something."

He'd said that last year but it had been the same as the others: the wolf spirit hadn't visited her dreams and none of the pups had chosen her to bond with them. After six failed attempts, other members of the tribe really started to talk. Incidents like the one with Torva were becoming more and more common.

Every year for the last six years, Astrid had waited. Each spring, she strained to hear or feel *something*. While her friends paired off with an Amarok, she remained behind. No song. No bond. No drive to find *her* wolf. Her other half.

Every year, nothing happened.

There were others like her, of course. Not every Skolvarg claimed a wolf. Not everyone wanted to be an Ulfsark and shoulder the warrior's burden to protect and provide for their tribe. Those who didn't want to hear the Wolf Song rarely did. As if the spirits could give the power to those who craved it.

Except Astrid.

Rarely did a girl with Astrid's drive and desire go wanting, however. A daughter of a legendary Ulfsark Pack Leader would be an immediate choice for any Amarok. Or should have been, by any account. The fact that she remained alone lingered like a bad feeling over the whole tribe. Though the Skolvarg never said it, Astrid knew what they thought.

Why did none of the young wolves want her?

"Do we need meat?" Astrid asked as she straightened away from her uncle's hold. "I can go hunting."

"No, the feast is tomorrow."

Astrid rolled her eyes with a groan. She'd forgotten about the feast with the Thyrlings.

"I don't want to go."

"Ah, come now, little wolf," he said with a booming laugh. "We must welcome and accept peace with our neighbors. Help me with the fire."

His face had become a vague silhouette in the night. He pulled away, reached toward a small pile of dried twigs and pinecones. Astrid leaned toward the fire pit in the middle of their hut and blew gently. A hint of bright crimson grew along a coal near the bottom. She accepted the dried orange pine needles Rolf handed her way and set them on top of the coal.

"I don't want to go either," he admitted. "Arguably, no Skolvarg wants to go to the feast, but we must. Maybe you can learn . . . a more diplomacy-based approach to keeping peace than a physical one."

Astrid's nostrils flared and she fought off a wince from her ribs. He gently meant to say that being an Ulfsark might not be her path. He'd been dropping those hints more and more often over the past year. She may have to learn to serve as a Skolvarg by other means. Talking to the nasty Thyrlings that they had just ended a years-long war with didn't appeal to her at all.

If she had to choose, she'd rather take another beating from Torva.

"You've just got to be patient enough to discover your purpose," he continued, oblivious to her pained expression. "That is a lesson your mother never really learned: there are things that, no matter how strong and powerful we become, are always—"

"—out of our control," Astrid finished.

Rolf chuckled and ruffled her hair, messing up the braids that held it back for the sparring.

"Now get some sleep. In the morning, we need more kindling and, if you can find them, some of those early spring mushrooms. They're good for wounds."

THREE

"Spotted, gray-topped mushrooms," Rolf said the next morning. "Yellow sap from the long-needled pine tree starts, if you can find it, as much as you can. And if you're lucky, some fresh bittergrass. Do you remember what it looks like?"

Her nose wrinkled. Bitter was an understatement once you picked it.

"I remember."

His smile widened. "Then be safe."

Relieved to be away, Astrid set off into the Wolfwood forest. The sun shone from a clear blue sky as she disappeared into the trees. It was only the fourth month of the year but the warmth felt more like a day in high summer.

She headed north, keeping the forest in her sight, eager to avoid Torva and the rest of the Ulfsark as they left for another hunt in the Wolfmoors.

Before long, she'd covered a handful of miles and found herself at the edge of a band of rocks that formed a short cliff. At the base, a pool had formed from the melting snow. Astrid found two of the plants Rolf had requested and carefully picked and stored them in her pouch.

She gazed around, then headed up the side of a nearby hill. At the top, she studied the distant view of the Wolfmoors. Without a wolf to ride, the plains felt vast eternities away, yet the plains were all she wanted.

A nudge to go east tugged at her again. Astrid obeyed. She could find the herbs wherever she went, so there was no reason not to listen to her instinct. Or was it something else pulling her there?

After a few minutes, she broke into a slow, steady jog. Eventually, a thick grove of pine trees appeared, stretched across two knolls directly before her. Within a bowshot of the pine grove, Astrid slowed her run to a walk.

She gasped, a stitch in her side. Her bruised ribs had mostly healed overnight, but the muscles around them still twinged every now and then. The pain in her elbow was gone, and her wound had sealed.

Sweat trickled down her face and her legs thrummed like a bowstring as she stopped just outside the copse of pines. Once there, an inexplicable trickle of cold slipped down Astrid's back.

Don't go in there.

Astrid took a step back at the unexpected, forceful thought, then stopped. She couldn't explain the reason why venturing into that thicket would be a bad idea, but she felt it. In direct opposition to the thought, the now-familiar pull urged her toward the pine grove all the same.

A wolf howled behind her and caused the nape of her neck to tingle. Wild Amarok wolves roamed the Wolfmoors and Wolfwood forest. While surprisingly docile under the eaves of the Wolfwood when they littered their whelps, the Amarok were still giant, wild creatures.

On instinct, Astrid crouched. The howl rose through the

pines again, forlorn and pleading. The hair on the back of her neck rose. Unlikely that she'd stumbled into an Amarok pack. All of them would have answered the lone, distant call. Nor did there seem to be any wolves within hearing distance to answer back.

For minutes, she waited. She heard no more howls, no indication that any living creatures were nearby. Yet she felt certain the wolf howl had come from inside the cluster of pines.

But that's how it was in the forest—everything went quiet right before it tried to eat you.

Or was she imagining this?

What if the wolf was injured? What if it needed help? Helping an injured Amarok would either be the last thing she did—or the *best* thing she did. Amaroks were intelligent. If she could help an unbonded Amarok, she might earn its trust. Other wolves existed, of course. Smaller ones, but they were rarely seen and hardly noteworthy in comparison. They knew the king of the forest, and it wasn't them.

What if this was the chance Rolf had been preaching to her to be patient for all these years?

Despite her better sense, her heart, stretching and pulling and yearning to become Ulfsark, pulled her right into the pine grove.

She stumbled through the trees, moving with none of the grace or silence she'd been taught. Branches, rocks, they were all just things keeping her from finding her wolf. She darted as fast as she could, leaping over fallen trees, crawling under tangles of branches. Every effort brought her closer to the soul of the grove and sent her heart hammering in her chest.

This could be *her* wolf.

Another howl sounded just ahead and she skidded to a stop. Bumps rose on her arms. She stood so close that the eerie sound reverberated through her bones. The wolf had to be just past the next bunch of branches.

Astrid shoved through them, heedless of the thorny undergrowth. Growling, she forced herself through, ignoring the cuts and grasping brambles. With a last burst of effort, she stumbled, then rolled out of the other side, expecting to find an injured wolf awaiting her.

Twigs and leaves stuck in her hair as she bounced back to her feet. Mud and blood smeared her face as she cast about wildly, looking for the wolf she knew had to be close.

There was no wolf.

But neither was she alone.

FOUR

Astrid froze. Her hand gripped her knife handle so tight
it throbbed.

Life in the Wolfmoors had exposed her to a
variety of dangerous creatures—gray bears, forest cats, snow
wolverines, enraged giant elk in the rut, and great-horned
bison, to name a few. Yet, she'd never seen or heard whispers of
anything that matched the . . . *thing* . . . before her.

The animal resembled a forest cat, but with twice the
muscle. Claws and teeth gleamed from short, charcoal-hued
fur. An eyeless, broad, triangular head studied her, then
released a menacing hiss through rows of long, needle-like
teeth. The space between furry ear tufts and a snub nose was
nothing but ashen fur.

Yet the beast knew she was there, Astrid had no doubt.

It hissed again, claws the size of a full-grown bear gouging
the ground as it stalked closer. She didn't move or breathe as
she quickly sped through her limited options.

Should she shout? Without it seeing her, maybe she could
fool the monster into believing she was big and strong. Sound
would definitely draw it closer, faster. Fighting would be fool-

ish. Even fully armored with a spear and a shield, Astrid didn't like her odds. Why hadn't she strung her bow before entering the glade?

A furious, high-pitched growl built in the monster's chest, rising to a scream that cut through the trees like an icy northern wind. The beast paced closer, fangs bared.

Astrid's gaze darted to her left. A tree, large enough to climb, was only a few steps away. With one eye on the cat, she quietly drew both of her knives and began to back toward the tree.

The beast matched her every step.

If it jumped, it could be on her in a single leap, assuming it knew exactly where she was. Where were its eyes? Her breath rattled from her shaking body as she kept in time with the cat. Nine steps to go. It snarled, teeth gleaming. A yowl came from the back of its throat.

Six steps.

She'd almost reached the tree.

Screaming, the monster swatted a claw through the space between them. The breeze of it swept across her, followed by the putrid smell of its breath. Astrid reared back, then threw a knife at the beast's triangular head. It clattered off the wide, flat skull, but Astrid had already turned and leaped for the tree.

She swung her legs up, caught a branch, and scrambled higher. Rough bark dug into her thighs, but she ignored that.

Behind her, the cat beat a hot pursuit. Claws snagged the tree trunk, just missing her left ankle. Astrid yipped and pushed higher. The cat snarled, and white hot pain flashed across the back of her leg as it flayed her calf open. Her left leg gave out beneath her, jerking her down. With a shout, she dug her fingers into the bark and held herself to the trunk.

One quick glance down confirmed her fear: the ashen cat climbed after her.

With two arms and one leg, Astrid dragged herself up the tree again. The thick old pine was straight as an arrow and dozens of feet tall with plenty of branches. Astrid focused on grabbing the next one, then the next. She didn't—couldn't —think about what would happen when she reached the top.

After hefting herself up five more branches, the thick tree limbs grew smaller. Her weight near the spindly top made the tree sway. Astrid risked a brief moment to glance below. The cat was half its body length below her. As if it knew she watched, its head tipped back to look up at her. The monster hissed.

Astrid growled back, teeth clenched in pain.

She raised her left leg and craned her head far enough at an angle to find a long cut across the back of her calf. Crimson stained her skin and her foot, along with white and a weird yellow color. The movement caused several drops of blood to fall on the monster. A long, purple tongue snaked out and caught one drop. Astrid shivered and climbed again, urgency flooding her with borrowed strength.

One hand, another. Drag foot. One hand, another. Drag foot. The sound of falling bark, shredded by claws like knives, clattered below.

As the tree swayed, and one branch snapped beneath her weight, she desperately clung to the trunk. She rushed onto a branch, hoped it would hold her weight, and drew her remaining knife. If she was going to die, she would die fighting to the last. This nightmare cat wouldn't get an easy meal out of her.

The monster screamed again, louder and longer, like iron drawn across stone. Astrid pressed her sap-covered, sliver-filled palms to her ears. The painful sound finally stopped.

A *thud* followed.

Astrid peered down, then startled. The monster was gone.

No, wait! She spotted a soot-colored form through the branches below. The cat lay at the base of the tree.

Had . . . had it fallen?

How?

Hadn't it just been screaming at her?

Astrid blinked and gazed around. Only the same forest awaited. She paused, her heart slowing. Did she imagine this? No. The cat definitely lay on the ground.

Minutes later, the ashen cat still hadn't moved. The angle of its head told her it wasn't simply playing dead, either. It appeared to be snapped unnaturally to the side. The cat couldn't have fallen out of the tree, because its claws had been too far embedded in the trunk.

"The beast is dead," trilled an unexpected, feminine voice. "You can come down now, *bannu*."

Astrid almost fell out of the tree. *Bannu* was a Skolvarg term of affection. One that mothers gave to their smallest children. One she'd certainly never heard from *her* mother, of course. Not even Rolf.

"Come on," the voice called again. "I haven't got all day!"

Astrid hesitated. Who was this woman? Why should she trust her? What if there were more of the cats nearby?

"Ah . . ." Astrid called. "I'd rather not."

"It's safe," the woman said in an exasperated tone. "Now will you please remove yourself from that tree? I went to a lot of trouble to find you today and then you almost got yourself killed before we could speak. A little gratitude would be nice."

Astrid slowly made her way down the tree, a wary eye out. Going down was harder than climbing up. When she finally dropped to the ground, landing with all her weight on her good leg, her hands throbbed from the rough bark. Her injured leg ached with a deeper burn. She grimaced, unable to rest any weight on it. Everything felt heavy and long now that the rush of the escape had faded.

Gripping her remaining knife, Astrid hobbled closer to the dead cat. Her nose wrinkled on examination. It smelled even fouler now. A few paces away, she knelt down—a difficult task with her throbbing calf—and grabbed a rock off the ground. She chucked it right at the rib cage. It landed with a hollow *thud*.

No movement.

Satisfied, Astrid looked around. At first glance, she saw nothing but trees and a swirling mist that didn't seem natural, given the time of day.

"Where are you?" Astrid called.

"Over here."

Astrid's eyes tracked back over the same space she'd just looked. A lone woman in a simple blue dress sat on a rotting tree stump, less than a stone's throw away. She hadn't been there before.

The woman hummed as she ran a comb through shimmering silver hair that fell to her waist. When their eyes met, hers were darker than Astrid had ever seen. Like two pools of night set in a lovely face. The woman gave Astrid a small smile, as if they were old friends who'd crossed one another's path again.

"Greetings," the woman said. Astrid tried twice to say something, but her mind couldn't manage anything but more questions.

Who was she?

"Astrid, isn't it?" she asked when the silence stretched too long. "I've been meaning to speak with you."

The woman looked distinctly Skolvarg. She had the same high oval face shape and firm features of Astrid's race, but something about her seemed . . . off. Her face made her appear young, almost . . . childish, yet something about her eyes gave an ancient impression.

Astrid couldn't bring herself to call her a woman, but she

wasn't a teenager either. She wore no shoes. Only a pale blue shift with a thin silver cord tied around the waist. There were no supplies or weapons in sight.

They stared at each other for several long moments. Her unnerving eyes, so dark the iris almost blended with the pupil, studied Astrid.

"Who . . . how?" Astrid asked. Part of a question, anyway.

"I am here," the lady said, "because I am meant to be here. That's all you need to know for now."

Astrid frowned. She didn't like riddles, particularly not when her exhaustion ran this deep. Almost-dying had a way of taking it out of her.

"Do you need help?" Astrid asked.

The lady threw back her head and laughed. A beautiful, ringing sound that Astrid might have enjoyed if it wasn't directed at her. Her face grew hot.

"Great snows, from a little thing like you?" she asked, her voice rising. "I mean, just look at the state you're in. You're half dead already."

"Hardly."

The lady laughed again. Astrid's lips pressed together until the laughter died away. The lady cleared her throat, then clasped both hands and pointed right at Astrid.

"My apologies, but really . . . you're a mess. Anyway, well, that was very kind of you to offer, Astrid daughter of Hildr. I'm here to help *you*."

Astrid's hand strayed to her remaining knife. The woman didn't pose much of a threat physically, but she was clearly mad.

"How do you know my name?" Astrid asked. "We've never met. I'm sure I'd remember."

The lady's face scrunched. "We haven't. I apologize for sounding so cryptic and confusing. And for that unfortunate encounter with the nyx cat. They have a nasty habit of slipping by at the most inconvenient times."

Astrid stared. In her weary state, there was too much there to untangle. She offered her pouch of trail food and her water skin to the stranger.

"I don't have time for riddles," Astrid said. "If you're hungry or thirsty, I have a little to share."

The lady shook her head. "I have no need of food or drink."

"Fair spring to you, then," Astrid said as she settled onto a log with a grimace. "I've got to get this bound up and back to my tribe." Her gaze slipped to the cat, then back to the woman. "Thank you for saving my life. I . . . I'm grateful."

The mysterious lady didn't take the hint. Instead of leaving, she remained on her stump, hands folded in her lap. Astrid ignored her as she used her knife to tear off a strip of her shirt, then gently wrap it around her leg. Pain shot through her calf and into her thigh. She sucked in a sharp breath, nostrils flared, and tried to ignore the pressure of the strange woman's stare.

"Not every Skolvarg hears the call of the wolf spirit," the woman said, matter-of-factly.

All Astrid's muscles tightened at once. She hesitated, then lifted her head. The lady leaned forward now, legs crossed, eyes tapered right on Astrid.

"But you know that. Don't you, Astrid?"

Astrid ignored her. Or pretended to, anyway. After another awkward moment, the silver-haired lady stood up and smoothed her dress.

"Well," she said brightly, "it's been a pleasure, but I must go. Take care, Astrid. Get home quickly. Nyx cats shouldn't be prowling around at all but where there's one there could be more."

Relieved to see her go, Astrid pulled herself to her feet and nodded once.

"Go safely," Astrid said.

The lady grinned, somehow having all her teeth still. "The same to you, *bannu*."

A thousand questions flooded Astrid, and she wanted to ask all of them. Why had the woman saved her? *How* had she saved her? What was a nyx cat? Where were its eyes? Why had she never heard of them before one had tried to slice her to ribbons?

Only one question surfaced.

"Who are you?" Astrid called. "Your name?"

The lady didn't turn back nor did she answer. As she sashayed away from the stump, she hummed. A gentle cadence, quiet as a lullaby, that reminded Astrid of gentle evening snowfall she liked to watch from the comfort of a dry place and a warm fire. In between notes of her song, a dark mist appeared that blurred and distorted the forest glade.

All at once, Astrid's head spun and the world tilted. Her stomach twisted, ready to retch. Wolves howled in the distance and the forest started to spin around her.

"The thing you seek will not be found among the Amarok or the Skolvarg," the lady's singing voice whispered.

Astrid pitched into a heady and deep darkness.

Astrid opened her eyes to the kiss of mist on her face. Coughing, she waved a hand to clear it. She scrambled to her feet, but didn't recognize her surroundings.

This wasn't the Wolfwood. The mysterious lady no longer stood before her. Instead, a vague nothing stretched around her. Dark, with shadows and lack of permanence or normalcy

Her gaze dropped to her left leg. No bandage. No pain.

A dream then?

The Skolvarg often spoke of visits from the spirits—the mystical beings found in the trees, hills, rocks, and rivers. Though the Matrons consulted with the spirits often, it was rare for someone without years of training to sense their presence as little more than a tingling, rarer still to speak with one.

Though not always easy to interpret and fond of riddles, spirits were generally helpful. When one appeared in a dream, it was said they could show a person a glimpse of their future or grant them good fortune. Astrid wasn't quite sure that was what she'd experienced. The old stories never said anything about being eaten alive by hellish cats in dream visits from the spirits.

A forlorn howl drew Astrid out of her thoughts and back to the strange area. In the ringing emptiness, the howl sounded morose. Hollow. Astrid's heart quickened. How could a wolf sound so plaintive? As if it lived alone, afraid. It sounded like the same wolf that had called her here in the first place.

"This is foolish," she muttered.

Or was it fate?

Only that thought propelled her forward. Hadn't a possibly injured wolf drawn her to this very spot anyway? There may still be a purpose for the strange cat, the strange woman, and then this.

Astrid ventured deeper into the dark mist. She held her knife, even if this was a dream. Another howl sounded, this time, more urgent than before, accompanied by a yip at the end.

A snow flurry burst out of nowhere. She blinked to get the sharp, stinging icicles out of her eyelashes. It dropped all at once, in the strange way dreams had of changing immediately. She rubbed it out of her way, feeling no cold. No pain.

Squinting, Astrid leaned forward to see sharpened logs at

the top of a wall. A wall? Logs? No, she'd never seen anything like this. The Skolvarg were nomadic. Even in the winter they lived in yurts made of pine poles and animal hides.

Whatever she saw here was a fortress. Built sturdily and broad. It flickered in the snow, as if it wasn't really there.

She walked through the wall as if it were made of nothing more than mist and snowflakes.

Now she stood inside a long structure. No visible ceiling soared overhead, but the snow had stopped. As if the dream moved her through a progression of time too quickly to trace. Astrid, wiser now, simply waited for the rest to unfold.

A single howl broke the air yet again.

The strange mist had disappeared with the snow and morphed into structures. Cages, perhaps. Snow heaped up the sides, fluttering by. Not all the way indoors, but not entirely exposed either. Gaunt, wherever it was.

A canine whine sounded nearby.

Astrid's heart drew out, pained. The whine was desperate. Frantic, even. Like a forgotten pup. Unable to help herself, she felt instant panic. A stir of something inside her. She had to fix this. Help the wolf. An Amarok wolf, perhaps? The mysterious lady's words slipped through Astrid's mind again.

The thing you seek will not be found among the Amarok or the Skolvarg.

"Are you showing me an Amarok that needs help?" Astrid whispered.

No reply came. Only the changing of what lay around her. The cages faded into a room filled with . . . equipment? Contraptions made of metal. Snares, spears, chains, and other things used to capture and control animals. A shiver ran down Astrid's back. These traps weren't used to capture animals for their meat or hides. The angles of the teeth were too low, even bent. They weren't meant to kill, just injure, slow, or cripple. These were purely for sport.

Definitely not Skolvarg.

Astrid strolled deeper in the building, past the rows of spikes and iron teeth. The spirits had brought her here, surely. They wanted her to see something. But why? What? The Amarok that she heard, perhaps?

Where was the wolf that called to her?

A tiny growl sounded from the darkness and Astrid whirled around. The vision around her blurred into black, but the low growl remained in the air, reverberating. A low feeling of misery and pain filled her next. Whatever it was, it suffered.

In the darkness, the growl faded into a whine.

"What have they done to you?" she whispered.

The dream disappeared.

FIVE

"Astrid!"

A rough hand shook her shoulder.

Astrid groaned but didn't open her eyes. The wolf. Where was the wolf? The panic, the pain, started to subside inside her. With it came a longing that drew her toward the animal. Her animal.

No, not hers.

Astrid blinked awake, startled to be back in daylight. The voice came again.

"Astrid!"

"I'm fine." She muttered a curse word when her leg ached again. "Where am I?"

"What in the name of the spirits are you doing all the way out here? Astrid!"

Two hands gripped her side and rolled her over. Freydis. How had Freydis found her? Freydis' dark auburn hair was braided out of her face in rows, a sure sign that she'd been about to hunt. She loomed overhead. Concern creased her sharp-featured face and bright brown eyes.

"Freydis?" Astrid murmured. "What're you doing here?"

Astrid's best friend rolled her eyes.

"Do you even know where *here* is? You're miles away from camp. I found you lying face down in the pine needles. I thought you were dead! Why are you out here? Have you been eating mushrooms?"

A pounding headache slowed Astrid's thoughts. She reached up to rub the pine needles and dirt off her cheeks. Memory returned with blurry images. The cat. The woman. The dream. Freydis helped her sit up. She brushed away dirt sticking to Astrid's shoulders.

"Well?" Freydis asked.

"Rolf asked me to replenish his plants. I heard a wolf howling in the trees and followed."

Astrid paused, heavy with a sudden, terrible suspicion. She knew who the blue-clad, silver-haired woman was after all. It came to her like a revelation—or a curse.

Not a random forest spirit as Astrid had first suspected. One of the *Seasons*, the four immortals that maintained the balance of the world. The so-called Greater Spirits. And not just any, but Margu, the Spirit of Winter. Which made no sense. It was spring, the time of Radi, who dressed in green and ushered in new life and growth.

The thought staggered Astrid. Had she really just been visited by a Greater Spirit? Margu, of all of them. The spirit of winter, darkness, and death. Yes, she felt it in her bones.

But why?

Questions came at her relentlessly, but she pressed them back. Only one thing was clear right now: she couldn't tell Freydis. She couldn't tell *anyone*. There would be too many questions. Most likely, the tribe would think her cursed in some way. Or crazy.

But had Margu shown her a real wolf?

What if that injured animal was a captured Amarok? *Her*

captured Amarok. Margu distinctly said that Astrid wouldn't find what she sought amongst the Skolvarg.

So where?

The very thought of not being an Ulfsark, not bonding with an Amarok, made her heart pound. She realized she'd spaced out for far too long, lost in thought. Freydis shook her again, her voice a low growl.

"Astrid!"

"Sorry. Sorry. What did you say?"

Freydis gave her a scrutinizing look. "Are you sure you weren't eating mushrooms? You know you're no good at telling the safe ones apart."

"No, I haven't been eating mushrooms."

Astrid swung an irritated glare her way. Everything felt all jumbled in her head now, tied up with questions about the spirits.

More to the point: how would she walk with her injured leg?

"There was this cat thing," Astrid muttered, trying to get it all straight. Her head tipped back to regard the tree she'd scrambled up. "It had no eyes and chased me up a tree, but then it fell out and—"

Freydis jerked upright, reaching for her sword. A rustle in the bushes followed. Astrid tensed moments before Syrhan, Freydis's Amarok wolf, slipped into sight. His fur had a reddish tinge, like his Ulfsark's hair. The hair on the nape of his neck bristled as he sniffed for danger. According to Freydis, a bonded Amarok and Skolvarg nearly shared a mind. Their communication became mere thoughts when needed.

"The cat thing is dead, over there by the tree." Astrid waved a vague hand in the direction. Casting her friend a concerned look, Freydis headed that way with Syrhan at her side.

"Is this some kind of joke?" Freydis called a moment later.

"Or did you hit your head harder than you think? There's nothing here but a pile of soot and charred bones."

"What?"

Astrid struggled to her feet and made her way over to the base of the pine tree. Sure enough, Syrhan sniffed at a pile of ash and blackened bones. Nothing else remained to mark the existence of the nyx cat.

"It was right here!" Astrid cried. "Look, see the gouges in the bark from where it climbed after me?"

She pointed to long marks sliced in the bark. The smell of sap and wet pine filled the air near them. Clearly, the gouges were fresh. Astrid remembered her injured leg and twisted to look at the back of her calf.

"And this! Look what it did to my leg."

As soon as the words left her mouth, her leg didn't hurt. A bloodstained cut ran through her leggings and boot . . . but her calf looked perfectly fine. No cut.

No pain.

Freydis stared at her with concern. "*How* many mushrooms was it again?"

"I didn't eat any mushrooms!" Astrid growled. "What do you think did this to my leggings? What about the marks in the tree?"

Freydis held up two hands. "Slow down and start at the beginning."

Astrid gave an exasperated sigh, irritated at herself more than Freydis. Nothing made sense. She repeated the story, but refrained from mentioning Margu. Just the thought of her sent a cold trickle down her back.

"I'm not crazy and I didn't eat anything funny," she finished as she batted a piece of hair out of her face. "I don't know why there's nothing but bones or how my leg got better but I'm telling you the truth."

Astrid and Freydis had grown up like sisters. In the last

several years, as Astrid failed to hear the Wolf Song, Freydis' friendship never wavered. Although Freydis was a full Ulfsark and had heard the Wolf Song in her twelfth year, she'd never made Astrid feel like less of Skolvarg for her lack of a wolf.

"I don't know *what* happened to you, but strange things are going on in the Wolfmoors," Freydis said at last. "Syrhan and I were running a message to the Matrons. Mother is worried about a sickness our hunters have discovered since the snows melted. Some of the deer, elk, bison, and moose were dead, but . . . not from usual wasting. All of the carcasses were . . . wrong."

"What do you mean?"

Freydis shifted her weight, her shoulders wiggling uneasily. "Just . . . felt different. No scavengers had touched them. When our wolves smelled them up close, they growled and their hackles went up. Syrhan couldn't communicate why, he just seemed uneasy. We cut one open and there was nothing inside but rot, even though the snows should have kept them from decaying. The bones were black and dark slime leaked out of their eyes and mouths."

Astrid grimaced at Freydis' ominous tone.

"I don't know how any beast would have turned into a pile of ashes after it died, but those bones are the same color," Freydis said, gesturing to the pile of charred debris. "It's too strange to be a coincidence. The Matrons are going to speak with the spirits and send runners to the other tribes who already left for the summer camps. They're worried it's happening all across the Wolfmoors."

"Seasons," Astrid muttered, then almost immediately regretted it. Now probably wasn't the best time to be blaspheming the Greater Spirits.

If enough of the herds sickened and died, the Skolvarg would have nothing left to eat. They could sustain on nuts and edible plants for some time, but the Amaroks required meat—and a lot of it.

"Now you're the one who looks like a wolf ate your dinner." Freydis cracked a grin. "C'mon, there's no need to be gloomy. It's probably just a seasonal sickness that will pass. We've got more important things to worry about, like making sure the Thyrlings mind themselves at the feast."

A delegation from Thyrden—the kingdom to the west of the Wolfmoors—would join the Skolvarg for their annual spring feast. A celebration of the transition from winter into spring.

After war between the two nations had ended six years ago, an uneasy truce settled between the Skolvarg Tribes and Thyrden's King Oskar. Freydis' mother, Odda, was chosen by the Matrons to represent the Skolvarg people in peace talks, hosted at their spring feast tomorrow.

"I heard about what happened with Torva, by the way." Freydis wrinkled her nose. "That rotten ogre! Torva's just jealous of your fighting skills. She's huge and you're far more limber and faster. What does size matter, anyway?"

Astrid managed a wry smile. "Thanks, Frey."

Freydis puffed out her cheeks and crossed her eyes, pretending to be Torva, and then folded one of her arms behind her back. Astrid laughed at the impression and Freydis threw an arm around her.

Together, they walked toward the edge of the glade.

"Let's go," Astrid said. "I'm starving. I didn't get all Rolf's plants, but I'll come back out. How did you find me in the middle of these trees, anyway?"

Freydis pointed to Syrhan, who was sniffing around a few flattened bushes near where the nyx cat had dropped. His shoulders brushed lower branches of the pines that were tall enough to brush her shoulder.

"He caught your scent, nearly jerked me off his back when

he did, then we went crashing right into the middle of all these trees. I almost fell off."

She added the last sentence as if mortally offended. Astrid nearly giggled. Falling off your Amarok was the height of a Skolvarg's embarrassment.

Syrhan turned toward them, tongue lolling out to the side in a big canine smile. He approached, giving Astrid an affectionate nudge with his nose and an inquiring whine.

"Yeah, you're a big hero," Freydis muttered affectionately, ruffling the fur on the wolf's massive neck. "You don't need to rub it in."

Astrid's eyes roamed across Syrhan's riding harness, a quiver of arrows, and a small pack of supplies. The Skolvarg didn't load down their wolves like a common pack mule. What would it be like to eat up miles of Wolfmoors on the back of a running wolf?

She'd find out this spring.

She *had* to.

Unbidden, her mind ranged back to the whine of the wolf she'd followed here. The strange dream that felt so real. A tug in her heart made her want to go back to that dark place just to find the wolf again. She shook her head to clear her thoughts.

Who knew if that was even real?

When Margu appeared, caution was the best path forward.

"There's still one out there for you," Freydis said in a soft voice. "Maybe as early as next week even, right? The Wolf Song should be starting soon. Any day now, I hear."

Astrid drew herself out of her thoughts, then opened her mouth to protest. She stopped and gave a little smile. There was no reason to burden Freydis with her deeper, darker thoughts.

"Right. Thanks."

Freydis put an arm around Astrid and gave her a side hug. "Come on, you've got a long walk back, mushroom picker!"

As she followed Freydis and Syrhan from the pine grove, Astrid glanced over her shoulder at the trunk where Margu once sat. She recalled her parting words with a feeling of dread.

The thing you seek will not be found among the Amarok or the Skolvarg.

Shivering, Astrid turned for home.

The next day, Freydis appeared at Rolf's hut while Astrid helped him hang the last of the herbs she'd gathered the day before. They'd dry in the spring air, shielded from the growing power of the sun, for them to use later. The blank expression on Freydis' face made Astrid's body tense.

"Mother wants to see you," she said in a flat voice.

"Everything okay?"

Freydis just widened her eyes. Astrid sighed and stepped away from the last bundle, which twirled from the piece of leather that anchored it to the top of their hut.

"I'm coming."

"Tell Chieftain Odda," Rolf called from the far corner of the hut, "that Astrid told me of the animal sickness. I've not seen or heard of anything like it, but I will send word to healers in the other tribes."

A note of concern edged his voice. Freydis nodded once.

"Thank you."

Astrid stepped out of the hut with Freydis at her side, a queasy feeling curling in her stomach. What could this possibly be about? Not the incident with Torva. That was too small to merit the Chieftain's attention.

Did she somehow find out about Margu?

"What does your mother want?" Astrid asked quietly.

"I can't say."

Chieftain Odda had a way about her that made their strongest Skolvarg cower. She never screamed or threatened. She didn't have to. Her powerful voice carried all the authority she required. The entire tribe knew Odda's prowess as an Ulfsark and a leader and they bowed to that authority.

No one questioned her.

"I don't know what this is about." Freydis dodged a little girl, legs caked with mud as she scampered by. "She didn't say. I don't think it's about Torva."

Astrid frowned, ignoring a searching, curious glance from another Skolvarg as she slipped by. Astrid's mother had been the second most important person in the tribe before her death. Her father had also served a respected and valued position as a warrior, just not an Ulfsark. He'd died years ago in the war with the Thyrlings—long enough that Astrid struggled in recent years to remember certain details about him. Astrid's inability to hear the Wolf Song was more than strange. It was . . . unheard of. It meant everyone in the tribe wondered at her oddity now.

She turned her mind from those thoughts and tried to imagine what the Chieftain could want. Moments later, they approached the largest hut in the village. Freydis sent her a bolstering look and swerved to the right. Astrid stood in front of a door made of wood planks strapped together that didn't quite reach the ground. She drew in a breath, then stepped inside.

A stern-visaged woman stood across the way. Shafts of light fell through the open hole in the roof where the campfire smoke would vent. Woven grass mats and furs covered the floor. Fresh, chilly air swept through the room, ushering Astrid inside.

Chieftain Odda was a broad-shouldered woman, but thin. She had soft features for a woman that carried so much authority, but a piercing stare. Dark brown hair pulled away from her face, trailing to her elbow in a braid on the left side. Strands of gray interwove it in a startling contrast.

A shield and spear leaned against the wall of the tent behind Odda. A rack bearing a polished mail hauberk coat marked Odda as an Ulfsark. Her blue-gray wolf, Grimfrost, hadn't been outside the yurt. He was probably off with the hunting parties while his rider managed the tribe's affairs.

Chieftain Odda shook her head at another Skolvarg, Utri, that stood nearby. He had always been known for his skill with fire and meat. Astrid's mouth watered at the thought of her favorite meals he often cooked.

"Three boars on individual spits is plenty for the feast. The Thyrlings should see us as prosperous, not gluttons and . . . Astrid, I'll be with you in just a moment."

"Yes, Chieftain."

Astrid stood straight-backed near the door until Utri left the yurt with a playful wink in her direction.

Chieftain Odda turned to Astrid, studied her, then gestured to a stump. "Have a seat."

Astrid obeyed.

Odda remained standing, a contemplative look on her face. "Spring approaches," she said. "Is, in fact, here already."

Astrid's stomach clenched. Oh, so that's what this would be about. The Wolf Song. Shine, but she hadn't expected *this* conversation. At least, not so soon in the seasons. She should have, in hindsight, but didn't.

"Yes, Chieftain."

Odda lifted an eyebrow, as if she expected something snarky, but Astrid had been sincere.

"The Wolf Song will be occurring soon with the new whelps." Odda hesitated. "There has been some indication amongst Skolvarg that it may have already begun."

Astrid's eyes bulged. A hole seemed to open in her chest.

"Already?"

Odda nodded once.

"Yes. Two whelps bonded with Bryka and Idun."

Astrid closed her eyes. Both were younger than her by years. Bryka, a solemn twelve year old that had a male twin. And Idun a rambunctious fourteen-year-old that talked too much and acted lazy during her fighting lessons.

"Good for them," Astrid growled.

"Nothing?"

Odda's voice lifted a little too much at the end. A hopeful question. Astrid thought back to the cry of the wolf she'd heard yesterday. No, nothing truly there. That had been a dream, at best. From all the accounts she'd heard of the Wolf Song, that wasn't it. Besides, the place with cages she'd seen couldn't house an Amarok wolf. A wolf, perhaps, but not an Amarok. The tone and strength meant it was likely a regular wolf and the regular wolves didn't have the spirit to hear or answer the Wolf Song.

The more time passed, the more convinced she became that it had all been a bad dream.

"I . . . can't say that I've noticed anything different, Chieftain," Astrid said. She shrugged helplessly. "What would I hear?"

Odda frowned. "It's not so much a sound as a . . . feeling. A connection. Like a relationship that blossoms immediately. You would know if you felt the Wolf Song answer, Astrid. It would consume you."

Astrid swallowed hard. She hadn't felt the Wolf Song yesterday, just compassion for a trapped animal. She hadn't felt it ever.

"Then no."

"Disappointing," Odda murmured, "but by no means over. There are still three more whelps in the pack that are likely to choose a rider."

Astrid knew that already. Each Skolvarg tribe was associated with a wolf pack, a larger representation of the bond between individual Amarok wolves and Skolvarg warriors. The Star Runner Pack partnered with Astrid's tribe and the alpha female had borne five pups in the heart of winter. Now the whelps were already the size of a regular wolf, and apparently choosing their Skolvarg quickly.

"Thank you, Chieftain."

Odda hesitated, then plunged right into the heart of the matter. "If you don't hear the Wolf Song by the end of this spring, I believe it's safe to say that . . . that you may never. I've never heard of a Skolvarg hearing the Wolf Song after nineteen winters."

Astrid's nostrils flared. She'd be twenty at the end of the summer. She grasped for hope. Maybe she'd be the Skolvarg that broke the age limit they'd seen before. Or maybe it was all a giant misunderstanding and . . .

She forced the thoughts to end. Bitter as it tasted, Astrid appreciated Odda's direct words and firm tone.

"Yes, Chieftain."

"There are many ways to serve the tribe, Astrid. The Ulfsark are one means for us to survive but not the *only* way. Change comes on fast winds. We'll need everyone in order to survive it."

The foreboding tone sent a little shiver through Astrid. She wanted to ask what that meant, but didn't dare.

"Yes, Chieftain."

"In the meantime, be thinking about what you can do that isn't an Ulfsark, just in case. You could still be a warrior, like your father. Spend time with the remaining pups as best you can, or as they allow you. Something will happen for you this year, Astrid. I can feel it."

Astrid nodded. She wanted to go. Get out of here. Feel

fresh air on her face and escape the note of compassion in Odda's tone. Towering, powerful Odda.

"Also," Odda added, "I heard what happened with Torva. I have spoken with her about using the term *omegr*. It's not allowed in my tribe, and you certainly are not one. I must speak with you also. You are a strong, brave young woman. I don't know what the Spirits have in store for you, but it is more than senseless fighting. Please, hold your temper?"

Astrid sucked in a breath, then nodded. Quietly, she said, "Yes, Chieftain Odda."

Odda reached down and laid a hand on top of Astrid's shoulder. Her calluses from years of labor with the sword and spear felt rough, but the gesture still gave comfort.

"Your mother would be proud."

Astrid bit back a welling of tears. How could that possibly be true?

"Thank you."

Odda leaned back with a heavy sigh, as if unburdened. "Let me know the moment you feel or hear anything, Astrid. I'd very much like you to join our Ulfsark. Now go make yourself useful in feast preparations. The Thyrlings arrive tomorrow and there is much work still to be done."

Astrid dipped her head in polite farewell, then rose and left the hut.

Six

The Thyrlings arrived the next afternoon, escorted by
a line of Ulfsark.

The Ulfsark led the way, half a bowshot ahead of
the Thyrlings on horseback. Both groups were still a short
distance from camp when Astrid first saw them. Even at that
distance, the Thyrling's horses clearly didn't want to be
anywhere near the gigantic wolves. The Ulfsark kept a
respectable distance ahead of the Thyrlings, allowing them to
keep their flighty, spooked animals in check.

"I'd never be caught dead on top of a horse," Freydis whispered to her. "How can those skinny legs take them anywhere?
Can horses fight? I doubt it. Not like an Amarok, anyway. Our
wolves are superior."

Astrid agreed with a low murmur.

The late afternoon sunlight gleamed on the shiny mail
shirts and polished helms as the Ulfsarks returned. The
helmets were Nistlefolk make, the brow featured a snarling
wolf's head.

Only Ulfsark were allowed to wear the wolf helms and
even then only for ceremony or a proper battle. Each Ulfsark

also carried a bow, spear, and a sword, which they kept belted at their waist. Skilled Ulfsark used their knees to steer, using subtle nudges and squeezes, to keep their hands open to fight.

Now, the Ulfsark dismounted.

The women spread out on either side of the long walk leading to Chieftain Odda's hut. Their wolves padded a dozen more feet away and laid down on all fours, heads and ears alert as the Thyrling horses approached.

"I heard their women have beards," Freydis whispered with a giggle, "and their men wear dresses."

Astrid nudged her with a sharp elbow to the ribs, but couldn't stop a smile. They stood next to each other as the Thyrling delegation closed the distance, only a minute away now. Their horses were skittish near the Amarok, but the wolves remained docile.

"Dresses," Astrid said in a low voice, "are a loose term. Those look more like skirts."

Freydis barely contained a squeal of laughter. She turned to Astrid, black-rimmed eyes dancing, and whispered, "Those are definitely dresses."

In preparation, Astrid and Freydis had braided their hair into several five-stranded braids in the back with smaller braids beginning above their temples. Turquoise beads glimmered along Astrid's smaller braids with winks of light.

Freydis wore magenta, as she always did. They'd taken thin pieces of charcoal and lined their eyes with black on bottom and top, the way all Skolvarg did during the long summer months, when the sun hurt. Today, it was more for show.

The stomp of feet approached, and Astrid fell silent.

A score of Thyrlings comprised the delegation, two standard bearers in the front, followed by the house guard known as *druzars*, then the ambassador and two more lines of warriors in the rear.

Indeed, it appeared they *did* wear dresses or something like it. Without their long, thick stockings, the druzars would have had no protection on their legs. Bare knees were visible even with a gentle chill in the air.

Most of them wore a black garment from shoulder to knees, bound in the middle by thick, leather belts where they hung pouches and weapons. Scale mail protected some of their shoulders and upper chests, but stopped near the waist. They carried round shields strapped over their backs bearing the great black bear on a green field of King Oskar's house.

They were armed similar to the Skolvarg—single-handed swords with shortened crossguards and spears. Astrid noted a few unstrung bows and quivers of arrows on their horses.

Their helms were conical in shape, with a mask over the eyes or a long nose bridge to their lips. Some of the druzars were almost the size of a Skolvarg, but built heavier, like a grizzled gray bear compared to an Amarok. Clearly, the Thyrlings could pack a punch, but would lack the speed and grace of the leaner Skolvarg, Astrid guessed.

Thank the spirits for that.

The Thyrlings marched on the main footpath through the Skolvarg huts, eyes fixed ahead. Their faces remained scrunched as the head druzars led the way behind the last Ulfsark.

"Their future Queen," Freydis whispered, with a nod toward a woman in the incoming part of the delegation. "Her name is Rosamund. She's acting as ambassador here today. Odda heard . . . interesting things about her."

Princess Rosamund, eldest child and only daughter of King Oskar, rode in the middle of the party. She wore split riding pants over a dress, yet bore no weapons or armor. A simple circlet sat on her brow over long, fiery-red hair. The Skolvarg always appointed warriors as their leader and Rosamund didn't look like she'd ever handled a weapon.

She appeared skinny, almost to the point of being sickly,

beneath her elegant, white, fur cloak. Her pale skin was a shade more fair than the mixed tones of the rest of the Thyrlings.

Despite her frail appearance, serious green eyes highlighted Rosamund's sharp features. She had the typical Thyrling high cheekbones and pointed chin. Astrid guessed they were close to the same age.

The Thyrling druzars dismounted first and stood at attention, faces impassive behind their helms. One took the reins of Princess Rosamund's mount as she swung out of the saddle with the natural grace of an experienced rider. The druzars straightened to attention as she passed through them. Rosamund stopped at the edge, near where the row of Amarok's waited.

At least she had the wisdom *not* to approach Chieftain Odda uninvited.

"Chieftain Odda," Rosamund called, her voice firm but bright. "It's my pleasure to visit you."

Odda nodded from the far end of the Amarok. "You and your delegation are welcome."

Odda wore plain hunting clothes and tall boots made of cream-colored doe skin. Skolvarg chieftains wore no crowns. A cloak with a blue fox-fur collar lay across her shoulders. Using twice the dark liner other Skolvarg had used, Odda cut an intimidating figure even though she only wore a hunting knife at her belt.

"I trust your journey was good?" Odda asked.

"We have been favored with an early spring on the western coast," Princess Rosamund replied with a short bow. "The weather was fair and traveling easy. I thank you in advance for your hospitality, Chieftain Odda. Is there a place that my retinue may establish our camp? We will sleep here tonight and tomorrow night before we turn home."

"You are welcome to all we have to offer," Odda said with

her arms spread. "There is a place by the river where you may picket your horses and make camp. Our wolves will not bother them, I assure you. Your people are welcome to join us under the lodge when they are settled. I will take you there now."

At a command from the princess, a half dozen druzars handed their reins to the others. Rosamund followed Odda, walking on her left and slightly behind. A natural Skolvarg position of respect and deference.

Well, Rosamund might not be so bad.

Her druzars followed a respectable distance behind Rosamund and Odda as they strolled down the path and in between other huts, speaking quietly. The rest led the horses and pack mules down to the river, heads bowed.

Freydis' nose wrinkled.

"Well," she murmured, "at least now we can get this over with and send them on their way."

After the Thyrlings set up a hasty camp by the river, a handful of higher-ranking Skolvarg in the camp—Rolf included—and some of the Thyrlings were invited to the council with Odda and Rosamund inside the yurt.

At the river, the Thyrlings had raised three large tents, made from giant squares of canvas. Each one was painted in white stripes and either red, blue, or green and looked large enough to comfortably house several people. Warriors milled around the edges of the camp, eyes darting and wary. Guarding it, no doubt.

The Thyrlings might have come as a peace delegation but it was clear old feelings still lingered.

Unlike the Skolvarg, whose warriors were an even split of men and women, the majority of the Thyrling druzars were male. Only a handful of women were in the mix but they were almost as sturdy as the men, though Astrid didn't see any hint of a beard or mustache among them.

Unimpressed, Astrid slid away from the willows where she peered out, and back toward the center of camp where Odda had ordered a large open-sided lodge built for the occasion. Fires sprang up around the perimeter. Drums and horns sounded throughout the camp, beating a rhythmic chant that soothed her agitation.

Time for the feast to begin.

Beneath the canopy, Utri and several other Skolvarg roasted meat and smoked fish. The dry scent of herbs spread through the air. Dishes of green berries, which were not quite ripe this early in the spring but still edible, filled wooden, carved bowls. A paste made from mashed seeds and a wet root filled others.

A large fire on each end of the structure illuminated the ground, with smaller fires spiraling into the night. It left an open, airy feeling to the place.

Also a sign of them moving into the Wolfmoors again.

Odda's Skolvarg tribe contained three hundred Skolvarg. To feed them and the Thyrlings, several dead boars, still thin from winter, hung on spits turned and tended by Skolvarg cooks. Fat sizzled on the rocks below the animals as it dripped into the fire.

Odda, Princess Rosamund, and a handful of other Skolvarg and Thyrlings sat at a table running perpendicular to the lodge. Rolf, Huntress Vanna, and the tribe's pack master, Hakon, sat at the table, along with two bearded Thyrling men with deep scowls. Skolvarg bustled behind them, carrying large water pouches and buckets made of woven grasses or pliable tree bark.

The rest of the Thyrlings outside the hut drank, shouted and sang like they were in their own halls back in Thyrden. Astrid caught one man, a dark-haired fellow with a thick beard, leering at her. She scowled back, then continued through the throng of people.

Princess Rosamund sat next to Odda and picked at her food with a two-pronged utensil she'd brought with her. The princess only spoke when addressed by the other Thyrlings or Odda. Her smile appeared . . . weary. Perhaps a touch bored. She cut her meat with the small fork and knife and each bite looked to be barely enough to feed a bird.

A voice called from just behind Astrid. She whirled around to find Freydis there, laughing.

"Where have you been?" Freydis shouted.

Even with the beating drums, the laughter and talking, she used a louder voice than needed. She slapped Astrid on the back and handed her a drinking horn. Astrid wrinkled her nose and sniffed the contents. She recoiled.

"This smells disgusting."

"It's just cider," Freydis said, then grinned. "And then a little bit of that stuff the Thyrlings brought. It's strong enough to set a forest on fire. Whew! Nasty drink called skar. Don't know how they stomach it."

"How much of it did you have?" Astrid drawled with another little sniff. Acrid and strong, the fumes curled in her nostrils, creating a metallic taste in her mouth. She shoved it back into Freydis' hands.

"Just a few sips," Freydis cried. She leaned in and spoke in a level tone almost swallowed up by the surrounding noises. "Our warriors are spread out all around the hut, just in case the Thyrlings have too much to drink and pick a fight. Wouldn't be very nice of them!"

"Has that been a problem before?"

Freydis shrugged. "I don't think they'll do anything stupid. At least not as a group. Some of them might need to be put in their place if they keep drinking skar, though." She hiccuped. "Stick around and watch my back, will you?"

Astrid appreciated the invitation, despite her lack of an Amarok to make her truly frightening. Freydis had a way of making her feel like less of an outcast through the little gestures.

"Of course. Always."

"Plus," Freydis added with a mischievous grin and a wink. "There's this Ochlander bard that came in with the Thyrlings. If he's as entertaining as he is good looking, we're in for a treat."

Astrid rolled her eyes. Skolvarg men were the only tribe members aside from Rolf, Odda, and Freydis that didn't have a negative opinion of her because of Astrid's lack of an Amarok wolf. They respected her skill with arms in the sparring ring because she'd knocked her fair share of them on their rears, but their true interest had nothing to do with her prowess in the ring.

More to do with her availability as a wife.

Given no Amarok, she'd be expected to fill other roles for the tribe. What that would be, Astrid wouldn't let herself guess yet. Warrior, most likely. She knew that it wasn't marriage or babies. Not yet, anyway. The attention from the Skolvarg men made her a stumbling mess.

Freydis, on the other hand, was happiest when she had a handful of young warriors strung along like creek trout on a fishing line.

"Now, where has that bard gotten to?" Freydis murmured. "I'll give you first crack at him, just because I'm a good friend like—"

Her words were cut off by a sudden blaring of horns and a round of shouts from somewhere down the line of tables. A group of four bards swaggered into view, dressed in bright blue cloaks that indicated their Ochlander origins. They carried an array of musical instruments between two men and two women.

Astrid had a mental image of bards as older, balding men with bouncing bellies and a fondness for loud talking and exaggerated tales. *These* bards looked battle-ready. Broad-shouldered with long knives at their belts, they seemed more natural holding shields and spears than lyres and flutes.

Odd.

Especially odd since this group seemed to have traveled with the Thyrlings from the west. Astrid hadn't thought the two countries were that friendly. And Thyrden was a long way from Ochland. They walked with a natural ease through the pockets of feasters, as if used to being the center of attention.

Freydis squealed. "There he is!"

The two men walked on the outside, with the women in between them. The man on the right had a lean frame and bright eyes. A hint of stubble graced gently-hollowed cheeks and a strong jaw. He looked to be about their age.

"Attractive, isn't he?" Freydis whispered. "His name is Ewan."

To her surprise, Astrid nodded once, her throat prickly.

Ewan smiled grandly and nodded at the feast-goers as he passed them. For a breath, his eyes tangled with Astrid's. He winked. She turned away, cheeks burning with embarrassment. Did he think she ogled him? Not true. Before she could feel properly horrified, he'd strode away, feet making a dull thud on the ground.

The chatter of attendees quieted when Ewan and the other bards stopped before Odda's table. He paused, then bowed deeply.

"Chieftain Odda." His voice boomed. "Princess Rosamund. Honored Skolvarg and Thyrlings. It is my plea-sure to perform for you tonight with my comrades. We wish you the best of health and the most fruitful of times with the continued peace between your people."

Odda and Rosamund nodded politely. With another

sparkling smile—which Astrid reluctantly admitted was a nice one—he turned and nodded to the rest of his group. They had already extracted instruments from packs and bags, and struck into a fast-paced dancing tune.

Freydis pulled Astrid closer to the group forming around the bards. The Thyrlings stepped right into the middle of the dance and hopped and strutted like roosters in a line.

Before she knew it, one dancing song transitioned into another and another. Everyone beneath the canopy and all around the feast fires joined. The levity brightened the cool spring evening as the sun slipped beneath the horizon.

Laughing as Freydis poorly attempted to mimic a Thyrling dance, Astrid slipped back a few steps. The air had grown thick with the scent of sweat and people. Thyrling and Skolvarg alike stood close together. She needed a chance to get her breath. The heat, movement, and sound made her dizzy.

A body appeared in front of Astrid, blocking her path. She jerked back, eyes wide when she recognized Ewan.

"Sorry, I saw you trying to escape and we can't have that." He held up a hand, half a smile on his face. "Let's go."

"Go?"

He jerked his head to indicate the middle of the dance, then grabbed her hand and pulled her into the throng with a wide grin. Skolvarg drums roared in a circle around them, pounding in her ears.

She grimaced and tried to yell, "I don't know what to do."

He shook his head, grabbed both her hands, and shouted, "Trust me!"

Before she could refuse, he put an arm around her waist, pulled her close, and swept her into a fast-moving dance. It wasn't a complicated one, but not knowing what to do made her stiff. Her feet kept tripping over each other.

"It's okay!" Ewan called over the music. "Relax. It's going to be fine."

Astrid hesitated, stuck in the overwhelming sound of drums interwoven with the high, melodic trill of a lute not far away. The bigger, older bard sang a deep bass above the music, an upbeat cross between a lullaby and a chant. The normally silent forest was so different from this . . . chaos.

But a lovely chaos.

Snatches of Freydis, red-cheeked from laughing and dancing, appeared here and there. Astrid relaxed. Maybe it wasn't so bad, even if it was different. The Skolvarg tribe played music, but they didn't dance much.

Finally, she nodded.

Laughing, the bard swung her around again as the music grew faster, drums thrummed louder. She stopped thinking about her feet and focused on the feel of the music. Her body seemed to naturally follow Ewan's clues. He guided them through increasingly complex patterns, laughing when they stumbled.

A circle formed around her and the bard. Everyone's gaze, including Ewans, trained on her.

Finally, the song ended all at once.

Ewan pulled them to a stop. His arm slipped away from her waist, leaving her standing alone in the middle of the circle. He smiled, chest heaving, and bowed.

"My thanks for the dance, lady. I have never found a more . . . worthy . . . partner to that song."

Before Astrid could feel her mortification more deeply, Freydis shouted her approval. An answering whistle came from the back of the crowd. A moment later, the crowd applauded and yelled. The bard took her hand and raised it in the air.

He turned to her with a delighted laugh as the crowd dispersed around them. A quieter song followed, this more mellow and taciturn.

"We're a sensation, you and I," he said, eyes alight. He

bowed low again, yet his eyes never left hers. She saw something in him. Something bold, fierce, and entirely too amused.

"Thank you," she managed to say past her tight throat. "But I . . . I need some air."

With that, she fled the celebration.

SEVEN

At the river, Astrid shivered.

She splashed water on her arms, slicking away the heat and sweat. The cool liquid on her face calmed her as she remembered how light and free and fun it had been to forget about the Wolf Song. To forget Margu and the cat and the dream wolf that wasn't hers. Odda's report of the beginning of the Wolf Song season and the utter, ringing silence in Astrid's soul.

For a few moments, everything had slipped away and that had been lovely.

"Is everything alright, lady?"

She glanced back, startled out of her thoughts. The dark-haired man that had leered at her earlier stood a few paces away. Two other Thyrling warriors stood nearby. Each held a skar horn in their hands and swayed slightly on their feet. Astrid tensed.

The dark-haired man held up a placating hand. "We didn't mean to scare you, lady. Just checking."

Two of the men advanced. Astrid took a cautious step backward. Cool water flooded around her foot, seeping into her shoe. Her alarm blossomed into panic. Down here by the river, no sound would carry up the hill to be heard over the drums.

The dark-haired man leered, hand still held out to Astrid.

"One who dances as well as you shouldn't spend the night alone and upset. Come here and let Ivar comfort you."

As the Thyrling made a clumsy lunge, Astrid planted her feet on the riverbank and drew her hunting knife. He hesitated, then his face broke into a wide grin.

"One of those wolf women, eh?"

A chorus of jeers rang from his comrades. His bloodshot gaze darkened as he studied Astrid from head to toe.

"I don't mind a good fight, either," he drawled. "How about we wrestle back at my tent? The weather's getting awful cold out here."

"Stay back!" Astrid shouted over growing guffaws. "If you touch me, I will fight back. I'm leaving. Stay here and no harm will come to any of you."

"Such a little thing," he murmured, eyes alight. "What could you do to hurt me?"

Astrid gritted her teeth and thought of just where she wanted to plant her knife to teach him his lesson—forever.

Ivar's laugh faded to a grin and then a scowl. "I don't like being teased, wolf girl. My bedroll or right here. I'm good either way."

"Go. Away."

The chuckles faded from his two associates. They looked between Astrid and Ivar. Ivar advanced another step. Astrid backed further into the river. Cool mud sucked at her feet, sliding around her calves as she stepped back. Careful to maintain her footing and control her rising panic, Astrid kept a wary eye on him as she moved. She used her feet to feel for her next step.

Behind him stood the two buffoons. One of them shifted uneasily. The other hissed his encouragement, clearly excited.

Ivar didn't stop.

"Better me than lying with a wolf, eh? Isn't that what your people do?"

Fury rose in her, but she stamped it down. Emotional reactions would only distract her, which might be what he wanted. He advanced faster now. She'd sloshed through the water to the other side of the bank.

"Last warning," she called. "If you don't leave me alone, I'll fight my way out of here."

He laughed.

"You're not going anywhere, wolf girl. Not until *I* say so."

Astrid charged. His slow reflexes from all the skar, and the uneven footing of the stream, set him off balance. She darted forward and slammed her shoulder into his thick belly. He made an *oomph* sound as she drove forward and tackled him to the stream bank. His head snapped back and hit the ground hard. Rather than dazing him, it seemed to clear his skar-laden mind.

"You rotten witch!" Ivar roared.

Astrid scrambled for his throat. He swung a meaty paw up and caught her in the ribs. The blow landed with a crack and sent her flying back into the stream. Icy water enveloped her, saturating her legs and back. Her knife fell, dropping to the rocks. She wheezed for air as she attempted to find it. Ivar righted himself and charged. Astrid abandoned the search for her knife and rolled through the icy stream, narrowly escaping his grubby hands.

The two Thyrling shouted from the stream bank while Astrid struggled to compose her thoughts, her breath.

"Go on, Ivar," shouted the largest of the two. "Teach that mouthy wolf whore a lesson!"

Ivar seized her moment of recovery and fell on top of her

like a bear. She slammed into the wet ground underneath him. He pinned both of her arms to the ground and shoved his foul face next to hers.

"How do you like this?" he asked, pressing close.

His sour breath sent chills down Astrid's back. Pain laced all the way through her chest, a whirling fire of agony. Her chest bucked as she tried to draw breath under his rancid, stinking weight. Ivar held her fast.

"I knew you'd change your—argh!"

Astrid slammed her knee in between Ivar's legs with a grunt. His grip slackened enough for her to slam her forehead into his nose. Pain ricocheted through her head at the contact as Ivar howled and grabbed his face. Blood spurted from his broken nose. Astrid scrambled toward the stream bank, but he reached for her with blood-slippery hands.

"Get back here!"

One of his bloody hands clamped around her ankle. He jerked her back into the water and hauled her to the other side of the stream. She sputtered, face down, for moments before he dropped her onto the ground near his friends.

"You thrice-cursed little whore! You'll pay for that now."

A terrible dread settled into her chest. She was all alone, with an enraged, drunken man she'd just injured and embarrassed in front of his equally drunken friends. She now sat in the middle of Ivar and two other Thyrlings.

No escape.

No help.

Astrid cast around in the dark, looking for her knife belt. This was no matter of honor anymore. She had little chance of fighting off three men, but the odds were even worse while unarmed.

"Looking for this?"

Ivar reached down and snagged Astrid's knife belt from where it was tangled in rocks on the side of the stream. He pulled a small blade free and tossed the belt aside. "I'm going to cut you to ribbons and feed you to your own wolves."

The Thyrling staggered forward, eyes wide, bloody face snarling. Astrid forgot the pain in her chest as she glanced back to the two Thyrlings behind her. One of them had paled. The other stammered.

"I-I-Ivar . . . let it go."

"Listen to Bori, Ivar," the other insisted. "The captain will have your head if anything happens to break the peace with the Skolvarg. It was fun but now it's not."

"Not if there's no body," Ivar growled. "And have you forgotten what those damned wolves did to our shield brothers?"

He lunged toward Astrid, knife overhead.

Everything happened all at once. Astrid threw up both hands, catching Ivar's wrist as he swung down. She side-stepped, let the momentum of Ivar's swing carry the big man right past her, and shoved his arm down and back as he passed.

Ivar stumbled and hit the ground with a soft grunt, the arm bearing Astrid's knife buried underneath his chest.

Stillness followed.

Neither Astrid nor the two Thyrlings breathed. Ivar didn't move. Blood slowly crawled out from underneath him as his face and body slackened. Terror welled up within Astrid.

"You killed him!" the reedy man shouted in a shrill voice. "You murdered Ivar!"

His companion dropped to the ground and rolled Ivar over. Astrid's heart froze in her chest. Her knife was buried to the hilt above Ivar's belly. She stumbled backward, body quaking, her mind a whirl of disbelief. It had all happened so fast. She'd had no option but to defend herself and—

"What is going on down here?"

A commanding voice cut through the night, breaking Astrid's spiral. A Thyrling captain descended the hill with half a dozen druzars, his hand on the hilt of an axe. Princess Rosamund walked behind him, within their protection, illuminated by the glow of the moon.

"Halt!" the captain shouted. "Reveal yourselves!"

The two Thyrlings swore under their breath and came to attention.

"Bori and Karl, captain," one replied. "There's, um . . ."

The captain stopped a few paces away. His cold, gray eyes fell to Ivar, face up with Astrid's knife in his chest, and then to Astrid. Shock, then fury, followed. She stared back, numb.

Princess Rosamund moved through the ranks of her druzars. She comprehended the scene all at once.

"Captain," she commanded. "Please send your guard to inform the Skolvarg chieftain. Tell her to come immediately."

Her gaze darted to Astrid.

"It appears our peace talks have been sealed in blood."

The next minutes passed in a blur.

Three men summoned chieftain Odda while the remaining druzars surrounded Astrid, Bori, Karl, and Ivar.

It wasn't me, Astrid thought. *I didn't hold the knife.*

It wasn't me.

Her broken thoughts gave no reassurance. She had two Thyrling warriors to give testimony against her own.

Would the truth even matter?

Chieftain Odda arrived quickly, flanked by a dozen Ulfsark, Freydis included. Freydis' eyes widened, then hardened. Astrid's throat grew tight, but she swallowed through it. Her hands trembled and her entire body flushed with cold. Odda studied the dead man and then Astrid.

Rage followed, but faded. "Are you all right, Astrid?" she asked gently.

Astrid nodded.

"What has happened here?" Odda asked no one in particular.

"My retinue and I were retiring to our camp for the evening," Rosamund said. Her impassive face showed no grief over Ivar. Nothing but a ruler's talent for blankness. "When we came down the hill, we found these four, just as you see them now. You were sent for immediately. I have waited to question my men until you were present."

When the princess finished, she looked to her captain. He stepped forward to Bori and Karl with folded arms.

"Bori, report."

"She killed him, captain!" Bori burst out. He pointed an accusing finger at Astrid. "We'd just—"

"That's a lie!" Astrid cried. "These men —"

"Silence," Odda commanded.

The captain turned back to Bori. "Continue," he said. "And know if you speak any lies, I won't take your tongue. I will take your head."

"We'd just come down to the river from the feast and the Skolvarg was here." Bori glanced to Karl, who quickly nodded. "We were just talking to the girl and she went mad. Challenged Ivar to a fight. He didn't even have a knife on him but she pulled hers and stabbed him, just like that!"

The Thyrling captain looked to Karl.

"Is this true?"

He hesitated, eyes flickering to Astrid, then nodded.

Astrid's entire body shook. Was this real? How could they possibly tell such a lie to their leaders? Wordless, Rosamund and Odda and the captain turned to Astrid with an unspoken question. Her voice trembled.

"N-n-no," she cried. "No! He wanted . . . he attacked and . . . my ribs. I . . . tried to leave. The stream and . . . he came at me and landed on the knife and . . . no."

Her tremulous words died in the night. Tears filled her eyes. She wanted to go home to her hut and away from the eyes on her. The darkness. Ivar's body. This wasn't supposed to happen.

"This poor girl is distraught," Princess Rosamund said. "And I would very much like to hear her version of events somewhere else. Chieftain Odda, perhaps we could return to your private hut and speak to her there?"

"Of course."

Odda waved her hand and the Ulfsarks surrounded Astrid, a wall of furious bodies that faced the Thyrlings. Whatever the Thyrlings said, her people didn't seem to believe them.

From the dark-clad forest eave, low growls emanated from the Amaroks. Somewhere behind her, Karl gave a whimper. The captain had the wisdom to eye the forest with a healthy level of fear. Meanwhile, Astrid turned her back to Ivar's body as Freydis threw her arms around Astrid.

"You're safe," she whispered. "Your tribe has you."

Astrid forced her legs to keep her weight, but leaned against her friend.

Before she knew it, she sat in Odda's yurt, a cloak wrapped around her. Everyone aside from Princess Rosamund and Odda waited outside. Away from Ivar's body, Astrid's thoughts started to clear. She stared at the ground, recalling each moment of the fight in terrifying detail.

How had they lied to Rosamund's face?

Rolf burst into the yurt and rushed to her side. He stopped, studied her, then moved close. Astrid leaned into him.

"Your niece has been accused of the murder of a Thyrling warrior," Odda said quietly. "You may now speak, Astrid. Please, tell us what happened?"

Astrid drew in a shuddering breath and, with an encouraging squeeze from her uncle Rolf's hand, told her story.

Princess Rosamund's face darkened when Astrid repeated Ivar's taunt about Skolvarg mating with wolves. Odda remained impassive throughout the entire recounting.

"He picked my knife up off the ground and attacked," Astrid said. "I dodged his strike and Ivar fell on my blade."

Princess Rosamund pursed her lips but said nothing. Odda's stony expression broke into a heavy scowl.

"I believe you, Astrid."

The firm words sent a shiver of relief through Astrid. She only nodded. Rolf's hold on her tightened to the point of pain, but she didn't push him away.

"Princess Rosamund." Odda turned to her. "Both of our people have been wronged tonight, but I hold this at your feet."

"The responsibility is ours," Rosamund said. Her gaze slammed into Astrid's. "Words are trite after such a traumatic experience, but please accept my deepest apologies."

"Do you believe me?" Astrid asked.

Rosamund hesitated. "Yes, I do. Whether or not you wielded the blade or if Ivar really did fall on the knife is of little consequence now. He's dead and two druzars speak against you. It will not be easy to return to my father with these tidings. But . . ."

She trailed away. *But.*

Astrid's heart fell into her stomach.

"But?" Odda asked.

"My father and his jaegars—nobles—may see it differently."

Astrid sucked in a sharp breath. Odda frowned.

"But they're lying!" Astrid cried. "Why would I make any of this up?"

Impassively, Rosamund said, "Prove it to me, Astrid. Give me irrefutable proof that no one, not even the king, could deny."

"I can't."

"I know." A note of mournfulness lingered in her words. "Without satisfaction or solid proof, I fear our noble houses may demand retribution that could damage our hard-won peace. Ivar was the second but favored son of one of our most powerful jaegars."

"Another war," Odda muttered.

Rosamund's lack of denial sent a frisson of rage through Astrid. She might be small, but her emotions had always been mighty. Before she could protest again—and uselessly, at that —Odda spoke up.

"How would your laws address this, Princess?"

"An interview with my father first. If needed, another with his jaegars and a secret vote of guilt or non-guilt."

"You must be joking," Rolf snapped. "Astrid in Thyrden? Of course they'd accuse her of murder and act against her."

Rosamund met his furious gaze.

"Not if I stood with her and issued my testimony of her innocence. I believe that together, Astrid and I could solidify her non-guilt, allow her to return free of fear from retribution, and prevent another war between our countries."

"So I'd have to go to Thyrden?" Astrid whispered.

Rosamund nodded. "Your willingness to come voluntarily before the king will speak to your innocence."

"This is your druzar's fault," Odda said with steel in her voice. "Why should Astrid have to be put through so much?"

"Allegedly," Rosamund said gently. "We have no irrefutable proof either way, but my father will have the testimony of two men, the friends of a jaegar's son. For him, it will be enough."

"While we have one testimony," Rolf muttered bitterly. "And in the courts of Thyrden that is as good as a declaration of war."

Rosamund said nothing.

Odda looked to Astrid, studied her, and back to Rosamund. "Why should I have to send my Skolvarg to your city to correct a wrong given by your people? By any other measure, we should be attacking you."

Rosamund met her gaze and bowed her head slightly. "That is within your power, Chieftain," she said, tightening her lithe fist. "But I plead with you for diplomacy. I believe Astrid and am willing to fight for her with my people as a show of peace and good faith. It's unfortunate this happened, but it happened. We must move forward now."

Astrid held her breath. If Odda wanted to deliver a crippling blow to Thyrden and get retribution for Ivar's act, she could kill Rosamund right now. The fact lay on the air, as if all of them could sense it at the same moment.

A long pause passed before Odda said, "I have no desire to harm you, Rosamund. Peace and stability and to be left to our lives in the Wolfmoors is all we desire."

A hint of relief appeared in Rosamund's expression.

"Then Astrid will return with me. The two others will each receive ten lashes of the whip and be branded on the cheek with a mark we give to those who force themselves on women. I have no doubt that is how this night would have ended had Astrid not fought for her life. The two men will be kept under constant guard as my prisoners until we return and report to the king. Once King Oskar is satisfied with my reporting, I will send a party of my personal, most trusted druzars to return Astrid home."

Odda looked at Astrid in silent question.

Astrid attempted to rebut the plan, but words failed her. Perhaps some Ulfsarks could escort them? No. The Thyrling horses wouldn't tolerate their presence for that long, and they couldn't be spared from the hunt. Early spring was a meager time as winter closed out and new growth wasn't ready to be eaten yet. Certainly not with deer and animals inexplicably dying in the forest.

If she didn't go, would war really break out? The solemn expression on Rosamund's face, though like glass, told her it would. Perhaps the Thyrling jaegars didn't crave peace like the Skolvarg. History spoke to other rulers that loved war before.

For several moments, Astrid floundered in her disbelief. Her rage. She hadn't asked for this! To be attacked and nearly killed? Right as the Wolf Song had started for this final year.

But . . . Rosamund had been right. It happened. Focusing on her frustration would help no one move forward and away. Still, her heart sank like a stone. The Wolfmoors and the Wolf-wood had been her only life. Her only tribe. Astrid had never wandered beyond either before.

Now she'd have to leave.

In the silence, Astrid thought she heard the plaintive cry of a wolf. She sighed, looked at Odda again, and nodded. Odda pressed her lips together, then turned to Rosamund.

"We agree to your terms," Odda said.

"Very well." Rosamund rose from the fur-draped stump she'd been sitting on. "I appreciate your willingness to fight for peace, and apologize for the actions of my warriors again. If you would excuse me, I will retire. We will leave just after first light. I wish we could remain longer as planned but I fear this incident may cause more violence between our people if we stay and allow it to fester."

Somehow, Astrid managed to stand and incline her head to the departing princess. The action made her dizzy, but Rolf still held her close. Princess Rosamund slipped away in the night.

"This isn't right, Odda!" Rolf hissed as the princess' foot-steps faded. "You let these foreign brutes insult our people and threaten my niece, then apologize for it? And now you would send her away to answer for *their* crimes?"

Jaw clenched, Odda whirled on Rolf.

"What would you have me do? Go to war? Lose hundreds of lives over an incident that, thankfully, didn't end in the rape or death of one of our Skolvarg? Tonight was a disgusting and unfortunate incident, but thank the spirits that Astrid was able to take care of herself before something worse happened. Our peace is now brittle, Rolf. Even with our best intentions, we may still end up going to war over this. I would delay that as long as possible."

"The rest of the tribe will revolt. They'll be furious when they find out."

"Were I acting in the name of our tribe alone, I would flay the other two and stake them out for the ravens and crows," she continued hotly. "But in this matter, the Matrons asked me to represent the entire Skolvarg people. And we cannot go to war with the Thyrlings again because of three drunken men. The Matrons would have *my* head for it."

Rolf's open mouth bobbed, then closed. His fierce brow relaxed. With a sigh, he shook his head.

"No. Forgive me. You conducted yourself as best you could in a hard position. I just . . ." His jaw tightened, darkened with a hint of stubble along the jaw. Fatigue and sorrow filled his eyes. "I wish it hadn't been my niece or any Skolvarg, for that matter."

Astrid wanted to close her eyes and go to sleep for days, but thoughts of Thyrden kept her awake. She squeezed an arm around Rolf's waist. Rolf shook, fists clenched, chest heaving. In a different life, her broad-shouldered uncle would have made a fearsome warrior.

"If there was another course I would take it," Odda said. The fire in her eyes ebbed into a fatigued voice. "By all means, if you know of another solution, speak now."

"The Wolf Song," Astrid whispered. Her throat felt as dry

as the desert lands of Emora. "None of the whelps will choose me if I'm in Thyrden. I . . ."

Odda let out a long breath. "I thought of that," she murmured. Astrid's final hope shriveled in her chest.

"Then I won't be an Ulfsark," she whispered.

The hollow sound of her own voice shocked her. She'd never whispered any words like it out loud. Rolf closed his eyes. Odda kept Astrid's gaze.

"I'm sorry, Astrid."

Odda turned away, her voice as thin as a leaf in the wind.

"Go home and make preparations to leave tomorrow. The Thyrlings have remained long enough. We will speak in the morning after we've all had some sleep.

Eight

Astrid dreamt of darkness and the whimper of a wolf.

The next morning, she woke up before the sun. Her head throbbed. Her ribs ached with nearly every breath, consuming her chest in tendrils of hot pain. She stared at the top of the hut and wondered where she'd sleep while waiting in Thyrden.

Under the stars?

She hoped so.

Rolf's voice broke the tepid morning air. "You're awake, Astrid?"

"Yes."

He sighed. "I don't think I've slept."

"I'm sorry."

"Don't be."

He shuffled around the hut. Minutes later, a spark of light appeared in the middle of the room. From it, Astrid saw a flash of her uncle. Her father, for all intents and purposes.

Rolf sat cross-legged in the middle of the room, near a pile of kindling. Slowly, he fed dried kindling to the weak flame. With his patience, it grew until he could prop larger sticks over the top. Once the gentle flames wrapped around the sticks and the crackle of burning sap followed, he stacked logs around it.

The flames consumed the wood.

Rolf looked at Astrid, pain in his gaze. He ran a hand over bleary eyes and through his graying hair. When had he started to age so visibly?

"Perhaps some good may come from it."

She scoffed and lay back again.

"While you are among the Thyrlings," he continued, "keep your eyes open. See how they fight, what they eat, how they hunt. Learn everything you can."

"So I am to be a spy?"

He tapped the side of his head. "You are to learn and grow wiser about our enemies. If you are not meant to be an Ulfsark, perhaps you are meant for something greater."

Tears pooled in her eyes. She'd been avoiding the truth, the thought. The horror of that sentence. *If you are not meant to be an Ulfsark.*

What else was there? Certainly nothing greater.

Rolf continued, oblivious to her thoughts. "The circumstances that put you in this situation were unjust. It is not ours to say how the stars will align—"

"—but to bravely face our fate," Astrid finished quietly.

She found a small measure of peace in the old Skolvarg words. Words her mother had once recited daily.

"I'll pay attention."

He gave her a weak smile. "Thank you." He lifted a finger. "There is one more thing. My sister would have kicked me for waiting so long to give it to you, but the time never felt right until now."

Astrid's breath caught as he reached for the other side of his sleeping furs. He produced a bundle wrapped in cured hides, about the length of Astrid's arm.

"For you."

Her hands trembled as she removed the leather cords that bound it. With shaking fingers, she untied the knots and reverently pulled back the hide.

Underneath it, a sword shimmered with a silver-white reflection, evidence of Nistlefolk craftsmanship. Dyed leather wrapped the grip. The pommel featured a star carved into a half circle on top. The guard was a gaping wolf's maw, as if the blade came from between its jaws.

Astrid's breath caught in her chest. Her hand hovered over the sword, too startled to pick it up. Rolf nudged her.

"Go on."

Still trembling, Astrid's fingers wrapped around the cool leather of the hilt. The grip was molded from years of use by her mother, but it fit Astrid's hand like it had always been for her. She hefted the blade, surprised at its lightness, and held it up to the burgeoning morning light outside.

"It's . . . perfect," she murmured.

"Your mother loved that sword."

Atka's age-whitened nose peeked inside, yellow eyes transfixed on the blade. A reverent sort of interest filled his gaze. Astrid paused as Atka padded into the hut, his shoulders barely fitting through the opening.

"What is this?" Rolf wondered aloud.

Atka stopped when his nose touched the hilt of the sword, just above Astrid's hand. The old wolf looked up at her with sad eyes. He hesitated, nudged the sword one more time, then strolled back out of the tent.

He lay down outside with a heavy sigh.

"I believe that's Atka's way of saying he approves of you having it," Rolf said.

"I thought we burned it with her?"

Rolf shrugged. "She made me promise to keep it back because she wanted it to be yours."

Astrid lowered the sword and Rolf offered the belt and

scabbard. Like the guard, the belt buckle and end of the scabbard were a wolf's head. The leather had been dyed a wine red, worn but well-oiled and cared for. Astrid slid the sword home and pulled the belt around her waist. A presence settled over her with the weight of the blade on her hips. Her mother, no doubt.

Watching over her from beyond.

"Well, you certainly look the part," Rolf said with a proud smile. He folded his arms and shook his head. "Too much like your mother by half. It's a good thing, even if you are smaller than her."

Astrid replied with a trying smile. If anything could have given her courage to face the Thyrling king and defend her innocence, her mother's sword was it. She wrapped her fingers around the hilt of the sword once more and drew reassurance from the cold steel. This would be her wolf instead. Her trusted companion during peace and war, just like an Amarok.

With it at her side, she could do anything and feared nothing. She took a deep breath.

"I think I'm ready."

Rolf stood in front of her, hands on her shoulders. "Take care of yourself, all right? Your job is to come back. Rosamund will see to your innocence. They won't kill you."

The implication remained in the air. *But they might imprison you.*

Which was worse?

Rolf put an arm around her, pulled her close, and whispered thickly into her hair, "You might be small, but you are powerful. You are strong. Whatever you do, Astrid, please come back to me. I couldn't bear to lose you both."

Astrid's feet moved of their own accord as she followed Rolf through the Skolvarg camp toward Odda's yurt. On a normal morning, the camp would have already been rekindling cook fires and fetching water. The morning after a big feast, however, meant fewer early risers than usual. Cool fog crawled along the bluish ground with a shiver, creeping into her thick fur-lined cloak.

Lost in her thoughts, Astrid didn't realize they'd reached Odda's yurt until Freydis called to her.

"Astrid."

Astrid glanced up. Freydis, Odda, and Vanna waited just outside the hut. The whole spectacle last night ran through her head like a distant dream. Something that happened, but maybe to someone else. It seemed only a moment ago she'd been fighting Torva in the sparring ring. An image of the ashen-colored cat and the Spirit of Winter, Margu, sprang into her mind. She pushed them away.

The spirits seemed to push her into the wrong place, wrong time, every time.

She thought of the young whelps tumbling over each other near the Amarok dens in the Wolfwood. She'd miss them.

She'd also miss her last Wolf Song.

"I volunteered to go with you," Freydis said in a low voice as she embraced Astrid. Her skinny arms were a warm comfort in the cool mist. "Odda wouldn't allow it. Don't worry, we'll have plenty of adventures together when you return. Watch your back around those stinking Thyrlings."

She pulled back, worry and love in her eyes. Astrid smiled through tears that she blinked away.

"I'll miss you."

Freydis squeezed her arm and stepped back. Rolf pulled Astrid into another warm, heavy embrace. When she pulled away from her uncle, it felt much too soon. He put a hand on her neck and pressed their foreheads together.

"Remember," he said, voice thick with emotion. "Remember what I told you. Remember who you are and come back to me. Soon."

Astrid nodded, wiped her face, and took a deep breath. The sun had risen over the hills casting a pale, golden light on the day. Astrid looked to Odda, who nodded.

"It is time."

NINE

L ess than two hours later, Freydis' oath to never be caught dead atop something as ridiculous as a horse looped through Astrid's mind.

She clung to the reins of the ungainly brown animal and swayed in the saddle with every step. Her knees, hips, back, and thighs ached, but she refused to show any weakness to the Thyrlings. Each time Princess Rosamund asked Astrid how she was faring, Astrid lied through her teeth.

Never mind that she'd almost fallen off the spirits-cursed horse the one time they'd halted. All her resolve and a good deal of teeth-gritting helped her climb back in the saddle.

Rosamund busied herself at the front of the column. She spoke often with her captain of the guard, a burly man with a barrel chest and a midnight beard named Jormund. They spoke in their native Thyrling tongue, so Astrid had no clue what they discussed. Astrid remained under guard between the two groups of Thyrling warriors, ahead of the bards that followed close behind.

A pair of scouts led the Thyrling riders around the

remaining snow drifts and picked the safest crossings over swollen streams. Bird song filled the air and hints of buds and greenery graced the tips of trees and bushes. A cloudless pale blue sky overhead and the smell of sunshine on damp earth made Astrid's heart ache for springtime in the Wolfmoors.

To distract herself from thoughts of home already creeping in, Astrid studied the Thyrlings. They laughed and talked quietly among themselves. A few of the party gave her hard looks, but none dared speak out. She kept an extra watch on them.

The bards rode on large, shaggy ponies. Their laughter rang through the air. She wanted to talk to Ewan again, but felt a rush of heat in her cheeks at the thought.

Astrid distracted herself from the boring journey by counting the number of axes, swords, and other weapons the Thyrlings carried. If wealth in weapons told the tale, the Thyrlings were a prosperous people. Each of the guards was as well armed as the best Ulfsark and better than the rest of many of the Skolvarg warriors.

According to the renewed peace treaty agreed upon by Rosamund and Odda, the eastern boundary between the Thyrlings and the Skolvarg remained at the Auroran River, a wide tributary known for its crystal-clear waters. The Auroran was so broad it reflected the Great Lights when they danced in the northern skies.

The Thyrlings would not pass east of the river nor the Skolvarg west. A raw deal for the Skolvarg. Miles and miles of the Wolfmoors lay to the west of the Auroran River. They had been Skolvarg hunting grounds for ages. No tribes had inhabited the area in a generation, but it still made the bargain a rough one to swallow.

Rosamund's voice cut through Astrid's mind. "We shall make a horsewoman of you yet, Astrid!" She nudged her horse closer to Astrid's side with a bright smile.

"Thank you, Princess."

"Please, call me Rosamund. Save the title for when we are at a formal gathering. I apologize that you have been largely ignored the past few hours. My captain and I have decided the best route to return home. He fears this warm weather has raised a number of the streams. We may be forced to alter our course."

"I'm enjoying the sunshine."

"I'm glad."

Astrid shifted in the saddle with a grimace she couldn't help.

Rosamund frowned. "Please excuse my ignorance, but have you never ridden a horse before?"

Astrid felt herself flush with embarrassment. She shook her head. "No. This is the first time I've seen one up close. Living with giant wolves around makes it hard to keep other animals."

Rosamund laughed, a clear, honest sound, but Astrid hadn't meant to be funny. Stranger still, the laugh wasn't some forced chuckle. Maybe the princess laughed *at* her? No, that wouldn't be good decorum.

"I'm sorry." Rosamund calmed, perhaps sensing Astrid's unease. "I meant no offense. I see what you mean about other animals. I wish we had been able to stay with your tribe longer. I find the Skolvarg way of life fascinating."

The tension at the back of Astrid's neck released. Rosamund wasn't making fun of her, at least.

"We spend the summers traveling across the Wolfmoors, hunting and occasionally trading. In the winter, we camp inside the Wolfwood forest."

"You already miss it," the princess said. "I can see it in your eyes. I often feel the same way about Tyrvik, our capital on the western coast. It's been almost two years since I've seen it. The entire city sits at the end of a fjord. Sometimes the sun sets just right so that it looks like the water flowing to the ocean is a road of golden-red glass."

"It sounds very beautiful."

Rosamund smiled, but it appeared a little tense. "Thyrden has its beauty."

For at least an hour, the two of them rode side by side without conversation. The closer they drew to the borders of Thyrden, the quieter the princess fell. Despite the questions buzzing in Astrid's head, she couldn't muster a single word.

Did Rosamund ride next to her as a sort of protection?

The thought made her teeth clench, but she forced herself to relax. She'd never ask for protection from any Thyrling. Small or not, she could protect herself. She'd proven that last night.

The thought sent a shudder through her. Then again, she didn't want to face that situation twice. Perhaps fighting for one's life outside the ring wasn't all she'd cracked it up to be.

Even when the party forded a stream near a broad spot, soaking the ground either side of its shallow banks, Rosamund didn't return to Jormund's side. Nor had she said another word. The wrinkle in her brow seemed to indicate deep thought.

Astrid gazed at a thick collection of logs, branches, mud, and rock that created a giant beaver dam as they passed. Her body still ached from last night. Rolf had tied a wrap around her ribs before they left, which helped support the sore area. Mostly, the pain had faded because Skolvarg healed faster than most, but she still ached. Whether it was the horse, or the fight, or her heart, she wasn't sure.

A male Thyrling with blond hair and a mustache so light it appeared white rode not far behind Astrid. His eyes haunted her all day. Despite the Princess at Astrid's side, he didn't attempt to mask his voice very much when he whispered to another druzar, "Have you heard the story about what happened with the Skolvarg?"

Rosamund tensed ever-so-slightly. Astrid watched her out of the corner of her eye and tried not to give herself away.

"Not much. They're keeping it under wraps."

"Think she's guilty?"

"Of course."

Astrid swallowed hard. She waited for Rosamund to stop them, or give some indication that she heard their low speech. None came.

"She killed Ivar. Even as little as she is? I wouldn't want to mess with her. Deceptive, you know? The rest of them are so big. They have unusual strength, heal fast, that kind of thing."

"Please," the woman druzar muttered. "It's all a bunch of tall tales if you ask me. If they were so brave and fierce, why did their chieftains hand over all the lands west of the Auroran?"

Unfortunately, Astrid had the same question.

Their discussion turned, then faded into nothing. Slowly, Rosamund relaxed. Her focus remained straight ahead.

Astrid did the same.

A breeze picked up in the afternoon, chilling Astrid to the bone. Unable to bear another moment in the saddle, she swung out and lowered herself slowly to the ground. A low, simmering pain laced through her ribs like a lattice of fire, then calmed.

"You've had enough of your horse for the day?" Rosamund asked.

"My legs would like a little break, I think."

"There is wisdom in that," Rosamund said, smiling. She swung out of the saddle with much more grace dismounting than Astrid. "Perhaps we can walk together? I have many questions about the Skolvarg, if you're willing to answer."

Astrid nodded.

Rosamund looked away for a minute as they continued to walk. At last, she turned back. "I hope you don't find this question too forward to start with, but I'm curious about this Blessing of the Spirits that your people speak of. May I ask what it means?"

Would an explanation give an advantage to the Thyrlings? One they could exploit through her trial or, perhaps, war? No, Astrid decided. The Blessing of the Spirits was no secret. Even if they didn't believe in it, the Thyrlings at least knew about it.

Rosamund seemed to sense her hesitation and gave her an encouraging smile. "I understand if it is not something you wish to discuss. I had only intended to learn more about your people, now that we are at peace with one another. Who knows? In the future we might even be able to call the Skolvarg allies?"

Astrid set aside the hope of diplomacy to answer the original question.

"The Blessing of the Spirits is what makes the Skolvarg different from other humans," she said. "I'm not . . . there's not much else to it. We're supposed to be naturally faster, stronger. We heal quicker and live longer."

"All of you?"

"As far as I know." Astrid didn't know if the Blessing of the Spirits was what enabled some of her people to speak with the spirits but that subject didn't seem appropriate to bring up with an outsider, even one as friendly as Rosamund.

"And is that how you bond with your Amarok wolves?"

Suspicion spiked in Astrid. Did Rosamund know about Astrid's situation? That was none of her business. Before she could answer, the princess seemed to sense something was amiss.

"I didn't mean to offend you! I'm only curious about life outside of Thyrden."

Astrid blinked and realized she'd had her horse's reins in a death grip. Rosamund had no way of knowing *why* Astrid didn't have her own wolf. She relaxed her shoulders and tried to push down the ache of missing out on what was probably her last chance at hearing the Wolf Song.

"That's something different," Astrid said, hoping to end the conversation or change the subject. "The wolves are the ones that choose us. It just. . . happens."

Or at least it does for everyone else but me, for some reason.

She didn't have the heart to tell Rosamund that when you came from a place where everyone was special, no one was special. Among the Skolvarg, the Ulfsarks were the truly blessed ones.

"I see," Rosamund looked away for a time. "I wish we had been able to stay with your tribe longer. I am fascinated by your culture. The Skolvarg worship the seasons, yes?"

"Four spirits that each represent one of the seasons," Astrid said, grateful to talk about something besides the Wolf Song. She wasn't much for religion—though her recent experience in the woods had her questioning things. "I've spent more time with a weapon than I have studying our beliefs, though."

Rosamund laughed. "I envy you for that! I'd much rather be outside riding or hunting than stuck in a hard chair listening to tutors and coin counters talk endlessly about the affairs of the kingdom."

That surprised Astrid. Given Rosamund's pale look and slight frame, she'd just assumed the princess spent her time gossiping about the court and doing needlework. Then again, she should have known better after spending her entire life being discounted for being the Skolvarg equivalent of a runt.

"This must be an enjoyable break for you then."

"Indeed it is," Rosamund said, nodding. Her voice fell quiet. "I am in no hurry to get back to court life. Believe it or not, I know what it's like."

"I'm not sure what you mean?"

"Having something so close that you want more than anything in the world but not being able to take it. It doesn't take a seer to see you want to be a wolf rider, Astrid."

Astrid pulled in a breath. Rosamund studied her, so Astrid finally nodded.

"Yes. Very much."

"Will you?"

"This trip makes it very unlikely."

Trouble crossed Rosamund's expression. "Then I'm doubly sorry for it. Ivar made a lot of terrible choices and caused pain in more than one way. I'm ashamed of him."

Unsure how to respond, Astrid only nodded again.

"When we arrive in Drakby," Rosamund continued, "I hope that one day you will—"

A horse thundered toward them from behind, cutting Rosamund's reply off. Both turned to see Ewan canter up with a broad smile. Astrid's stomach flipped. She'd ignored him most of the day, unwilling to be distracted by his attractive face. Now that she saw him again, she realized that it had been foolish.

She'd been distracted by him all the same.

"Snow roses for the princess and the Skolvarg maiden?" he asked with a melodic tone that reminded her of his songs last night.

In his outstretched hand, he held two flowers.

Snow roses weren't roses at all, but a strange cross between a flower and a pinecone sprig. They grew on evergreen bushes and turned white in the springtime. Astrid looked from the flower to him. He grinned, teeth surprisingly white for a man his age. Twenty five, she guessed. It appeared he'd kept all his teeth.

"Thank you," Rosamund said with a gracious smile. Captain Jormund called for her at the front. She turned to Astrid and said, "Excuse me, Astrid. Thank you for speaking with me and breaking up the dull ride."

Rosamund mounted her docile horse, then guided it around her druzars and back to the front. Astrid kept her gaze ahead, unerringly aware of Ewan at her right side as he dismounted and walked next to her.

If Freydis were here, she'd know what to say.

"We heard about what happened last night," he said, low. All the humor and playfulness had dropped from his tone. He reached over and laid the snow rose across the front of her saddle. The delicate white flower set against the dark horse hide was a brilliant, striking contrast.

She tried to say *thank you*, but the words stuck in her throat. Ewan knowing about the embarrassing incident felt like too much, but she didn't know why.

"We wanted you to know that we are happy to offer our protection, should you need it," Ewan continued.

Astrid glanced to her left as the other bard, thick bellied but jovial, drew up close. He gave her a bright, but gentle, smile. Auley, she'd heard Ewan call him.

One of the druzars glanced back, but Ewan gazed around with a wistful expression that belied the gravity in his tone. When the druzar faced forward again, Ewan turned to her.

"The Thyrlings aren't bad people in general, but I wouldn't call them trustworthy."

"Like bards, you mean?" She'd meant it as a joke but it had come out closer to an accusation.

He grinned anyway. "Against the Thyrlings?" he scoffed. "Yes. We may not be perfect, but at least Oskar isn't our king. That alone makes us far more trustworthy."

The mention of the Thyrling king sent a stab of nerves through Astrid. Perhaps it wouldn't be a bad idea to have friends on her side when she had to face his possible judgment. That she had to make this trip at all was ridiculous.

She couldn't help one last jab, however.

"So I'm to trust the reputation of the Ochlanders based on the words of a bard?" she asked. "That doesn't seem wise."

"Quick," Auley said, laughing. "Very quick. I like this girl!"

The responding smile that Ewan gave didn't seem off put, and she couldn't deny having them at her flanks did feel better. Memories of Ivar remained bright. Her paranoia around the Thyrlings would exhaust her by the end of the day. Particularly with a horse to ride for far too long.

Astrid drew in a deep breath. "I can care for myself, but thank you."

"You've got a fire in you," the other bard said. "Still, if the need arises . . ."

Somehow, the implication that she was too small to look after herself seemed less an insult from him than from others. Astrid managed a wry smile.

"Thank you."

"Just back here if you need us, then."

Auley turned his horse and disappeared. Astrid's mouth opened. For a moment, she wanted to ask Ewan to stay. Riding the horses was boring, and she felt less swamped by the Thyrlings with them there. She closed her mouth before it could come out.

No, a Skolvarg could take care of herself.

Astrid shoved that thought aside with a little growl. It wouldn't serve her now, true or not. Ewan remained at her side without another word. They plodded along in an easy quiet that she appreciated.

In the silence, Astrid thought she heard the plaintive cry of a wolf.

TEN

For the next week, they traveled out of territory Astrid knew.

While still in the Wolfmoors, the unfamiliar country cast a shadow over the sunny spring day. Astrid had never been so far from home before. The growing distance sat like a rock in her gut. How would things have been different if she'd minded her own business and never left the feast?

Unknowingly, Ewan's gregarious antics kept her from plunging into despair. He always sang, anything from comical funeral dirges to epic ballads. If he didn't make music, he cracked jokes and made himself laugh harder than anyone else. The Thyrlings started bets on what the bard would find funny.

A lot of money was exchanged.

The other bards acted equally as bright. Auley and one of the twin girls had several comedic routines they volleyed back and forth. Druzars relaxed in their saddles as they laughed. Even Rosamund cracked a smile.

Ewan had a long dagger that he kept belted to his waist. Too long to be a tool for eating, but he'd never drawn it. Not even to participate in the Thyrling's knife throwing contests in the evening. She watched him with it. He didn't grasp it often, but it seemed cared for. Amidst his saddlebags, she spied a sword, and several other possible weapons. Both the male bards tended to ride closer to the Thyrlings, keeping them away from the female bards.

Auley and the twins, however, were a different matter than Ewan all together.

One of the twins never spoke that Astrid could tell, and the other never stopped. They both had dark eyes, but the quiet twin had a more pinched chin and drawn face, as if she worried all the time. Ewan called her Lara. The other one, Liss, had bright, apple cheeks and a way of laughing that felt contagious. Their singing was beautiful, even to Astrid's untrained ear.

Auley hovered protectively over them in a gentle, big brother fashion. The only thing *he* carried more of than songs was weapons. A startling array of small knives, hatchets, and an impressive two-handed sword he called a claymore. The accoutrements appeared in his hands at random moments, like they were little trinkets he liked to collect and show off.

The more she got to know them, the more Astrid wondered whether they traveled with the princess by happenstance or invitation? Astrid couldn't tell.

In the front of the traveling group, Rosamund spoke only to Jormund, occasionally Astrid. The conversations were short, quick.

No further problem came from the druzars that had been with Ivar. The pair had their weapons taken the night of the fight and walked or rode bound at the wrist with leather straps. An escort of other druzars accompanied them. How that prevented them from taking off into the Wolfmoors, Astrid had no idea.

But then, what Thyrling would want to be loose in the Wolfmoors?

Most of the Thyrlings ignored her. While she didn't actively fear for her life, neither did she trust any of them. No matter when she went to bed, she woke every morning with Ewan and Auley close by. As if the bards intentionally sought to help, even when she didn't ask.

Rosamund's wisdom in waiting to deliver the punishment —or verdict—when they returned to Thyrling lands struck Astrid during their travels. Distance and time had cooled much of the heightened anger, allowing more space for truth. Action that night, at such a delicate time, would have been more likely to result in less discipline for the Thyrling druzars. They might have retaliated against Astrid or the Skolvarg and truly sparked a war.

Not that the Skolvarg would get out of this so easily.

The flutter of bird wings late one morning drew Astrid out of her thoughts. She glanced up just as a russet-colored bird flittered by and landed on Ewan's shoulder. It preened, chirping gently. He tilted his head, laughing.

At the bird?

The song?

Ewan had a strange affection for the little creature. Must be some sort of pet, because it had followed them for days now. Just as Astrid summoned the words to ask, the thunder of hooves interrupted her chance. A horse, then the rider, appeared from some trees ahead.

"Princess!" called a voice. "Princess?"

"Here!"

The rider, a young boy with dark locks and broad lips, pulled the horse to a stop. It tossed its mane, halting a few paces away from Captain Jormund's thick mount.

"We're half a day from Drakby," the boy announced. "The river isn't far. We should be back this evening."

Relief welled up in Astrid. Finally, an end. Rosamund had explained that King Oskar currently held court in Drakby, a relatively new town on the western banks of the Auroran river. She allowed herself a hope that if things went as the princess promised, she would be on her way home in a month. Or locked away and forgotten in a dungeon. Astrid forced herself not to think about that, though she couldn't help but wonder if anyone from home would ever come looking for her if she never returned.

"Thank you," Rosamund said. "That is wonderful news indeed."

The Auroran river barreled by like a stampeding bison in a spring storm.

It crossed the countryside like a blue-bleeding wound, frothing around the edges. In some places, ice rimmed it. The depths looked black as a starless night and twice as long. Astrid shivered as she stared at it that evening.

"We tried building a bridge across it." Rosamund pointed to an abandoned structure not far down the other side of the river. "But there was no way to set timbers in the middle to stabilize, even at low tide. Instead, we use the barges."

A number of large rafts bobbed on the racing river on the far side. Tall timbers had been driven into the high banks, then ringed with massive stones. A thick rope strung between the timbers, each barge, and across the river to other trees. Opposite them, a barge shoved away from the nearest bank with a push of long poles.

"Inventive," Astrid murmured, for lack of anything else to say about it. She hated to praise a Thyrling, but it was ingenious.

"You, the bards, and Captain Jormund and I will cross

first," Rosamund continued. "The rest will come on the other barges. That at least allows us to cross first and see King Oskar to update him on . . . recent events. The accused will be on the final barge."

As she spoke, other Thyrlings moved toward the remaining barges still tied up. Astrid's throat tightened. So many people. All of them unfamiliar, chattering in a language she didn't understand. A chest-tightening, over-whelming feeling threatened to consume her, but she staved it off.

Not the time, nor the place.

She turned her focus to the barge and the river. In the recent years of the uneasy ceasefire, the Skolvarg tribes had avoided the lands near the eastern banks of the Auroran because of Thyrling proximity. Crossing to the west bank felt like stepping into another world, one entirely out of Astrid's grasp.

The midday sun shone bright, reflecting patches of snow scattered across the other bank. The river ran high and fast. Four men on the barge somehow managed to keep it on course with a rope angled downstream. The current propelled them toward the opposite bank.

Shouts rang out as they approached, barely audible over the river. A number of warriors and other settlers gathered on the far bank waved.

"My welcoming party," Rosamund said, though she seemed far less enthusiastic than the people waving and cheer-ing. Astrid wanted to ask why but decided it was best to keep the question to herself.

Within minutes, the waiting Thyrlings numbered in the dozens. Just as Astrid counted two hundred, more joined the throng.

Was Drakby that large of a town?

The people on the shore alone rivaled the size of most

Skolvarg tribes. An uneasy feeling swelled in Astrid's stomach. Did all of these people live together? How close?

In reality, she hadn't actually left her homeland yet. Drakby was part of the Wolfmoors, as much as the Wolfwood forest on the other side. But the teeming crowd at the waterfront, framed by Drakby's wooden palisade walls in the distance, were a stark reminder of just how far out of familiar territory she'd come.

If Rosamund noticed Astrid's concern, she made no comment.

A moment later, Captain Jormund called out orders for the crossing, which ended the conversation.

The barge docked on the bank only a few steps away. The jarring *thud* of wood hitting ground shook Astrid out of her thoughts. One of the bargemen extended a plank, then bowed.

"Your Highness."

Rosamund acknowledged him with a nod.

"Welcome home, Princess Rosamund." The barge operator was a salty old man with a gray beard, sprawling shoulders, and a missing front tooth. His words issued with a slight whistle. "We'll have you safely across the river shortly. River is high, but the ropes are new and firm. You're safe with me!"

"Thank you, good sir."

Captain Jormund stood to the side of the board and held Rosamund's hand, giving her additional balance as she crossed the board without getting her feet muddy. As she stepped onto the craft, each person bowed and murmured.

"All right," Jormund called as he spun to face Astrid and the bards. "Let's get on with it."

Ewan snorted.

"That's what his wife said on their wedding night," Auley muttered, then jabbed Ewan in the ribs with a wink. The two of them snorted. Astrid rolled her lips to suppress a laugh just as an oblivious Thyrling from the barge took the reins of

Astrid's horse. She gratefully let it go, then followed Rosamund's beckoning wave. Ewan and Auley framed Astrid on either side, one ahead, one behind, without a word.

Plenty of room remained in the barge after they stepped on, but the operator barked a command and the remaining Thyrlings shoved away. Rope handles tied to the inside of the barge gave them something to hold onto. Likely, it could hold up to twenty armored warriors, depending on the river. Worn planks and logs lay beneath her feet. Had the same vessel carried warriors over to fight the Skolvarg just a few years ago?

Undoubtedly.

She hated Drakby already.

The waves lapped the sides of the rocking craft, but the barge rode the high water without problem. Six bear-like men hauled at the ropes, their sheer brawn pulling the craft across the water. Skolvarg in general might have been stronger than Thyrlings but Astrid would have bet any one of these men could hold their own against the biggest Ulfsark.

As they neared the western shores of the Auroran River, Astrid glanced back to the east. In the shadows of the Wolf-moors, she thought of her uncle, her tribe, and the only life she'd ever known. A silver-haired figure robed in blue stood near the bank, far downstream from the other Thyrlings in the approaching group. When Astrid blinked, the figure was gone. No, it couldn't be right. She'd only imagined Margu.

With a dismissive thought, Astrid turned ahead, to the unknown world that awaited.

After she crossed the Auroran river, the only thing Astrid wanted was a breath of fresh air. Never had any gathering she'd attended—not even trading camps or the mid-winter gather-

ings with the other Skolvarg tribes—smelled as filthy as
Drakby.

"Here ya go," called the operator. He gestured toward a
crowd of horses. One of the bargemen lifted the board that
Rosamund had entered the barge on and dropped it across a
muddy patch of ground that led to the horses. Another
servant ripped off a coat and laid it on the ground next to a
smaller, but magnificently cared for, horse.

"Thank you," Rosamund said.

To her credit, no disgust showed on her face. Nothing but
a bright, shining sort of relief. Meanwhile, Astrid tried not to
gag at the stench. Even the bards had fallen uncharacteristi-
cally silent. Ewan's bird tucked itself into the collar of his shirt,
ceasing its happy chirping.

With help from a nearby servant, coated with mud almost
to his waist, Rosamund crossed the board and mounted the
regal horse herself. At a nod from the operator of the barge,
Astrid slipped across the mud and stood next to a black horse
several hands higher than the last.

It reached back, teeth bared, and snapped, a hands-breadth
away from taking a chunk of muscle out of her leg.

She whacked it in the ribs with a growl.

"I'll take a bite out of *you* next."

The horse faced forward again with a shake of its head and
low sound of protest. Wretched animals. If she had the choice
to ride or walk home when this was all over, she'd go on her
legs even if it took her until the snows flew to get back to her
tribe.

Rosamund spoke brightly with Thyrlings clustered
around her. Only Captain Jormund seemed to pay attention.
He eyed the road ahead with some trepidation. A channel of
thick mud awaited.

A gaggle of girls waved from down the way, hair held back
with stained, dark kerchiefs.

"Welcome home, Princess Rosamund!"

She waved, and her horse started forward. Astrid's horse followed without command, so she let it go. Next to her, Ewan rode a gray horse with spots along the flanks. He peered around, a steady curiosity in his expression.

Minutes later, Astrid's horse sank almost to its knees in the mud. Undaunted, it continued after the lead horse, which navigated with startling ease. Astrid breathed through her mouth as they passed huts, people, and more dirty streets.

The sheer number of Thyrlings crammed into poorly built log cabins was the biggest cause of the stench. Human refuse, animal waste, and old vomit lay thick in the air. So many bodies crammed inside palisade walls, slopping together with livestock, mud, and woodsmoke reeked.

The Thyrling's occupations added to the stench. Following no logical layout, the settlers' cabins mixed with skinners, tanners, and butchers. Vats of dye and curing furs stretched over piles of trash.

Blood trickled through the road, collecting in muddy puddles along the way. Mounds of half-butchered deer, elk, moose, and caribou carcasses piled against the palisade walls. The carcasses were a haven for half-wild dogs, who lumbered around, so swollen and bloated with rotted meat they could barely move. Not a single tree stood on this side of the river within a quarter mile, all of them stripped and gathered into stacks of logs, planks, and timbers.

People shouted greetings to the princess from their cabin doors. Merchants hawked their wares in loud voices up and down the streets, pausing to take a breath and wave as the royal procession went by. The constant movement, noise, and stench of it all made Astrid dizzy.

When they finally made it out of the busy settlement, the air improved—slightly. The smell lingered, but the crowds thinned. The constant shouts lessened when they approached a large hill at the west end of town. The hill overlooked the rest of Drakby and had its own palisade fence.

"Impressive hill fort, Princess," Auley called. He rubbed at his red beard, which sprouted frizzy hairs from his chin. "There's many an Ochlander chieftain who would be jealous of your stronghold."

Princess Rosamund smiled. "Thank you. King Oskar has put a significant amount of energy and time into its creation and upkeep."

If nothing else, the hill provided an escape from the cursed mud of Drakby's streets. The slope had a gravel track running all the way to a second set of gates, which were thrown open. Numerous flapping pennants cracked in the wind. A black bear on a field of green, the standard of Oskar, King of the Thyrlings.

A horn sounded somewhere inside the hill fort. Several horns throughout the city answered moments later. Finally, a booming drum banged somewhere on the wall.

"Now," Rosamund murmured, "we may officially return to my father's personal quarters. He calls it his fort. The long house is his, and I have a smaller building in the back."

She passed first through the wooden gates, and Jormund followed. The moment Rosamund slipped inside, a raucous cry sounded that intensified as the captain followed.

Astrid trailed Jormund, cheeks hot. She kept her head high. A lone Skolvarg had no distinguishing characteristic that might set her apart from the Thyrlings in an obvious way. The Thyrlings had such a variety of people that she could blend in easily enough.

Except for her clothes.

She wore the typical Nistlefolk-traded fabric and deer-leather pants of the Skolvarg. Her hair, a glossy blonde color, hung to the middle of her back when she didn't braid it in coils and pin it to her head. Another thing that the Thyrlings rarely saw.

So what would they say when she entered King Oskar's fort?

They wouldn't know what history lay behind her coming, but they would know it wasn't usual for a Skolvarg to attend a princess. She braced herself, expecting the worst. Behind her, the bards rode four abreast, with the two women in the middle.

"Courage," Auley said softly. "We've got your back."

Astrid relaxed just a little, but gave no reply. Later, she'd thank them. For now, she focused on memorizing her surroundings. If she wanted to keep herself safe, she had to know all her exit points.

The interior of this palisade that surrounded all of Drakby had ramparts made of packed earth for additional support. The center of Oskar's keep was a long lodge, several stables, storage buildings, and what appeared to be outbuildings behind it. Cooking, perhaps? The largest of the buildings was most likely to be Rosamund's.

The peak of the lodge rose higher than the rampart walls, marking it as the largest structure she'd ever seen. At least twice as tall as Chieftain Odda's expansive lodge.

The eaves were painted in greens and gold, patterned in diamonds. The windows had shutters of carved wood featuring snarling bear heads. Each of the six enormous pine columns holding up the front of the lodge were also carved with the likeness of full-sized bears standing on their hind feet.

In the doorway stood King Oskar.

He looked just like the bear he appreciated so generously. Tall and broad-shouldered, with a thick black beard that spilled onto his chest and shone with oils in the afternoon sunshine. His aging face creased with what looked like a permanent scowl.

A heavy cloak of gold and green draped over his imposing frame. On anyone else, the cloak would have served as a large blanket. To him? It fit just right. Ringed fingers rested on a jeweled belt as if inspecting his warriors, not welcoming home a child.

Rosamund rode almost to the porch of the lodge before dismounting. Each rider followed suit, then knelt. Reluctantly, Astrid did the same. As she did, Rosamund approached her father and gave a half-bow.

"My King," she called, her voice bouncing off the palisade. "I return with good news from the east. The Skolvarg have agreed to peace terms with our people."

"As expected, my daughter." His eyes slid from Rosamund to the bards, and Astrid in particular. "But these hangers-on you have brought back to our halls?"

"This is Astrid of the Skolvarg."

Rosamund swept to her side and placed a hand on Astrid's shoulder, indicating she should rise. Astrid obeyed. As she rose, she met Oskar's scrutinizing gaze. His hard brown eyes scowled back. He held her stare for a moment, then looked to Ewan in silent question.

"And this is Ewan, an Ochlander bard," Rosamund said. He rose as she touched his shoulder. "We encountered his small band on our journey to meet with the Skolvarg. I invited him to return with us to Drakby and the celebration with your other leaders."

The king spared only a glance at Ewan before his hard stare returned to Astrid. His fingers curled around the belt below his barrel chest. How much Skolvarg blood was on those hands?

"You're young for a Skolvarg," he called. "Or maybe you're just short. I wager you never fought in the wars?"

Astrid gritted her teeth and shook her head.

His scowl broke into a toothy grin. "I could tell you a few stories about those battles, Skolvarg."

Astrid set her jaw and refused to answer. The longer the silence persisted, the wider his smile stretched. She resisted the urge to place a hand on her mother's sword.

"Perhaps a tale or two from our bards this evening?" Rosamund suggested. Her words cut the growing tension in the air. Oskar waved a dismissive hand, as if he didn't care.

"If he has any tales worth telling or songs worth singing." The king turned, as if he knew the answer would disappoint him before it was given. "Come Rosamund, I would speak to you in private. Jormund, see that our guests are given quarters. The stables will do for now."

Without a parting word, or waiting for his daughter, the King turned and disappeared inside the lodge.

"My father is a military man," Rosamund said, quietly enough so only Astrid and the bards could hear her. "As such, his memory of the Skolvarg war is as deep as his love for song and saga is shallow. I will try to make sure he remains respectful this evening. I will also search for other accommodations for you other than the stables, but it will be tricky. The jaegars are coming from different parts of Thyrden and the lodge and our inns are already promised out. Nevertheless, I will see what I can do for you."

She stared at the lodge, shoulders tense and pulled back. Her jaw remained tight. Still, Astrid sensed some relief in her, as if Rosamund had dreaded the confrontation with her father as much as Astrid.

"Thank you," Astrid said, but her hope wasn't great. She doubted a grizzled gray bear could keep a leader like Oskar in line, let alone Rosamund. It didn't take a diplomat to see the King had little regard for his daughter, at least based on their first impression.

"Perhaps I can prepare a few of my songs and tales of war that may be more to his liking," Ewan said with a bow.

"That would be appreciated, thank you Ewan," Rosamund said. "We will speak soon. Until then, please make yourselves comfortable and rest from our travels. I'll send a messenger for you when we have dinner prepared."

ELEVEN

To Captain Jormund's credit, he kept a straight face as he led them into a stable that lay on the other side of the inner palisade wall. Thanks to a slope in the hill, Oskar's lodge and outbuildings weren't visible. The stable looked over Drakby a little below them, elevating them out of the stench.

Servants accepted their muddy horses and led them toward a different stable while Jormund showed Astrid, Ewan, and the other bards the spare stalls that had just been filled with fresh straw.

"I am certain the princess will find quarters for you in the lodge after the meeting with the king concludes," Jormund said. His flat voice didn't sound convincing at all. Or like it really mattered to him.

"I'm sure you're quite right, thank you," Auley said. He slapped himself on the stomach. "We'll do as the princess suggested and make ourselves comfortable until we hear from her. Thank you again for your hospitality."

Jormund gave a stiff nod, then left the stables. The bards scattered to separate stalls and Astrid found herself alone in between the wooden walls of her own stall. The fresh straw smelled better than Drakby, at any rate, and it was out of reach from Oskar's immediate influence. She doubted he'd come here.

In a way, this was perfect.

"Well, then." Ewan whistled and raised a hand overhead. His finch flew up into the rafters, chirping in apparent satisfaction at its new home. Ewan then fell backward into the stall, out of sight. Astrid shuffled to the side and peered in to find him laying back, hands stacked behind his head.

"We've had worse places to lay down our heads," Liss said. She gazed around, then looked at Lara, who frowned at the straw and said nothing. "We'll like as naught be moved into the hall as soon as the king is done meeting with the princess."

Lara appeared no less appeased by the thought. She nudged some hay around with her foot while her pretty scowl deepened. Meanwhile, Auley kicked some of the straw around his stall until it made a gigantic pile, revealing hard-packed dirt underneath.

"We've had better accommodations, too," Auley said, then flopped onto the straw with a sigh. "Still, might as well get comfortable before our performance tonight. Don't want to mess up in front of Oskar."

Ewan's expression had changed to one of deep thought as he studied the underside of the rafters.

Astrid undid her belt, then hung it on a nail that stuck out of the wood. She withdrew her mother's sword, then tucked it under the straw. Later tonight, she'd clean it with the straw and make sure it shone. The Nistlefolk steel required little upkeep. She could hide it in the back, underneath all the prickly stuff, while she attended the dinner. Undoubtedly, Oskar wouldn't let weapons inside and she didn't trust it in the keeping of his guards.

Lara pulled out a flute and fiddled around with it with

delicate fingers, no doubt attempting to distract herself from the current circumstances. Liss quickly undid her braid, humming as the strands fell to pieces. She studied Astrid as she worked, then finally broke the quiet with a question.

"How old are you, Astrid?"

Astrid glanced up. She hesitated, then said, "Nineteen winters."

"Ah. Our age."

Lara's light blue eyes met Astrid's with a shot of curiosity, then turned back to her flute. Dark hair loose on her shoulders framed a heart-shaped face and a smatter of freckles crossed the bridge of her nose. Liss differed almost drastically. Light yellow hair. Deep green eyes. Her nose was long, her lips a bit more pouty. She was taller and lean, where Lara rounded. The two couldn't be more different for being twins.

"Don't mind her," Liss said. "Lara doesn't like to speak, though she's our best singer."

Astrid nodded.

"We haven't spent much time among the Skolvarg," Liss continued. "Do you always have the wolves around?"

"They live with us."

Ewan straightened up. Around the corner, Auley peeked his head out as well.

"They're not wild?" Liss asked, her pitch rising in surprise. "I heard the Amarok live in packs and only come when their riders call them."

"Some are wild. Some are tame. Even the tame ones will go out in the forest on their own. They usually respond to the call of their Skolvarg, but apparently they sort of . . . share a mind."

"Where's yours?"

Liss' question was innocent enough. Her wide-eyed gaze innocuous with curiosity. Astrid swallowed past a dryness in her mouth.

"I don't have one."

"So you don't all have a giant wolf?"

Astrid shook her head. "No, not all of us."

"Interesting," she murmured, then lowered her voice. "Did the wolves eat the Thyrlings during the war?"

Her gaze darted around, no doubt searching for Thyrling stable hands that might overhear.

"Ah, no," Astrid replied, feeling more and more uncomfortable with each passing question. "They don't eat people."

"Damn shame!" Auley called out from his stall.

"How about we give Astrid a little space, eh?" Ewan stood up, his lithe body moving with an unexpected grace. "We'll do plenty of talking tonight at dinner. No doubt, we'll have a lot of time to get to know Astrid while we're here."

What that comment meant, Astrid could hardly fathom, but she appreciated the space it gave her to settle into her straw, bury her sword inside, and think.

Rosamund sent word that night that Oskar canceled the dinner, but servants from the lodge brought food for Astrid and the bards.

"Get used to it," Auley grumbled. "Oskar likes to be in control and *prove* he's in control. He'll keep us waiting until his pride is satisfied."

Nevertheless, the meal was a hearty one. Each of them received a fist-sized loaf of dark bread, fresh from the oven, and a steaming bowl of fish stew. Carrots, wild onion, and potatoes flecked the warm broth.

The change in pace was welcome. Instead of resting, Astrid's mind had spun over the possibilities of what King Oskar would say the moment he heard her story. The few minutes she'd been in his presence hadn't lent her much hope of acquittal.

If he blamed her, what then?

The bards gathered in the hallway of this part of the stable on small, empty ale barrels and bumps of hay. "Come, Astrid!" Liss called. "Sit with us. We're just planning out our songs for . . . well . . . we don't know when, do we?"

She burst into giggles. Auley had a booming laugh that filled the barn, warming the air. Astrid joined them and listened while they tossed ideas back and forth. As they chattered, the spring evening grew dark and chilly. Astrid downed the stew, tore the loaf into pieces and quickly chewed them, then felt lost when her hands no longer had anything to do.

Astrid wrapped her cloak tight around her as the plaintive, low cry of a wolf came from outside. The back of her neck prickled.

"Hardly!" Ewan scoffed as Auley tilted his head back and roared at a joke he'd told, probably at Ewan's expense. Both of them had ignored the wolf's howl. "I'll have you know, I had every eye in that hall wet with tears, fighters or not."

The keening wolf cry came again, this time louder.

"Do you hear that?" Astrid asked.

The bards quieted, then paused. Ewan tilted his head to the left slightly. "Hear what?" he murmured.

"The wolf."

Quiet fell, broken only by the occasional sound from the yard or call of a stablehand on the other side of the stable. Astrid strained to hear, but the mournful note didn't repeat.

"Sorry." She shook her head. "I . . . I could have sworn I heard it."

"Might have," Liss said with a little smile. She nudged Auley with an elbow. "Auley's so loud you can't hear anything else when he's talking."

Auley gave a mock frown and splattered her with a little soup from his bowl and she gasped in outrage.

Lara laughed.

Astrid peered past them, to the window, too focused to pay any attention to the fact that Lara had broken her silence. A leather hide had been tacked to the edge and hung halfway down. Cool air rolled in through the gap. On the other side of the hill, torches burned low and clear along the palisade wall, cutting into the dark night sky. A thousand stars speckled the night.

She frowned.

Why had the wolf gone silent?

She hadn't imagined it, she knew that. The sound sent a chill all the way to her bones, and her skin still puckered. Although she couldn't be sure, she'd swear it was the same cry she'd heard before. Astrid forced herself to relax, but still felt on edge as she attempted to hear it again. The bards spoke more quietly now, and Ewan watched her with greater attention.

After relentless focus, her head began to pound. She felt drawn and tired. An hour ago, she'd taken her braid out and brushed her hair, which had eased the building headache. Now, it flooded back, tightening the skin around her eyes. Her neck felt as tight as a bow.

Perhaps she was more tired than she thought.

"I . . . I think I'll go to bed," she said, and stood.

Liss smiled at her. "Sleep well. We'll keep it down over here." Lara gave her the same appraising, curious look that she gave everyone. Auley reached over and tapped Astrid on the back of the arm.

"Night, lass."

Astrid turned to leave. A few steps from their little party, a hand touched her arm. She glanced back to see Ewan there, concern in his features. The low light of the stable away from the torch Auley had taken from outside cast him in shadows.

"Everything all right?"

"Tired."

"Is that all?"

No, she wanted to say. *No, I'm lost and far from home and maybe my life is in danger and I'm hearing a wolf and I just want to go back.*

Instead, Astrid swallowed.

"Yes. It's all new and will look brighter in the morning."

Ewan hesitated, then gave a nod. "I'm the next stall over if you need anything. Auley is on the other side. He snores loud enough to scare off any troublemakers. I'm a light sleeper, and so is Lara. You'll be safe with us."

To her surprise, his reassurance provided some comfort. Having never ventured outside her tribe, Astrid hadn't been sure what other groups of people were like. She hadn't expected any immediacy of friendship.

"Thank you," she murmured.

She felt Ewan's eyes on her back as she slipped farther into the shadows, stopped at her stall, and lay down. The straw prickled into her back, neck, and scalp as she pulled her furs farther over her shoulders, and closed her eyes. Moments later, sleep stole over her.

As the last dregs of awareness slipped away, she thought she heard a wolf cry.

Astrid awoke to Ewan and Auley's quiet murmurs in a pre-dawn light. She bolted upright with a low breath, then held it. The stable was familiar enough after a few moments, and shades of the night passed away. She relaxed.

"Not sure," Ewan whispered. "Princess Rosamund will try

to show some control, I would imagine, but has little. Last night, she invited us to dinner and then had to quit."

"Think Oskar finagled that?"

"Of course. I think there's a power play between her and her father. She's going to try to establish precedent and he'll push back at every opportunity. The little things, you know? It's how Oskar has always been."

"Last night could be a coincidence," Auley murmured. "Just a dinner. We'd all just returned from traveling."

"Is it?"

Astrid swallowed, her mouth and throat dry. Ewan's question went unanswered for so long, she wondered if Auley heard at all. Across the way, the two lumps of Liss and Lara still lay in their shared bed of straw, visible from where Astrid sat. When traveling, apparently, true privacy was rare.

Ewan and Auley silenced.

"Good morning!" Ewan's head popped over the neighboring stall with a broad grin. He cocked his head to the side, eyes tapered in amusement. "Did you sleep in the hay or roll in it? If the latter, can I join you next time?"

Auley burst out laughing.

Flustered by his roguish grin and the sense that he made a joke she didn't understand, Astrid scrubbed the loose stalks off her arms. Wakefulness continued to clear the cobwebs from her mind.

No wolf.

No princess.

What next? At home, she'd already have her tasks set for the day and would be accomplishing them. Now that the Ulfsarks would be hunting more plentifully again—and the Wolf Song underway—she'd have all her free time taken. Here? Here she . . . she had to search for some kind of purpose until Oskar decided the Thyrling's response to their violent warriors.

Just the reminder of all she missed, and wouldn't be able to help with, threatened to tip her into a terrible mood. The mystery of the wolf call didn't help either.

Ewan distracted her.

"A servant from the lodge just brought breakfast. Come and eat. They said we're to meet with the princess this morning. I doubt we have reason to fear, but when with the Thyrlings, always be ready."

He gestured toward her sword belt, then disappeared.

Breakfast turned out to be a startling affair. Small chunks of honeycomb for each of them, fresh bread, and a pitcher of white liquid that bubbled at the top and steamed lightly. The bards gathered around the same place as the previous night. Lara pulled her cloak around her, still rumpled and grizzled and half-awake. Liss chirped an annoying song, not unlike the bird flittering around Ewan's shoulders.

Astrid peered into the wooden bowl of white liquid.

What was this?

"Won't eat you, if that's what you're wondering," Auley quipped with a grin. "It's just cow's milk. Fresh from the udder too, and unstrained. See how it's warm? It'll keep you full for a while like that."

"Cow's milk?"

He nodded.

She lifted an eyebrow and watched Ewan down an entire mugful without taking a breath. Her more tentative approach yielded a mouthful of something rich, warm, and not . . . unpleasant. Auley sent her a silent question.

"It's good."

He smiled.

A silence stretched around the table, broken only by snippets of warm conversation from Liss and observations on Thyrling life from Auley. The bards had been unexpectedly kind to her the last several days. For better or worse, they were stuck together. They may end up being the only trustworthy friends or people Astrid would know here. With Ewan's observations on Rosamund and Oskar, Astrid's uncertain future became even more tempestuous.

Perhaps, it was time to extend their friendly favor.

"Did you sleep well?" Astrid asked Auley, because he seemed like the safest best. Just looking at Ewan tied her tongue into knots.

"Yes, I—"

A druzar swept into the stable with a deep glower on his face. His head swiveled around, landed on them, and approached with heavy thuds. Without a word, he passed them, checked the stalls, and returned.

"Safe, Your Highness."

Ewan and Auley shoved to their feet the moment Rosamund entered the stable. Liss and Lara popped up like floating sticks right after. Only Astrid was a little too late to respond to the unexpected visit. She rose to her feet, feeling small next to Auley's and the druzar's tall forms.

Rosamund smiled at the bards, but her gaze landed on Astrid. The Princess seemed to have nearly transformed overnight. Her hair shone, scrubbed, curled, treated with oils, and twisted into a coiffure that was then decorated with gems. Her skin showed no sign of fatigue or dust. Her dress, a blood-red silk that dropped to the floor, clasped her arms to the wrists.

Princess, indeed.

"I apologize for our poor hosting," Rosamund said. "It was not my intention to house you in the stables but . . ."

She trailed away, then shook her head and smiled a little *too* brightly.

"But we'll make the best of it for now. I've had some servants go into Drakby this morning. They've returned to tell me that all available inns or large houses are already occupied, or will be soon when the jaegars come to Drakby. This stable is the best we have for you at this time."

"We've stayed in places far worse than stables," Ewan said with a reassuring smile. "It was warm and the food delicious. Thank you for your hospitality."

Rosamund acknowledged his gracious reply with a slight smile. "Thank you, Ewan. I appreciate such an attitude. I would also like to extend an invite to join King Oskar and myself for our meal tomorrow evening. For certain, this time," she tacked on quietly. "The King himself has sent the invitation."

Auley gave a sweeping bow. "We would be honored."

"Excellent," Rosamund said with a thin smile that hinted at a rough night. "If you've finished your breakfast, perhaps all of you will join me for a short walk? I would like to show you the rest of the city."

Astrid nodded. Any opportunity to understand where she stood—and what to avoid—would give her a sense of relief. With so much newness around her, she groped for anything that could make sense.

"That sounds like a good idea," Astrid murmured. "Thank you."

Rosamund's smile brightened. "I'm glad you think so and will come. There is something I would like to show you that I think you'll find interesting, Astrid. Please, come outside. The grooms have already prepared fresh horses."

Astrid bit back a groan.

Auley and Rosamund spoke as the group stepped out of the stable. Liss slid up to Astrid's side as she crossed into the sunshine. "Don't worry," Liss murmured, a friendly hand on her back. "The soreness will wear off. The first time always hurts, doesn't it?"

She finished with a knowing wink and a big smile.

TWELVE

Even with morning sunlight cutting through the misty river, Drakby was still ugly.

The fur-clad people looked the same. Dour expressions, dirty hides, and soupy roads. Astrid rode at Rosamund's side while the princess pointed out various parts of the town.

"The new smithy," Rosamund said with a touch of pride. The *clink clink clink* of hammer on anvil preceded the hiss of hot metal shoved into water. "Gregor is his name. His son has impressive skill with swords."

Astrid squeezed the handle of her mother's sword between her ribs and her arm, where it rested while she rode. No Thyrling sword would ever match a Nistlefolk blade. Thankfully, the Nistlefolk refused to go anywhere near Thyrden or have any dealings with Thyrlings.

Eventually, the eastern gates loomed ahead of them.

"We're not going back across the river, are we?" she asked.

Rosamund laughed. "No. We'll turn north here, and follow the trail along the wall. It's easier for the horses to manage and less muddy."

A well-managed trail led the way, wide enough to accommodate a single horse or two people walking side-by-side. The whole thing had been graveled, removing the calf-deep mud that coated all the other roads.

Astrid followed behind Rosamund, who called over her shoulder. "The arena is something we adopted from Kerys. I'm told theirs are made of marble and quite grand. Ours is much smaller, and of dirt and wood for now, but hopefully you will all find it . . . entertaining nonetheless. In addition to the fights, some of our own skalds also tell tales and sing songs in the sand. We have other uses for them as well, as you'll see today."

Astrid processed Rosamund's news with surprise.

Arena.

Sand.

Fights?

The lurid vocabulary sent a pit into Astrid's stomach, but she didn't know why. The Thyrlings had no reputation for clean, fair fighting. At least, they hadn't during the war. Oskar hadn't been afraid to use any advantage, and honor be damned.

She had a feeling whatever waited ahead would be the same.

They continued around the base of the wooden wall before pulling away to the north, toward a stand of dark pine trees. Just on the edge of the forest, a bowshot's distance from Drakby's walls, lay a circular ring of wooden walls interspersed with wide, doorless entries that seemed to lead inside. Only crossed gates closed across them, hinting at open ground. The structure loomed larger than any sparring ring among the Skolvarg, and certainly bigger than Oskar's lodge.

They crossed onto a well-trodden path leading to the ringed structure. Before entering, Rosamund dismounted and handed the reins of her horse to a guard stationed outside the walls. With a wave, she indicated for them to do the same.

After Astrid dismounted and passed her horse to a waiting druzar, Jormund appeared from within. He bowed before the princess.

"Is everything in order?" Rosamund asked.

Jormund gave a curt nod. "Everything has been prepared as you commanded."

"Good. Lead the way then, Captain."

Astrid followed with uncertain interest. Wherever they went, she had a dour feeling she wouldn't like it. Ewan and Auley hedged a little closer to her and Liss and Lara.

They passed through the outside walls and approached a series of wooden stands that ringed the interior of the circular arena. Warriors and a few townsfolk sat on benches built into the stands. Lean-to structures dotted the inside of the wall, some of them lined with empty cages or weapon racks.

Rosamund, shoulders back and chin tilted high, led them past one of the lean-tos. The whimper of an animal caught Astrid's ear. She turned to see a pair of black bears locked inside.

Astrid stopped, cold all over.

The two bears were skinny, with scars on their hides and missing patches of fur. The larger of the two grunted, nose in the air toward Astrid. The smaller lay back, body sprawled on the ground. Nausea welled up in Astrid's throat.

What was this?

"Come," Rosamund called, oblivious. "You'll be able to watch the next event from over here."

Only a few steps away, next to another lean-to, Ewan had paused as well. Auley, Lara, and Liss followed Rosamund, but even they appeared uneasy. Astrid forced her feet to move, her heart racing.

The wolf? Had she heard a wolf that was locked up here?

Her heart pounded at the thought. No animal should be caged up like this. She didn't need to see more of the arena to know *why* these animals were here.

Thyrling savages.

A needed reminder of just *where* she'd come.

Astrid swallowed back her nausea as they passed other cages. Mountain lions, a musk oxen, and a ferocious bull bison that bellowed in between charges at his enclosure gate. Driven by an insatiable curiosity to prove she hadn't imagined the whole thing, she searched each cage for one of the eyeless cats she'd encountered in the forest. None were apparent.

The Skolvarg hunted for necessity and sport and with honor. They respected each animal, granted them quick deaths, and suffered no fools on the hunt. What the Thyrlings did here was cruel and cowardly.

Rosamund stopped halfway around the ring. In front of them waited a sprawling cage, as big as two stable stalls. Rusted iron bars ran vertically and horizontally along each of the four sides, providing maximum protection from whatever lay within.

As they drew closer, Astrid understood why.

A great gray bear, large as a horse, lay on dirty straw inside. The putrid stench reached yards away from the cage, and Astrid fought the urge to gag. Lara turned her face, skin green around the edges. Liss held a piece of cloth to her nose.

"Allow me to introduce you to Gorm the Grizzled," Rosamund said. "He's my father's special pet."

She said it with little inflection to her voice. Astrid had no indication what Rosamund truly thought of the bear, but wondered what it could be. Rosamund seemed to treasure all of Drakby and Thyrden, as gory and ruthless as it may be.

Each square opening between the bars was about the size of a grown man's hand, enough to make out the sleeping form of the bear. Unlike its black bear cousins, this monstrosity's coat was shiny and well-kept, laying over rolls of hard-lined muscle. It appeared better cared for than any animal she'd seen yet.

Rosamund gestured around the arena with a note of disgust in her voice. "Behold King Oskar's menagerie."

Rosamund said the final sentence almost as an aside, but it twisted Astrid's gut all the same. King Oskar didn't strike her as the kind of leader to do anything out of sheer civility. No, he wanted them to witness something possibly barbaric and violent. She mentally braced herself.

They followed Rosamund up a ramp, then a flight of stairs, to a small viewing tower above the benches. They gave a full view of the fighting grounds. Instead of mud, a smooth arena filled with sand lay before them. King Oskar must have had it hauled up from the river bank. Two thick logs were driven upright in the center of the sand but otherwise the area lay empty. Another wooden wall circled the arena, standing at the height of two men.

A number of Thyrlings already filled the stands despite the hour, maybe two hundred all together. Nowhere near the capacity of the place.

Rosamund strode to the front of the box and gestured to a druzar above the pit. A moment later, gates across the arena opened. Two men were dragged out by four druzars, one on each side.

Astrid's stomach clenched.

The two men had been with Ivar, back in the camp.

Druzars shoved the pair forward, their hands bound behind their back. They stopped near the end of the pit and tilted their heads. Rosamund loomed above them, her eyes snapping with rage.

One of them swallowed.

The other started to shake.

The fear in their expressions, and the way their gaze darted over to Gorm's cage, made Astrid wonder just what would happen here.

Is this what Rosamund wanted her to see today?

Rosamund called to the crowd. "These members of my guard stand before you to receive punishment for their actions while in the Skolvarg camp. I have gathered you here so that you may witness what happens to those who break their vows."

The weight in Astrid's stomach intensified. She glanced at Ewan. His lips pressed together, his hands held behind his back. Without making eye contact with her, he nudged a bit closer. Auley closed on her other side.

Astrid's breath came faster. None of this made sense. Rosamund had said she'd have to speak to Oskar before declaring this matter settled, else risk war. So why would she punish them so publicly?

Had King Oskar already ruled?

"By now," Rosamund continued, "I am sure various tales have circulated through your ranks as to the crime these two committed. Listen carefully to what I say. These two men stood by as another attempted to force himself upon a Skolvarg woman at our peace meeting. Their actions could have broken that peace and started another war. More importantly, they soiled my honor, and your honor, as warriors and Thyrlings. For this, they will be punished."

A startling change had come over Rosamund. The firmness in her voice. Her rigid spine. The way her chin angled slightly up, as if challenging them to defy her. *This* was a Thyrling princess.

The stands remained silent.

One of the men below spat on the sand. He glared at the overlook tower, nose wrinkled in a snarl.

"Am I allowed to speak, *Highness*?"

The way he twisted the word made Jormund's upper lip

curl, but he remained silent. Solid as a pillar, and cold as ice. Rosamund nodded once, her face impassive. Her arms remained at her side, but her fingers were clenched together.

The man gazed around the stands, then called, "The one who committed this crime is dead! Why are we being punished? If punishment is to be given, it should be to the Skolvarg woman. She's the one that fought off Ivar and caused him to fall on the knife! Instead, she sits at a place of honor by the princess. How, I ask, is that justice?"

Rosamund took in a sharp, low breath. Next to her, Jormund tightened. Astrid blinked, the words echoing in her ears.

The Skolvarg woman. She's the one that fought Ivar and caused him to fall on the knife.

He'd just exonerated her.

"In your own words at the Skolvarg camp," she cried, "you told us that this girl killed Ivar in cold blood and denied the allegations of Ivar's intended rape. Do you recall your story now?"

His mouth opened and closed again. Rosamund arched a brow. He paled, the truth seeming to dawn on him.

Rosamund had set a trap and he'd fallen into it.

She'd pressured him into telling the truth because she knew he lied at the camp. This was a clever way of augmenting —in front of hundreds of witnesses—Astrid's story. Bori had admitted it in front of his comrades, the bards, even Jormund. A swell of hope, and perhaps a little fear for the princess, tripled through Astrid.

Who *was* this woman?

"And what else would I have said in a camp full of Skolvarg?" the man finally shot back. "Better to face punishment here than to face death at the hands of savages."

"Enough!" Jormund roared. "You're fortunate Princess Rosamund has not asked for your tongue by now. You had your chance, Bori. Face your punishment like a warrior, instead of a word-twisting coward."

Bori's face screwed into a look of hate. "If the Skolvarg-loving princess wants my tongue, she may come and take it."

Jormund tightened, expression mutinous. Rosamund set her hand on his arm before he issued an enraged reply.

"I will deal with this, Jormund."

"Your Majesty! This insult must not—"

"Obey me."

The weight of her words hung in the air. Jormund frowned, gave a short bow, and stepped back. "Yes, Your Highness."

Rosamund turned to Astrid and the bards, placid. "Please remain here," she said evenly. "I will return in a moment."

Rosamund appeared in the arena moments later, flanked by a pair of druzars. They crossed the sand quickly. In what seemed only a few strides, Rosamund reached the two men.

The one that had been quiet dropped to his knees.

"Please, Princess," he called. "Mercy. Please."

"Silence!"

Rosamund turned to Bori. He continued to glare defiantly, although his gaze didn't quite meet Rosamund's. At his side, his fist opened and closed. As if he couldn't stand the silence that followed, he cried, "Go on, then. Let's see if you've got the guts to—"

Rosamund curled her fingers into a fist and struck the man across the face. Bori's head snapped back and he crumpled to the ground. Rosamund stood over him, studying the nails on the hand she used to strike. Bori groaned and spat blood. Two white dots freckled the sand.

Teeth?

Spirits. The blow had been as hard as any full-grown man could deliver.

"How did she do that?" Ewan whispered.

Astrid watched Captain Jormund to gauge his reaction. He hadn't taken his eyes off the scene below. The muscles in his jaw worked.

Movement caught Astrid's attention again. In the arena, Rosamund hauled Bori to his feet with little effort and shoved him against an upright pole. It was hard to tell at a distance, but the princess seemed to be shaking. With rage? Pain? A hit like that could have broken her hand. She held the man by the neck, just far enough off the ground that his face reddened.

"I would love to take your tongue," she called. "You insult me, my father, and our people with your cowardice and twisted words."

Bori's tied hands thrashed around, but she ignored him. His flailing legs didn't deter her at all. Astrid's heart pounded in her ears as Bori's kick weakened. His face deepened to a blood-red crimson, and his wheezes grew further apart.

"Never again," Rosamund shouted.

She stepped back.

Bori dropped to the ground with a thud. He sucked in a deep breath, then hacked a cough. His body curled on the ground as Rosamund strode across the arena, ignoring him. When she passed the guards, she nodded once. The guards crossed the sandy pit, the female drawing a sword. When they reached Bori, the bald guard hauled him to his knees and stepped back.

The woman drove her sword into Bori's ribs.

With a gasp, then a muted, guttural cry, Bori fell.

Rosamund crossed the bottom row of the stands and back up the ramp to the tower. Astrid and the bards turned as she re-entered. As one, they stepped aside so she could walk to the opening.

Auley, Lara, and Liss shrank back. Shock kept Astrid near Rosamund. The princess' breath came fast and she stared ahead, refusing to look at anyone in the box. In the back of her mind, Astrid swore she saw dark purple veins receding down Rosamund's pale neck. She blinked and they were gone.

"Let the remaining prisoner receive ten lashes, and be branded with a mark on his face that denotes his crime," Rosamund cried. "May this serve a warning to any that serve the kingdom of Thyrden and my father's house."

Concerned looks passed between the bards as the surviving man was tied to a pole face-first and his shirt stripped. The guards gagged him with it, then strode away. Uncurling a long whip, a guard proceeded to strike his bare back. His muffled screams made Astrid sick to her stomach.

He would have raped me, she thought. She kept that thought at the forefront of her mind, but it didn't stop her from twitching as the blows fell or make the agony easier to bear.

By ten strikes, the gagged screams had faded to a low moan. When he slumped against his bonds at a dozen, Rosamund raised her hand.

"That is enough. Take him to be cared for at the barracks. The rest of you are dismissed."

Rosamund turned to Astrid, her delicate features unreadable. Up close, it seemed impossible that she'd nearly strangled a man with a single hand and ordered another lashed within a stroke of his life.

"I hope the punishment given today will demonstrate our commitment to the cause of peace."

It demonstrated something all right, but whether it had anything to do with peace was left to be seen. How had Rosamund done that? Astrid managed to nod, her mouth dry and throat tight.

"Yes, Your Highness."

"Then shall we return?"

"Yes," Astrid whispered.

"Come, let us leave this wretched place," Rosamund muttered. "I'll make sure you return safely to the stables to prepare for the dinner tomorrow."

As Rosamund turned to go, Ewan moved to stand beside Astrid. They didn't touch, but having him at her side felt like a gentle reminder of a friend. His flared nostrils and deep breaths seemed to indicate he felt as much horror as Astrid.

Auley's brow grew contemplative as he gazed on Bori's still form in the arena. Why did he seem so unbothered? Seeing had only been half of it. Astrid would hear the screams the next time she had a quiet moment, and likely long after.

Lara let out a little cry as Rosamund strode away, so Auley wrapped his arm around her shoulder and pulled her close. Liss stared at the spot where Rosamund had disappeared, expression pale.

"Well," Liss whispered hoarsely. "That . . . that wasn't what I expected."

"A good reminder," Auley murmured.

Ewan nodded.

A very good reminder, Astrid thought, *of just how far I've come from home.*

THIRTEEN

That night, Astrid dreamed of the wolf.

Instead of darkness, she came to awareness inside a barn-like structure. Several things appeared to her as before in the dim light that shadowed rows of traps or cages. More details existed now. Rusted chains. Boards spotted with old blood. Enough that if she saw this place in real life, she would recognize it right away.

A whimper caught her attention.

Astrid moved into the dream, seeking the canine sound yet again. The whimper had increased a pitch, as if the distress had also gotten worse. She reached a hand down to her mother's sword, but nothing was there. Fog crawled around her legs, dark as night and reaching. The tendrils curled around an ankle, then faded away.

She whistled, low and quiet.

Nothing responded.

A cage sat in the back of the area. Iron, like Gorm's. Not quite as large, though, and with slightly wider gaps between the bars. These bars were rusted and narrow, but still sturdy. Crouched in the back was a furry . . . something.

Astrid headed toward it.

The distance between her and the cage immediately disappeared, in the strange way that reminded her this might not be real. Inside the cage waited a wolf. Not an Amarok. Not even an Amarok pup. Relief flooded her that an Amarok wouldn't be chained here, but guilt followed. Amarok or not, this was a wolf. As a Skolvarg, it was a cousin.

Still worthy of saving.

Frantic now, Astrid gazed around. There had to be a key, or a hammer, or something she could use to break the lock and free the wolf. The dim light of the moon shining through the top window revealed no such tool.

Margu's strange words replayed through Astrid's mind. *The thing you seek will not be found among the Amarok or the Skolvarg.*

Whatever she sought, it certainly wasn't a young, half-starved wolf. One that, in all likelihood, could be imprisoned by Oskar to fight in his bloody arena. Or maybe the wolf wasn't anywhere near Drakby, and all of this meant nothing. Nothing but Astrid's frantic state of mind being so far from her people.

Rolf would suggest that *she* was the wolf and the spirits had attempted to tell her something about herself.

Astrid seriously doubted that.

Her wits sharpened and the haze-like acceptance that accompanied dreams fell away.

The ball of matted fur that she could barely make out in the cage let out a growl. Two yellow eyes appeared in the night, tapered to half-open in warning. The depth of the growl stopped Astrid from moving closer. She could only see an outline. A vague color of grayish fur, and the eyes. The scent of rotten meat and urine wafted toward her for the first time.

Those eyes.

"I'll find you," she whispered.

The eyes watched Astrid.

She turned away to examine the rows of traps and chains hanging from the walls or sitting on benches. Nothing. Resolved not to leave the wolf alone, Astrid made for the edge of the dream. She'd find something.

"I'll be back," she whispered.

The farther she pushed into the darkness, the more the wolf disappeared. Panic seized her at first, but then all faded to black anyway. The sound of a clank made her whirl around to find two large, double doors. Barn doors? No, something else.

She pushed one side open, but it only budged a crack. Pale moonlight spilled inside. The heavy door forced her to lean into it and drive with her legs to open it. A shocked voice broke the silence in the dream.

"Who are you?"

Astrid gasped and stepped back. Her hands rose and she dropped into a crouch. A ghost of a man, little more than a skeleton with skin stretched over the bones, stood before her. A plain, sackcloth robe flowed over his narrow frame. Pale eyes circled in dark lines studied her. His hairless head turned to the side.

"How did you get in here?" he asked in a hushed, hoarse voice like stone dragged across steel.

A vague reverberation distorted his words. Although a frightening vapor, she had the odd sense that he couldn't hurt her here.

Astrid straightened.

They stared at each other.

"Well," he murmured, "aren't you a surprise?"

Something about his ethereal appearance and the soft, quizzical tone of his voice sent shivers up her spine. The same chilly feeling from when the ashen beast glared at her.

The emaciated man stepped forward, stretching a bony palm in her direction. "Who are you?" he called.

"Your worst nightmare," she muttered.

His lips moved in what might have been a smile, but looked more like a corpse's grimace. He covered the distance between them in a breath and raised a single, pointed finger to her eye level. She sucked in some air.

He waited.

His finger paused in front of her, one long, cracked nail hovering a breath away from her skin. The way he peered at her seemed to indicate he *sensed* her, but didn't see her.

Without a word, he poked Astrid in the forehead. "Go," he whispered. A cold shock sprinted through Astrid, then a jerking sensation. As if the man had shoved her right out of the dream and sent her sprawling on her back.

She gasped.

Her eyes flew open.

Darkness met her, but a familiar one. One that smelled like hay and horse manure, and rang with the staccato of Auley's snores. Liss murmured something in her sleep just across the way, little more than a dark blur.

Chills ran through Astrid's body, and an icy sweat trickled down her face. Sucking in air like she'd been running for days, Astrid collapsed back onto the straw and stared at the dark ceiling.

Back in the stables, she told herself. *I'm back in the stables.*

The strange panic began to recede. Over several minutes, she calmed. The fur she'd been sleeping on was damp with sweat. Her legs tangled in her cloak. The pale man had disappeared.

Her fingers searched by memory and finally curled around the handle of her knife. A ripple of relief followed. A weapon. At least she had a weapon again. When she'd calmed enough to set it down, Astrid pulled her knees to her chest and wrapped her arms around them.

The plaintive whimper from the wolf. The stench of

urine. The general sense of desperation that had permeated the dream. Even the call of the wolf, the lonely howl she'd heard every now and then, shuffled into a weird sort of puzzle.

This wolf, she knew, needed her.

It was a normal wolf, maybe nothing special or even beyond saving. But it was still a cousin of the Amarok, and though the Amarok wolves seemed not to have chosen her to be an Ulfsark, Astrid was still a Skolvarg.

At dark tomorrow, she'd *find* that wolf. Then she'd set it free. She'd meet with Rosamund sometime after the dinner, clear her name with the Thyrlings for certain, and then she'd be gone.

She flopped to her side, cloak pulled over her shoulder. The only thing that bothered her now was the reality of this dream. A dream . . . no. It had to be more than a dream. On some level, it must be real. Admitting that created a heavy cost, because if the young wolf existed, which she felt certain it did, that meant that husk of a man was real, too. Not only that, but he'd sensed her. Could know her.

And in the dark of night, Astrid did not want to think of such things.

A late season snow greeted them the next morning.

Not a light dusting, either, but almost a foot of the stuff, wet and heavy like most spring storms. The flakes twirled down when breakfast arrived, along with a note from the princess.

The king does not wish to have guests with the snow. He has suspended my return feast. Please remain in the stables.

. . .

She bit on her bottom lip as Liss read it again, then shook her head. Why did it feel like Oskar put off something *else* and not just this dinner? Or were Thyrlings this loose and slippery? To the Skolvarg, honoring guests and following through was held above all. Perhaps, however, that wasn't the Thyrling way.

Or Oskar's way.

Apparently, Oskar's way involved caging innocent animals, being a nuisance to his guests, and bullying others into compliance. Astrid pushed these thoughts aside. Today, she had to think of a way to get the animal out. With King Oskar as a wild card, she needed a plan she could enact immediately.

Breakfast waited in a steaming wooden pot with a lid, a wooden spoon, and several smaller wooden bowls. "Porridge," Ewan murmured when he pulled the lid off. His nose wrinkled. "Thyrling's favorite breakfast food. Not all that appetizing."

Her first few bites confirmed his grimace. Bland and lumpy, but still better than going hungry. Astrid's growling stomach didn't care, so she ate her portion and listened while Liss and the others dove into what she wanted to speak about most—the arena with Rosamund yesterday.

"These people are monsters!" Liss cried. She stood at the end of her stall, not far from Lara. Savage now, she stirred her porridge with too much force and spoke through individual bites. "And that princess is just as bad as her father if you ask me."

Ewan pressed his lips together and cast a wary glance to the door of the stable. No one stood there, however. No Thyrling wanted to be anywhere near a traveling group of bards *and* the Skolvarg that spurred the events yesterday.

She couldn't wait to get out of here.

"Rosamund might be the only sane one in the whole court," Auley said. He sat in the straw across from Liss and

Lara, his back to the wooden barrier. Astrid stood against the end of her own stall, watching him.

"How did she pick up that man?" Ewan muttered. "She looks like a good wind would snap her in half and yet she lifted him like a flower. I've never seen anything like it."

Auley shrugged. "There are many strange magics across the lands of Vigard. Methinks there is more to this princess than meets the eye."

Astrid wasn't quite sure she understood what Auley meant. Even so, she didn't like the sound of it.

"The princess had that man killed, and watched the back get peeled right off the other without blinking," Liss hissed. She threw a hand in the air. "She's no better than Oskar." Liss looked up to Astrid, eyes suddenly wide. "Though," she added hastily, "I'm glad you're safe, Astrid, and the punishments were properly seen through. Bastards, all of them."

Astrid nodded to reassure her she'd taken no offense.

Ewan cast Astrid a glance she couldn't begin to fathom. His continued attempts to calm Liss down only met with failure. Eventually, Astrid hoped she'd tire herself out. In the meantime, her attention waned and wandered through the dream with the wolf.

"True, Rosamund didn't seem bothered executing punishment," Ewan said quietly, "but remember they were both her subjects. Her druzars. They deserved what they got. And worse."

Auley hauled his body out of the straw and slapped the loose strands off his pants. "Don't forget, we don't study law or mete justice. We came here to entertain. Now it's looking like one wrong word from any of our hosts and we'll have our hides flayed off as well, so keep your mouth shut unless you're singing."

"Let's go home," Liss said, arms folded tight against her

chest. "I never want to see anything like that again and I don't want to be here."

Ewan lifted both hands in a gesture of surrender. "I think everyone has been through a lot and we could all use some peace of mind before something drastic is decided."

"Drastic?" Liss leaned toward him, eyes sharp as flint. "I'll tell you what's drastic. Having my back shredded to ribbons!"

"No one is going to be whipped, and I shouldn't need to tell you that's nonsense," Ewan said in exasperation. "We are here as guests of the princess, not beggars or thieves off of the street. I'm sure we'll be fine."

"But what about—" Liss snapped her mouth shut almost as soon as she started. Her teeth clacked from the effort. Ewan's silencing glare had something to do with the unexpected end to her comment, perhaps? Astrid studied them.

Were the bards hiding something?

"There's no need to make snap judgments before we've even performed." Ewan looked to Astrid as he pushed away from the stable wall. "I'm in no hurry to leave just yet."

Astrid's mind went to the wolf, and she said nothing.

The day inched by.

Astrid sharpened her weapons, paced the stable, and watched the snow fall. The Thyrling's movements outside the stable were non-existent—everyone had disappeared inside huts, outbuildings, houses. When the mud-strewn roads were covered and the stench of Drakby suppressed by the moisture, the place didn't seem half bad.

Only the bards kept the day from being interminable. They practiced jokes, anecdotes, songs, and stories. Astrid laughed with Auley when he attempted to come up with a new rhyme that ended with *dud*, and fell quiet when Lara sang a sweet, child-like melody that reminded Astrid of a new baby.

Once the stable settled into darkness, Astrid stared at the ceiling and waited for them to drop off to sleep one by one. Auley fell to sleep first, his growl-like snore cut through the air. Ewan would be harder to tell as he was quieter in everything. Liss had a calm hum-like sound she made, and Lara went still as a grave.

At least an hour passed before Astrid felt confident they'd sleep through her departure. She didn't want to answer any questions. Inevitably, anything they asked would end with her answering, *I'm a freak who can't hear the Wolf Song. I fight strange animals in the forest and spoke with one of the Greater Spirits. I'm visited by odd men in my dreams but I have no idea who they are. Also, I need to save a wolf.*

None of that would be wise.

Astrid rose and crouched at the end of her stall. Finally, her small size would be to her advantage. No movement or indication of consciousness came from the others, so she stole down the path and toward the main window. There would be guards in the other part of the stable, so she couldn't use the regular exit.

Using the tallow from a still-warm candle, Astrid greased the hinges on the window shutters. The almost-cool wax thickened on the end of her fingers, but did the job. Cool night air rushed past her when she pulled them open. A sliver-thin line of moon and starlight raced past her, falling to the stable floor. Sometime between sunset and now, the snow must have stopped. Only a clear sky unfurled overhead, replete with stars. She closed her eyes and drew in a deep breath. *Spirits help me.*

When no reaction came from the bards, she stole into the night.

FOURTEEN

T he setting would have been a perfect night to escape if there wasn't over a foot of snow ready to betray her.

A full moon illuminated the world enough she could pick her way across the bright grounds without much fear, but the snow guaranteed she left an easy track. Annoyed, Astrid made her way to a main road, following already-existing paths created by servants, no doubt. She had yet to come up with a good excuse if she were caught creeping around, but she'd deal with that if it came.

The streets lay quiet and empty at the late hour. Anyone out past the inn's closing wouldn't want to be seen anyway, and most working citizens couldn't afford all-night revelry with fields to prepare. She worked along the edge of the street until a low growl stopped her. She froze in the shadow of a hut, then relaxed.

Across the way, a small dog, no larger than a fox, nosed through a pile of refuse. Astrid growled back. The pup yipped, then skittered away. Could dogs sense the blood of wolves in her? It may have been used to avoiding humans. The former thought made her feel better, so she kept with it.

By the time she'd climbed the wall around Oskar's keep, crept across the grounds, and made it to the arena path, her side already hurt. Jogging had kept her warm, particularly because she had to work hard to mask her tracks. Doubling back a different way, following established foot trails. Anyone would be a lunatic—or completely unable—to track exactly the way she went.

Even if there were no wolf to free, she liked being out and about on her own. Compared to the amount of time in solitude she spent at home among the Skolvarg, her new life felt stifling. The thrill of being on her own helped her enjoy herself, potential danger or not.

Thankfully, by the time she left the town and arrived at the arena, plenty of foot traffic had trampled the snow around the outside. It seemed to be Drakby's most popular place. She stepped onto an icy, but worn path and headed toward a set of gates. To her surprise, they weren't locked. No guards patrolled, either.

Feeling uneasy, Astrid slipped inside the arena's walls.

At first, she couldn't tell where she was. Not the same entrance that Rosamund had brought her to, of course. She'd avoided that on purpose. The change of scenery disoriented her, particularly in the shadows, but she had a hunch that kept guiding her. She stayed close to the inner arena wall and walked. She followed her instinct to the right. Eventually, an open walkway led to outside the arena, where the roof of a dark outbuilding caught her attention.

Astrid walked toward it, curious. The whole structure was built of logs with the thatched roofs the Thyrlings loved.

A barn.

A prickling sensation stole across her neck. The barn was no doubt full of mice and fleas, as she'd come to learn in her time in Drakby. Worst case scenario, Astrid could climb on the roof and cut her way through to the inside. Before committing to that option, however, Astrid surveyed the back of the log barn.

The building was close to the outer palisade wall of the arena, with just enough space in the back to form an alleyway wide enough for a horse pulling a cart to fit through with space on each side.

Astrid covered her mouth to conceal a retch when she turned the corner, even muted as the smell was by the snows. At the end of the alleyway, pieces of dead animals piled on top of a cart. Most were killed in the arena or chopped up to serve the caged predators, she guessed.

Ducking back around the barn, she found large double doors, similar to the stables within King Oskar's keep. With a muttered prayer to whatever nearby spirits might be listening in the forsaken lands of the Thyrlings, she slipped inside.

Cages, some filled, some empty, lined the walls of the room she entered. On smelling and hearing her, several animals whined. One snarled. The pathetic sounds cut to her heart, but she forced herself to focus. She'd never be able to call herself a true Skolvarg if she left the wolf imprisoned here. With any luck, she and Rosamund would clear up her own glorified imprisonment by tomorrow evening.

Then she'd be free.

"Wolf," she whispered. "Wolf. I'm here for the wolf."

Still, her gaze darted around, searching for the sickly, strange man that had occupied her dream. The memory sent a chill down her spine that she forced away.

After feeling along walls, Astrid found her way to the back. A doorway waited there. She pressed inside quietly, then quickly closed the door behind her. The room she stood in was oblong, as bathed in darkness as all the rest. Only a little moonlight allowed her to make her way around, slanted through high, open windows that let in the chilly night. But something about the room registered in the back of her mind.

She stilled.

This was the place.

A guttural, low growl filled the air.

Astrid sucked in a sharp breath and whirled to the right. She knew that growl. Her braid smacked on her back, right near her spine. She held her breath.

"Wolf?" she whispered.

Silence.

Her heart thudded so hard she felt it in the back of her throat. Each muscle tensed, ready to spring into action. Of course, this could be the pale, strange man's lair. Maybe he lived a hermit's life among the caged. She could have just walked into her death.

She doubted it.

As in the dream, Astrid ventured forward a step.

"Wolf?" she whispered. Of course, it wouldn't answer, but she felt better with her voice in the air. In the dim light, the outline of the cage appeared a few paces away. Astrid paused, then shuffled forward two more steps. The rumble intensified, but she didn't stop.

A shaggy creature stood within. It lurked at the back, as far away as possible. The wretched, thin outline left no doubt.

This was the wolf.

Stepping clear of a mess of chain coiled near the cage, Astrid slipped around to the far side. The animal pivoted with her. Slowly, she squatted down an arm's length from the bars. The wolf scuttled to the opposite corner, eyes true on hers.

Memories of the Amarok pups slipped through her. Some of them acted like this at first. Bristling and defensive. *Tough guys*, Pack Master Hakon always said with a little laugh. *They're trying to prove themselves already*.

A few words, a well-placed hand, and they'd be pouncing

on her with wolf-pup kisses within minutes. They loved her, all of them.

They just never chose her.

"Do you remember me?" Astrid murmured. She slipped a bit closer, putting her face into a line of moonlight. "We met in my dream. Were you there? I hope so, because I don't know what's going on. I sort of hoped that you did."

The wolf growled, but with a little less effort. Emboldened, Astrid leaned forward. With a stretch, her fingertips brushed the iron bars. In a flash, the wolf lunged. Astrid jerked her hand back and fell flat on her rear, eyes wide.

Tail tucked, the wolf retreated.

"Well," she muttered, "that wasn't very nice."

Her frustration softened. If she'd been caged for who-knew-how-long, she would have reacted the exact same way. Lean ribs gave way to a poor coat. A girl, Astrid thought, but didn't know why. The light was too dim to be sure, but her hunch guided her. Compassion swelled in her chest. She didn't fight it. This wolf needed a friend, and she knew just how that felt.

"If you promise to be quiet," she murmured, very slowly backing away. "I'll see what I can find for you to eat."

Deliberately easy with her movements, she passed around the cage. A door in the far well led outside, as Astrid suspected. Not far away lay the alley with animal carcasses no doubt intended for the caged creatures. The cold prevented flies from buzzing around, at least. She found what looked like a mangled deer leg and worked her way back.

Inside again, Astrid approached the cage from the front. When she reached her original sitting spot, she lowered. The wolf hadn't stepped into the light, but she heard the gentle rush of air that meant it was sniffing. Astrid stretched the remains into the cage, wedging them in between the bars. The wolf didn't move, but its mouth opened to pant. She licked her lips, but didn't take her gaze off Astrid.

Astrid scooted back, hands visible.

"Go on."

The young wolf continued to eye her, teeth half bared. After a few minutes, her muzzle fell back down over her fangs. Within thirty seconds, the wolf stretched its scrawny neck as far as it could reach and jerked the leg through the bars. Moments later, the crunch of a bone filled the air.

Astrid relaxed back.

For almost an hour, she waited while the wolf ate. The wolf kept one eye on her while she gnawed on the carcass. A low growl came from her throat as she ate, making Astrid chuckle quietly. She scooted forward, into the light, and studied the dim barn.

Without more light, the dark was too deep to spot a key to the cage and she couldn't risk a torch. Just being here was suspicious enough. Enough to give Oskar cause to incite a war? To kill her?

Maybe. Life seemed cheap in Drakby, even for the natives.

While the wolf gently whined and chewed on the bone, though, she knew it was worth it. Amaroks were special wolves, touched by the spirits to make them bigger, smarter, and stronger. Astrid wished that all wolves enjoyed the same blessing, but then dismissed it. That wouldn't work at all.

The cold kept Astrid awake as she watched the wolf, lost in thought. For the first time since leaving her tribe, she finally had time entirely alone. Although kind, the bards were always present. For the brief chance she had, she sank into the quiet, peaceful night, broken only with the occasional happy whine, then suspicious growl, of the wolf.

Her thoughts wandered to the princess. Did Rosamund know the wolf was held in the barn? Even if the princess didn't, she knew perfectly well what went on in all the other pens and cages in the arena. Then again, what could Rosamund do? The arena was, clearly, Oskar's domain.

Although Astrid had no way of knowing how much time had passed, she had a feeling dawn was on the way. Her legs ached from not moving after so much running, and the light of the moon had disappeared as it tracked across the sky.

"I can't set you free tonight," Astrid said quietly as the wolf worked on a small, remaining part of the bone. "I'm sorry. You might not like it, but you've got me on your side. I'll be back tonight or tomorrow."

The wolf looked up long enough to stare right at her. It might have been her imagination, but the unblinking, unmoving look held little sign of the hate she'd seen before. The wolf didn't trust her, but it clearly didn't hate her.

Astrid pressed her hand to the bar.

"Goodbye."

FIFTEEN

King Oskar's lodge made Astrid feel more naked than running through a snow drift without clothes.

The next afternoon, she trailed behind the bards as Captain Jormund led them into the long house. King Oskar had summoned them without explanation, presumably to prepare for the dinner tonight. Astrid tagged along, for lack of anything better to do and with Rolf and Odda's admonition to learn as much as she could, ringing through her ears.

The lodge held a maze of people, tables, and servants. Everything seemed to move all the time. The towering, peaked ceiling, dim lighting, and long walkway made the building look bigger than from the outside. Massive tree trunks formed the main pillars of the area, and all were carved into the likeness of bears standing on their hind legs. How many thousands of years of trees had ended to build this court?

Torches hung in brackets along the wall, but there was only so much to see. Smoke made the area dim. It hovered around the rafters like a spectral ghost. They passed several hearths busy with fires, spits, and cooking pots. Astrid longed for a breath of bracing, fresh air and she'd only been inside for two minutes.

Captain Jormund stopped unexpectedly when they came to a wall at the end of the lodge. A doorway seemed to indicate a room behind it, not to mention two guards on either side. They stared straight ahead. Lara skidded to a halt, a breath away from crashing into Jormund's back. Ewan steadied her from behind.

"Astrid of the Skolvarg," Jormund said as he turned around. "King Oskar wishes to speak to you alone."

Her heart leapt into her throat. Astrid nodded once, then swallowed hard when Jormund turned around and rapped on the door. He stood there, back to them, while the distant sound of approaching feet issued from behind the wall.

Instant concern appeared on each of the bard's faces, but none as much as Ewan. He turned, canting his body so his back was to Jormund. "Do you want me to go in with you?" he asked, low so only she could hear.

Yes, she wanted to say, but shook her head. "No," she said, then added, "Thank you. I can take care of this. I'm not afraid of him."

Ewan frowned, his brow heavy. "He did this on purpose," he said with a tone of warning. "He wants to see you without the princess. Do whatever you can to stall. I'll find Rosamund."

The door cracked open and a single eye peered out, saw Jormund, then opened a bit wider. Without a word, Jormund stepped back and motioned to Astrid. The eye seemed to scowl, then the door shut. Before she could comprehend what that meant, it opened again.

"Come. He's waiting."

The eye belonged to an elderly man not much taller than her. His twiggy body was nearly bent in half, and all limbs as thin and long as willow branches. Astrid stepped forward, but his scowl stopped her.

"Armed!" he squeaked. "Are ya mad? He'll have your head."

Astrid hesitated, her hand on her mother's sword. Reluctantly, she undid her belt, then handed it to Ewan with a silent question. He accepted it with a nod, and his confident handling of the blade reassured her.

"Thank you," she said with feeling.

The old man grabbed her sleeve and yanked her inside. He shoved her forward, clucked, then disappeared out the door as quickly as she'd come in it. Astrid blinked and found herself nearly alone in a startlingly broad room. The open windows gave a chill to the air, but cleared all the smoke. Here, she could see. She didn't choke on her own breath, at least.

Her gaze fell on a hulking figure waiting at the other end of the room.

King Oskar.

Sheer panic kept her from gazing around, hoping for Rosamund to be there. Did the princess know about this? Doubtful. Astrid would have to figure this out herself if she wanted to get home soon. Thoughts of the wolf intruded and concern wrapped her heart.

No, she'd have to play this *very* carefully.

Uncertain what to do next, and not wanting to give offense, Astrid held still. Within a few moments, her eyes skimmed the area. A banister lay behind Oskar, indicating an entrance to the second floor balcony running along either side of the lodge. The sun had already started to set, casting the windows in a pinkish hue. Animal heads and hides, shields and weapons. They populated the wall, as arrogant as boasts.

"Come closer, Skolvarg," Oskar called.

He waved a massive paw of a hand. Even at a distance, he seemed to rise above the shadow to sit on his throne.

Astrid attempted to keep her face blank, but she'd never been great at that kind of thing. Which is just why Torva always picked on her. She couldn't help but wonder what would happen if she had her knife and attacked the king. Could she take him by surprise and end his blood-soaked reign? It was utter madness, yet a wild part of her played the possibility over in her mind.

As she approached the raised wooden throne hung with furs, she refused to take her eyes from the monarch. King Oskar stared back just as intently. If he was offended by her gaze, he gave no sign. Amaroks circled their opponents before a fight in much the same way.

"Rosamund tells me you've met Gorm the Grizzled."

His booming voice reverberated in the wide room. Tonight, it held an edge of something. Warning? Threat? Madness? She couldn't say for sure.

"He's quite the bear," Astrid said.

He leaned forward a little in his chair. "Do you know why I keep him?"

She'd heard the tales from other Skolvarg before. Tall tales, she'd always assumed.

Until now.

"I heard you fought with the king of gray bears once. Rather than kill him, you took him as a prize and nursed him back to health."

Oskar sat back in his chair with a grim smile that parted his mustache from his beard in blocks of yellowed teeth.

"Close, but not quite. Stories are always twisted on their way across the Auroran to other campfires." He half shrugged. "While I would love for that story to be true, he makes a far better ally than enemy."

He'd just given her an opening, she sensed, and chased the hunch that told her to keep him talking. Flattery, for most men like Oskar, worked better than gold. She had no desire to stand here without Rosamund, anyway. Hopefully, Ewan could be good on his word.

Unprompted, the king continued, staring past Astrid, into a fire pit that burned in the center of the great hall. "It was late in the war against your people. I led one of our largest armies north, to the wildest reaches of the Wolfmoors, where the Skolvarg skulked in the shadows instead of fighting us with honor."

Astrid bit her tongue.

He continued, ignoring her.

"My warriors were weary, hungry, downtrodden. For months, my war council advocated pushing east to the Wolfwood. They thought if we could capture your Matrons, we could win the war. But I knew better. The last thing I wanted was unknown numbers of Ulfsark at my back while we marched leagues through enemy lands. Instead, I struck out for your summer camps, determined to give the Skolvarg such a battle that it would swing the tide of the war."

The next part Astrid knew, or thought she knew. But instead of talking about the Battle of the Bloody Heath, as it was known amongst the Skolvarg, the king took a different turn.

"We marched for weeks, the Skolvarg always one step ahead of us. You led us on a chase, but what else could I do?" He spread his hands. "If I turned around, my warriors would think me weak. Your wolf riders would attack as soon as we showed our backs. So we pushed north.

"One summer night, the temperature dropped. My warriors were uncomfortable, weary as snow began to fall. Some were dying. I once again contemplated retreat. At the point of madness, I walked alone beyond camp. There, I beheld a great gray bear. He stood over a moose carcass. He was beautiful in the night, so dark against the setting sun. Then? An Amarok appeared from the tree line."

Oskar lifted a hand, more in his mind and the story than the lodge. Astrid watched him warily, unwillingly entranced herself. A gray bear against an Amarok? She wanted to say the Amarok would win every time, but it wasn't true. Gray bears like Gorm were ferocious predators, and would fight to the death before running.

The Skolvarg believed that summer snows were an omen from the spirits to attack, so attack they would have. King Oskar had better instincts than she expected.

"Whether Gorm had killed the moose or stolen it from an Amarok wolf," Oskar continued, "I couldn't guess. I watched this lone Amarok and the bear test one another. Each wanted to know which would back down and surrender the prize. I have never seen such a battle in all my days. The bear held the lone Amarok at bay for hours. The new fallen snow ran red with the blood of both until they were equally at the edge of death."

Oskar looked right at her, his expression studious, intent. Astrid held his gaze until the world became a fuzzy tunnel around them.

"At last," he whispered, "the mighty Amarok relented. It limped away, tail between its legs. No sooner had it gone than Gorm fell to the ground. I returned to my camp and ordered my warriors to return for the bear, on the edge of death. They obeyed, if reluctantly. They lashed him to a wagon and brought him here. Back then, Drakby was only a war camp, not the town you see today. Inside his cage, Gorm the Grizzled regained his health and I claimed him for my own."

Oskar straightened. Astrid blinked, her mind racing over the memory of the ferocious, monstrous bear.

"You know the rest of the story," he said brightly, "yes? The Battle of the Bloody Heath."

His tsk resounded through the air.

The Battle of the Bloody Heath was a story that seemed

older than time now, though only six years had passed. Her father had died there not long after her mother's sickness, on the heath-filled fields where the summer snow fell, when the Skolvarg attacked. For three days war waged, but neither side could claim the upper hand. When the fighting finally stopped, both sides withdrew.

It became the biggest turning point in the war.

Two years later, the Skolvarg were forced to accept a truce that ended their lands at the Auroran River. For King Oskar and his bedraggled force, The Battle of Bloody Heath was a victory that played out years later, even if it didn't seem like it that day.

"Gorm the Grizzled taught me a valuable lesson," Oskar said, one finger upheld. His gaze tapered slightly, as if imparting a great lesson. "An Amarok wolf may be mighty, but in the end, it bleeds like any creature. Eventually, it will tuck its tail between its legs and slink away, if you hurt it enough."

Astrid's teeth ground together so hard her head started to ache. She forced her face to relax by taking in a deep breath and pretending to study him. Finally, she said, "I don't think you met the right Amarok that night."

Oskar sat back in his chair with a booming laugh. With hands so meaty they rivaled Gorm's, he wiped away moisture at the corners of his eyes, set in a thick face.

"I like you, wolf girl. You've got iron in you." He gestured between the two of them. "Let me share some wisdom with you. Peace makes you soft. An enemy is the only thing that will keep a person strong and wary. Spears do not stay sharp without war."

He waved a hand, clearly not wanting a response. But his eyes had grown beady and tight. He studied her, as if anticipating a reaction.

"I believe you'd agree, considering what my daughter has told me about you. You killed one of my men."

"Yes."

It would make no difference to this man if she reasoned or justified it.

His brow rose.

Astrid didn't have a chance to read whether his expression was startled, amused, or filled with rage. A side door that Astrid hadn't seen opened up, admitting the princess.

"I see you've gotten a head start on your evening," she said to Oskar, voice tense. She moved quickly. Her fast breaths meant she'd rushed to get here, but a fixed smile indicated she tried to hide it.

Spirits bless both her and Ewan.

Oskar frowned at his daughter. "Where are the singers, dancers, and fools you have invited to my table?"

"Awaiting your audience with Astrid to end," Rosamund said. "Can the feast begin without the king?"

Oskar grunted and leaned back, like the last thing he wanted to do was attend his own dinner.

"Cancel it. We'll have it tomorrow."

"But, father, this is the third—"

"Cancel it!" he roared.

Astrid sucked in a sharp breath. Cancel a third time? But why? Rosamund's nostrils flared as she nodded.

"Very well. Tomorrow then."

With a slight movement of her head, Rosamund indicated that Astrid should follow. Astrid cast one look back at the king, who stared into his drink with a contemplative expression, then followed.

"Astrid of the Wolf Riders," Oskar called to her back. She froze midstep, but didn't turn around. "I look forward to our next discussion. We still have much to talk about. Namely the murder of my druzar. There is a blood price to be settled."

Unable to help herself, Astrid spun around.

"A pack of wolves will kill a bear every time," she said, barely able to control her voice. "Even Gorm."

Oskar's smile stretched wider than she'd ever thought possible. He lifted his drinking horn to her. "And what of a little, lone wolf?"

Teeth clenched tight, Rosamund grabbed Astrid's arm and tugged her out of the room. Astrid followed behind, his words ringing in her ears.

The only discussion she wanted to have with Oskar was on a battlefield with a sword in her hand and the Ulfsarks at her back.

A sodden darkness hid Drakby as she, and the bards, trekked back to the stable after the meeting with Oskar. Tensions ran high between Liss and Ewan. Liss's grumbled demands that they return back to their homeland followed behind.

"Thank you," Astrid said as she glanced at Ewan. "For finding the princess."

He nodded.

"I . . . appreciate it."

The edge of his lips twitched.

"It's amusing, is it?" she asked with a little laugh. "My gratitude?"

He held up two hands. "Rare, that's all."

"I'm not ungrateful!"

"Maybe not," he admitted with a little shake of his head. The skin around his eyes crinkled a little when he said, "but you are very quiet."

"Yes."

"Is it a Skolvarg thing?"

"An Astrid thing?" She shrugged. "I don't know. Freydis,

my best friend, talks a lot more than me. With her around, I never needed to say anything."

"Ah. I think I am the best friend in that situation. My mother said she couldn't shut me up when I was a little boy. Singing *or* talking."

Astrid laughed again, and it felt good. The image of a smaller, chattier Ewan amused her to no end. She hadn't realized how much she missed Freydis until the name crossed her lips. Weeks had already passed, but her mind went to Rolf and her tribe constantly. Had the Wolf Song finished?

Did they think of her?

The conversation fell flat for several moments, belying his claim to discussion. What did the bard have on his mind? His usual way of flittering effortlessly from topic to topic failed him now, when Astrid actually wanted to talk.

The russet-colored bird appeared from the sky, alighting on Ewan's shoulder. He tilted his head toward it and the tiny thing rubbed against his neck, preening the way it might in a water bath. Ewan made a sound in his throat as the bird snuggled into the collar of his shirt, feathers a bit ruffled in the wind.

"How do you do that?" Astrid asked.

"Do what?"

"The bird," she said, nodding her head at Ewan's pet.

Ewan smiled and Astrid sense a story coming. "The Skolvarg have the Four Seasons but Ochlanders worship the Three Muses. Those of us who train in the ways of bards are said to develop a special affinity for the songbirds that are sacred to the Muses."

"So the Skolvarg ride giant wolves into battle and you have pet canaries?" Astrid's wit surprised even her as Ewan let out a rich laugh.

"I suppose that's one way to put it. We're not really bonded the way your Ulfsarks are."

Astrid sensed an opening to bring up something else she couldn't stop wondering about. "You're armed quite heavily for a traveling minstrel."

"Thyrden isn't an easy place to travel to and now that you've seen Drakby, would you want to come here unarmed?"

"Why come here at all?"

She couldn't imagine anywhere in all of Vigard she would have wanted to visit than Thyrden, if she had the choice.

Ewan shrugged. "That's what we bards do: travel the kingdoms."

That didn't seem like the whole story but Astrid sensed she'd only get more smiles and misdirection if she pressed the bard further. And she realized more every day that she understood precious little about the world beyond the Wolfmoors. She knew bards sometimes visited with Skolvarg tribes who summered to the south, closer to Lake Vyla and the Ochland border, though none had ever visited Odda's people before. Maybe Ewan's explanation was really all there was to it. If she couldn't trust the Ochlanders, who could she trust in Drakby?

The little songbird rustled against Ewan's neck, eyes closed in sleep. He reached up with a gentle finger and rubbed its silky feathers.

"Can you speak with him?" Astrid asked.

"He understands me but we can't swap tales, unfortunately," Ewan said with a wink. "What about you? Did you leave your wolf at home?"

She sank her teeth into her bottom lip. Did she want to reveal her squishy spot? The thing in her life that robbed her courage more than everything else? It would be easy to say yes and leave it at that. She didn't want Ewan's pity. The Skolvarg had always judged her as weaker than others because of her small stature and lean size. Without an Amarok, she'd been even *less* regarded.

Would Ewan do the same?

"I . . . I haven't heard the Wolf Song," she said quietly. "Not everyone hears it. The wolf pups, at a certain age, pick their Skolvarg. None of them have picked me."

"Oh."

Trouble brewed in his expression. Relieved to speak to *someone* about it that wouldn't give her mindless platitudes— like Freydis, though she meant well—Astrid continued to explain.

"I want to. Desperately. My mother made a name for herself as a great warrior with her Amarok, and my father died in the Thyrden war. My uncle has raised me the past six years and he, too, has a place in the tribe. I will too," she added quickly. "It's just . . ."

"Not the one you want?"

She sighed. "Exactly."

"I know how that feels."

The lonely note in his voice caught her attention. She wanted to ask what he meant, but he spoke before she could.

"Tonight has, at least, demonstrated one thing," he said before she could ask. "We must watch this king. He's intentionally unpredictable, which is dangerous for any man in a position of power. There's no love lost between him and your people. We must also watch ourselves around the princess. She may not be the ally she made herself out to be. I will always believe that Rosamund has her own interests at heart first, no matter how friendly she acts."

Astrid fidgeted at that. Rosamund had been the closest thing Astrid had to a friend since leaving home. She'd protected her against her own guard, after all, and believed Astrid when she didn't have to. Rosamund interrupting Oskar's interrogation only made Astrid's thoughts more complicated.

"Perhaps," she allowed.

Ewan watched her, but said nothing.

While they crossed the outskirts of Drakby and headed back to the stable, Astrid turned her thoughts back to the wolf. She'd visit again tonight. Only tonight, she'd find the keys. Hopefully set the animal free.

After that?

She had only to free herself.

A voice came out of nowhere, whispered through the silence of the darkness. It made the hair on the back of her arms stand up.

Astrid.

Margu. Astrid sucked in a sharp breath, eyes on the band of darkness ahead of their torch. If Ewan heard the voice, he gave no sign. Just frowned as he led them through the snowy roads, a step or two ahead of her now.

The distant howl of a wolf punctuated the air, as if to affirm Astrid's suspicion.

"I'm coming," she murmured.

If the strange woman really was one of the Greater Spirits, the last thing Astrid needed was her interference. All the old tales said it was bad luck to dismiss one of the Greater Spirits, but since running into the ashen cat and the mysterious lady in blue, Astrid's life had been a series of ill luck anyway.

Although, after meeting Oskar and the dire warning in Ewan's tone about her people and the Thyrlings, she started to wonder if leaving was the wisest path after all.

Astrid dismissed thoughts of Oskar, the Spirit of Winter, and her growing curiosity about Ewan. Instead, she focused on the wolf and how she'd get back there tonight without drawing suspicion.

Sixteen

Returning to the arena shouldn't have been so simple.

The snow had melted or been trampled through the day, giving her more options to get there without concern. The trails from the night before had disappeared, and ice had taken its place. Still, Astrid had spent most of her life navigating frozen forests and difficult terrain. With her light feet and small body, she slipped back into the arena in half the time it took the night before.

When she stepped into sight of the wolf, the growling began.

Prepared this time, Astrid jerked open a leather pouch, sat with her legs folded in front of her, and tossed a few pieces of meat saved from dinner into the cage. Whether the wolf received regular water, she couldn't tell, but the pungent scent of urine meant she must get some.

"Hope you had a better day today," Astrid murmured, then tossed a piece of meat into the kennel. The wolf sniffed, eyes on Astrid, then gobbled it in a second. Astrid scooted closer and ignored the bared teeth that came next.

"Weird day for me."

She spoke quietly, easily. The Amarok whelps often settled at the sound of a familiar voice and some Skolvarg believed that whelps could choose the person they'd imprint with just by voice. This was a wolf—nothing like an Amarok—but the principles likely applied.

Besides, it soothed Astrid to speak the words and hear something except the eerie, ringing silence. She tossed a crust of bread into the cage. The wolf grabbed it as it dropped into the pen. Instead of snarling, the upper lip lowered. A slight tilt of her head indicated more curiosity than ferocity, but one unexpected movement from Astrid brought the growl back.

Astrid ignored it.

"My plan is to get you out tonight, just . . . not sure how. Those metal bars are a definite problem, but I'm sure we can figure something out."

She threw her gaze around. A table with a stack of parchments and vials stood against the far wall. Astrid produced a pheasant wing she'd scavenged and dropped it into the crate.

The wolf sniffed, then settled down with the wing between her paws. Seconds later, the crunch of bones broke the night air.

Giving the adolescent wolf a wide berth, she approached the table and scanned the parchment and other instruments. None of the words in ink made any sense, but that wasn't a surprise. Whether this was the common written language or a special text of the Thyrlings, Astrid had no idea. The Skolvarg runes were carefully guarded from outsiders. Skolvarg children learned to write with no other alphabet, although they could speak other languages.

Astrid debated stealing the papers, but shoved it aside as soon as the thought crossed her mind. What would she do then? Ask Ewan to read them for her? It might be nothing more than a list of the creatures in the arena. If Oskar had her possessions searched and found them, she'd be flayed open as a spy.

Leaving the papers, Astrid ventured down the wall. Some hanging tools, small hatches, a mallet, some leather-making instruments, and bottles of different ink cluttered a counter.

No sign of a key.

Through the dark, Astrid attempted to make out the construction of the cage. Could it be opened anywhere? Broken, perhaps?

She approached tentatively. The wolf remained silent at first, but bared her teeth when Astrid closed in. Still a long way from friends, then, but she could work with that.

"Hey girl, just looking at your cage, all right?"

Her voice went farther to soothe the wolf than her words, no doubt. The wolf still didn't like her near. She pressed back, then barked once, growling low after. Astrid ran her fingers around the outside until they stopped on something smooth —and then a defined hole. She crouched next to the cage.

The wolf snarled, teeth bared.

Astrid ignored her.

A pair of locks made up one side of the bars. The key would be circular on top, like any key. She reached for her small knife and tried for several minutes to crack it open, but no such luck. The pommel of her mother's sword didn't break the metal either.

She scowled.

For an hour or two, she searched each nook and cranny of the room to no avail. Frustrated, she leaned away from a woven basket filled with odd scraps of metal.

There had to be *something*.

Why was the wolf in here alone, anyway?

Fatigue made her thoughts sluggish. Last night, she had no sleep, and caught only a few hours before being forced to get up in the morning. Tonight, she'd need more rest if she was to return with reinforcements.

"I'm sorry I can't do more tonight," she said to the wolf, "but I will find a way back after dinner. Although, really, who knows if we'll even have one?"

The wolf studied her in return with narrow eyes as Astrid stood up, walked to the door, and glanced back. A little whimper came, but Astrid couldn't tell if it was one preceding another attack, or some sort of regret.

"Tomorrow," she whispered.

Then ducked back into the night.

SEVENTEEN

The next evening, Astrid reluctantly joined the strangest and most uncomfortable feast ever known to Thyrden, and probably all of Vigard.

Astrid sat along the edge of a long table that swept up and down the long hall. Oskar sat at one end and Rosamund the other, each separated by twenty druzars on one side. Scents of the feast lay thick in the air. Roasted pork. Crispy fat. Apple pastries drizzled with what Liss called cinnamon, a spice Astrid had only heard of.

Her stomach growled, ready to dive into a plate, except Oskar kept holding the food off. Auley stood near the fire, reciting a humorous war ballad about a Thyrling warrior decades ago that she'd never heard of. Oskar laughed uproariously, then demanded more. The food steamed and piped on the sideboards, ignored by the king.

An hour later, and the entire assembly started to get edgy. If Oskar noticed their frustration, he gave no sign, just laughed with his massive belly and demanded another from Auley.

Astrid sat alone, flanked by two jaegars that pointedly ignored her. She got the impression being seated by the

Skolvarg was meant as an insult. Mud on their pants and fatigued expressions indicated that they'd just arrived. Both of them were men with gray-flecked hair. The first had rotten teeth and a mean disposition.

The second jaegar was a normal-enough man with a skinny, sickly boy sitting next to him. Twenty years old, perhaps. He kept darting furtive glances to Rosamund. They'd clearly just arrived, the first of Thyrden's jaegars coming for the council.

Relieved that she wouldn't be forced into conversation, she studied the lodge, the servants, and attempted to overhear conversations. Auley, Lara, Liss, and Ewan worked frantically to keep the crowd entertained.

"Let's eat!" Oskar roared unexpectedly, halfway through Auley's recitation. He interrupted Auley mid-word. Auley's mouth snapped closed, startled into silence. Half the room gasped, then turned to look at the king. His cheeks had deepened to a ruddy, pinkish color. Heat built in the lodge, thick and hazy from the cooking fires.

Loaves of dark bread and small cups of pork gravy graced the table first, then platters of roasted boar. Astrid paused, watched a few Thyrling males help themselves with fistfuls of meat, and she selected a small loaf of bread first.

Only a few chairs away, Rosamund sat with her shoulders back, head high. She spoke with an impressive calm despite the ruckus of voices that arose with the food. A polite smile accented some of what she said. Her impeccable tidiness with her food stood in stark contrast to Oskar's ravenous feasting.

The man ate like a bear. He tore into his meat without cutting it, grease and gravy draining from his lips into his black beard. Perhaps the oils she assumed he used had actually been grease all along.

An hour into the feast, as appetites began to slow and

speech slur, a bellow rippled down from Oskar's side of the table.

"Astrid of the Skolvarg!"

Her head popped up. She glanced at the King, who stared at her with a drinking horn in hand. He smiled, but it appeared more sneer than amusement. Flecks of bread filled his beard, and he emitted a low belch that must have been accidental. The entire room silenced as one.

Her answer rang in the sudden quiet. "Your Highness?"

"I'm told you handle yourself well in a fight, given your size."

Her thoughts hardened. A hint of humor accented his voice, as if it held a laugh he didn't dare release. The king was goading her.

But why?

Overstating her skills would be her greatest mistake. A round-about approach would be best, and hedge at whatever he had planned for her. The warning in his words when they'd parted yesterday still rang in her ears.

"I would like to think so, Your Highness."

He grinned again. She hated the hint of madness in his eyes. Feral and unpredictable, like a rabid dog.

"Is that so?" he called, straightening. "You've already pitted yourself against a Thyrling. Why not test it again?"

She frowned. "Your Highness?"

"What if we put you in the arena against one of my beasts?"

Her stomach turned cold. Not far away, Rosamund's jaw tightened. Spirits, but his game with her had begun. The calculation in his eyes confirmed it. The only thing she knew was she could not get in that arena against an animal. She'd be forced into something against her very nature.

"I find no sport in fighting caged creatures for entertainment."

He shrugged, skar sloshing out of his goblet. Intelligence —even challenge—flashed through his eyes. He acted sloshed from drink, but she wondered if that's all it was. An act. A leader of a country that didn't trust his own people and lied to them constantly to see what they thought.

"It's not entertainment. So much as . . . justice."

His warriors had wanted to rape her, yet *she* had to answer to justice? She gathered her thoughts back together. Loss of control was exactly what he wanted. The details of his game shuttled together now.

Oh, yes, now it all made sense.

Only a few warriors in the hall tonight because they would take up space for the *real* people he needed. The jaegars. The wealthy. Oskar had delayed this feast for them. Maybe to put on this spectacle.

For this moment.

Astrid cleared her throat. "To what end, Your Highness?"

"Your freedom."

"I fight one of your beasts and you let me go?"

He nodded once.

Astrid's gaze narrowed on him. A heavy fog lay on the feast now, compounded by the pressing weight of all their stares. Out of the corner of her eye, Astrid caught sight of Rosamund's long, perfect fingers fiddling with a napkin.

"Am I a prisoner now?"

"You killed one of my warriors in cold blood. I would say that requires justice."

"Three against one didn't seem very honorable. One of them admitted I was not the one to start the fight."

Oskar's eyes gleamed. "A man about to face death will say many things, won't he? Addled minds, and all that. I heard a convincing story that *you* attacked him."

Rosamund hissed, barely within earshot. "Say nothing, Astrid."

Astrid listened, grip tightening on her knife so hard her palm ached.

Oskar scowled at his daughter. "No?" he drawled. "Well, that's disappointing. Because I was going to involve your friend."

He nodded to Ewan, who leaned against the wall with a shrewd gaze. Only a slight widening of his eyes betrayed any surprise. The king leaned forward and spoke with this goblet pointed to Ewan.

"Let me tell you something—you can't fool me with silly songs and pretty words, minstrel. I hear you wear a sword. I am curious to see if you know how to use it."

Rosamund stood. "The bards and Astrid have the guest-right of protection, my King."

Her voice remained even, but firm. Underneath it, Astrid sensed layers of fury that Rosamund held back. She didn't dare look at her.

Oskar's rabid smile returned, as if he was glad for Rosamund's interference. "Of course you'd remind me of something I needed no reminder of. I have found the bard's songs and poems lacking. Did you hear them tonight? For an hour or more I gave them an opportunity . . . is it not their profession to entertain? Well then, I wish to be entertained! They have failed! The guest-right has now failed."

His booming voice left a hollow echo. Liss had paled in the far corner, where Lara clutched onto her from behind. Auley stood a few steps away from Ewan, expression intent as he gazed on the king.

"Perhaps we could arrange another display of entertainment that would please you?" Rosamund said. "I'm sure they would be willing to do a demonstration or—"

"Silence!"

The dishes rattled as he thumped a heavy fist on the table, shaking it all the way to Astrid's end. Only Rosamund appeared unfazed by the emotional display. Oskar pointed at his daughter.

"You have no power here, daughter. Not while I sit on this throne. A fight I desire," he called, voice rising, "and a fight I shall have. Bard, you will fight in my arena or your friends will be in my dungeon pits."

Rage flickered in Ewan's expression. His gaze darted down the table, no doubt to Rosamund.

"Forgive me," Rosamund said. "I thought only of our reputation for hospitality. When neighboring countries hear the tale of two guests that died at our animal's hands, I fear for the ramifications."

Astrid fought off a wave of annoyance with the hope that Rosamund simply played the game back. Hospitality? She had to be desperate now. Oskar wouldn't care about hospitality. Astrid's hand reached to the small dagger in the side of her leg, hidden under her pants. She could fight and win against the animals.

She just didn't want to.

"Dear daughter," the king said in a patronizing tone. "You were too young to remember our wars with the Skolvarg. I assure you, they are the hardiest of people. Is that not true, Astrid? Or has the blood of the wolf thinned in the new generation?"

The direct jab to her pride couldn't have been an accident. She spoke through her teeth in an effort to maintain control.

"I assure you it has not thinned, Your Majesty."

"So the question remains: are you going to be in the arena to help him, or will you let him face this himself? His pretty hands might work a lyre and put the animals to sleep, perhaps?"

The hardening of Oskar's expression told Astrid everything she needed to know. Oskar wanted one of two things to happen. One: a reason to go to war with the Skolvarg. Astrid's self-defense attack might have been sufficient reason, had his daughter not worked so quickly to discredit the account of the warriors in front of so many people.

Two: something else entirely. Something else she couldn't yet see, couldn't fathom, and would surely change her life.

His motivation? Who knew what Oskar really wanted? Except for more power. There was no choice here.

There never had been.

Astrid swallowed and inclined her head. Although she was small, she made sure her voice carried over the heads in the room.

"As you wish, Your Highness."

"Well then!" King Oskar clapped his large hands together and the sound echoed throughout the hall. "It is settled. The Skolvarg and the bard will fight two animals of my choosing at a time also of my choosing in the arena."

***

The rest of the feast passed in an awkward silence.

Oskar brooded on his throne, lost in skar. Rosamund gave up on faking conversations and the bards reverted to their instruments, with no songs. The two recently-arrived jaegars fell into a solemn silence, their expressions empty and not revealing. When Oskar finished eating, he belched loudly, wiped his greasy hands on a cloth, and threw it on to his plate.

"Leave me."

Before he could turn away, half the people in the room stood to depart. Astrid blinked, shocked by the unexpected flow that rushed away. Oskar disappeared through the double doors behind him with a slam.

Astrid let out a long breath.

Rosamund rose, looking anything but pleased. The calm, cold young woman who had ordered a man executed reappeared here. This time, however, she had a pinch of helplessness about her. Like a determined child, but a lost one.

Jormund came to her side and whispered something in Rosamund's ear. When he finished, she turned to Astrid.

"Thank you for your presence this evening. My father has requested that a guard escort you back to the stable in order to assure your safety. You . . . they will be available to you through the night as well."

Astrid almost laughed. Her safety? More like his entertainment. He'd essentially locked them into the stable and slammed the doors on her prison.

With that, two guards stepped closer in a clear indication that it was time to leave. Ewan stepped up next to Astrid, followed by Auley, who walked close to the twins. She couldn't deny the comfort of a friend at her side as they left the hall.

The guards escorted them back to the stables, then stood on either side of the entrance without a word. Darkness filled the calm air outside. With it came a wet scent. Another spring storm was on its way, no doubt. Astrid hardly had a moment to take stock of the weather, she was too busy trying to figure out how they'd best Oskar at his own game.

Minutes after returning, Auley, Ewan, Lara, Liss, and Astrid had gathered as far from any window as they could, back in the darkest stalls of the half-empty stable. Astrid hadn't even leaned against the wooden stall before Liss' words barreled out.

"We're going home tomorrow."

Ewan rolled his eyes. "I have a fight in two days and a guard to make sure I'm there, remember?"

"After it. We won't spend another minute here with these . . . these monsters!"

"And leave Astrid?" Auley asked, his carrot-orange eyebrows lifted high.

"Oh." Astrid straightened. "Don't factor me into your decisions. If I—"

"We're not leaving you to fend for yourself," Ewan said firmly. "And that's that."

"I can take care of myself."

Ewan's brow rose almost to his hairline. "We're the only friends you've got here, like it or not. If you think the princess has your best interest in mind, you're wrong. Oskar has his eyes on you. Any plans he has now are only going to lead to war—somehow. You need friends."

Her frustration flared, but she forced it back. No, now wasn't the time for a fight, as much as she wanted it. Tomorrow would be soon enough to prove her prowess with a sword.

Yet, Oskar's hope for entertainment likely stemmed from seeing a little thing like her fighting a massive animal like Gorm. In a sense, her independence might give Oskar exactly what he wanted.

She turned away.

"There's no way around it," Ewan said. "We're under guard now and any attempt to leave will only give Oskar the excuse to do something worse."

"But what about—"

"No more discussion." Ewan rapped his knuckles once on the stall wall, a tired hand passing over his eyes. "We're going to win and all of this will be fine. Get some sleep. All of us are going to need it." His gaze lingered on Astrid. "Especially you."

EIGHTEEN

Avoiding the guards that night was far easier than Astrid anticipated.

Perhaps they weren't worried, since Astrid and the bards were still trapped inside the palisade keep, even if they escaped the stables. One of them fell asleep just after midnight. The other left him to snooze as he completed one of his rounds. Astrid slipped out the window, raced along the edge of the stable roof, and disappeared into the night. How she'd get back without drawing suspicion, she'd think about later.

Muddy ground slowed her path back toward the arena, caking around her ankles and calves. She fell three times, coating herself with icy sludge. She forced her mind off her numb toes and frozen fingers to focus on the wolf.

The only thing possibly in her control.

She had an idea of stealing away in the night with the wolf now that she'd cleared the stable, but sent that back into her mind. No, Oskar would somehow turn it against the Skolvarg and likely Ewan and his troupe. Would use it to dishonor

Astrid. The wolf pups that never chose her dishonored her enough, she didn't need it from a Thyrling king.

Besides, what if he sent Ewan into the fight alone? The thought made her stomach twist. No, she wouldn't abandon him or the other bards, even if they did have to kill an animal together.

Ewan had a point about Rosamund. Yes, she'd proven to be helpful to Astrid, but had it been on her own agenda as well? Astrid wanted to figure it out.

What felt like an eternity later, Astrid reached the base of the mound that formed the palisade ramparts. In the almost-silence, she realized someone followed her.

Astrid strained to hear more than the scuff of a boot or a whisper of movement. She could slip over the wall, but her pursuer might wait for her to return, or leave to notify the guards at the keep. Better to know who tailed her.

One of the guards? No, that didn't seem likely. They would be more likely to sound an alarm or tackle her to prevent an escape.

A small woodshed to her right caught her eye. In an attempt to act like nothing was amiss, Astrid headed for it. The narrow building stood near a workshop. The overpowering stench of decaying animal hit her nose a moment later. She recoiled at the putrid smells.

A tannery. Doing her best not to retch, she breathed through her mouth and walked casually around the bend of the woodshed.

The length of the building guaranteed that her pursuer would have to risk being seen or lose sight of her when she rounded the bend. Several hides were stretched out on boards to dry, everything from foxes all the way up to elk, providing additional cover on the opposite side. She pressed herself against the corner of the shed and drew her knife.

The muffled sound of boots on gravel continued. Astrid gripped her knife in her right hand, farthest from the approaching person to give her room to swing. Always ready to strike.

The walking stopped.

Astrid risked a quick glance behind her. Nothing. Her mind raced to determine her next step. She wouldn't attack an unknown someone, but neither could she wait there. Barely audible, the person took a slow step forward and drew her attention back to the moment.

Another step.

She held her breath.

The pursuer was almost to the corner now. She tightened her grip and hauled her arm back. A shadow figure appeared. Astrid lunged, throwing her body weight on top of them, her knife held out to the side. The two of them landed on the ground. With the element of surprise on her side, she pinned an arm back with her free hand and raised her knife.

"Quiet!" she hissed.

The cloaked figure turned its head. As they did, the hood fell back. Astrid's eyes widened. Ewan grinned at her from the shadows.

"Really, this seems a bit forward . . . especially for you."

Astrid shoved herself off Ewan, glad for the darkness that hid a flush to her cheeks. The bard held out a hand for her to help him up, but Astrid glared at him instead.

"You were following me."

The smile faded from Ewan's face. "Yes."

Astrid planted her hands on her hips. "Why?"

"I was worried." He shrugged. "You're so—"

"Don't you say small!"

"—secretive," he said with a roll of his eyes. "I wanted to

make sure that you were safe. King Oskar clearly has a vendetta against you and I wanted to be able to help if you needed it."

"An assumption that I can't take care of myself?"

"No." He met her gaze. "Just a friend watching out for another friend."

She struggled to find a response. Whatever she had expected him to say, that certainly wasn't it. Astrid swallowed, then let out a long breath. The tension in her shoulders eased. For all his ability to entertain, he didn't appear to be anything but sincere right now. It disarmed her.

She lowered her weapon, then slid the knife back into the sheath.

"Next time, can you just come with me instead of sneaking behind?"

The bard sighed and ran a hand over his face. His dark, loose curls jostled with the movement.

"Yes, of course. I apologize. I should have said something."

Fatigue showed in his slack face and pale expression, even in the moonlight. Like clouds slipping in front of the sun, lines of worry shadowed Ewan's gaze while he studied her.

More questions ran through Astrid's mind. Had he been spying on her? What did he hope to see? She had no energy to ask them—not with the wolf and the fight at the forefront of her mind.

Perhaps she needed his help.

As sore as it felt against the force of her pride, she admitted it would be easier to set the wolf free with Ewan than without him.

"I'll tell you what I'm doing out here on two conditions," Astrid finally said. "One—you promise not to tell the others. I just . . . I'd rather this stay between the two of us."

"Depends on what you tell me."

She couldn't fault his honesty, then finally nodded once.

"Fine. And two—you have to tell me what you're really doing here in Drakby."

Ewan hesitated, eyes mere glimmers in the moonlight. So many heartbeats passed that Astrid wondered if he'd heard her. Just when she opened her mouth to say something, he stopped her.

"Agreed."

Satisfied, Astrid grabbed his arm and tugged him away.

They climbed over the wall, Astrid first, followed by Ewan. Once they were both on the ground outside the city, she started a light jog, slow enough they could both talk. Ewan followed her easily, listening to her breathy explanation without interruption.

Halfway to the arena, she slowed down.

"So you're setting the wolf free?" he asked.

"Hopefully. I haven't found a way to do it yet, but maybe with both of us there we can come up with something."

"I'm in."

She sent him a look out of the corner of her eyes. "Well, I'm glad you don't think I'm crazy."

"I never said that," he drawled.

Astrid grinned and gave him an elbow in the side. As before, she guided him to the arena, then swung around to the back, where the barn waited. When they reached the rear door of the barn, Astrid paused. Ewan stopped next to her, lean and strong at her side. She held up a hand to indicate to wait and he nodded. The night was cool and quiet with just enough light to examine their surroundings. No sound slid through the evening chill. She counted to two hundred.

Hearing nothing, they pressed inside.

Once Ewan slipped through the open barn door past her,

she closed it. A quick glance confirmed no one but the wolf waited in the interior again, and she let out a breath of relief.

"Let's get this done," she murmured.

As expected, the wolf growled at their presence. She hunkered down in the far corner, teeth bared. Astrid stepped into a slant of moonlight.

"It's just me again."

The rolling growl slowed as the wolf regarded her, then rose again when it caught Ewan's scent. Astrid froze as the wolf threw itself at the bars, snapping and snarling louder than ever before.

"Can you do anything to calm her down?" Astrid asked, thinking of his connection with the songbird.

Ewan dropped to one knee, a few paces from the cage. He held out a hand, seemingly oblivious to her snarls. A low, barely perceptible hum followed. After a few moments, the wolf calmed. Her rump lowered until she sat, panting. No sign of fear or alarm remained.

"What did you—"

The wolf shot her what could only be described as a warning glance, then turned back to Ewan again. The bard continued humming, hand outstretched toward the cage. He closed his eyes. All too soon, Ewan's humming died.

"What's wrong?" Astrid asked.

"There's only so much I can do for a creature in this state," he said. "She needs something to eat and drink. She's thirsty and hungry, for sure." He ran a trembling hand through his hair.

"Of course."

Astrid stepped outside, rummaged for a meaty bone, and returned less than ten minutes later with a skinned foreleg. It wouldn't be much, but it would distract her. The wolf growled in her chest as Astrid slipped the bones through the cage, then stepped away.

Ewan hadn't budged from his spot on the floor. He slowly stood up. The wolf ignored him, intent on the bone.

"We've got to get her out," Astrid said. "I've looked for the key but there's no time for that anymore. What if I break some of the bars on the cage?"

"And even if that works, then what? As soon as you open that cage she's going to run. If she gets outside the barn without raising a racket, do you think she'd just run right to the gates and off into the forest? She'll be lost and scared and likely wake the animals outside. The entire garrison might be activated and we will still be here."

She opened her mouth to reply, then stopped. Irritated that he was right—she hadn't thought this through—Astrid swallowed.

For the sake of the wolf, she set aside her pride and quietly asked, "What do you suggest?"

A twinkle appeared in his eye, as if he knew the struggle it took to overcome her own independence.

"I promise I'll help you get her out of here," he said gently, "but if we just turn her loose it's more than likely she'll be killed. This is important to me too. But we need to build trust with her first. Then perhaps we can at least get a rope around her and try to lead her out, or find a way to wheel her out in the cage then release her when she's free of the arena."

The force of Astrid's feelings when she said, "I want her out of here," surprised her. Ewan's expression softened.

"Me too."

"What if we're too late? What if she has to fight tomorrow?"

His shoulders lifted as he studied the wolf. "I'll ask around, see if there's a wolf fight planned anytime soon."

Astrid nodded. "Fine, but I won't leave Drakby until she's free."

"I understand."

While the wolf remained occupied with the joint and a wary eye kept on them, Ewan refilled a small bowl of water from a frosted rain barrel outside and handed it to Astrid. She pushed it close enough the wolf could stick her nose through the bars and lap up the water. They did this four times before she stopped drinking.

All through it, Ewan regarded the wolf with deep concentration. Astrid remained silent, her heart curled up in a tight ball. In her mind, she'd already freed the wolf. To walk away *again* was . . .

. . . awful.

"I can't get much of a read on her," Ewan said when Astrid replaced the bowl on an obscure shelf near the far wall.

"What do you mean?"

Ewan turned to her with a little smile. "I think it means she likes you better than me. Not surprising, since she's seen you more, but I don't think that's all of it. You said you had dreams?"

Astrid nodded.

"Did the wolf seem responsive in the dreams?"

"Yes."

Ewan ran a hand through his curls. "Can Skolvarg bond with regular wolves?"

"No. The Blessing of the Spirits extends only to the Amaroks." Astrid ran her bottom lip through her teeth, then shrugged. "At least that's what legends say. But what's happening here isn't the Wolf Song. Not like my people describe it, anyway. It's . . . something else."

Or maybe I want it to be something, Astrid thought. But she remembered Margu's words and couldn't help but wonder if greater forces were at play.

"Whatever it is," he threw up a hand, "I can't explain it." His expression altered slightly, almost coy. "Maybe you still smell like wolves?"

"Hey!" she cried. "I don't smell like a wolf!"

He cracked up, laughing harder when she smacked his arm. A wooden thud sounded from across the barn. The front wooden doors closing? Astrid slammed her lips together. Ewan sucked in a low breath. They glanced at the door, then one another.

In the next instant, they bolted.

Astrid led the way, hand on her knife, half expecting an armed Thyrling to meet them as they rushed outside the barn through the back door. When no one came into sight, she kept running, past the carcasses, crates, and barrels, all the way out of the back alleyway until they reached the edge of the arena.

"Whoever it is might have gone to awaken the garrison if they heard us," Astrid said. "We need to get out of here. Can you keep up?"

His grin hadn't diminished. "Keep up?" He scoffed. "I'll probably beat you back."

With a growl, she took off after his already-retreating form.

Nineteen

They snuck back to the stable an hour before the sun climbed over the eastern pines. Astrid settled into her straw pile, hot from exertion. Despite the successful escape, her mind remained back in the barn.

Did anyone see them?

Could it have been a trick of the wind?

Was the wolf okay?

"Bit long for a midnight stroll, eh?" Auley growled from two stalls over, half asleep. His lips smacked in a yawn.

Astrid tensed, but relaxed when Ewan whispered, "Lost track of time I guess. Tell you about it in the morning."

A gentle snore responded. Ewan sent her a wink she barely saw in the darkness. Unable to help it, she gave him a little smile.

Ewan's bird flitted around Ewan's stall, popping up here and there. When Astrid sat down, her heart began to slow. So did her body. Then tension bled from her muscles as she stared into the dark. An exhaustion she'd never experienced before swept into her mind. She needed sleep. More sleep, anyway.

With the wolf caged, however, she doubted she'd get much of it.

One moment, Astrid thought of what Ewan said about building trust with the wolf and how long that would take. She closed her eyes and the next moment, Lara peered at her from overhead. Escaping tendrils of hair framed her face in dark strands. Morning light filled the stable, flooding it with brightness. Lara's subdued eyes, almost olive, blinked.

Astrid rubbed her face. Had she fallen asleep? How had the night passed so quickly? Her stiff body made it clear she'd been sleeping. Deeply.

Lara disappeared.

"You're going to get yourself killed!" Liss hissed from not far away. "Both of you!"

"You're a fool if you underestimate her, Liss."

Fatigue shucked itself quickly in light of Liss' opinion. Ewan's defense of her, however, warmed Astrid through. She struggled to maintain control over the begrudging sense of affection for Ewan that followed.

She realized too late that they hadn't even spoken about the fight last night.

"I say we leave," Liss said. "Get out of here. We can take Astrid with us."

"Astrid won't leave yet, and I won't leave her here."

Liss threw up her hands. "What obligation could you possibly have to her? There's a time and a place to be a hero, Ewan, and this isn't it. I like Astrid too, but we can't put her above our obligation. We have a job to do and we can't do it if you're dead."

"You definitely could."

His unaffected voice prickled the back of Astrid's neck. What exactly did *they* have going on?

Auley's gruff voice interrupted their back-and-forth. "If we leave now, we'll never get another chance. Ewan can fight and he'll have Astrid with him. Together, they'll figure it out."

Silence followed. Astrid counted seven thudding heartbeats before Liss spoke again.

"This is it, Ewan. If you and Astrid somehow manage to survive the fight tonight, then we're done. If you refuse to leave, Lara and I will return by ourselves if we have to, and Muses curse you if we find any trouble along the way."

He sighed. "Liss, stop being dramatic. Let's see how the fight goes tonight and decide in the morning. Agreed?" His tone lowered. "I believe . . . that is . . . yes, there *is* something here. Soon, we'll tell Astrid everything. I think she can help."

"Tell her?" Liss sputtered several more times. "Are you mad? That's . . . I . . . there's no putting sense into your head!"

The sound of retreating footsteps came next. Ewan sighed. Straw rustled, as if Lara had gotten up to follow her sister. After it, a reluctant assent followed from Auley.

"Has to happen," he murmured. "The fight *and* telling Astrid."

"You trust me?"

"I do."

"You trust Astrid?"

Auley hesitated, then must have given either a nod or a shake of his head, because he said nothing.

"And you'll be all right without me tonight?" Ewan asked. His tone had dropped, all business now. He sounded nothing like the light-hearted bard he showed himself to be most of the time.

"Course." Auley scoffed. "Be easier without you, since you'll be distracting so many people at the arena, anyway."

Astrid's eyes felt full of sand when she blinked them open again and slowly sat up. Their words churned in her mind, a slow, gradual storm despite the dull throbbing that echoed in the back of her head. Thoughts of the fight had her nervous enough, but knowing for certain that the bards hid something potentially dangerous felt like missing a step.

Hearing her movement, Ewan's head popped around the corner of the stall. A smile appeared there, even if it held a touch of uncertainty. Did he worry about what she'd overheard?

"Good morning, late sleeper. Rough night?"

She glared daggers at him.

He laughed.

How was he so fresh and chipper?

Astrid mumbled something meant to be unintelligible and yanked straw from her hair with the thought that she desperately wanted to bathe. Another body appeared at the end of her stall.

"You look terrible," Auley said with a wink.

"Thanks. What time is it?"

"Lunch just came. With it, a message from Rosamund. Your fight will happen at dinnertime." Auley raised a bushy eyebrow in an expression that reminded her of annoyance. "His Highness wishes to eat while he's entertained."

TWENTY

E scorted by sunshine, warm weather, and a sense of foreboding, Astrid, Ewan, and their guards arrived at the arena an hour before the scheduled fight time. A lunch of smoked ham and hard bread sat uneasily in her stomach. It hadn't tasted good, but hunger had forced it down. Besides, they'd need every advantage tonight when they fought in the ring.

Drakby and the surrounding countryside became a sodden mess, turning the ground into something like soup. Outside the city, the blankets of snow had peeled back to reveal spots of green. Between the wet storm and the sunny weather after the snow, everything would soon be in full bloom.

The warmth was a tantalizing caress against her cheek. Astrid leaned into it as their guards led them up the hill. Judging by the number of people jostling to enter, the stands would be packed for the fight. This wouldn't be like any sparring match she'd ever participated in before.

Rosamund met them at the gate.

She held her head high. A sunshine-yellow dress capped her shoulders and extended with sleeves past her elbows.

Velvet, was it? Astrid had only heard of the expensive, shiny cloth before. She wanted to touch it, feel if it was as soft as it looked. Rosamund's light hair lay tucked at the bottom of her head in a bun, brightening her blue eyes despite her somber gaze.

"Please," Rosamund said as Astrid and Ewan approached, "allow me to apologize for the barbarity of this fight and assure you that I've attempted to change his mind. It hasn't worked. He gets an idea in his head and . . ."

Her neck tightened as she drew in a breath, then let it out.

"We'll give him a show and it will be done and over with," Ewan with a dismissive wave of his hand. Astrid gripped her sword to hide her nerves. Sparring had always excited her, but fighting an animal?

She just wanted to be back with Rolf in her simple life, back when the biggest worry was what Amarok pup would choose her.

Streams of Thyrlings populated the countryside at their back as they flowed to the arena. Oskar must have somehow declared the match, because Drakby spit out all her residents. They chattered noisily, dresses and pants stained with the tenacious mud that clung to the low points of most roads and hills. In the far distance, cattle roamed through pastures, abandoned but for the young cowherds as their owners gathered in the arena.

Astrid breathed through her collecting anxieties.

Rosamund bit her lip and glanced between them. "There's something else you should know. When I realized my father wouldn't call off the contest, I persuaded him to change the rules. Instead of fighting Gorm, you'll face his two strongest household warriors. Two berzars. The fight is to yield, not death."

Ewan's eyes widened. "He was going to put us against Gorm?"

Rosamund nodded, lips pressed. The apology in her gaze made Astrid wonder if that had been a wise move after all. His berzars had been strangely absent in their interactions, so she had no idea what they'd face.

"Lovely," Astrid muttered, thinking of Oskar's vicious mind. When a funny look crossed Rosamund's face, Astrid quickly added, "Thank you. I . . . you may have saved our lives."

Rosamund nodded.

In the hours that had followed lunch, Astrid and Ewan had planned out potential fight strategies. All of them revolved around a four-legged nemesis. Too late, Astrid realized she should have seen this coming. Torva would have. Maybe even Freydis. Oskar would have allowed the rules of engagement to change unexpectedly, of course. Perhaps he planned it himself, only Rosamund gave voice to it. The mad king overturned the game board whenever he saw fit.

"May Tyraz watch over you," Rosamund said, invoking the Thyrling god with a lingering glance on Astrid.

She spun, her dress rustling as she slipped back through the gate. Astrid watched her go, torn between frustration, gratitude, and an impending sense of doom. Ewan set his hands on his hips and heaved a giant sigh.

"Well, at least now I won't have to embarrass you in front of all those Thyrlings. Killing Gorm myself would have been a blow to the honor and pride of the Skolvarg."

She rolled her eyes, appreciating the attempt at levity, even if her smile was forced. "No one could kill Gorm alone." Even a fully-armed Ulfsark with an Amarok wolf be in for a fight for their lives against the great gray bear.

"Think of it this way," Ewan said brightly. "You've always wanted to fight a Thyrling, haven't you? Now you've got the chance to fight two of them in front of a whole crowd of *more* Thyrlings."

Astrid opened her mouth to reply, then realized he was right. She'd been sizing the Thyrlings up since they first visited the Skolvarg camp. This was the first real opportunity to test her warrior skills against them.

"Sometimes you make sense," Astrid admitted. "But I don't think this fight is much safer."

Ewan's brow creased. "You're probably right."

"He's a bully. He'll likely call foul play if we win, then it'll be easy to make up some excuse to execute us for it. If we lose, he's lost nothing except a nuisance. Something tells me these berzar of his won't be holding their blows back."

He contemplated that for a moment, but their guards shoved them in the back, toward the arena, with a growl. Astrid followed, and they began a slow trudge through the gates.

"Whether or not he has another intent, let's work as a team as much as possible. We have no experience in a sparring match together to base our footing from, but with your quick feet against their brawny bodies, we'll have a chance."

"A small one."

His lips twitched as he met her gaze. "You know as well as anyone that size doesn't determine everything."

"You nervous, Skolvarg?"

Ewan muttered the question from where he stood next to her, in the center of the arena. Thyrlings filled the stand with flecks of color and waves of noise. The last hour had been interminable, but at least it had passed. Waiting for doom or destiny had Astrid on edge.

Astrid's fingers started to ache from gripping her sword too tightly. She loosened her grip, paying attention to the amassing crowd.

"No."

He scoffed. He had it right. She'd lied. Of course she was nervous. This would be much different than the training ring back home and that was all the experience Astrid had. Inside, a growing knot of tension started to build.

The finch on Ewan's shoulder gave him an encouraging nip at the ear and a chirp. The bard forced a smile and whistled something in response.

"Does your bird have a name?" she asked, grateful for something else to think about.

"Maury. He's a good friend . . . most of the time. Cursed little thing gets into his fair share of trouble, though."

"Can you speak with him as well?"

Ewan shook his head. "Maury is smart as finches go, and I can teach him bits of song, but he won't start doing anything a finch couldn't do already."

"Not like a bard that could double as a warrior?"

Ewan cracked a grin. "If I swoon when they first attack," he shaded his eyes with a hand and made a show of studying the people in the stands, "just promise you'll catch me?"

To her own surprise, Astrid laughed. Part of her question had been serious. She wanted to know more about a bard that could, presumably, hold his own in a fight. His utter lack of fear, and the discussion he had with Auley and Liss earlier today, only amplified her curiosity. Not to mention his broad shoulders, a heavy sword, and no lacking stability in the way he held himself.

Something didn't fit here.

"Can't do anything about nerves until you step in the ring anyway," she said, just to keep the conversation rolling. "At least, I've never been able to stop them."

"You spar a lot, don't you?"

"Had to," she said quietly.

He gazed over. "Because you're smaller than all the other Skolvarg?"

Her lips tightened and she nodded. The reminder didn't thrill her, but she'd brought it up. Besides, there was no judgment or mocking in his tone. He made a sound in his throat and went back to his perusal of the stands.

"So you just endure the nerves you feel before the fight?" he asked. "You don't plan it out? Try to work through every possibility?"

"I'd go mad."

He laughed again, and she hated how easy this seemed to be for him. Perhaps he put on an act now. Imagined this was nothing more than a song to sing to the people of his kingdom.

Across the arena, shouts began to ring out. After a few moments, a body strode toward them. Captain Jormund. Sand shuffled under his feet as he approached, boxy expression plain and unreadable. Astrid imagined him like an owl. Virtually expressionless but packed with things to say that never escaped.

"You won't be fighting with sharpened weapons," Captain Jormund said as he stopped in front of them. "I'll personally inspect all four to make sure they're equally blunted and will bring the opposing fighters with me."

"Oh good," Ewan said. "We'll just break our necks instead of losing a limb."

Jormund ignored the joke, and held out a hand for their weapons.

Astrid reluctantly handed her sword over. She felt sick seeing her mother's sword in the hands of a Thyrling, but there was nothing to do for it. The king had made no threats, but she had a feeling there would be consequences if she and Ewan didn't play along. Jormund had given her no reason to trust him, but at least he'd shown the most loyalty toward

Rosamund, not Oskar. She'd have to hope her sword would be safe.

"Thank you, Jormund," Ewan said.

Jormund cast him a sidelong glance, then tilted his head across the way, through the gates leading to the sands of the arena.

"Head down there. Now."

Padded jerkins and leather helms awaited them in the middle of the white-sand circle.

They stood alone, the filling stands surrounding them. Astrid ignored the welling nausea in her stomach as she tied Ewan's straps in place. He did the same for her. Thyrlings booed and chanted. She tuned them out by imagining they were Torva again.

"Can you see our opponents?" Ewan asked as he knotted a string of leather near her shoulders. "Any sign of the other two?"

She frowned. "No."

No one else lingered in the arena. Unfortunate, because Astrid felt good about their chances against any of the weak-appearing Thyrlings in the immediate vicinity. She pushed the thought away to focus on all the lessons driven into her by Huntress Vanna.

Astrid had little experience fighting with a partner. Skolvarg warriors-in-training learned to fight as individuals, at least until they passed the age when they could hear the Wolf Song. Since Astrid had clung tooth and nail to that hope, she had yet to join the warriors in their group training.

Today, it seemed, she'd get a crash course.

"I think I look quite dashing in this." Ewan flashed her a

questioning look from beneath the front of his helm. "Does it suit me?"

Astrid snorted.

He smiled all the wider.

"You won't be so charming if you get your nose smashed like a pumpkin in the next few minutes."

"True." He paused and seemed to seriously consider the prospect. "But I won't."

A roar rippled through the crowd on the other side of the gates, sending a thrill of excitement and dread through Astrid. In the box where they'd stood for the execution, Oskar sat behind a table. A flash of light indicated a fork or goblet had just been lifted to his face.

Astrid scowled up at the box.

King Oskar rose to his feet, leaning over into the wall. Princess Rosamund stood next to him, appearing less pleased. Lara and Liss, looking uneasy, stood behind Rosamund's left shoulder.

Where was Auley?

"It'll be worse for the twins, don't you think?" A note of forced humor entered his tone, belying the sense of grimness underneath. "At least down here, we don't have to smell Oskar's stink."

Astrid said nothing. The jokes weren't landing any longer.

Oskar raised his hands. Somewhere behind them, a horn blew. By the time its last note sounded, silence reigned. He gestured to Astrid and Ewan.

"My people," he called, voice booming through the thin, open air. "We have before you two who would test their might against us! A Skolvarg warrior and an Ochlander bard!"

More boos reverberated through the air, but the greater part of the crowd remained silent. Astrid studied their faces, desperate for a clue. Did they love their king? Did they want this sort of bloodthirsty show? King Oskar might have enjoyed this more than any of his subjects. He'd also done a good job setting the fight up as an "us" versus "them" for the crowd.

"Given that we are now at peace with the Skolvarg after a long, hard-fought war," he continued, "I thought it only fitting that we have a friendly spar, without blood, as a test of skill. And, as our good friend the bard is a master of entertainment, he offered to join the event as well."

"Not quite how it happened," Ewan muttered.

"Not even a little," she replied.

"But since these are special warriors," Oskar continued, "I have decided to match them with opponents worthy of their skill and prowess."

Oskar waved a hand at the gates below his tower. They swung open. Two men—the burliest men she had ever seen —swaggered into the arena behind Jormund. They were no taller than Skolvarg, but twice as thick. Each wore a helm with a half-circle mask over the top of their faces, fashioned so it looked as if their heads sat inside the top half of a snarling bear's head. Both had bare chests and arms, but wore bear skins over their backs. The king's household warriors, indeed.

These massive berzars were almost bears themselves.

Their powerful strides brought them within a few paces in moments. They sneered, eyeing Astrid, then Ewan. She ignored them, her stomach a hot pit of frustration. Jormund stopped and held out two wooden swords.

"For you."

"A wooden sword?" she cried. "Are you kidding? Look at their swords. They're almost twice as long."

"Don't worry, little Skolvarg, it'll snap you right in half," the one on the right said with a jeering laugh. "At least you'll go quick, all right?"

"Let me feel them." Astrid stepped toward Jormund, a hand held out. "I want to compare weights. Those are big enough they're probably hollowed out and filled with iron inside."

Jormund said nothing.

Ewan grabbed her shoulder and hauled her back. "We'll figure it out," he said. His voice was too even. Too steady. In the hands of those two hulking warriors, the weapons would be as dangerous as a mace. Easily capable of splitting a skull or breaking a bone.

But what could they do?

"Thyrling honor," she hissed.

A flinch flitted across Jormund's face. With a growl, Astrid yanked the offered short sword out of his hand. A shield slipped off Jormund's back—she accepted that as well.

Behind them, Oskar's voice resounded through the arena again.

"Today, I am pleased to introduce the warriors from my household. They have risen above all others to a position of highest honor, the berzar."

"Just stay at my side as we discussed," Astrid said, low. "And don't get hit. Those swords will break bones."

"Thanks," he drawled. "I hadn't surmised."

Astrid hid a tiny, nauseous smile.

"And now," Oskar bellowed, his face visibly red from here. "We celebrate the arrival of the spring and the last of the snow. Let them fight!"

The moment the first note of the horn sounded, Astrid moved.

Jormund had barely gotten a step away from the berzars when she charged head first, hoping to take one of the bear-men out of the fight right away. With two bounding steps forward, she let her warrior's mind take over.

The third step brought her in range of the Thyrlings while the horn still sang. The big berzar on the right swung his sword horizontally, much faster than Astrid expected. She barely had time to get her shield arm up to catch the blow. The wooden two-handed sword with the leaden core hit Astrid's shield like a battering ram. She struggled to stay upright, almost knocked off her feet. In her lack of stability, the other berzar struck her with a shoulder charge.

Astrid flew off her feet and landed hard in the sand.

"What happened to staying low?" Ewan shouted to be heard over the raucous cheers as he helped Astrid to her feet. Anger burned away her pain.

Cries from the spectators rippled through the arena as Astrid hurried to her hands and knees. Her lungs were paralyzed. Desperate for breath, Astrid attempted to suck in air. Finally, as darkness edged her vision, she drew in a deep lungful.

The other berzar laughed at her.

"I didn't think . . . they'd be so fast," Astrid muttered between gasps. "Thought I could . . . catch them."

"Somebody caught somebody, all right," Ewan said. He turned to face the two Thyrlings, shield raised. His gaze tapered into slitted, assessing lines.

No room for pride on the battlefield.

"You're right," she muttered and raised her shield in response. "Together."

"Keep low," Ewan murmured as the giants lumbered back around to face them again, bright gleams in their beady eyes. "Stay to my right as much as you can. If possible, let's separate them. With us in the middle, they can't work together. Get your back to mine. I'll take the guy on the left, you go right. I think the one on the right favors his left knee a bit, so press your advantage in the sand."

His quick assessments shocked her into silence. Indeed, the one on the right *did* seem to favor that leg—just a little. He anchored it more, moved with it less.

"How did you know?" she asked.

"I'm a bard," he said with a little grin, "not an idiot. I—"

Before Ewan could finish, the berzars bull-rushed them.

Being left-handed made it difficult to fight with Ewan on her left, but Astrid gritted her teeth through the impracticality. She turned just enough so the back of her shoulder faced the Thyrling, then met his attack with her sword. As his weapon came down in an overhead blow, Astrid met it.

The *crack* of wood slapping wood nearly sent her reeling. Had her blade snapped? Pain sprinted through the bones in her hand and wrist, but her grip held by sheer willpower. The wooden blade held, by some miracle of the spirits.

Pushing forward, she locked the hilt of her sword against the berzar and swung her shield hard into his exposed elbow. The giant grunted. When the weight of his two hands lifted ever-so-slightly, Astrid pushed back before he disarmed her.

"Little girl," he sang. "I'm not even trying."

To his credit, she believed him.

Astrid stepped out of reach of his blade, then darted back in with a growl. She launched a flurry of blows with her sword, attempting to impact his inner thigh. A dull weapon wouldn't draw blood, but if he fell on his back, she had better access to his knee. Bruising—or a shattered kneecap—would stop him.

The Thyrling countered her attempts almost effortlessly. His long reach and heavier sword made it almost impossible to contact his body with hers. She may not be tall, but she would parry ruthlessly.

Finally, her relentless attacks drove the man back and to her left. Out of the corner of her eye, she could just see Ewan holding his own. Chest heaving, Astrid hammered away as fast as she could, not giving the man a chance to take the offensive position.

Thrust.

Slash left, slash right.

Duck.

Her body moved through the attacks until she sank into the rhythm of the fight. Perhaps her *only* hope was to tire him before she tired out. But would she make it that long? Beads of sweat raced down her face, soaking her hair. Her arm tingled from the force of the wooden swords colliding.

The Thyrling might have been stronger, but his sword-work was sloppy—maybe because he didn't think he needed more skill to beat her. He swung heavy, as if he'd been trained more for overwhelming power than skill. Several times he attempted to use sheer strength to overpower her, but her small size allowed her to dart away. Like a wolf chasing down much larger prey, Astrid wore at him, nipping here and there, never letting him rest.

"Astrid!" Ewan called. "Close in."

Ewan parried somewhere behind her, the clash of wooden swords ringing in the distance. The crowd's cheer rose and fell with each heavy hit and smash. Astrid attempted to tune out her concern for Ewan based on what she heard.

She focused on surviving . . . until the berzar decided he'd had enough of being toyed with.

Gritting his teeth, he swung out wild with a broad, horizontal slash that would have cut her in half had it been a real sword. Astrid ducked and raised her shield. At the last second, she swung her shield with the attack, diverting the blow rather than absorbing the force of it.

The swing left her opponent wide open. She used her momentum to dart inside the reach of his sword, struck him hard in the right thigh just above the knee, and planted a kick to his abdomen.

The Thyrling shouted as his leg gave out. He fell, crashing like a massive tree. Astrid pushed aside a clumsy, half-hearted attack and raised her sword arm for a downward stroke to the neck.

"Astrid!" Ewan shouted. "Look—"

The force of an angry bull slammed into her back. Astrid lurched to the side, banging into the ground with her right shoulder. Wheezing, she forced herself to scoot away, half-heartedly raising her shield over her head as she fought for breath again. The other berzar towered over her, grinning.

A second later, Ewan yanked her to her feet and away.

"He kicked sand in my face and rushed you," he cried, still blinking and shaking his head. The skin around his eyes had reddened as he swiped at it. "Are you all right?"

The berzar she had dropped struggled to his feet next to his comrade, using his sword as a staff to rise. Her original idea to tire the monster out clearly wouldn't work. She didn't have the stamina herself. If she were an Ulfsark . . .

No, that wouldn't have mattered either.

She glanced quickly at Ewan. He bled over his left eye, a gash in the skin there. Blood smeared his forehead, hastily wiped out of his eyes. Something bubbled up around his bottom lip, but he gave no indication of being in too much distress.

Watching the two Thyrlings together, a plan formed in her mind.

"Take the one on the right I was fighting," she said to Ewan. "He's favoring his right leg even more now. Go hard on that side."

"What about you?"

"I'll take care of the other guy."

"That's it?" He panted, chest heaving as he stared at her. "You're not going to tell me what you're going to do?"

She shook her head. "Just keep him busy. Attack when I tell you to."

"Fine," he muttered. "I'll trust you."

Later, she'd have to thank him.

They advanced together, Astrid on Ewan's left so her

stronger sword arm would be free to maneuver. As she approached, Astrid slipped the straps of her shield down so it hung loose on her arm.

Given the high guard the berzar favored with his weapon, his lower half remained open. A couple of paces separated them, just enough that Astrid could fling her shield sideways into his knees.

She braced herself.

"Go home and sleep in the filth with your dirty wolves," the new berzar opponent called. He raised his weapon as she approached. "What are you, anyway? A Nistlefolk half-breed? You're too small to be a human. No match for –"

"Now!" she shouted.

She flung the shield.

The shield slammed into his left kneecap, just the way she planned. A *crack* of bone followed and the Thyrling shouted, then screamed. He dropped his sword to catch his fall, but Astrid was on him by then.

As hoped, the berzar wasn't fast enough to bring the weighted wooden sword back up. Not while in so much unexpected pain. With a lightning-fast thrust, Astrid struck him hard in the ribs. He swung with a shout, but Astrid stood too close. She shouldered aside the hilt of his sword and swung again. The wooden sword cracked the man across the head. The bear helm rang with a *ding*, and he stumbled backward.

The wolf does not wait for the prey to rise before it strikes, Huntress Vanna whispered in Astrid's mind. *You take advantage of every weak thought, emotion, and moment that each battle gives you.*

Astrid leapt on him.

Using both her hands to swing her lighter, shorter weapon with all her strength, she pummeled the injured berzar. The Thyrling blocked once, twice, then the weighted sword fell from his grip. He threw his arms over his face, shielding himself with his hands.

"Enough!"

Astrid barely heard the command. Through the haze of desperation that had become her mind, the word rippled into her thoughts. She paused for only a moment. Had she imagined it?

"Astrid!" Ewan called. "Stop."

The horn blast cut through her mind. She backed away from the berzar, her sword held in front of her. She picked up his sword. Weighted, for certain. Nearly double the weight of hers. She hurled the longsword far out of his reach with a snarl. Her chest heaved when she stumbled back to Ewan. He was down on one knee, holding a profusely bleeding nose.

The remaining Thyrling leaned heavily on his sword. His white-as-snow expression indicated great pain. He grimaced, unmoving. The knee around his right leg was swollen. He stood only on his left leg.

She couldn't conjure any regret. They'd made fun of her for her size, and that size had helped her win the game.

King Oskar raised his hands in a slow clap that seemed too loud, even from so far away. Each beat of his palms echoed in the arena.

"Our foreign friends have fought my berzars to a draw," he cried. "Well done, little Skolvarg."

Astrid gritted her teeth at the subtle jab. The king looked anything but pleased, despite an amiable tone. His deep annoyance made every ache worth it.

She resisted the urge to scowl at the king. She had a good chance of finishing off both the berzars and winning the match, but Oskar likely knew that as well. The weight of his glare crossed the arena and settled right on her.

She didn't look away.

Thyrlings in the stands began to filter out. The uproarious

shouts from before had faded into a gentle buzz. Jormund headed their way, as well as several of Oskar's household warriors that looked similar, but had different uniforms. Oskar turned away, Rosamund still at his side.

A muttered curse escaped Ewan. Astrid spun around as he spat blood. It dribbled down his chin, into the sand.

"Are you okay?" she asked.

"We barths have a thaying," he said in a thick voice. "Doth tempth the Muthes with the wordth you utther."

"Your nose is broken," Astrid observed, with a straight face.

"Yeth."

Astrid fought back a smile. She was the one that cautioned Ewan to be careful or his nose would be smashed like a pumpkin.

"I apologize. Here, let me see."

His eyes widened. "You can fith it?"

In answer, Astrid, reached for his face.

Ewan pulled back. "Don't tuhth it!"

"My uncle is a healer. Just let me look. He's set plenty of noses after an accident in the ring, including mine."

"You broke your noth?"

She glared. "Don't insult me."

He shrugged.

"I just want to look. I'm sure there's a Thyrling healer who can fix it so your pretty face isn't ruined."

Still eyeing her like a suspicious animal, Ewan slowly lowered his hands and let Astrid approach. Ignoring the two berzars limping out of the arena with other druzars at their sides, she gently placed her hands on either side of Ewan's nose. It faced slightly to the right. He must have taken a punch or hilt to the face. Blood chugged down his chin in a crimson stream.

"I left you with a downed opponent," Astrid said, gently

feeling around the area. Ewan winced under a slight touch, but he didn't pull away. "How did he break your nose?"

"Ith that importhant ribe now?"

"Yes."

Ewan tried to smile and winced again. "Outh! Why are you looking at me like that?"

Astrid let a coy smile play on her lips. She dropped her tone to a lower register, eyelashes fluttering.

"Like what?"

His voice lowered, husky and uncertain. "Like . . . thad."

Astrid leaned in. "Like this?" she murmured.

Her heart raced a little harder. He smelled like sand and wood and sweat. The tips of her fingers found the right place on either side of Ewan's break, but he didn't seem to notice the soft probing.

"Like you're going to kith me."

Astrid's eyebrows rose. "Well, what would you say to that?"

"I'd thay . . ."

The bard's eyes closed as he leaned in. Astrid would have laughed if she hadn't wanted to keep him so focused. With a quick jerk, she set the nose. Ewan screamed. Her hands fell away as he stumbled backward. Rage spilled across his features as he looked at her, hands at his nose again.

"How dare you!"

"There you go, charmer," she said, laughing. "I bet you won't even have a bump!"

TWENTY-ONE

D espite her fatigue and aching body, Astrid couldn't sleep that night.

The howl of a wolf echoed through the night. She couldn't tell if it was real, or if she imagined it. Perhaps Margu gave her the sound as a reminder of the wolf in the cage. Either way, Astrid couldn't forget the caged animal.

The wolf resided too deeply in her mind.

While the bards snored quietly in their own stalls—Ewan seemed to sleep the deepest this time—she pulled on her wool cloak, laced up her thickest leather shoes, and crept to the closest window. Her muscles still ached from the fight, and her body begged for rest, but she couldn't help herself.

When they'd been escorted back to the stables, no guard had remained. Astrid supposed the king wasn't worried about them sneaking out of the enclosed keep or maybe he was still pouting over the outcome of the fight. As Astrid darted through the sleeping city, a spring breeze swept past her, laced with warmth instead of cold.

The movements that took her closer to the wolf seemed almost routine now. She slipped gently along, letting her thoughts brew in the background. Now that the fight finished, her chest tightened every time she thought about it. Like she experienced it again, even though it was far away.

Skill as a Skolvarg or not, they shouldn't have won that fight.

Ewan's skill with the sword might have been the one thing that saved them. If he hadn't been able to sufficiently distract the other berzar, then Astrid would have had both against her. Not even the greatest skill could have given a small girl like her a victory against those two behemoths.

So how did Ewan know so much anyway?

The memory that he did, indeed, hide something from her continued to creep up her back, but she restlessly shoved it away. Later. He'd promised her he'd tell her the truth, and she'd call on that promise in the morning.

First, the wolf.

Her agitated thoughts calmed slightly as she worked her way back toward the arena. Although it was the last place she wanted to go, Astrid forced herself to press forward.

The alleyway outside the wolf's barn reeked of metal and death again. Flies buzzed above several discarded carcasses this time. Breathing through her mouth, Astrid used a stick to poke through the pile, then extracted a leg of something—a sheep, she thought—that looked the freshest of all of them.

No other sound or person revealed themselves, so she slipped inside.

A low growl in the darkness greeted her.

"Just me," she whispered.

The growl quieted. Astrid paused, feeling the room out. No sound of breathing. No shuffling. When no indication of anyone else near came, she advanced farther.

The night was darker than usual, but not pitch black. Astrid could just make out the outline of the wolf pressed back against the bars on the other side of the cage. The wolf tilted its head, sniffing higher in the air. Astrid worked the mutton leg into the cage. Before it could hit the ground, the wolf snagged it with a chomp and began to chew.

Astrid watched her, thoughts whirling with other things.

Instead of backing away, she sat next to the cage. The wolf eyed her, paused, then resumed eating, but split her attention from the bone every few seconds. Finally, the wolf settled into a gnawing and licking rhythm while Astrid let her thoughts roll out.

For some reason, it was easier to think here than back in the stable. When she sat closer to the wolf, her mind organized itself more easily.

Time passed as she thought about the fight, Oskar's frustration with her when she won, the way the wolf continued to be caged away from the other animals, but didn't appear to have been in the arena.

Finally, her thoughts ran back to home. Freydis. Rolf. Her Skolvarg tribe. Her throat thickened, but she blinked the tears back. She still had to *get* back home.

Tears could come then.

A gentle whine brought Astrid out of her thoughts. Startled, she glanced up to see the wolf peering at her, eyes lightly glowing in the slivers of moonlight that fell from the high window.

Astrid blinked.

"What," she murmured, "am I going to do with you?"

Ewan's warning about setting the wolf free to run through the arena alone played back through her mind. How else would they take care of the wolf? Doubtful that she could get a rope around the wolf's neck and lead her out. Too much noise, too much opportunity to lose a hand.

How else to lead a normal wolf?

An Amarok wouldn't need to be told, they'd sense the danger. Plus, if the Amarok had bonded with a Skolvarg, as an

Ulfsark pair, the Skolvarg would be able to guide the wolf where to go through the connection they formed. *It's all mental,* Freydis had said, *it's like we see* and *know each other's thoughts.*

"Too bad regular wolves don't do that," Astrid murmured to her.

The wolf canted her head.

A dozen other concerns followed those. Why hadn't someone caught Astrid yet? Weren't they suspicious? Even in the dark it was easy to tell the wolf didn't appear as gaunt anymore.

Someone here knew about the wolf.

The niggling sensation that Oskar could be using the wolf against Astrid came to mind. Perhaps he allowed her to care for the wolf so that he could use it against her. The concern had occurred to her before.

Yet, she would still continue to feed it.

"It's not fair, is it?" Astrid asked. Slowly, she lifted one hand and put it on the bars outside the cage. "Have they thought nothing of you because of your small size, the way they think of me?"

The wolf let out a low, disgruntled whine, and licked her lips. With a yawn, she gazed around, seeming bored. Astrid's lips twitched. Bored was certainly better than violent.

"I'll be back tomorrow. Because I feel that both of our fates are somehow tied together, although I don't fully understand it myself. I'm done in Drakby, I think. As soon as I can find a way to get you out, I'll leave as well. We'll have to do this together . . . somehow. Just don't let them put you in the arena before then, all right?"

The wolf settled into sleep with a thud of her body hitting the ground. Only small flecks of gristle remain on the floor beneath her, the rest of it consumed. Astrid sighed, bid another farewell, and slipped back into the night.

Astrid had never considered herself clever, or sharp-tongued. It didn't take much stretch of the imagination to call Torva an ogre, after all, but Ewan's vanity proved her only defense against the bard's quick wit.

"I take it back," she said. "I think your nose does have a bit of a bend in it when I look at it from this angle."

Ewan scowled behind two black eyes. He still blamed her for putting the notion of his nose breaking to fate before the fight. The bones were still a bit swollen, and some bruising flowed out to his cheeks, darkening the delicate skin below his eyes. Despite the grotesque colors, his face still cut a handsome figure.

Astrid laughed, then quelled it after another dark look from him. Bluster, most of it. Ewan was too lighthearted to stay angry for long, and she *had* set his nose. She suspected his frustration came more from a thwarted kiss than the pain of his nose, at any rate. A thought that she constantly set aside to consider later.

"You know, that stopped being funny days ago," he said.

"The fight was only two nights ago!"

"Now I'm worried you might actually be telling the truth," Ewan said, ignoring her. One of his fingers probed the nose, and he sucked in a sharp breath.

"A Skolvarg always tells the truth," Astrid replied. She leaned back, the sunshine warm on her skin. "I said I'd seen my uncle do it, not that I'd ever fixed a nose before."

His gaze darted to hers in shock, but she smiled to show him she was joking. Ewan leaned forward, his forearms resting on his knees. They stood on top of one of the palisade walls overlooking the river.

Nearby, a pair of guards glanced their way, wary of their presence even though Astrid and the bards were given somewhat free reign inside the keep. As long as they didn't try to enter the king's lodge or leave through the gates and were in the stable by nightfall, no one bothered them.

All day yesterday, Astrid had attempted to find a way out for the wolf. Oskar hadn't said a word after the fight—probably gathering his pride back together—and Rosamund had been oddly quiet. Except for a note that expressed her relief at their safety, the royal family had been laying low for two days.

The gathering jaegars, however, likely had something to do with that. Another anticipated jaegar had arrived, meaning two others remained before Oskar could press into his great meeting whatever it was for.

Beyond the palisade wall where they stood, Drakby hummed with new life. Wagons from more distant Thyrling cities in the west rolled into town on difficult roads. The mud had dried, but left thick, tenacious tracks and ruts in its way. Broken axles and wheels kept Drakby awake and busy.

Not to mention the bustling inns, busy with jaegars, their attendants, servants, and more. Astrid had never been so grateful to sleep in a stable.

At this point, common convention with the Thyrlings had been satisfied. The King brought no trial against her, she'd participated in an entertaining fight at his hand, and had eased general decorum—all while sleeping in a stable. Her aggressors had even given their own confession of guilt.

Nothing waited here for Astrid.

Except the wolf.

And the lingering threat of Oskar's interest in her death. She had the feeling that if she ran, he would follow. Perhaps he wanted her to run. Astrid couldn't decide, so she waited, plotting an escape for her and the wolf together.

"I have to make my money on these good looks you know," Ewan said, tapping his chin and drawing her thoughts back to the present. He glanced at her with a sidelong glance, a light humor in his gaze.

"That's good. Because you won't be able to hire on as a mercenary anytime soon."

"Ouch." He rubbed his chest as he laughed. "That hurt right here. I thought I handled myself very well, thank you. Admit it!"

"You were better than expected." Her gaze tapered on a lighter spot not far from them. She nodded to it ever-so-slightly. "There? Is there an opening in the palisade below there?"

Ewan continued to look contemplative, but his gaze moved round. "No. But the bush does look more manageable over there."

"It's not too far from the arena. If we could get a rope around her neck then we'd be able to bring her there."

"She needs to get through the palisade somewhere."

Astrid frowned. The wooden palisade walls that encompassed Drakby and the arena grounds were the biggest problem in her bid to set the wolf free. Both the town and arena walls were manned by guards. At night, they closed the doors to the town and locked them with giant timbers set into hooks.

"I'll take your compliment on my fighting prowess," Ewan said a little too loudly. "But to be fair, my fighting skills are better than your singing."

The *thuds* of approaching guards clued Astrid in. He was trying to play the part of an innocent bystander. Astrid held up two hands. Her eyes continued to rake the countryside on the other side of the wall, however.

"I won't argue with that. I never could sing."

"Don't the Skolvarg have any songs?" he asked as he leaned back against the wall, facing the other direction. "Anything besides wolf howls?"

Astrid laughed. "We do, but I've never bothered to learn any of them. I could tell you a few of our sagas, but I'd probably leave out some of the important parts."

"You probably skip all the romance and go straight to the battles, don't you?" Ewan asked, an eyebrow cocked.

Astrid nodded. "Yep. Ulfsarks don't have time for romance."

"Ulfsarks. That's right."

He didn't press any questions, for which she was grateful.

"Well, I'd still like to hear one of your stories sometime." Ewan straightened as the guards strode past, ignoring them completely. "I don't know any Skolvarg sagas or songs."

"Perhaps on your journey home you could make a stop with my tribe again."

He grinned, sending an odd whirl into her stomach. "I'd like that. I bet the others would too."

The guards faded away and silence fell between them until Astrid motioned ahead. They continued to walk, this time toward the arena. Not only did she want to scout out the escape route for her and the wolf, she wanted to see the activity around the barn during the day.

Was the wolf left alone? Did someone see her?

"I imagine this is all strange to you." Ewan gestured to the fields off to their left. "All this civilization. Much different from living more nomadically in the Wolfmoors."

"Yes. Isn't it for you?"

"We have quite a few established towns, though nothing the size of Tyrvik, I'm told. As bards, we're used to traveling and seeing different sights."

"So why did you choose to come to Thyrden? You can go anywhere and sing to anyone." She lifted her hands. "Why here?"

A warm wind whispered past again, brushing the hair off

Astrid's neck. The cool uplift of wind under the looming spring sun felt delicious on top of her skin.

"There isn't as much freedom to being a bard as you might imagine," Ewan said with a little lift of his brow. He folded his hands behind his back. "It may look like we're always wandering free and easy, but there's more to it."

"Such as? You still owe me some explanations."

She'd been so preoccupied in freeing the wolf, she'd all but forgotten his promise to reveal secrets.

Without missing a beat he said, "Tonight. The others have agreed. I owe it to them to be present."

"Even if they aren't happy about it?"

His eyes cut to hers, startled. Astrid realized she'd given herself away. She'd heard his conversation with Liss, but hadn't eluded to it until now. She held her breath, wondering if he'd be upset, but he chuckled and said, "Even then."

Relief rippled through her. Whatever information she could gather before she left, she'd take. If they told her tonight, that meant she could gather some more food for the next two days, finalize her plan with the wolf, and be out of there tomorrow evening, just after sunset.

The night would give an added advantage. She doubted anyone would miss the wolf, but Oskar might try to pursue her. It seemed Astrid represented the Skolvarg and the war the king did not seem ready to forget. Astrid wondered if the king had truly wanted peace or his hand had been forced by his jaegars. The latter seemed more and more likely.

"So," Astrid said, just to keep her mind off those thoughts, "tell me about the Ochlands. Are hills really covered in blankets of flowers?"

Ewan grinned. "Yes indeed."

Maury flitted about his head while Ewan dove into a song to describe his homeland. All fighting talent aside, he had a strong voice, a knack for melody, and an easy way around the words. The deep reverberation in his tones sent a little thrill all the way through her. Not to mention the opportunity that the song gave her to study the land while she listened.

So, there *was* joy to be found outside being an Ulfsark after all.

Twenty-Two

The bards gathered in the stable that evening.

Ewan stood in the middle of the stable hallway just after sunset. A torch on the nearby wall, and several smaller candles that Lara had lit throughout each stall, illuminated the space with a soft glow.

"Thank you for attending." Ewan bowed, his voice comically deep and resonant. Lara rolled her eyes, but Auley chuckled.

"First of all," Ewan said, voice clearing, "as we agreed together, we're here to tell Astrid about our purpose with the Thyrlings."

Despite his pale, freckled skin, Auley's expression darkened considerably. "In for a chord, in for the song," he half-growled. "You must understand, there's no going back once we reveal what we know to you, lass. Right now, if things go awry, you can tell the princess you knew nothing about us."

Could it be that terrible? Their solemn expressions didn't give her any hope of this being a joke.

"I will not speak of this to anyone else but the Skolvarg leaders," she said with a measured tone. "I cannot promise you anything more than that. I will keep your secret but that doesn't mean I wish to be involved."

Ewan looked surprised. "Why?" he asked.

"Because I'm leaving the moment I can."

Something registered in his expression, then faded. He nodded and his voice dropped slightly.

"Very well. What you said the other night at the tanner's was near the mark. We are not in Drakby to perform for Oskar. The High Bard sent us to gather information on the Thyrlings."

Her lack of surprise seemed to shock all of them. Astrid processed what he'd said with a little nod.

"That much," she murmured, "I surmised."

Auley sighed. "Perhaps we're not as good at this as we'd like to think."

"Rosamund and Oskar aren't suspicious?" Astrid asked.

Ewan ran a hand through his hair. "They probably are now that I competed and won, although I tried to throw it as much as I could."

Astrid glowered. "You what?"

"I fought!" He held up two hands, then a roguish smile stole across his face. "I just . . . maybe I messed with it a bit so I didn't look *too* skilled."

Astrid shot to her feet, enraged.

"You—"

"It's all part of a game the different kingdoms play," Ewan said, holding up a hand defensively. "Everyone has spies, Astrid. I certainly wasn't faking my broken nose."

Astrid opened her mouth to say the Skolvarg certainly didn't have spies, then realized she didn't know for certain if that was true or not.

"More than likely there are spies in the Ochlands for the Thyrlings as well," Liss said with a dramatic sigh. Lara sat next to her, eyes wide, looking small against the backdrop of straw that had been trampled nearly flat.

"We wanted to be here for the gathering of jaegars," Ewan continued. Astrid's immediate ire had calmed, but it still simmered under the surface. He'd been even *more* competent than what she'd seen in the ring? Granted, she'd been more focused on the berzars than him.

But still . . . what kind of spies were they, exactly?

"We believe Oskar is scheming with Kerys to wage a war against Ochland and the Skolvarg," Ewan said. "And he can only sail his longboats down the Auroran until he reaches the Slidrfalls. The waterfalls and cliffs there are too steep to move an army through. We were sent here because if the rumors were true, the easiest way for Oskar to march his warriors against us is by crossing the Auroran and cutting across the southern part of the Wolfmoors."

The blood drained from her face when she realized what that would mean. "The Skolvarg won't let that happen. It would break the treaty with my people."

"Aye," Auley murmured. "We don't think the Thyrlings will honor your peace treaty. And they won't want you at their backs, even though the Skolvarg and Ochlanders aren't allied. It's a good excuse for Oskar to break a peace he probably never wanted all along."

She leaned back against the stall, ignoring Ewan's assessing stare.

"We believe this council with the jaegars is when—or where—Oskar will decide the next course of action," Ewan said. "If the jaegars support it, the Skolvarg have reason to fear. If they don't?" Ewan shrugged. "Let's just say that there are many reasons for us to stay a little bit longer."

Astrid didn't miss the look he gave Liss, though Liss pretended to rub dirt out of the lines in her knuckles.

Astrid drew in a breath, her head spinning with implications and thoughts. Perhaps it had been better she didn't know about all of this sooner. It would have tainted her interactions with Oskar, with Rosamund.

"But then Oskar will be fighting a war on two fronts," Astrid pointed out. "He'll have to hold a line across the Wolfmoors to get to the Ochlands."

"It may be that Thyrden's role is to keep you out of the war," Auley said. "Our lands neighbor one another—this alliance may think the Skolvarg pose a threat if you joined our side."

"That's ridiculous!" Astrid said. "The Skolvarg stay out of the affairs of the kingdoms. We only went to battle against Thyrden because they invaded our lands."

"Times change," Ewan said sadly.

"And Rosamund?" Astrid asked. "Do you think she knows?"

Ewan's shoulders dropped. "We don't know, but we doubt it. It's no secret that Oskar would prefer to give his throne to one of his younger sons, but tradition won't allow it. Or he sent Rosamund to make peace with the Skolvarg knowing he could use that against her with his supportive jaegars."

"He's likely playing Rosamund as much as the Skolvarg," Auley muttered.

"Then we tell her!" Astrid cried.

"Rosamund isn't a fool," Liss said with a snap. "She either knows about it, or she doesn't. If she knows, then she's going along with it. If she doesn't, then she'll probably tell the king what we've said or use it to her own advantage."

Words crowded Astrid's mind, but every attempt to speak them only led to more frustration. She closed her mouth. Ewan reached out and put a heavy hand on her shoulder.

"You can't tell her, Astrid," he said quietly. "If something went wrong, I couldn't guarantee that we could get away before we ended up in chains."

"Or with our heads on pikes," Lara said in a flat voice, speaking for the first time.

"The river is too high to cross without a barge anyway," Auley pointed out. "We'd have to head west or north or south, and that would just send us deeper into Thyrling territory. It's not a good time to escape."

"Staying is little better," Liss added.

Astrid didn't realize how tight she gripped her mother's sword until her finger bones began to ache. Her fingers loosened by conscious willpower. She met Ewan's gaze, shifting back a step so his hand fell away.

"I need to leave."

She started for the door, determined to gather what supplies she needed and find the first horse possible.

"Be smart, Astrid," Ewan said, voice full of warning. He stepped in front of her, blocking her path. "You can't leave tonight. Listen to me. We can't act before the council of jaegars takes place. If we manage to learn anything about King Oskar's plans in that gathering, we'll be much better equipped to help both our people."

"If I don't do something right now," she hissed, "the first Skolvarg tribe the Thyrlings come across could be killed without warning. What if he acts immediately? What if he's already started?"

Ewan's eyes remained on her, steady as endless pools. "I don't think so. Oskar can't march to war without the support of his jaegars and Drakby is the only place they could gather an army and cross the river in force. That's why we have to stay."

"My people don't have the numbers to resist the Thyrlings unless we band together, and that would take well into the summer season to get the word to all of the tribes across the Wolfmoors."

"Then you have at least a week to wait, right? A week before you *have* to go. And this is all worst-case. The jaegars may have no appetite to go to war again."

Her mind raced. Did she have *any* time? The panic slowed as she thought out his question. She did have time. If she could make it far enough north of Drakby, there were plenty of fords where the Auroran broke into dozens of smaller rivers. She'd ford the smaller ones and get across, then find a Skolvarg camp. The Ulfsark would spread word to the Matrons and the other tribes.

She could reach *some* Skolvarg tribe within a week, maybe two. Certainly before Oskar mobilized anything, she imagined.

And maybe the jaegars would not agree to march to war again, though after meeting their king Astrid wouldn't hang her hopes on Thyrling mercy.

Ewan's voice dropped, drawing her back to the present moment. "With a little luck, *she* will last another week as well. It buys you time to save the Skolvarg and the wolf."

Astrid sucked in a sharp breath. His calmly stated words sent a shock through her. Ewan was right. She couldn't act out of panic. Not only might she draw attention to them and the Skolvarg, but she'd miss pivotal information that the Matrons would want. She let out a long, controlled breath.

"Then I'm stuck here?"

He cracked a smile. "Only until the meeting. Then you're free to go save the world if you need to."

She didn't like it, but he spoke sense. "So what do we do? Sit around and wait for Oskar to decide he's ready to march?"

"Pretty much," Auley said.

Lara's frown deepened.

"We listen," Ewan said, "and learn. The jaegars are almost all here. Oskar will wait for all five to arrive before he holds the meeting. There's two left. If we can avoid suspicion, there is a good chance we'll perform at the nightly feasts following the first council. No matter how secret the king wishes to be, his jaegars will talk. Word will get around. When the time comes, we will be ready."

The following morning opened on an overcast sky, forgoing hopes of warm sunshine.

Astrid lay in the straw, her hand wrapped around the hilt of her mother's sword. When pale dawn crept through the stable, she arose, dressed, and stood at the window. People bustled in and out of the keep already, with several servants clucking at horses in the paddocks not far from the stable.

In the earliest light, Oskar had left on a grand spring hunt with the jaegars that had already come. That left Rosamund in charge of Drakby.

Somehow, Astrid wasn't relieved.

Ewan appeared from behind his stall, eyes still sleepy. Despite the early hour, his hair gleamed with moisture and the teeth marks of a comb. Hints of a beard showed on his face. Did he shave without a mirror? The Skolvarg men used the water when they could. A few Skolvarg had the silver-backed Nistlefolk mirrors, but they kept them well out of reach.

"Up early, eh?" he asked.

"Restless. What are you doing awake at this hour?"

"Can't sleep with Auley around," Ewan muttered. On cue, a loud snort rang out. "As soon as the flowers get close to blooming, his head gets all stuffy and you can't get a bit of sleep around him."

Astrid laughed. "My uncle, Rolf, has the same problem. I've lived with him my whole life, so I can sleep through anything."

"Your parents?"

Too late, she realized she revealed more than she meant. A

reply rose to her lips to turn him away, but she stopped herself. No, Ewan deserved the truth. They were . . . friends. Perhaps the only person in Vigard, aside from Freydis, that held the title.

"Dead," she said.

A dart of pain showed in his expression. "I'm sorry."

She nodded.

The cranky call of a servant from the castle rang through the air. "Breakfast," he growled and a thud at the stable door followed.

Ewan sighed. "Another scrumptious meal, no doubt," he said drily. "I'll get it this time."

He turned toward the outer door, and Astrid drew a deep breath in his absence, relieved to have a chance to pull herself together. Something about his sleepy gaze and the early morning light set her stomach on fire.

Moments later, he returned with a tray. In an easy quiet, they ate while Auley snored away, and an occasional, low hum issued from Liss. They'd just finished when Jormund appeared with an expression stricken with fatigue and something close to resignation.

"The princess wishes to see you." His heavy-heeled boots stopped just short of the makeshift table where they sat. "I am to bring you as soon as you are ready."

Astrid stood.

Ewan moved to follow, but Jormund lifted a hand. "Only Astrid was requested," he said.

Astrid gave Ewan a little nod to show she didn't mind, then followed Jormund out of the stable. Two guards flanked them on either side as soon as they stepped out of the building. She cast them a sidelong glance.

"Where are we going?" she asked as they turned from the path to the main gates and instead took a footpath. The area inside the keep wasn't big, but Astrid had never gone this way before.

"The princess wishes for you to join her at the arena."

The narrow path forced them into a single file line, with Jormund ahead of her and the two guards behind. As they rounded the hill, a small gate, big enough for a single person, was built below two wooden towers on either side. She marked the location with interest.

Escape hatch for her wolf, perhaps.

Two guards posted at the door lifted a wooden bar to allow the small group to pass. Astrid grew more excited—the gate was barred from the inside and the bar was manageable for a girl her size. She set that aside and focused on where they went now.

They headed toward the arena on foot. Tips of the dead brown grass had just started to turn green, issuing the slightest aroma of fresh growth. Astrid's entire body tensed, memories of berzars still lingered from the fight, even though her body had already healed.

Reaching the arena, Jormund led them around the back, toward the lower gates she and Ewan had entered for their fight. The two guards halted at the edge of the arena, but Astrid followed Jormund.

When they entered the sand-covered area, archers fired at targets and warriors cast javelins. Others fought with spear, shield, and sword. The *thunk* of staves striking shields combined with focused grunts of exertion. The sounds filled Astrid with a longing for home. She missed training with Freydis.

At the far end of the arena, they found Rosamund. The princess sweated in the brisk morning air as she wielded a spear through several drills against a padded dummy. Rosamund fought in forms and steps Astrid had never seen before. Instead of a shield, she held the spear in two hands. She attacked with the head and defended with the shaft, much like a quarterstaff.

Whether she noticed their arrival or not, she continued through her stances and thrusts. As the timing and momentum of her routine built, she spun on her back foot and thrust the spear through the heart of the dummy with a shout. The wooden chest burst into slivers.

"Spirits," Astrid muttered.

Amidst his fatigue, pride shone on Jormund's face.

Where did this savage strength come from? All previous judgments of weakness in Rosamund bled away like snow in a rainstorm. Her skill, paired with her political power, made her a fearsome warrior princess.

Rosamund yanked the spear head back through the dummy and twirled it with a flourish. The butt of the weapon rested on the ground when she turned to Jormund and Astrid for the first time.

"Good morning to you both," Rosamund said with a smile as they approached. A nearby aide handed her a cloth to wipe her face. Before the cloth covered her face, her eyes seemed unnaturally dark and dilated.

Did Astrid imagine it or were those some dark veins receding out of sight? Rosamund's lean, too-skinny shoulders rose and fell from exertion, but she seemed satisfied. She handed the towel back to her attendant and once more Astrid wondered if she'd imagined things.

Rosamund's bright gaze turned to Jormund. "Thank you, Jormund, that will be all."

He hesitated, then gave a salute before spinning on his heel and leaving.

"I hope you had time to eat breakfast," Rosamund said to Astrid. "I should have given you notice last night that I wanted to meet you here this morning,"

"It is no problem, Your Majesty."

Rosamund waved a hand. "Please, while I train I'm just another warrior working on her craft. Call me Rosamund. And I apologize again for the farce my father made pitting you against his berzars." Her lips tightened. "I didn't think you would want to return to the arena today, but perhaps you would have enjoyed an earlier invitation? You're free to train here whenever you like."

Training again *would* feel nice, but allowing the Thyrlings to observe her skill firsthand seemed like a lapse in judgment. "Thank you. I will take you up on the generous offer."

"Would you like to spar now?"

Astrid gaped at Rosamund, who peered at her in curiosity. "Spar?"

Rosamund fought back a smile. "I've seen you do some remarkable things, Astrid. I'd like to see how my abilities rate."

A grin slipped past the serious exterior Astrid was trying to hold. She *wanted* to fight again and couldn't wait.

"That would be fine with me."

"Fetch some armor for Astrid," Rosamund said to her attendant. "A shield and wooden sword too, please."

What felt like moments later, Astrid stared across a medium-sized ring drawn in the sand. The attendants outfitted her with leather armor and protective padding, but neither of them would wear a helmet. In place of her spear, Rosamund held a quarterstaff and Astrid a wooden sword and shield.

"You may have seen me practicing when you arrived," Rosamund said. "I should warn you, my style with the spear is probably not like anything you've seen before."

Rosamund's confidence sounded like a challenge. Astrid twisted her grip on her sword and the handle of her shield, shrugging to get the loop onto her forearm just in the right place. Rosamund was taller than Astrid—as were most people

—but it was her other unexplained feats that gave Astrid pause.

Still, if Astrid could handle a berzar, she could handle a princess.

"I'll see what I can do," Astrid said.

Rosamund grinned. "Then let us begin."

She launched herself at Astrid, spear held low in a long thrust. Astrid dropped her shield to block the blow to her waist and barely registered a thrust toward her right shoulder. She pivoted away as the blunt end of the staff brushed past her.

Astrid attacked.

Her shield back in place, she sent a downward slash at Rosamund's neck. The princess twisted and danced back. She could use her longer weapon to her advantage from a greater distance.

Astrid pressed the gap, trying to close in. As she did, Rosamund's spear flashed like a striking snake. The princess jabbed high, low, left, right, so fast Astrid had to commit to each, not knowing which was a true strike and which was a feint.

Against her will, Astrid moved to the defensive, driven back by the flurry of blows. The small, rapid attacks frustrated her. Using her shield to absorb the strikes, Astrid pressed in again. Rosamund skittered back. Still, she had a sense of the edge of the ring. Her footwork moved her in a circle just inside the edge.

Impressive.

Astrid batted aside an incoming jab and slid to her left. Sweat drenched her neck and hair. They'd only been fighting for a short time, but her muscles burned with the required speed to keep up with Rosamund. The same look of joy, focus, and concentration showed on Rosamund's face.

A pattern of attacks began to emerge. Rosamund struck

low first, then left, then right, then higher, near the throat. Astrid went through the motions of each attack and when the higher jab came, she shoved upward instead of using her shield. Then she stepped inside and made a horizontal cut. The attack should have caught Rosamund in the ribs, but she used the momentum of Astrid's swing and struck out hard.

The spear shaft became a club. Impossibly, it collided with Astrid's shield like a blow from a charging bull. At the same moment, Astrid struck Rosamund in the ribs. Rosamund cried out and bent over, while Astrid flew off of her feet and slammed into the ground.

As a pair of attendants shouted, scampering over to see the princess, Astrid lay in the sand, arm throbbing. Her fingers wiggled. A good sign. A slight edge had eased away from the dull ache, so her arm probably wasn't broken.

"I'm fine." Rosamund waved away the fussing attendants. "Please, leave me alone."

The princess straightened with a wince. She shot a half-smile, half grimace of admiration to Astrid. Struggling to her feet, Astrid shook off her shield, wincing from the ache in her arm. She gave a small bow.

"Well fought, Rosamund. I don't think I've ever been struck that hard in my life."

"I could say the same." Rosamund held her arm close to her side. "Nothing broken, however. You?"

"I'll have a nasty bruise, but I've had worse."

"We will do this again," Rosamund said, "once we both recover. Will you walk with me back to the lodge?"

Astrid agreed with a nod. Together, they made their way around the outer circle of the arena. The princess led them the long way around. With a thudding heart, Astrid realized they'd soon pass by the barn. Although the barn stood outside the arena, she'd be able to see it through the open doors that fed inside.

Could she see the wolf?

Or whoever kept her there?

Astrid spotted the doors of the log building ahead and had to force herself to hear Rosamund.

". . . thought it strange that a monk, of all people, would use a spear . . ."

They were almost upon the doors leading to the barn now. Astrid's mind raced. There were no guards, but then again, why would there be? The arena teemed with druzars and none of them seemed inclined to help the animals.

"Astrid?"

Astrid jumped in surprise when she nearly collided with the princess. Too late, she realized she'd been tuning Rosamund out.

"I'm sorry, Your Highness."

"Is something wrong?"

"No, I apologize." Unable to help herself, she gestured to the barn. "Do you mind if I ask . . . what do you keep in there?"

Rosamund's concern changed into confusion. "I don't know. Some sort of storage, I'd wager. Maybe empty cages or something of the sort. Why do you ask?"

"Curiosity," Astrid managed, then gave a small smile. "Seems such a strange addition to have a barn outside the fighting arena."

Astrid turned to keep walking, but the door to the barn opened. A person emerged to gaze at them. A jolt of alarm shot through Astrid.

The pale, hollowed-out man from her dream.

Only here he was . . . different. For one, the man before her was not as thin as a corpse, but on the heavier side. In place of his gaunt, dull eyes were bright green, cheerful ones. Instead of dark shadows, laugh lines creased his face.

The complete opposite.

Astrid took all of this in in a moment. The man carefully closed the barn door behind him, giving Astrid the briefest glimpse of the wolf. She seemed to be back in the far corner of the cage.

The man wiped his hands on his robes, which were gray with elegant scrollwork, belted at the waist with black-and-white woven rope. A religious man, perhaps. The monk who trained Rosamund with the spear? Astrid didn't know of many religious orders, especially among the Thyrlings.

"Your Highness," the man called, beaming. "Good to see you!"

His accent had a tilted wrap to it. Perhaps a far outreach of Thyrden or someplace else entirely. He bowed as deeply as his large belly allowed.

"Good morning, Uzell," Rosamund called.

His lively green eyes flickered to Astrid. "Is this the honored guest I have heard so much about? I'm afraid I missed your fight in the arena, but word of your victory spread nonetheless. It's good to meet you, Astrid of the Skolvarg."

Astrid managed a nod.

Rosamund gestured to Astrid. "Uzell, this is Astrid. Astrid, this is Uzell. He's an advisor in my father's court."

Astrid nodded to him again. She couldn't bring herself to speak or else he'd hear her voice hum with rage. Was this the man that kept the wolf caged? The animals? Why else would he be in the barn?

Her mind spun with questions. Why hadn't she seen him before? Why did he keep the wolf locked up? Where did he come from? She blinked those away.

Uzell said in a kind voice, "I hope we may speak again."

His last words sent a shiver down Astrid's spine as he slipped away, humming.

"He's an odd man," Rosamund murmured after they'd passed through the gates of the arena and into the main fields outside. In the distance, glimpses of the Auroran river were visible. "He's always been kind to me."

"What does Uzell do for the king?"

Rosamund shrugged. "I'm not sure. He's not at all like the war priests of Tyraz. Calls himself a *vodi*, whatever that means. But he has successfully seen signs of droughts, storms, illnesses among our herds, that sort of thing."

"I see." It almost sounded as if this Uzell could speak to spirits like the Matrons. That couldn't be the case. The Matrons guarded their secrets carefully and they were even more sacred than the bonding of Skolvarg and Ulfsark. Likely this Uzell was a fraud. . . but then why did he remind Astrid so much of the starving man from her dreams?

Rosamund let out a long breath. "Well, let's find some water and then I must return to my duties. The last of my father's jaegars arrive this afternoon and the tournament begins tomorrow."

A subtle tightening of Rosamund's voice sent Astrid's instincts into a whirl.

"Tournament?"

Rosamund's jaw tightened for just a moment. "Yes. You're invited, of course. I hope . . . well, if you desire to come, please do. You're under no obligation. All the same, Astrid. Thank you for our fight. It was a most welcomed reprieve."

"I'm glad I came."

It felt strange to hear the words coming out of her mouth, and stranger still that she meant them so deeply.

TWENTY-THREE

E wan handed Astrid a wrapped bundle that clinked together later that afternoon.

She glanced up at him. He smelled like the heather that started growing on the hillsides behind Drakby. His cheeks were pink, as if he'd been running, and his eyes bright.

"What is it?" she asked.

He grinned, a little breathless. "Something I picked up while talking to the blacksmith earlier today."

"Oh?"

Ewan talking to anyone in Drakby didn't surprise her. She'd never met a more social person in her life. Somehow, he managed to not only talk to everyone, but make friends of them as well.

She slid the fabric away and peered inside. Five long, thin, black rods lay there. None of them were much longer than her hand, and all thin as twigs. They had a rough exterior that snagged her skin when she ran a finger over them.

Her brow furrowed. "What are they?"

"Files."

"Of course!"

His smile grew. "They're sort of expensive these days, since Drakby is so far away from everything else, but I thought you could use them for your . . . friend, since you can't find the key."

"I can't pay you, but—"

He waved a hand. "My pleasure. Surprisingly, Oskar's court has been fairly generous when we perform. I'm assuming Rosamund is paying the bills, but I'm not sure. And with the king out on his hunt, no one bothered me when I left the keep, though I think I was followed the whole time. Anyway, take them."

"Thank you, Ewan. This . . . this means so much."

His expressive eyes softened. "I know it means you'll be leaving soon, which I don't like." He ran a hand through his hair with a little chuckle. "I confess that I almost didn't get them for you. Thought they would just drive you away, but that's idiotic. As soon as you can go, you need to. You *and* the wolf."

Several moments passed before Astrid could conjure up a reply.

"Well, I appreciate it."

The lazy way he smiled as he disappeared, strolling as if he didn't care, belied the sense of sadness in his gaze. Astrid stared at the files. Given some time, she could file down one of the bars on the cage. With any luck, the wolf would be skinny enough to slide through. Two bars, if she had too. Could take awhile, but if she arrived early and no one interrupted, she could make it work.

Her brow furrowed. With Uzell in the way, though, she didn't know how early she could go to the wolf. Her excursions had been later in the night up to now, but she'd need time to make sure the wolf went free. Did Uzell live there? Work there? Had it been a coincidence that she'd seen him with Rosamund earlier that day?

None of her questions had any obvious answers, so Astrid curled her fingers back around the files and looked at the spot where Ewan retreated, feeling unaccountably sad herself.

The next evening came on the heels of a massive influx of Thyrlings into Drakby. Given that most of the newly plowed and planted fields were on the south and west side of the city, the meadows and open space between the town and the arena filled with tents as the last two jaegars arrived with their households and warriors.

Every inn and street in Drakby swelled to bursting. Rowdy patrons stayed up until dawn. Animals, merchants shouting, and general chatter filled the air until darkness quieted most streets. Any available nook and cranny had been taken, which only made Astrid more grateful for where they stayed.

The quiet, out-of-the-way stable made it easy to hide from Thyrlings. The stable hands had loose tongues they didn't hold back for the bards' sake, as well, which meant that Auley had never gleaned so much easy information.

Too soon, the bards and Astrid stood outside the arena again, near the elevated platform where King Oskar sat. Rosamund walked across the dusty sand and toward them, a dark silk dress fluttering around her thin legs. With a smile in their direction, she walked up the stairs. Astrid thought of their sparring session yesterday with a sense of vague disbelief.

Had such a thin little thing really bruised her?

Yes, she had.

Astrid's cheeks heated at the unfair thoughts about Rosamund. Weren't people always underestimating her because she was short? She'd inadvertently done the same.

"You aren't going to fight the princess now, are you,

Skolvarg? I see you eyeing my daughter. She's tougher than she looks."

Oskar's low drawl had no drunken slur in it, but Astrid shuddered all the same. He leaned over the wooden railing, studying the pair of them. His hair trailed around his face and his cheeks hung down in fat, unflattering lumps. Behind him lurked several people she didn't recognize. The jaegars, no doubt.

"Your berzar provided plenty of entertainment," Rosamund said.

"Fortunately we shall have a less disappointing show today," he called with a pointed look at Astrid. "One I would invite you to stay for. It occurs to me in all your weeks we have hosted you, my beloved bear has not given you a show of his prowess."

The playful taunt of his voice set her stomach on edge. Next to her, Rosamund turned a delicate shade of white.

While they spoke, warriors and guards filled the training arena. The double doors below the king's pavilion opened, revealing the caged form of Gorm the Grizzled. For a split second, Astrid feared the king would feed both of them to the terrible bear. Instead, he dismissed them with a wave of his hand.

"Join me and the jaegars, little Skolvarg. I would not want you to miss this display."

Reluctantly, Astrid followed Rosamund up the back stairs, to an elevated platform. Commoners and the household servants of Oskar and the jaegars filled the stands. The heady scent of body odor wafted through the air. Jeers, bets, and odd wagers filtered through her ears. Her upper lip curled.

Only a Thyrling would bet on life and death.

Once on top, King Oskar beckoned them to his side with an impatient wave. Astrid's stomach turned. She had to *stand* next to him? Seeing no way out of it, she followed Rosamund over.

Astrid studied the jaegars as they walked past. Four men stood in an awkward sort of group, ranging from early to late middle age. A white-haired woman joined them. While she clearly wasn't all together accepted, they didn't appear to shun her. She looked young enough to still swing a sword, if the notion struck her.

All of the male jaegars carried swords and a glare that promised violence if she stepped out of line. With her tribe in mind, Astrid forced herself to turn her back to them and give the king a short bow of respect, much as it pained her.

"Did you hear the good news, daughter?" Oskar asked.

His booming voice rolled through the stands near them, drawing attention beyond the jaegars. No doubt on purpose. Although he feigned nonchalance, everything Oskar said had purpose. The white-haired woman kept a steady eye on Rosamund, her gaze thin.

Rosamund shook her head. "No, Your Majesty."

Oskar clapped a hand on her back. Despite the force, Rosamund didn't sway or look at him.

"I decided that the winner of the tournament will be given your hand in marriage. Not bad, as far as prizes go, eh?"

Astrid bit the inside of her cheek so hard she almost cried out. Every eye in the vicinity swung to Rosamund, who stared at her father in an open mixture of disgust and surprise. Oskar's grin widened. The moment it appeared, Rosamund's smooth mask returned.

"This is unexpected news." Rosamund turned back to the sand. "I look forward to the results."

"It's time," King Oskar snapped at her, seeming irked by her bored reaction. "You are my eldest child. If you are to be my heir, you must have a strong marriage. And I reserve the right to refuse the winner." He glanced back at the jaegars collectively. "The match will be advantageous for everyone that matters."

Astrid caught a series of startled glances between the jaegars. Rosamund's open hand in marriage added all new implications to the tournament that none of them had expected or prepared for.

Rosamund ignored him. Her silence inflated his temper.

"There will be no discussion," Oskar barked. His voice shook. Rosamund continued to stare straight ahead, oblivious to his building rage. Like a bristling bear, the king snarled behind his black beard. "The decision is mine!"

"I have not contested your power to do so," Rosamund said.

Oskar's fists clenched, trembling. His face had turned a splotchy red. Whatever response he'd expected from his daughter, she hadn't given it. Oskar turned to face the arena and raised his massive paw of a hand.

"Bring them in and release the bear!"

Astrid turned her attention to the arena as the doors opposite them burst open. Two men were shoved forward by several guards. They stumbled and fell into the sand. Before the guards shut the gate, they tossed in two long boar spears. The heavy iron-banded gates closed with a dull thud.

Trembling, one of them reached for the closest spear.

The other one gaped.

A roar issued beneath the pavilion where Gorm waited. The creak of a pulley came next, releasing the door that held Gorm captive. A moment later, the bear lumbered like a rolling gray boulder into the arena.

Astrid turned away, acid in her throat. The clean, quick execution of the smug soldiers had been bad enough. This would be nothing but a pure blood bath. As if she sensed her thoughts, Rosamund shifted a hand over. Her fingertips touched the back of Astrid's hand, lingered, then moved away.

King Oskar raised both his hands. "Gorm the Grizzled!" he shouted. "Have you missed him? Are you ready for the entertainment that he lives to provide?"

The cries continued, deepening the ache in her chest. Not only did they imprison Gorm and force him to fight, but they sacrificed people. Trust a Thyrling to lose all respect for nature *and* humanity.

Oskar focused on Gorm, his teeth gritted. His meaty hands grasped the edge of the wooden railing in front of him. His dark eyes appeared wild with rage and hate. Astrid took a step back, hand reaching for her sword hilt.

Who controlled who—the bear or the king?

Gorm roared as he rose on two legs. The pair of men fighting Gorm appeared pale, underfed, and dressed in rags. Neither looked like they knew anything about fighting. Even fully armored, well-rested, and well-fed, she doubted they would have a chance against Gorm.

Spittle flew from between Oskar's clenched teeth now. His eyes grew wider, frantic. He raised his two hands and smashed them on the wooden railing. Astrid felt the vibrations through the end where she stood.

Gorm roared, dropped on all fours, and charged.

A paw the size of a shield knocked one man's spear aside like a green willow twig. The man stumbled, Gorm charged, and one wrench of Gorm's massive jaw later, the man went silent.

The second man charged, spear at waist level. Gorm spun, blood covering his gray nose. The sudden movement glanced the spear off Gorm's neck and made a deep cut into his shoulder instead.

Oskar shouted, a hand going to his right shoulder. Almost as one, bear and king roared. Oskar shouted to Gorm.

"End this!"

The bear rose to his hind legs. At his full height, Gorm

could climb over the walls of the arena if he wished, but he appeared to be under King Oskar's control. The remaining man cast his heavy spear again, but it fell short.

The man turned and ran.

He darted behind one of the thick poles stuck in the middle of the arena as Gorm advanced. After a moment of trying to keep the pole between him and Gorm, the man ran again. This time, he sprinted to the pavilion.

"Please my king!" he screamed, voice shrill. "Spare me!" He threw himself into the sand before Oskar and sobbed. "Please, I'll do anything you ask! Mercy!"

Oskar's eyes glinted with a wild, distant color. He appeared to stare past the begging man and toward the hulking bear. Gorm lumbered slowly toward the prisoner, huffing. Blood still stained his snout.

The crowd roared with approval as Gorm closed in on the prostrate man.

"*Please my king!*"

Goosebumps spread across Astrid's skin. She pressed her lips together, ready to vomit. Although worse than Rosamund's execution, she couldn't look away. Couldn't move, couldn't speak. She watched as Gorm approached the man. Could Oskar call Gorm off now? Gorm, not Oskar, clearly held the reins.

Gorm loomed over the man and roared. Rosamund flinched. Astrid took a step back, hand on her sword, as Gorm's yellowed fangs and bloody maw opened wide. The man tucked his face into the sand. Gorm dropped the weight of his body on top of the man's back with a sickening *crunch*.

The prisoner died in an instant.

Oskar released a long sigh and sagged against the wooden railing. Rosamund took an involuntary step back, bumping into Astrid, who stood frozen in place.

"Father," Rosamund said quietly, "we should remove

Gorm from the arena. The blood could send him into a frenzy—"

"He must feed," King Oskar said in a flat voice.

Astrid turned away as Gorm the Grizzled set upon the dead men. The sun shone bright above, and all around, the people cheered.

TWENTY-FOUR

"I'm leaving tonight."

Astrid said it a few hours later, to Ewan, Liss, Lara, and Auley. The five of them gathered in the stables. The sweet, dusty smell of fresh hay and straw, delivered while they watched at the arena, filled the air with motes. Rays of light streamed in from the far window, warming the stable with fresh, spring sunshine.

Auley glanced at her, then nodded. Liss did the same. Lara peered at her, as if curious, but said nothing. Ewan's sickened expression turned into a frown that Astrid didn't try to read. The resounding cheers of the Thyrlings as Gorm fed on the prisoners rang through her mind.

The wolf—maybe Astrid—would be next.

The files Ewan had given her lay heavy in her pocket. She ran her finger along the edge of one, ponderous. The rough edges snagged her fingertips, but she didn't stop.

"He's mad," Auley said. "Connected with that cursed bear somehow. It's not natural. There's no way to trust anything he does or says. I say we all leave. Our lives aren't worth it. We can warn the Skolvarg who can post scouts on the river and give us advance notice if Oskar makes a move. It's the better path."

Ewan didn't respond at first. Instead, he turned to Astrid. "I'll help you get the wolf out tonight and be on your way. We'll be faster with the files if we work together." He turned to Liss. "Then I'll be back to help the three of you pack and leave."

Liss folded her arms across her chest. Her petite features narrowed into a stern glare. "Didn't hear your name in there with us. What do you think you're doing?"

"I'm not leaving."

Auley threw up his hands. "Don't be a fool, Ewan! If we leave but you don't, Oskar will feed you to his bear within a day."

"He might already!"

"We don't know it. You come with us, or we don't go at all."

"We have to know Oskar's plans. And I don't intend to wander around out in the open. I'll stay in disguise just long enough to hear the outcome of the council. This is the only way."

"Maybe it's not," Astrid said. She chewed on her bottom lip as all of them turned to face her. With a shrug, she said, "Rosamund is different from her father. I have to believe she really wants peace. If that can't happen, maybe she can tell us enough to warn the Skolvarg and the Ochlanders."

"Rosamund is helpless to do anything," Ewan countered. "She just . . . she tries to pretend that she's not."

Astrid opened her mouth to argue, but stopped. As much as Rosamund tried to make it seem that her interests were separate from her fathers, when it came down to displays that mattered, she had none. Her pending nuptials to the tournament winner were confirmation of that.

"Maybe if Rosamund were the second or third in line to

the throne," Ewan said as he dragged a hand through his hair, "it would be different. But her position as eldest—and the one that inherits the throne—means that she's his biggest pawn. Oskar will strengthen his ties with his most powerful jaegar by marrying his daughter to them, then asking them to go to war with him. All he needs is a couple and the rest will have to follow. That's if any of them are opposed to war in the first place."

Ewan reached out and gave her shoulder a squeeze. She sucked in a breath, then let it go. The skin beneath his warm touch burned. His hand fell away, feeling like the final sounds in an announcement of demise.

"One of us has to stay," he said with finality. "It will be me. Even if I hide out in the town, there's no way the decision made at the council won't spread. I just need to lie low long enough to find out. For now, we should get some rest."

Darkness surrounded Astrid again.

She'd returned to the weird dream place and could feel the fogginess of it all the way to her bones. It settled in like it meant to stay, weighing her down. Astrid gazed around, eye sharp for a flutter of blue dress or silver hair. A strange laugh. Any sign of Margu.

None came.

Slowly, something materialized in front of her. Bars of a cage. The sharp, overpowering smell of urine. Vague shadows —traps and other items. All at once, she realized she looked at the barn from the wolf's cage.

She lifted a hand to her face, but nothing happened. A scraping noise issued from the front doors of the barn. Astrid swung her attention to the left. Uzell appeared—skinny and pale. She tried to stand, but nothing happened. A growl issued from somewhere close by. The wolf?

How had she fit herself in the cage, anyway?

As the emaciated man approached, her vision jolted backward. The growl increased to a snarl. Uzell smiled, a ghoulish, empty thing that didn't reach his eyes. Fear trickled through Astrid, mixed with something stronger. Hate? Uncertainty?

With a cold rush of blood through her body, she realized what she saw: the world through the eyes of the wolf.

"Where is your friend tonight?" Uzell asked. His cold voice was fit for a grave. "Has she abandoned you?"

Astrid felt another shot of horror.

So Uzell knew about her trips. Maybe he'd been watching —or allowing them—this whole time. In reply, Astrid—or the wolf, rather—lunged forward with a snap. Uzell paused, raised his head, and looked about the barn, appearing to sniff.

"I sense her, but I do not see her. And yet . . ."

Uzell studied the wolf. She thrashed, trying desperately to move, to do anything but face his disconcerting, probing stare. How could she end this dream? This . . . connection? What was happening here?

A voice rang through the air. "Well?" The tones were familiar to the wolf, at least, but Astrid couldn't make it out well enough to pinpoint. The wolf shrank back, afraid yet again.

"I don't think she has visited in some days." Uzell tapped a finger against his chin. "The connection seems to have faded slightly."

"Then you have failed," the other voice hissed. "Our work has been for nothing. Your promises were nothing but lies."

Seeing and hearing through the wolf made it impossible to identify the second speaker.

"We are not done," Uzell said easily, unbothered by the

frustration. "Bring her here. Force her, if you must. We will test their connection."

A silence sounded. Astrid stopped trying to think, she just listened. Thinking would have to come later.

"Be warned, priest. My patience wears thin. We have very little time to prove our success."

"I do not take you for a fool." Uzell fought off a yawn. "Observe, if you will."

Uzell stepped forward, his skin nearly translucent in the moonlight. He began to speak in a low, guttural language. One step at a time, he stalked closer to the wolf. Eyes forward. Skin pale.

Fear and hate rose in the wolf, echoing through Astrid. The wolf snapped her teeth, slamming her body into the cage to get free of his gaze. Pain burst with each hit, but she didn't stop. Astrid felt the pain. Smelled the strange stench of Uzell. Felt the wild panic without words in the wolf's mind.

An overwhelming desire to kill the pale man by sinking her teeth into his neck filled Astrid. Anything to get the chants to stop.

Uzell's words fell in cadence with his foul incantation. The distance closed between Uzell and the cage. A dark purple-black aura flared around him, outlining his skeleton-like form. Another figure appeared behind him. Thin, lithe. Silhouetted in the purple aura like flames. A black cloak rippled along the ground, hiding whoever hid inside.

Astrid felt the wolf's panic overtake her. She thrashed and screamed inside a body that would not obey. An overwhelming terror followed. A blast of purple shadow swarmed Astrid, wrapping itself like a thick fog around the cage. Astrid's vision blurred.

She knew no more.

Astrid leaped awake.

Sweat drenched her shirt and hair as she scrambled all the way to her feet. She whirled around. The stable. She'd returned to the stable. Memory brightened slowly. Talking to the bards about leaving. Laying down to take a nap.

The dream.

Hand pressed to her head, she peered outside. Night had just started to fall and a few stars popped out of a darkening sky. Raucous sounds came from Drakby. Even more near Oskar's lodge.

She leaned back against the stall and let out a long breath.

Orientation came slowly. She relived the wolf's terror in snatches. Comprehending what she saw funneled through an animal's mind wasn't easy because the wolf thought differently. She could recall Uzell's words now, for the most part, and make sense of them, but many were blurry. Uncertain. His voice strangled up in the wolf's fear.

Finally, she remembered the other person, the cloaked figure in the shadows.

Oskar?

Her throat felt raw and her head pounded like she'd been thumped too hard in the sparring circle. She glanced around, and found Liss asleep in the straw. No sign of Ewan or Auley or Lara. Preparations, maybe?

Something told her she'd been screaming and kicking. Sweat drenched her shirt and the soft leggings she wore to sleep. Her chest heaved as she tried to calm her breathing while she sucked in air like she'd been running outright for miles. Her arms, legs, and ribs ached and throbbed with pain.

A voice broke her thoughts.

"You look awful, *bannu*."

Astrid's head jerked to the corner of the stable. Margu leaned against the wall, idly examining her nails.

"What in the Seasons are you doing here?" Astrid whispered.

"Is that any way to speak to me?" Margu straightened, her voice a drawl that didn't sound all that annoyed. "I'm only here to help, after all."

"Can't you make an appearance *before* something bad happens?"

Margu lifted an eyebrow. "Perhaps you should be grateful I showed up at all, instead of leaving you to fend for yourself."

"Right after I met you last time, I was attacked and forced to leave home, then brought here, where Oskar clearly wants me dead. Then, he'll incite a war with my people. Forgive me, but I'm not sure if you show up at the end or the beginning of my troubles."

Margu trilled a fake laugh. "Pure coincidence. I thought you'd be glad to see me . . . given your latest predicament."

Astrid studied her. Margu appeared exactly the same as before. This time, her dress had a gauzy appearance, like fabric made of blue smoke. It moved, barely covering any part of her body. At any given moment, Astrid expected the cloud-like material to completely evaporate. Margu's shimmering silver hair had been drawn to the side, resting on a pale, bony, and bare shoulder.

Despite Margu's mesmerizing appearance, Astrid's mind shuttled back to the wolf. To the draw she felt for the animal, even though she couldn't explain it.

Now, she had to assume that Oskar had been behind this entire farce. A trap was a trap. For some reason, he wanted a Skolvarg to see the wolf. They said something about her connection to it.

She should leave immediately and head home. Get out while she could. On her own, she'd be fine. Even if they tailed her, she'd make it back without any problems because she'd be faster through the Wolfmoors than they would.

Yet . . . she couldn't abandon the wolf.

Margu drew her out of her thoughts. "If you're going to daydream and don't want my guidance, I *do* have other things I could busy myself with."

"Can you help me with the wolf?"

Margu smiled. "I *can* help you with anything. If I *will* is a different matter."

Astrid swallowed hard. "Then I apologize for my rudeness and would appreciate your help. Assuming it's not another one of your riddles?"

At length, the Spirit of Winter smiled a wolf smile that showed her teeth against pale skin.

"You'll do Astrid, daughter of Hildr. If you manage to keep that hard head on your shoulders, anyway. You may not be a hero, but you'll do. Your mind still lingers on the hope of becoming an Ulfsark, yes?"

She had a hard time meeting the woman's eyes when she answered.

"Yes."

Once more, Margu studied Astrid for a long moment. Her cold, dark eyes chilled Astrid like the darkness just before dawn in winter.

"You may yet have a chance," Margu murmured. Her brows drew together. Far from a guarantee, but it felt like a gasp of breath as she drowned.

"How? When?"

"When you're ready and not a moment before."

"You'll make me an Ulfsark?"

"Not exactly." Margu winked. "Things are already in motion, Astrid. I see farther than you do, so I anticipated this very thing. Until then, be wary. The king is not the real danger in Drakby."

Astrid opened her mouth with a dozen questions, but the Greater Spirit winked, raised her hand, and snapped once.

Astrid's entire body jolted, as if she'd been shoved off a step. She gasped, then blinked. Someone loomed over her, and a wavering voice rang through her ears.

"Astrid?"

"Ewan?"

"Are you okay?"

She put a hand on her head a second time. The throbbing had faded. Any trace of fatigue had evaporated. Whatever Margu had done, she'd cleared Astrid's head. The plan now felt . . . certain.

Astrid stood up from where she sat on the floor. Ewan crouched next to her. Margu was nowhere in sight.

"Nightmare?" Ewan asked.

"Something like that. Doesn't matter now. I need to go."

He let out a long breath, then glanced over his shoulder to the window outside. His expression remained drawn and tired.

"Time to set your wolf free."

TWENTY-FIVE

"You shouldn't have come," Astrid repeated for the dozenth time since they'd left the stable.

They were almost to the gates of the arena now, which fortunately remained open. Or was it on purpose? Astrid berated herself. She was being too skittish and paranoid. If she didn't get a grip it would drive her mad.

All she understood was the frantic push to be there with the wolf, an undeniable feeling that something was about to happen.

"Could this be you trying to prove something?" Ewan asked as they crept closer to the barn. No sentry in sight. Instead of reassuring her, it only made her feel worse. Would Uzell be waiting for her inside?

Oskar?

Astrid stopped as Ewan's words sank in. "What do you mean?"

He grabbed her arm, tugging her across the alley and around the back of the barn. Once the door whispered shut behind them, he let go of her.

"You want to be an Ulfsark but it hasn't happened yet. I'm

assuming, based on the relative age of the other Ulfsarks that I saw and the general desperation on your face when we first met at your tribe, your time might be almost past. So maybe you're saving this wolf to . . . I don't know. Prove to the Amaroks that you're worthy?"

Rage, then fatigue, followed Ewan's statement. She didn't have the room in her heart to fight for her spot as an Ulfsark anymore. Maybe it was time to accept that it wouldn't be her path. Margu had said as much—in her vague way.

But if she could at least save the wolf from a short life of pain then death, didn't that prove . . . something?

Astrid realized she had no answer to Ewan's question.

"I just want to make sure," Ewan said, gaze darting around as he tried to read the shadows, "if this is worth it to you."

The answer came out of her before she could think it.

"It is."

He nodded once. "Good enough."

Almost silently, they crept through the caged animals and to the back of the barn. Instead of regret, she felt pulled forward. Like a string existed in her stomach to draw her closer to the wolf.

As soon as she stepped inside, Astrid drew her sword. She'd break the lock because they didn't have time to file the bars down. It could chip her mother's blade, but she had to take the risk and have faith in the Nistlefolk steel.

"Look!" Ewan whispered.

Astrid followed his pointed finger. A still form lay on the floor of the cage, pressed against the iron bars. With a cry, Astrid dropped her sword and fell to her knees at the side of the cage.

"Oh no!"

The wolf made no movement, no jump of surprise or twitch. She stuck a hand through the bars and ran her fingers over the wolf's fur. The ribs stuck out from the animal's side in an alarming way, despite all Astrid's sneaky feeding.

But then, against all hope, the soft rise and fall of faint breaths followed. The wolf wasn't dead after all.

"She's alive, but we have to hurry!" Astrid whispered. "Keep watch."

"The files!"

"Too long."

Rising, Astrid picked her mother's sword up. A glint of Nistlefolk-forged steel pierced the darkness to fill Astrid with hope and strength. She took the sword in both hands and swung down hard on the lock.

The ringing of metal-on-metal filled the barn.

She winced, the sound rough on her ears. Ewan stepped back, near the doors, but kept glancing at her over his shoulder. A chip appeared in the blade, but she ignored it to lift again.

Her second blow landed in the middle of the lock, glancing down. A spark flared, then faded. Astrid grimaced. Another crack in the once-perfect blade, she'd wager. With a deep breath, she re-gripped the sword. Her arms quaked from the force of the previous swing.

The third attempt hit true. Her overhead swing met resistance against the lock for a brief second, then carried through to the ground. The lock buckled in half with a *clang*. Astrid grimaced, but sheathed it.

She'd sharpen out the damage later. Hopefully.

"Hurry," Ewan called softly. "Someone would have heard that."

Astrid yanked open the cage door and gathered the half-starved wolf in her arms. The wolf gave no resistance. The acrid stench of caged, underfed animal came with her, but Astrid ignored it. In her arms, the wolf felt so small. So light.

Ewan abandoned his lookout post and ran a hand over the

wolf's head. "She's still alive but barely. The faster we get her to fresh air, water, and food, the better."

A voice issued from the loft, calm and soft.

"I'm afraid I can't let you do that."

Uzell peered down at them from overhead. His rounded face, still pale but not deathly, looked eerie in the darkness. He remained the regular, rotund Uzell that Astrid met in the arena with Rosamund, except for the faint outline of dark purple flames gathering in his right hand.

Ewan stepped in front of Astrid and the wolf. "What have you done to this poor creature?"

Astrid had never seen Ewan—or possibly anyone—so angry in her life. His voice radiated with rage, his features taut. He had his hands clenched at his side, one of them on the hilt of his weapon. She couldn't help but notice that his little finch, Maury, was missing tonight.

"I have only tried to make her more than she is," Uzell said, hands spread out. "Greatness comes at a heavy price."

"The princess will hear of this!" Astrid promised.

Uzell laughed, then leapt from the loft. He landed hard on his feet, the ground cracking near his heels. Astrid gaped. Ewan backed up, arms spread out to put Astrid in his grasp. The jump should have broken Uzell's ankles, but he didn't flinch.

Now both of his hands glowed with the violet flame as he rose to his full height. The priest was Astrid's height, but no longer appeared a soft, fat man. Determination and power radiated from him.

"You will not leave here to tell anyone," Uzell said. His eyes were two pitch black coals and purple veins snaked across his face and bald head. He raised his hands and the flames began to swirl around them. "We still have more learning to do."

"Run, Astrid!"

Still holding the wolf, Astrid bolted for the door. Ewan charged the priest, knocking him to the ground. The flames disappeared, flickering into nothing. Astrid skidded through the doors and stopped outside. When no one else appeared, she lay the unconscious wolf on the ground and darted back in.

Bard and priest wrestled on the floor. Maury flitted over their heads now, diving in to peck at Uzell whenever he saw an opening. A filmy, bluish smoke rose from the two of them, but Astrid couldn't tell where it came from. She charged forward, sword drawn. The priest lashed out with both legs, knocking Ewan backward. Ewan slammed into the ground and gasped.

Astrid swung her sword as Uzell rose to his feet. In the inch before the blade cleaved into the side of his neck, Uzell raised a flaming purple hand and caught the blade. With a grunt, he pushed up. Astrid spun backward, managing not to impale herself only by sheer luck.

She rushed back to her feet, hair obscuring her eyes.

"What are you?" she whispered.

The priest laughed in a low, rumbling sound. Both of his eyes were completely gray, devoid of emotion or life.

"I do not wish to kill you, Astrid. You could be very useful. Even valuable. But if you continue to resist . . ."

His words trailed off. With a few steady steps, he approached her. Astrid tightened her grip on the sword, then charged again, shoulder low to drive right into his gut.

Uzell spun to the right, moving with the fluid motion of a fist fighter. Astrid quickly turned and pulled a swing into a horizontal cut on her right. Uzell raised a forearm and purple flame blocked the sword stroke as easily as a shield. Astrid retreated to clear some space to swing, but the man pressed his advantage, keen to stay inside her reach.

Panicked, Astrid lifted her arm for another swing, but the priest caught her wrist. Icy cold filled her arm, spreading through the sword to her other hand. The blade fell from her grip, chilled as if she plunged it into a frozen river.

Black flames ignited on Uzell's hands, turning into a putrid smoke as they burned through Astrid's clothes and met her arms. The flames didn't light on her skin, however. Instead, they sat there like a cool kiss, unmoving. The priest frowned, grunted, and squeezed harder.

Astrid cried out and dropped to her knees. The force of his hold and the cold crackling through her blood, all the way to her heart, was too much to bear.

"Stronger than I imagined," Uzell hissed. His slate, empty eyes remained fixed and unblinking. "But my strength is greater. You shall never overpower me."

The *crunch* of a large bear trap connecting with the side of Uzell's head broke the strange air. Uzell fell in a motionless heap, releasing Astrid. The moment Uzell's touch fell away, warmth slipped through her again.

Ewan stood over Uzell, teeth bared, holding the chain of the trap. Astrid glanced at the trap, Ewan, and back. He'd swung it like a mace.

"Nice work," she muttered.

"Thanks."

She reached with a shaking hand for her sword and, after three attempts, managed to get it back in the sheath. Cold tendrils still worked out of her system, away from the blossoming heat that took back over.

Ewan held out a hand. She grasped it and he gently pulled her to her feet. His hand clasped her shoulder as he peered into her eyes.

"Are you all right?"

Astrid nodded once. "What in the spirits was that?"

"I don't know, but we need to get out of here. Kill him or risk it?"

A dark bruise bloomed on the side of Uzell's pale head.

Blood oozed from a jagged cut near his temple. In spite of that, Uzell's chest still rose and fell.

"I . . . "

The words *kill him* lingered on the tip of her tongue, but never manifested.

"I can't kill him," she finally whispered. "He has no way to defend himself, and he had offered surrender to us more than once. He should get the same chance."

Ewan's nostrils flared, but he nodded.

"Let's bind him and gag him, then. We need to get out of here now."

A short time later, Astrid shifted the wolf in her arms. Her muscles burned, and her chest ached, but she didn't complain.

They pressed farther away from the arena. It lay somewhere behind them to the south, not far. The torchlight from the palisade wall and the arena itself was still visible. No resistance—or even guards—had been at the back gate. Whether they lucked out in between rotations, or Oskar didn't have all gates manned, Astrid didn't care.

Now, she crossed an open space before the forest, in the dark, with Drakby at her back. Freedom had never tasted so good before.

Ewan glanced back. "I can carry her for a while?"

Astrid shook her head. Even in a sick and unresponsive state, it felt good to hold the wolf close. Every now and then, their heartbeats mingled. She shook her head again.

He opened his mouth to protest, and she wondered if he was about to say something about her size compared to the wolf. In the end, he turned forward again and kept pressing away from the outer wall.

All the better. She didn't have to explain the jealousy she

felt at the thought of someone else holding her. The sensation of attachment and need. If she released the wolf, would she lose it?

Astrid wouldn't take the chance.

Fortunately, the tree line wasn't too far from the arena, albeit at the top of a large hill overlooking the Auroran river in the distance. By the time they hiked to the top, sweat dripped down her spine. The wolf remained limp and unresponsive as Astrid reluctantly laid her in the grass.

"We'd better not stay here for long." Ewan used both hands to wipe his forehead and push back dark curls from his face. Maury flitted above his head with a light chirp.

"We?"

He glanced at her. "I think my plan to stay for the Council is a bit off-kilter now that we fought with Uzell, kidnapped a starving wolf, and broke out of the city at night. Besides, the Council won't take place until after the tournament, anyway. I might be able to go back in disguise, or something. For now, I'll have to just be gone."

The reminder of Drakby and all its dark news settled back on Astrid. Her mind had been looping around Uzell, her dream, and the wolf all night long. Part of her wished she'd dreamed of the strange magic instead of experiencing it.

"What about the others?" she asked.

"Auley will get them out and I'll get a message to them. Besides, they have each other. You have . . . well . . ."

The rest went unsaid. Astrid would have protested, but she was grateful for the company. Getting to the Auroran river with an unresponsive wolf, on her own, would be challenging enough. With his help, they held a better chance.

Too short of a time later, Ewan motioned to the south with a nod. "There's a camp. Let's head north, swing around, and then head back east away from them. We should hit the river soon."

Astrid nodded, drew in a deep breath, and reached for the wolf. She didn't stir as Astrid draped her over her shoulders, hands around her legs. Her faint breaths gave Astrid enough reassurance to keep moving.

Darkness slowed their progress.

The lack of a moon left them nearly blind, venturing toward unknown dangers. The possibility of stumbling on a Thyrling lumber or hunting camp lay at the forefront of her mind. With every step, her weary body grew a little more tired.

When pale sunlight shone down through the branches, Astrid set the wolf down near a small, chipper spring. Morning arrived in full. The smell of dew, pine trees, and the rich loam of the forest filled her nose. Birds chirped and a squirrel chattered from a dead pine limb.

"It's lovely."

Ewan nodded.

They each took long drinks from the cool stream and splashed their faces with water.

"I know we didn't plan on her being hurt," Ewan began carefully, "but what do you plan to do with her once you get across the river? We're almost there, aren't we?"

The wolf's ribs rose and fell in a steadier rhythm now. As if she drew power from the forest itself.

"I'll carry her until she's better." Astrid shrugged. It wasn't really an answer, but there also wasn't another acceptable alternative. She couldn't carry her forever. Hopefully, she wouldn't have to.

Ewan tapped his teeth together while he peered into the stream. He crouched there, clothes damp from dodging through the dewy forest all night. Leaves and a twig littered his hair.

"We don't know what that priest's magic did to her. I've tried to reach out to her but . . . I can't sense anything right now. It could be because she's asleep but . . . there's a chance that she might never—"

"If I had freed her earlier it wouldn't have happened," Astrid said a little too sharply. "This is my fault. I shouldn't have waited so long."

Ewan looked like he wanted to say something else, then let out a sigh. "Will you at least let me take a turn?"

He was right. Uzell would eventually be found and search parties set out for them. They needed to move fast, and her body struggled as it was. Her arms, back, and chest were on fire. Reluctantly, Astrid nodded.

"Then we should be going."

Kneeling down beside the wolf, Ewan ran a gentle hand over her matted fur. Maury fluttered to the ground in front of the wolf's nose and cocked his head to the side with a soft, questioning chirp. Ewan's hand lingered on her side for a moment, then he reached beneath the wolf to lift her in his arms.

The moment he stood, the wolf's eyes shot open.

Astrid gasped.

The wolf panicked. Ewan grunted as the animal planted her hind legs in his stomach and jumped free of his arms. She hit the ground running and disappeared in a flash of grayish-red fur, swallowed in the forest before Astrid could blink.

Astrid darted into the trees to follow. For minutes she scoured the ground, searching for prints or obvious paths or any sign. Finally, she sank to her knees, panting. A gaping hole lingered in her chest.

Eventually, a hand came to her shoulder.

"I'm so sorry, Astrid." Ewan panted as he tried to keep up. "I don't know what I did. She woke up and must have noticed she was out of the cage. It makes sense she would have taken her first shot at freedom."

Sadness weighed like a blanket on her. An emptiness overtook her soul. A dearth. Somehow, she'd tied her own fate to that of the wolf. Even though the wolf now ran free, Astrid felt like she'd just lost everything important.

"It's all right, Ewan," she said, voice thick. "You did nothing wrong. I . . . I should have had a rope on her or something."

"She would have bit you."

Astrid held back a laugh—mostly a sob—but it came out anyway. What had she really expected to happen when the wolf woke up?

Some small, but vibrant, part of her had still hoped that the dreams of the wolf meant that something had formed between them. That although she'd accepted she'd never have an Amarok, maybe she'd have *this* wolf.

As if physical distance could break those supernatural bonds, the feeling of security, connection, perhaps even affection, ebbed.

A tear dropped down her face. Astrid let it go. "We accomplished my goal," she whispered. "She's free."

"And so are you."

Astrid forced herself back to her feet. They'd done the right thing. A good thing. If an Amarok or even a regular wolf couldn't—or wouldn't—bond with her, then the spirits would present a different path.

She had to believe that.

"Let's go," she said, her voice a rasp. "We need to get out of here, and now we can move faster."

Twenty-Six

E wan led them northeast, along the river.

Here, in the heart of the forest, it was easy to believe there wasn't another person for miles. But Astrid knew better. With the number of warriors camped in Drakby, Oskar would send searchers in every direction. There would likely be a prize from the king for whoever found them. Oskar would not rest until they were fed to Gorm.

Each snapped twig caused Astrid to reach for her sword. Each moment she expected to hear the shouts of hunters drawing closer through the pines.

Unlikely or not, Astrid never stopped searching for the wolf.

A part of her insisted the wolf might have only been scared and now searched for Astrid, but she quieted that thought. It didn't make sense. Wherever the wolf had gone, Astrid hoped Uzell hadn't hurt her beyond whatever healing she could manage in the wild.

A few hours later, the Auroran river proved a welcome distraction.

"Well, that was certainly an adventure," Ewan said. "Might

as well try to cross soon, don't you think, instead of skirting it for too long?"

The trees thinned, leaving them on a short cliff that dropped into a narrow, but steep, gorge. In it, the Auran river roared with foamy, watery life. Farther north, the lower parts of the mountains known as the Grimstens would shed their winter coat of snow and raise the river for weeks. The Auroran peeled off into dozens of smaller tributaries near the southern spur of the Grimsten range the farther they went.

"Crossing the Auroran anywhere will be a challenge," Astrid said, elevating her voice above the roar of the river. "But heading farther north will give us the best advantage."

She'd always spent her daydreams wishing she could become an Ulfsark, but at the moment, Astrid might have traded any chance of bonding with a wolf to be able to speak with a water spirit that might ease their river crossing. Or a forest spirit that could hide their tracks from any pursuers.

"We've already been going north all night and today."

"Farther," she insisted. "It isn't safe to cross this low even if we could. Once we make it to the east bank, the Thyrlings will be hesitant to follow us into Skolvarg lands."

I hope, she thought but did not add.

He sighed. "All right, but keep an eye out. If we find a good place, I want to cross it there."

"What about the others?"

"Ah-ha! That's the easy part." He whistled and Maury took off from his shoulder, darting through the branches until Astrid lost sight of him above the forest canopy. "Maury will find them and Auley should have gotten them a head start before Uzell was discovered. We discussed it and his plan was to head north of the city as well."

Stretching out on a boulder, Ewan motioned her next to him. The sun had already warmed the rock. She sighed as she curled up on the warm face, her clothes still damp from sweat.

"Take a nap," he said. "I'll keep watch for Maury, and you need to recover some energy. We'll eat when Maury returns."

Her eyes closed, and Astrid fell asleep moments later.

The dream world awaited her, this time without Uzell.

Immediately, she could tell that she saw through the wolf's eyes again. She slipped through the forest, low to the ground, senses alert. Smells assaulted her all the time. Some familiar, some new. Some concerning. She veered away from those, padding through the new growth.

Her nose dropped to the ground, scenting out the depths of unfamiliar territory.

The desire and pull of home guided her, but she couldn't seem to make up her mind. At times, she felt a tug to the north. Her mother and pack lived there. How far away, she didn't know.

Another instinct told her to head east in an irritating, confusing pull. Why that direction? Nothing familiar lay in the east. Her pack was not east of the great river. The Grimsten mountains called. Home called.

Why was it so hard to answer?

A sharp pang of hunger reminded her that she hadn't eaten anything but a rabbit since she'd awakened, free of the cage. Miles away from the stranger who'd held her in his arms, she had finally considered he wasn't a danger. His scent was the same that had visited her while locked in the darkness.

The other was the one who came to her most often. The woman that fed her and gave her a drink. She wasn't like the others who'd hunted her when she roamed free. They had chased her with dogs, chained her, and caged her.

A flood of memories streamed through her mind as the wolf continued to roam, heading more northeast than anything. Endless days in the dark, broken by visits from the pale man. They prodded, they poked. Sometimes the man hurt her. She expected pain when his hands glowed and the strange sounds came from him. Inside, she sensed it changing her in ways she did not understand.

She paid attention to the scents, eager to avoid any that smelled like the men and dogs that had chased her.

All that was behind her now. If she could ignore the tug to the east, soon, she would run with her pack again.

North, north. North.

She padded faster through the forest, keen to return.

"Astrid, wake up."

The weight of a deep sleep peeled away from Astrid's mind. A warm hand lay on her arm, nudging her further out of rest. Astrid sat up, disoriented. They lay at the end of the Auroran river still.

"Why are we going east?" she murmured, the dream still wrapped around the edge of her mind. "She's north."

"Who?"

Astrid blinked.

"We're not heading east." Something propelled Ewan's voice. Excitement, maybe? Sleep continued to shed, opening her mind.

"Maury has returned. The others aren't far south. Are you feeling strong enough to get started again?"

Astrid rubbed her face. The others? Who would be . . . oh. Right. Auley and Liss and Lara. They were supposed to connect. But her heart drew out, farther north, to the wolf that searched for her home.

Just a dream, Astrid told herself. She blinked several times.

Her clothes had dried while she lay in the sun. She felt more rested than before, though still weary.

"How long did I sleep?" she asked.

"You slept like the dead for a couple of hours. I wouldn't have woken you but Maury returned."

The little finch was nowhere to be seen. "Where did he go?"

Ewan gestured with his head downriver. "To lead them here. I'm not sure how far away they are. It's hard to get an exact distance from a bird."

"I admit, I am impressed," she admitted ruefully. "I didn't think he did anything but sang and annoyed people."

"Are you talking about Maury or me?" Ewan asked with a roguish wink that sent her stomach into flips.

Chuckling, Astrid stood and stretched. "Both of you, I guess. Get some rest. You should have woken me long before now." She stopped when he tried to protest and raised a hand. "Both of us will need it and I feel much better. Now . . . sleep."

Ewan pulled his pack close to use it as a pillow. "Fine, but I'm keeping this with me. Otherwise, we'll be out of food by the time I wake up!"

Swiping a kick at the bottom of his boot, Astrid walked to the edge of the gorge and sat on the ledge.

The rushing waters hurried by as she pieced together her dream. In the aftermath, longing for the wolf filled her. Real or not, she still felt a yearning for her at her side. Perhaps worse now. But still . . . the dream had *felt* so real. Like she really moved with the wolf.

Was this the Wolf Song?

She considered Margu's involvement in all of this. Was it all tied together? Did Astrid experience some sort of connection with the wolf because of Margu? Did it have anything to do with Uzell and his strange magic?

The fact that she'd dreamed about the wolf despite the distance meant something, Astrid felt certain of it.

If they were real dreams, what did it mean that she had them? The wolf continued to move north anyway. There was no way to tame a wild animal like that. If the dreams continued after she returned to her tribe, she'd ask someone about them. Rolf, perhaps. Maybe Odda.

Until then, she had to get home.

Eventually, Astrid left the river and positioned herself deeper in the woods, near a natural footpath that meandered from the south. Away from the river, she could hear better.

While she inspected the chips in her mother's blade, Astrid's thoughts continued. Her musings carried her into the afternoon, until shadows stretched across the far side of the gorge. The distant sound of horseshoes on stone caught Astrid's attention.

She shook Ewan awake, a hand over his lips. His eyes flew open. He nodded, and she let her hand fall away. Ewan straightened. A moment later, Maury landed on a nearby branch with a triumphant series of chirps and whistles.

Ewan grinned.

"They made it."

Auley, Lara, and Liss appeared on the animal path near Astrid's looking out. Five horses followed behind them, stepping carefully over the uneven ground. Auley seemed chipper enough for a man his size. Liss, however, had seen better days. Her face was pale, with heavy bags under her eyes. She yawned every other moment. Lara's hair had fallen out of her braid and lay in frizzy strands on her shoulders. Both of them looked ready to sleep while standing.

Astrid's relief startled her. She hadn't realized how concerned for them she'd been until she saw them again.

Ewan stood and tossed his arms around Auley.

"It's good to see all of you safe. We've been worried."

Auley released him with a shove, then pulled Astrid close. She melted against his fatherly embrace.

"By the Songs, it's good to see the pair of you," Auley cried. "What happened?"

"We'll tell you everything," Ewan said after he hugged Liss. Lara smiled at him, but stepped away from his touch. "First, did you have any problems getting out of town?"

"No, but just as we'd made it to the forest, we heard alarm bells ringing along the palisade wall," Liss said wearily. She rubbed a hand over her tired eyes. "Best to believe they're looking for us, I think."

Ewan pointed to himself, then Astrid, with his thumb.

"Us, actually."

Lara's brow rose to indicate interest, but as usual, she said nothing.

"We rode for as long as we could, as fast as we could," Auley said. "When the forest thickened, I thought it best to go on foot. We led the horses over ground that couldn't be tracked as easily."

"Good call." Ewan nodded. "Hopefully, the Thyrlings will assume you forded the river or went farther south. We'll rest until first light. No sense walking in the dark and risking our legs or the horses. Astrid and I will help you get settled. Liss. Lara. Sit down. You both look like you're going to collapse."

Ewan helped Astrid lead the horses to water, let them drink, then tied them in a grassy spot where they could graze. The trees surrounded them, keeping them out of sight if the Thyrlings made it to the gorge.

"Leave the saddles on," Ewan told her. "Just in case we need a quick escape."

Astrid nodded.

Meanwhile, Liss, Lara, and Auley splashed their faces in the stream, drank as much as they could stomach, and pulled a loaf of bread out of a pack. When all five of them settled down in the tree line, darkness began to fall. Without a fire, night fell fast. The moon struggled to shine through the tall trees.

"I'll be heading home with you," Ewan said. Auley, Liss, and Lara stared at him with sober faces. "There have been . . . interesting developments."

Without leaving anything out—and Astrid filling in a few details from her point-of-view—they told the other bards everything, up until the moment they found the gorge. Astrid left out her recent dream.

"Why didn't they come for us sooner?" Liss asked in a low voice. "If the king knew he was going to war again, why not seize us long ago?"

Lara snuggled deeper into her cloak, and shuffled a little closer to Auley. He put a friendly arm around her shoulders, and she burrowed into his side like a small child. Her eyes closed and head drooped seconds later.

"I've wondered that myself," Ewan murmured. His eyes had a gentle gleam in the darkness, barely visible. "Perhaps Oskar wasn't as sure as we think. Some among his jaegars could be tired of war and have no desire to join a war against Ochland or renew one against the Skolvarg."

"Oskar could cross the Stallofell mountains if he was determined to get to the Ochlands," Auley pointed out. "No, he *wants* to fight the Skolvarg. In his mind, the war isn't over."

"I'd take my chances against Skolvarg before I fought Stallogres," Liss said, with a shiver.

Astrid nodded in agreement. The Stallofells were inhospitable mountains that began south of the Wolfwood and ran all the way west to the sea, broken only by the massive Lake Vyla. Aside from towering peaks and dangerous, narrow passes that bred storms, avalanches, and rockslides, there were the Stallogres.

Nearly twice the height of a grown man, horned and broad in shoulder and belly, the race of ogres all but made passage through the Stallofells impossible, from the few tales Astrid knew. They didn't enter the Wolfwood or the Wolf-moors, but Astrid had heard the Stallogres sometimes raided into both Ochland and Thyrden.

"Wait. How did *you* get here?" Astrid asked.

"Went west into Kerys and sailed up the coast on a bloody boat," Auley muttered with a scowl.

"Then rode across nearly the whole length of Thyrden to track down Princess Rosamund," Liss said, rubbing her lower back as if the memory made her sore.

"Well, the good news is we'll see some new scenery on our way home," Ewan said.

"That's a worry for another day." In the faint light, Astrid could just see Auley stretching his arms over his head. "Astrid, you've got your first watch. Ewan, second. I'll take third. Liss and Lara, get some sleep. We can worry about wars when we're free of the accursed Thyrlings."

Later that night, Astrid opened her eyes in the darkness of her dream world. For a third time, she saw through the wolf again.

It all seemed so natural, so *right*. She accepted the scents and sounds of the forest as they stole her attention. Wolf eyes picked out details much better than humans. Trees, boulders, and fallen logs. They appeared as normal as if it were an over-cast day, not a half-moon at the zenith of night.

Weariness filled the wolf, but it was no match for the burning desire to reach home. Instinct gave her direction and, more importantly, strength.

The wind shifted. The wolf stopped, nose in the air as fresh scents swirled toward her. Eventually, she carried on. No smell of man, horses, or hounds. No scent of other wolves, bears, or bigger predators. Unfortunately, no scent of her next meal, either.

With a huff of resignation and annoyance, she carried on.

A small meadow opened before the wolf, surrounded on all sides by trees. In the center lay a slab of rock, jutting out of the ground at an angle. The wolf froze the moment she saw it. Her muscles tensed and instinct prickled through her.

Through the wolf, Astrid sensed an unknown power, stronger than the wolf's desire for home, that drew the wolf toward the meadow. The wolf followed it willingly to the edge of the trees, then paused before her paws tread into the grass.

Astrid blinked.

In the strange way of dreams, she left the wolf and found herself in her own body at the same meadow. The intensity of sounds and smells faded. Her thoughts weren't so single-minded now, but unfurled as usual. She spun a slow circle, assessing.

The same, distinct rock was visible from where she stood, only from the other side of the meadow. To the left of the rock, the auburn wolf gazed back at her. Her yellow eyes, luminous and bright, glowed in the night. The wolf stood just inside the edge of the forest, nearly hidden in the trees.

Astrid's heart skipped. She didn't dare speak, didn't dare move, lest she scare the wolf away again.

Overhead, and framed perfectly around the treetops, lay a collection of stars the Skolvarg called the Great Amarok. It shone directly onto the glade. As she watched, the stars around the Great Amarok gathered together, brightening the shape and definition. The Great Amarok had an illuminated outline that now shone more luminously than the moon.

Astrid held her breath. Whispers flitted on the wind. Hushed voices rustled with the grass all around them.

A single howl, cold, chilling, yet somehow familiar, filled the air. It seemed to reverberate all around her.

To answer, a chorus of wolves added their voice to the first. The forest echoed with their forlorn cries. Astrid tore her gaze away from the Great Amarok constellation and back to the auburn wolf. Relief that she was still there—alive and within sight—swelled in Astrid.

The wolf studied her for a long moment, then tipped her head back. She howled, her higher-pitched notes adding to the dozens of calls.

This was the Wolf Song.

The dreams and visions and emotions and pull to the wolf could have been nothing else. It pierced Astrid's heart. Filled her with a warmth she'd never known. Tears ran down her face as the howling increased. The stars of the Great Amarok shone so bright, Astrid raised her hand to shade her eyes. A sense of oneness filled her.

Margu's voice whispered through Astrid's mind, *Go to her.*

Without hesitation, Astrid crossed the glade. The wolf padded slowly out to meet her in the center at the base of an oddly-angled rock.

When they drew close, Astrid knelt on one knee and stretched out her hand.

The wolf lowered her head and dipped her ears. The moment Astrid's hand touched the auburn fur, the howling ceased. The stars of the Great Amarok flashed once overhead and the night sky returned to normal.

Yet Astrid would never be the same again.

The howls of her new pack continued inside, bouncing around her soul. Filling her. Strengthening her. Every wolf that had ever walked on Vigard and every Skolvarg that ever bonded with the wolves lived within her now.

Amarok or not.

She removed her hand from the wolf's head and the wolf gave a little whine. Slowly, the bright yellow eyes lifted to meet Astrid's. Unable to help it, Astrid giggled. She laughed and cried while the wolf barked and leaped all around her. Warm satisfaction glowed from deep within.

Her wolf.

Maera.

The name came unbidden in Astrid's mind. At once, she knew it was the wolf's name. Knew it like she knew the leaves would turn golden in the fall and the flowers of the Wolfmoors would bloom in the spring.

Maera's gaze revealed the depth of countless generations of wolves. Of history. Of Skolvarg. Of bonding and love and emotion and connection. Astrid never wanted the moment— nor the feeling of rightness— to end.

But as the darkness fell about her, a single thought overcame all else.

Find me.

TWENTY-SEVEN

Astrid woke in the dark with a huge smile.

She reached a hand to her face and found her cheeks wet with tears. Were it not for the still forms of the sleeping bards around her, she would have shouted. Screamed. Maybe even danced.

The Wolf Song.

Nothing on all of Vigard could compare to what she'd just experienced. Although she didn't feel stronger or faster or wiser, she knew somehow the call of her people had changed her forever. Now, she had to answer.

Somewhere out there, Maera looked for her.

Nothing else mattered.

Auley sat a short distance away, on the last watch of the night. He drew her gaze as he made a little snorting sound, his head tipped back to regard the moon. Moonlight bathed his features. A pang of guilt overcame her then. She knew she had to leave.

Would any of them understand?

Such an experience would be hard to comprehend if not

experienced firsthand. Maybe Ewan would get it, given his connection to Maury.

Besides, none of the bards needed Astrid to accompany them. They could cross the Wolfmoors without her—had done so before they came to her Skolvarg camp, in fact. Yet, it felt like an abandonment all the same.

These bards had become her friends.

But Maera was *her* wolf.

Astrid gathered her few belongings together as quietly as she could. Rising, she paused to look at Lara and Liss, then last and longest of all, to Ewan. She hoped to see the bards again someday. Perhaps it was best this way.

Saying goodbye to Ewan wouldn't be easy no matter how it happened.

She stepped carefully away from the others and walked to the edge of the camp where Auley kept watch. Only his orange mustache and nose poked out of his hood in the dim light when he turned to her.

"You're up early, lass," he said quietly. "Won't be another hour or so before sunrise. Are you . . ." His gaze seemed to drop to her pack. "You going somewhere?"

"The wolf," she whispered. "I just saw her in a dream. She's looking for me and I know where to find her. It's . . . a Skolvarg thing."

Auley remained quiet for a long time. Then he sighed. "I can hear it in your voice. You're decided. Ewan'll have my hide for this when he wakes, but if you say you must, then I believe you. Let me send you off proper, eh?"

The big man opened his arms and Astrid embraced him in a hug she thought might split her ribs.

"Be safe, Astrid. And may the spirits watch over you."

Astrid turned away from the camp and entered the dark isolation of the forest. She'd head north, skirting the river, and let her heart guide her from there. His words looped in her mind.

May the spirits watch over you.

She swallowed, readjusted her pack, and set her pace.

That, she thought grimly, *is also what I'm afraid of.*

As soon as the light grew enough to see the ground, Astrid increased her speed. She headed vaguely northwest, driven by a certainty that Maera waited somewhere in that direction.

Within the hour, her breathing became labored. Her legs burned from the constant jumping and dodging over and around rocks and fallen trees. The forest grew thicker the farther west she went. It was impassable for horses, even ones led on foot. If Auley couldn't deter Ewan from following her, the terrain certainly helped.

Morning passed into day and Astrid continued northwest. The overwhelming instinct left no doubt that she went the right way. Onward, always onward. She stopped only to drink and eat. Just long enough to catch her breath.

Her mind raced with questions as she answered the call of the Wolf Song, but she pushed them aside for later. Once she found Maera, they'd ford the Auroran. Then Astrid would search the Wolfmoors for another Skolvarg tribe. They could send word to Odda with an Ulfsark.

Of course, she first had to find a wolf in the forest, guided only by a newly developing sense that she'd never experienced before. All the while avoiding capture by Thyrlings, freezing, starving, or being eaten by any number of predators.

Midday became afternoon. The buds of shadows grew across the forest as the western sunlight shone down through the branches. Her legs felt light and unsure, her muscles exhausted. Being small gave her some advantage.

She navigated the forest far more nimbly than Ewan or Auley would be able to, but not enough to save much time.

She moved closer, though. Could feel Maera in her bones and her heart. As she stopped for a long drink of water, a lone howl sounded through the forest. A thrill of recognition made her choke and sputter.

Maera.

"Here!" Astrid shouted. "I'm coming!"

The inexplicable joy at hearing Maera's howl washed over her like a refreshing plunge into a cold river. This hadn't been the search of a day, or even months. She'd reached a turning point in a journey of searching for *years*.

Abandoning all caution, Astrid tore toward the sound of the howl. After a short time, it came again. This time, she heard more of an excited yip than a searching cry.

"Maera!" she called. "Maera, where are you?"

She laughed as she ran, hurtling carelessly over any obstacle in her path. Giving into the instinct, she let her feet take her. Then, in a small clearing between the trees, she saw Maera.

Maera froze as their eyes met. Astrid sensed Maera's mistrust, fear, and hatred of humans through their bond. She focused her mind on a sense of love and caring, like chords of the Wolf Song that brought them together.

Slowly, hesitantly, Maera padded closer. Astrid lowered carefully, her breath still fast. She held her hands low, palms out.

"It's okay, Maera," she murmured. "I won't hurt you. I won't let anyone hurt you. We belong together now, you and me."

The wolf let out a whine and dropped her ears back against her head. Another flash of fear and pain from Maera's months in the cage ripped through Astrid. She gritted her teeth, furious with Uzell again. Maera paused and let out another whine, tail tucked between her legs.

They were still a few paces apart but Astrid didn't want to push her. As far as she knew, no Skolvarg had ever bonded with an adolescent wolf. Most bonded as puppies so the wolf grew with the bond. But then again, she knew of no Skolvarg who'd ever bonded with an ordinary wolf at all.

Maera's experiences in the cage *and* her age would be a challenge for their bond. The fact that Maera had returned at all was a miracle.

An idea struck her. Astrid un-shouldered her pack, fished out a strip of dried meat, and held it out. Maera's nose twitched. She scooted forward, still hunkered down. She sniffed, then stretched her neck out for the morsel. Only a pace away now, Maera gave a small whine. She refused to come closer, no matter how much Astrid encouraged her. Last time, Maera had been stuck in the cage. In a way, the cage had protected her from Astrid.

Now, Maera really had to trust her.

"Good," Astrid said. "You're brave."

She tossed the strip of trail meat to the ground in front of Maera. The wolf snatched the food out of the grass and swallowed it whole. She licked her lips, head tilted as she peered at Astrid again.

Astrid produced another piece, this time holding it. Maera scooted forward, then snatched it before sinking back a safe distance away to eat the meat.

This continued until Maera accepted the food out of Astrid's hand without Astrid stretching her arm out. Any sudden or new move and Maera scampered backward. Eventually, she'd return.

While she fed her, Astrid studied the wolf. Her deep red-brown fur stretched over a gaunt frame, evidence of the months of captivity and starvation. Astrid wasn't sure if it was the lack of food and captivity, but Maera looked to be the runt of the litter. It was hard to guess how old she might be. Size and strength aside, the gleam in the wolf's eye hinted at an unbreakable spirit. That would be enough.

Astrid leaned back against a rock. Her muscles had grown stiff in the aftermath of the past couple of days.

"What are we going to do now?" With a grimace, she slowly wrapped her cloak around her. She couldn't risk a fire. Maera had almost made it to the foothills of the Grimsten mountains, which meant the air lay cooler now. Too far away for Thyrlings to pursue, Astrid imagined. Why come this far for a wolf or a Skolvarg girl?

Maera sat on the ground and stared at her, occasionally licking her lips.

Astrid gazed to the south and wondered how far the bards had traveled over the course of the day. Had they found a crossing for the river yet? She'd seen a few options when she'd jogged by.

Now, she had Maera to think about. After months of captivity, torture and little to eat, Maera wouldn't be in any shape to push hard. Both of them needed rest. Besides, she could hardly keep her eyes open. Tomorrow morning would be better for making decisions.

"Time for a rest," she said, chin drooping down to her chest. "We'll go without a watch to . . . tonight."

For the first time in days, Astrid's sleep was deep and undisturbed by dreams or visions.

TWENTY-EIGHT

Astrid blinked awake.

Sunlight streamed through the boughs of a tree overhead, dropping a small patch across her left eye. Blunted morning shadows disappeared around her. She felt like she'd just closed her eyes.

She yawned and started to stretch, then froze. Maera lay curled up against her legs, sound asleep. When had the wolf joined her? The warmth and comfort melted Astrid all the way to her bones.

With a gentle touch, she set a hand on Maera's shoulder. The wolf stirred, but remained asleep. Maera's auburn fur shone like a brilliant autumn canopy, hues of red and brown mixed with wolf gray. Though matted and filthy, Astrid thought her perfect. Her too-skinny ribs rose and fell, highlighting her thin frame. Uzell deserved what he'd gotten and more for the things he'd done to Maera.

Astrid pushed thoughts of vengeance from her mind. There were more serious, pressing concerns to worry about. The food she'd manage to scrounge up before they left wouldn't last past tonight. Spring was too early to forage for greens, nuts, roots, or berries.

If she didn't find the bards or a Skolvarg tribe again soon, she and Maera could starve.

Her gaze dropped back to Maera. Her eyes were closed, nose tucked in her paws. She appeared more like a half-grown pup than a wolf.

Maera's head shot up.

Astrid startled, but didn't make a noise. At once, Maera hopped to her feet, attention trained south. A low rumble rang through her chest. She sniffed, body tense.

A chill ran through Astrid.

She stretched out a hand and wrapped her fingers around the hilt of her sword lying close by. Maera's hackles lifted. Then Astrid heard it.

The unmistakable baying of hounds.

"No!" Astrid hissed. "No, no, no! How?"

She scrambled to her feet despite her tight, sore muscles from the day before. She hastily buckled on her sword belt while Maera growled nearby. Seconds later, her pack thudded onto her back over her shoulder.

"Maera," she whispered, "come on!"

They turned toward the Auroran and ran.

Trees passed Astrid like bats in the night as she summoned the last of her strength in an all-out sprint for the river. The hounds would lose their scent in the water—if they could just get across and disappear before the dogs caught up.

She ran on instinct, nudging them toward the east. Maera matched her step for step, running almost effortlessly in spite of her weakened condition as they jumped, ducked, and changed directions to avoid the natural clutter of rocks and fallen trees.

Yet all the while, the baying hounds grew closer.

Chest heaving, Astrid had to slow to a half-stumbling run as the forest cluttered. She sucked in deep gasps of air, toes stubbing on broken tree limbs. Maera bounded several paces ahead, then paused. She'd turn to Astrid with a low, distressed whine.

"I'm . . . coming . . as fast as I . . . can."

Several bowshots of distance later, Astrid could only focus her attention on staying upright. One foot landed after another. The area began to thin out. A long baying sounded not far behind them, followed by eager yips as the hounds closed in on their quarry. Between the hounds, the low rumble of the river crashed against rocks.

"Seasons help me," she panted, "and spirits give me strength."

Dredging the last of her will, Astrid threw herself toward the river. Maera growled, postured in place just ahead of Astrid. She snarled at something behind Astrid's right.

The crack of a stick, and an answering call, rang next. Astrid glanced desperately ahead of them. The river glinted between the trees, black and gray and snapping with white rapids. She swallowed hard.

Too late.

Cursing, Astrid dropped her pack, withdrew her sword, and whirled around to face the approaching hounds.

The first—a black beast rumored to be the King's favorite —burst through a young growth of pines. The slavering teeth jumped for her, eyes full of hate. Astrid swung. The sword struck the hound between the shoulder and neck. It fell in a heap at her feet with a short, high-pitched yelp.

She tugged the blade free, but before she could bring it to bear, a brindled hound appeared. It jumped, aiming for her arm. Astrid stumbled and fell, arm raised to fend it off. A second before she expected teeth to crush her bones, a flash of auburn struck the brindled hound.

Snarling, snapping teeth followed.

Fear of Maera being harmed overcame all her fatigue. Astrid bounced back to her feet, sword in hand, advanced. Even well fed, Maera would be less than half the size of the hounds, but she fought with the ferocity of an Amarok.

Before Astrid could come to her aid, another hound appeared. Then another. They clustered around the pack leader bleeding into the ground. Growls filled the air like a chorus.

A brown one lashed out at Maera.

Astrid advanced.

Teeth gritted, she dispatched the attacking hound the same as the pack leader, but the rest of the pack had arrived by then. Before she could pull her sword free, teeth sank in her arm.

She screamed.

The hound wrenched to the side, nearly dropping Astrid to the ground. Through the haze of pain, she scrabbled for her knife. White hot bolts of agony nearly sent her into darkness.

She fought to stay awake for Maera.

"Maera!" she screamed. "Back!"

Her free hand found the knife. A moment before she pierced the hound in the eye, a sharp whistle pierced the air. The hound released her.

Six Thyrling druzars flooded the area, spears leveled, chests heaving. The hound fighting Maera backed away, slinking toward a druzar on the right. Astrid tucked her bleeding arm against her body and cast about for her sword. Instead, she saw Maera, lying on her side, fur covered in blood.

Maera struggled to stand, growling at the new intruders.

Alive. For now.

Astrid wanted to scream. To tell the Thyrling hunters she'd fight any of them. She'd kill them all if her wolf died. But the pain made speaking impossible. Astrid braced her legs apart to keep herself upright as Maera tried to crawl through the soil to her side. Astrid advanced a step. The Thyrling warriors lifted their spears, but Astrid stopped when she stood between them and Maera.

"Hurt my wolf and I'll kill you."

Her threat should have fallen flat. She panted. Her body throbbed with pain. Blood dripped onto the ground and ran down her arm, where thick, black gashes oozed more of it. But the intense promise in her voice sent a troubled expression across the closest druzar's face. He backed up a step.

A call behind them, however, distracted all. As one, the warriors parted. Rosamund advanced from the back, peering at Astrid with an unreadable expression.

"Astrid."

Astrid nearly choked on her own tongue.

Rosamund's brow dropped into something unreadable. "I'm sorry this had to happen," she said. The look of pity and concern deepened Astrid's confusion. "I didn't want it like this."

"You?" she whispered.

Rosamund sympathetic look darkened. "I'm afraid there is much you don't know or understand. One day, perhaps you will. For now, the best I can hope for is your cooperation as we return to Drakby."

The pain radiating from her savaged arm blossomed again, like waves of heat. The desperate sprint this morning, after an equally arduous day yesterday, and little food to eat, made her head dizzy. Everything hurt. How much blood had she lost?

The world began to tip to the side. Astrid leaned the other way, then nearly fell on her backside.

Maera whimpered.

Astrid sank to her knees to make the whirling stop and put a hand on Maera's head. Her growling calmed. Maera licked Astrid's hand. Astrid blinked, the vision of Rosamund blurring.

What had she been about to say?

Her head was very heavy, yet she fought not to float away. Rosamund's voice echoed in Astrid's ears.

"Astrid?"

"Don't touch my wolf," Astrid slurred.

And knew no more.

When Astrid came to, darkness wrapped her.

She lay on the ground beside a crackling fire. Unfamiliar voices murmured to one another off to her left. Her pounding head occupied most of her thoughts at first, but then an ache shot through her arm.

Everything came rushing back.

Sucking in a sharp breath, she tried to sit up. Something held her in place. They'd lashed her legs together at the knees and the ankles, then bound her wrists with rope as well.

Where was Maera?

Astrid twisted her head left and right, finally spotting the wolf's auburn fur next to her. Maera lay on the ground beside her, all four legs and muzzle bound. Someone had washed away the blood from her fur. In the dim light, no wounds were apparent. Maera's chest rose and fell rhythmically.

Was she sleeping or drugged?

A twinge of pain near her arm drew Astrid's attention, and she glanced down. Someone had wrapped her arm where the hound bit her, but her sword and knife were nowhere in sight.

Rosamund appeared out of the glow of the fire and sat down on a fallen log beside her.

"You're awake."

The princess wore tall boots, dark leggings, and a green tunic belted at the waist. Aside from their training session in the arena, it was one of the few times Rosamund didn't wear a dress. A short distance away, the Thyrling warriors sat near the fire. A rabbit turned over a spit. The smell made Astrid's mouth water.

"What did you do to Maera?" Astrid croaked.

"Is that her name?" Rosamund's voice lifted with interest. "I didn't know you'd given her one."

"Is she drugged?"

"The wolf will be fine. Both of you were treated by our healer. You're fortunate we had one among our group. Once he took care of your wolf, Navi put her into a sleep. We can't have her running off or attacking someone. It will be a more pleasant experience for her this way."

"Just let her go."

Rosamund gave a tolerant smile. "Don't think me as foolish as that, Astrid. I know you bonded with her. If I let her go, she wouldn't leave. She'd fight every last warrior and hound in our party until we were forced to kill her. And then all these weeks of effort would have been for naught."

Astrid's gaze narrowed in question. *All these weeks of effort?*

Rosamund produced a small biscuit from a pocket in her tunic. Astrid eyed it, then said, "Please, save it for Maera."

Rosamund lifted an eyebrow. "Your wolf will eat bread?"

"Thanks to Uzell," Astrid muttered, "she's starving. She'll take what I give her."

"You seem hungry yourself."

Astrid just stared at her. Rosamund returned the look, then shrugged and tucked it back into her pocket. She reached for a leather skin. "I'll make sure the wolf receives it when she wakes. At least have water."

That, Astrid accepted. Rosamund gently assisted Astrid to sit. Even helped Astrid prop her back against a tree behind her, then tilted the water into her mouth. Astrid drank until she took it away, the rabid thirst barely satiated.

"So," Astrid muttered, "I assume you *are* in your father's pocket after all? Is that why you're here?"

In fact, Astrid had no idea what Rosamund's appearance that morning meant, aside from her possibly being involved in Maera's imprisonment and torturous life. Rosamund would not be held as accountable as Uzell in Maera's sufferings, but pay, she would.

Rosamund sighed. A contemplative expression crossed her face before she finally said, "Believe it or not, Astrid, I would not have let any harm come to you in Drakby. You didn't need to sneak away. Now my father is angrier than I've seen him in some time. You're lucky I'm in the search party that found you."

Astrid ignored Rosamund's promise of safety, as Rosamund hadn't exactly stood in the way of the two berzars.

"You didn't answer my question."

"My father sent me, yes," Rosamund said, "but I willingly came, because I knew you'd meet far more mercy from me than anyone else."

A second unanswered question. Like a true royal, Rosamund expertly skirted the difficult questions with non-answers.

Which meant *she* was as guilty here as Oskar. The thought tightened Astrid's stomach, particularly when she thought of how much she had started to trust Rosamund.

Like a fool.

"What is my crime?" Astrid asked instead.

"The bards." Rosamund's expression tightened slightly. "Spies from the Ochlands. You were with them. My father is declaring you a Skolvarg spy and sentencing you to death along with them. The bards, when they are found, will suffer the same fate."

The words should have struck more fear inside of Astrid, but they didn't. The whole thing was ridiculous. Instead, she laughed.

Had she finally broken?

Was she mad now?

"Is your father going to feed me to Gorm?"

Rosamund pressed her lips together and whispered, "I will do what I can for you, Astrid."

Well, that wasn't a no.

Astrid looked into the darkness. Rosamund's response was as good a *yes* as the word itself.

"Ease your conscience however you must, princess, but I don't particularly like the Thyrling idea of friendship."

Rosamund opened her mouth to speak, closed it again, then turned and walked away. Astrid stared into the growing flames with a sense of dread. Somehow, she'd gotten herself into even deeper waters.

This time, she had Maera drowning with her.

After a long, uncomfortable, and sleepless night, the healer came to examine Astrid. In the background, the Thyrlings broke camp with the hiss of doused flames and the shake of tents folding.

"I'm Navi," he said.

He stood in front of her wearing a simple robe. Beneath it, leather pants and a plain white shirt. Dirt stained the edges of his clothes. His eyes, a muddy gray color, appeared tired in his wrinkled face. His head was completely bald, save for bushy gray eyebrows. Based on his bronze skin, he might have been from Kerys, but Astrid couldn't place the healer's accent. She nodded warily.

Navi moved slowly as he crouched next to her, surprisingly

spry for a man of advanced years. With practiced skill, he unwound the bandage on her arm, revealing shiny pink scars. Astrid blinked.

"It's already healed?" she asked. Members of the Skolvarg tribe healed quicker than others because of the Blessing of the Spirits, but she'd never seen it happen *this* quick.

He shrugged. "Not really. The flesh under the skin will take longer to heal. I see no signs of permanent damage."

"How did you do that?" Astrid said.

The healer gave a thin smile but it seemed more sad than baleful. "All in the king's menagerie have their talents."

Astrid nodded to Maera.

"And my wolf?"

"I don't have much experience tending to animals." He glanced at Maera, a hand casually propped on his knobby knee. "But your wolf should be fine as well. I gave her a simple sleeping draught that will keep her asleep until we return to Drakby. You're fortunate the king's hounds didn't kill you both."

Astrid said nothing.

After Navi left, Rosamund returned. She nodded in approval at Astrid's arm. "Much better. Navi said you're well enough to ride."

"Great," Astrid muttered.

Rosamund pretended not to hear her. "Your wolf will remain bound. If you try to escape, or threaten any in this party, I will have her killed without question. Do we understand one another?"

Astrid nodded. She would comply as long as she must to lower their guard. *Patience*, she thought. *Wait for the right opportunity to free Maera*. The reminder as to where Rosamund truly stood was welcome.

Astrid couldn't afford to let that get out of sight again.

"The bards will be across the Auroran by now," she

couldn't help calling to Rosamund's back as she turned to leave. "Do you really think the Skolvarg won't find out about Oskar's plans?"

Rosamund paused, then kept walking.

While two warriors stood over with her drawn swords, a third cut Astrid's bindings and tied her hands back together—albeit with a bit more room to navigate reins. The Thyrlings, none too gentle in their treatment, seemed to have different thoughts than Rosamund.

With help, Astrid limped to a nearby horse, gritted her teeth, and managed to pull herself into the saddle without assistance—pain in her arm notwithstanding. Once she was situated, the Thyrlings loaded Maera's limp form atop a mule. None of the warriors looked pleased to care for the wolf. Astrid shook the thought of escape off. Both of them were alive, which meant they could wait for a better opportunity.

"Remember, no tricks or the wolf dies," Rosamund called.

A warrior grabbed the lead rope to Astrid's horse, putting Astrid in the middle of the Thyrling warriors. Soon, they headed south, back to Drakby and all its stench, violence and deceit.

TWENTY-NINE

On horseback, the return to Drakby required only a day. They entered the gates in the evening, after the sun had set.

A scout riding in advance sent notice of their arrival. Captain Jormund appeared near the gates, accepted Astrid's horse, Maera's mule, and led them to the barn. Astrid didn't care where she went—stable, barn, forest—she wanted nothing to do with Thyrlings, Rosamund, or Oskar.

Jormund set Maera in a cage not far away. Astrid watched him closely. For being a Thyrling, he had a gentle side, because he took care of her wolf. For that, Astrid might not deem him fit for death like all the rest.

"A cage is your place to stay before you meet your end with Gorm the Grizzled," Jormund said, his expression as neutral as ever.

Astrid gritted her teeth. "Any idea when that will be?"

"No. Princess Rosamund has requested you be fed three meals a day. At meals, you will be allowed to relieve yourself outside. A guard is posted on the other side of the doors. They are not allowed to speak to you. Uzell, Princess Rosamund, and King Oskar are the only people allowed inside. There is no escape," he finished darkly.

His gaze slipped to Maera, then back to her.

Astrid slitted her eyes.

With another pause to drive his point home, Jormund left. The door slammed in his wake, a dark reverberation.

The cage was one used to hold the fighting animals in the arena but large enough for Astrid to stand in and take a couple of paces across. The coppery smell of old blood and urine stained it. Darkness filled the room. She slumped against the iron bars and sighed. Quiet. No horse. No Thyrlings. In some way, this was perfect. At least she could wrap her head around what had happened and make a plan.

She should consider herself lucky. Her head remained attached to her shoulders, the cage was tall enough for her to stand or lie down in, and her companion was Maera, not Gorm the Grizzled.

Maera twitched, still sedated by whatever Navi had given her. Perhaps for the better. For now, Astrid wouldn't be able to comfort her. Astrid slumped against the cage, then down to the floor.

Exhausted, she tilted her head to the side, closed her eyes, and fell to sleep.

Astrid jerked awake to the sound of Maera growling and keys jangling. She shoved to her feet, half asleep. Uzell peered at her through the bars, jowls hanging around his jaw in a sad way.

"And so the wayward Skolvarg has returned to us," he said in a quiet voice, barely above a whisper. The curiosity in his gaze startled her. She backed away a step, alarmed more by his neutrality and the lack of agitation.

"I should have let Ewan cut your throat," Astrid snapped. "Or allowed Maera to eat you."

Uzell sighed as he turned away. "I can understand why you'd say that. I believe she probably feels the same way." He cast a long-suffering glance toward Maera, then shook his head. He held a tray in his hands as he shuffled to the wall, where a table stood. The smell of broth filled Astrid's nostrils. Her stomach growled, but she ignored it. She had no friends here, certainly not Uzell. For all she knew, the broth was poisoned.

Astrid pressed forward, hands wrapped around the metal bars.

"What do you want?"

"To bring you food and give you a chance to relieve yourself." He moved a few things around on the tray. "During which time," he continued in a melodic singsong, "you will try nothing foolish. Although I may have regrets for what happened to the wolf, I have accepted it as a necessity. I will do what is necessary again."

The dark look he shot her sent a shiver through Astrid. She swallowed and asked, "What kind of magic did you use against me?"

He smiled, revealing uneven, yellowed teeth. "Some secrets are for trading, not telling, my snowdrop. Why don't you try again?"

Astrid prickled like a porcupine at the term of endearment, but shoved that aside for later.

"Why did you hurt Maera and put her in a cage?"

Uzell's eyes widened. "Ah, a question I can answer. I never wanted to harm the wolf. She was . . . how should I say, an experiment? I have wandered far, learning many deep mysteries of spirits and wraiths alike."

Wraiths? Astrid had never heard the term. Rather than

interrupting, she let Uzell continue, hoping to learn more about his strange powers.

"Rosamund and I hoped to recreate the bond between Skolvarg and the Amarok wolves. Such an unmistakable bond in more civilized hands would make a powerful army. One that even the Ulfsark could not defeat. Getting our hands on an Amarok whelp was out of the question, so we settled for what we could. But the wolf was only half of the bond. When Rosamund ventured to your people, she hoped to find an excuse to bring a Skolvarg back with her. From what she has told me, you made it all too easy."

Her stomach twisted in on itself.

"Rosamund?" she whispered.

He lifted an eyebrow. "Who did you think was behind this?"

Her mouth moved wordlessly. Uzell gazed at her with something like pity, then shook his head.

"Oskar? No. Though he has played a pivotal role in our research he is more a participant than anything else. He's so lost in the memory of old wars that Gorm has driven him mad. There is more to that bear than meets the eye, as you may have already guessed. A twisted spirit of vengeance has taken host in Gorm and Oskar both, though the king is too blind to see his peril. We learned as much as we could from that pair—it was time to pursue the true purpose of my research: to fashion the bond between Skolvarg and Amarok. It seemed almost fated when Oskar sent Rosamund to lead a false peace envoy to the Skolvarg."

Astrid looked away, lips pressed together. She no longer felt hunger. No thirst. No urgency to escape. Nothing but a sickening sense of mis-reality.

"Maera and I have been an experiment the whole time?"

"Yes."

Astrid's mind spun with the connections.

Despite Ewan's warnings to keep Rosamund at arm's length, and Astrid's own realization that Rosamund served herself first, she'd foolishly believed Rosamund better than this. The disgust Rosamund showed for Oskar's caged animals. Her ambivalence toward . . . any of it.

A ruse.

From the back of her cage, Maera withdrew down into a crouch. A low growl rolled out of her. Astrid blinked herself back to the present moment. Whether her imagination or not, Astrid felt the rage and hate seeping out of her wolf.

Astrid mentally shook herself out. She had to stay in the moment. Get information out of Uzell. If they faced Gorm soon, it may not matter. But she'd go down swinging. Ire boiled under her skin, giving her power again.

"It won't work."

She didn't tell Uzell that she'd seen Maera in her dreams long before ever coming to Drakby. Better to let him think she blindly denied his claim. Deep down, however, a part of her wondered if he might be right.

"Are you so sure?" Uzell asked. "Your fylga is connected to the wolf through my power."

"A what?"

"Fylga." Uzell waved his hand as if searching for an explanation. "Your . . . spirit body, yes? I observed your many visits to the wolf this way, before you came to her cage in person. And little by little, tethered you together."

Astrid had no idea her spirit was wandering around Drakby where it had no business being, but Uzell's explanation made sense. Her love for Maera wouldn't change but the thought of his twisted magic influencing their bond made her sick. And hadn't Margu hinted she might find a wolf, long before she'd ever come to Drakby?

And yet. . .

"I saw you!" Astrid realized, thinking of her strange

dreams in the barn. "You don't look the same. You were skinny, starving."

Uzell nodded. "Observant young woman! Yes, I was there. I continued to watch you interact with the wolf, hoping, wondering..."

"That's not how the Wolf Song works," Astrid said, still refusing to believe Uzell had bound her to Maera. "We don't *make* Amarok wolves. The wolves choose us."

Uzell gestured to Maera and raised his eyebrows. "And yet, here we are. A link exists between you that was not there before. And this is no Amarok wolf. Don't think you can fool me. Rosamund was right. I can see it. I can *feel* it. Now that we've successfully done it—somehow, I confess again that I'm not exactly sure how—I believe it can be done again. I must do it again," he said mournfully. "For you are slated to meet Gorm."

He glanced at the window where the sunrise grew light on the horizon, then back. Astrid had to force herself not to shrink away. The thought of Uzell trying his dark magic, purple and strange, on anyone else—human or animal—made her sick. Maera's terror of him replayed through her mind in a dire warning.

But she had bigger bears to battle now.

"When?" she asked.

"Today."

Astrid snarled. Maera joined, snapping at the priest. Uzell stumbled backward in surprise and fell hard on his rear. A female guard with close-cropped hair rushed into the room and cracked a stick on the bars of Astrid's cage.

"Calm down!" she cried, "or lose water and dinner for your wolf."

Astrid turned away. "Maera," she called quietly. "It's all right. Calm down."

Through their connection, she attempted to impart peace.

The wolf quieted, but her lips curled at the guard, who looked between the two of them, frowned, and disappeared out the door. Only after she left did Astrid realize that Uzell had slunk away in the chaos.

Astrid pressed her back into the cage and slid to the floor, face buried in her filthy hands. All along, ever since the Thyrlings visited the Skolvarg camp, Astrid had played right into Rosamund's hand.

Rosamund had never wanted her for a friend. Astrid had been the perfect opportunity to attempt a study of the Wolf Song. In a cruel twist, Astrid fit right into their plans. Almost by divine design.

Margu slipped through her mind. Had she known all along? Astrid's current situation seemed like something she would get some kind of twisted satisfaction out of. Only the intervention of fate itself could have paired Astrid with Maera right under the watchful eye of Uzell and Rosamund.

"I'm sorry, Maera," she whispered with a shake of her head. "I'm probably not the best Skolvarg for you to be paired with. I really messed this up."

Maera glanced at her, head tilted slightly to the side. Her curious expression sent a stab of pain through Astrid. Finally, she'd found her wolf. The Wolf Song finally sang in her blood. And within hours, she stood to lose Maera and her life.

"I'm sorry. Let's do this together."

Maera whined, pawing at the floor near Astrid. The guard rapped on the bars with the head of a spear.

"On your feet, Skolvarg. The king is coming to speak with you."

Of the two of them, Astrid wasn't sure if she or King Oskar was the worse for wear.

His hair was wild and unkempt around his crown. A tangled, untrimmed beard grew below gaunt eyes. Lines creased his face, aging him ten years, and dark circles gave him a deathly appearance. Astrid recalled what Uzell had said about Oskar and Gorm. What demons drove him? Had he chosen this madness? She almost pitied him.

Almost.

Rosamund followed at her father's side, chin tipped slightly up.

"Tell me all you know of the bards," the king commanded as he approached. He ignored Maera's escalating snarls as he gripped the bars of the cage in his two large hands. For the first time since her return, Astrid was grateful for her cage.

"Maera," she called, "calm yourself."

The wolf settled. Oskar lifted an eyebrow, but Astrid hadn't taken her eyes off him. "I know the bards are from the Ochlands. They prefer the lute with their songs, and Liss and Lara's favorite song is—"

"Toy with me, Skolvarg, and meet Gorm now. What of the bards?"

"I don't know where they are. We split ways so I could find my wolf after we freed her and they could go home. They didn't want to sing the wrong song and get fed to your bear."

Oskar glowered at her, teeth bared behind his beard.

"Last. Time. Where are they, Skolvarg?"

Astrid had already anticipated their questioning. The Thyrlings would know the bards were trying to head east. If she was convincing enough, she could buy Ewan and the rest more time. Ironically, her capture might have delayed the closest searchers on Ewan's trail.

"They started to the south to find a place to ford, but Ewan disagreed. He said they were in too much of a hurry."

Rosamund turned to her father. "You see? We already knew this."

"Do not speak to me in that tone," Oskar muttered, dangerously calm. "I am no fool. The dark-haired bard wouldn't leave the Skolvarg, no matter what anyone says." He tapped the side of his head with a finger. "I am king because I think of things no one else does. I saw the way he looked at you. The bard went north with her, I'd bet it. The two groups met together, and you'll find the rest in the north woods. When we capture them, I shall make them sing a more honest tune. Kill the Skolvarg and her wolf now."

The utter lack of mercy on Oskar's face sent Astrid into a mad spiral of panic. There was only one thing left to do. Her life and the life of all her friends rode on one single chance.

"You speak of power," Astrid cried, "then why not put it to the test? I challenge you to a duel, King Oskar of Thyrden."

Oskar's anger bled away at once. He paused, regarded her, then threw back his head and laughed.

"A duel?" He studied her as he calmed. "I have nothing to prove by fighting a Skolvarg whelp. A bear does concern himself with a mouse."

"I'm a wolf, not a mouse," Astrid called, her tone rising. "And I fear no bear!"

Oskar stared at her, startled into silence. Finally, his brow rose. "Prepare Gorm!" he shouted over his shoulder. "We shall see how brave you are this afternoon."

Astrid's heart fell into her stomach.

Rosamund paled. "That was not what we agreed to! You said you were just *threatening* to send them to Gorm. If you kill her, we will have no chance to unravel the secrets."

"I need no secrets or tricks to defeat the Skolvarg!" Oskar said, halfway across the room now. He stopped, whirled around, and stared at his daughter. "Were it not for my cowardly jaegars, the war would not have ended in a truce. We would be victorious, even now! A king of Thyrden uses power to take what they are owed. A king doesn't use tricks. That is the lesson I don't think you will ever learn." Oskar drew himself taller, though he appeared to hide a grimace. "Yet another reason you're not fit to sit in my throne when I am gone."

Rosamund's eyes widened. She stepped closer to Oskar. "Father, no," she whispered, "I need Astrid . . . "

"You need a husband to slap some sense into you," he snapped.

When he turned to Astrid, a cold smile stretched across his face. She saw only Gorm in the deep lines and hungry gaze.

"As you wish, whelp. You may fight Gorm if that is how you choose to die. Perhaps your silver-tongued friends will come out of wherever they are hiding to rescue you, and I can feed them to my bear as well." He growled. "Once he has had his fill of you."

Oskar's ferocity belied her only hope.

"Should I defeat Gorm, I want your oath that you will let myself and Maera go free."

"No!" Rosamund shouted. "If she dies or escapes, all of our progress will be undone. Our hope for a more powerful army will be erased. Uzell needs more time to study her and the wolf. Father, we've worked so hard!"

Astrid kept Oskar's gaze, taunting him with it. This was her only chance. Subject herself and Maera to spirits-knew-what kind of testing, or put herself in front of one of the most ferocious animals that ever existed.

She'd rather face Gorm.

Oskar ignored Rosamund, and Astrid knew she had him then. The pride and fury of the great bear was too much for Oskar. He extended a hand inside the cage to Astrid. Maera's growl grew louder, but Astrid stepped forward and clasped the king's forearm. As soon as he had her in his grip, Oskar jerked her closer. She struck the bars with her shoulder. Oskar squeezed and Astrid realized her mistake too late.

She'd given him her wounded arm.

His fat fingers dug into the sores, which raged with pain. By sheer grit and willpower, she kept herself from screaming.

"Swear . . . it . . ." she muttered through gritted teeth.

"You have my oath," Oskar hissed. "Daughter! Witness this."

Rosamund turned away, but muttered, "I witness your oath to allow Astrid to go free if she wins against Gorm."

Her sentence died at the end, giving Astrid a morbid sense of satisfaction. Oskar's wild eyes seemed to laugh at her.

"I shall enjoy watching Gorm break your bones and eat your flesh for dinner, Skolvarg. Prepare yourself. You die tonight."

He released her forearm and shoved her as hard as he could with one hand. She slammed into the bars behind her, then fell. Maera leapt at the king, teeth snapping. Oskar strode away, the doors slamming behind him. Astrid felt, more than saw, Rosamund remain behind.

Rosamund shuffled closer to Astrid's cage.

"Don't speak a single word to me," Astrid hissed. "You are honorless for what you did to Maera and what you were willing to do to both of us. Get out of here," Astrid commanded quietly, "spirits take you and your father."

Astrid lifted her gaze to meet Rosamund's. It was bare, blank, unreadable and empty at the same time.

"If I ever have the chance," Astrid whispered, "I will destroy everything your family stands for."

A soft intake of breath preceded Rosamund's long pause. Astrid didn't move. Her heart thudded in her chest as she waited, unwilling to acknowledge the princess for another moment.

Finally, Rosamund turned away and departed.

A flutter of feathers caught her attention. When she looked up, her heart clenched. Perhaps Oskar was more cunning and less of a raving madman than she thought. Equal parts dread and hope filled her as Maury fluttered down and landed on her knee.

"Hello," she murmured.

Tears filled her eyes as the little finch ran his beak along Astrid's finger in a gentle, affectionate gesture. She didn't understand Ewan's connection with the bird, didn't know if Maury could somehow communicate her words back to his friend, but she had to try.

Astrid held up a finger. Maury hopped onto it. She slowly lifted him until she could peer into his tiny black eyes.

"Tell him not to come. The king is expecting it. There is a trap. Tell them they need to go to the Skolvarg and let them know about everything. Do you understand, Maury?"

The finch chirped and bobbed its head from side to side, as if inspecting something above him. Astrid hoped it meant something. Better for her to take matters in her own hands against Gorm and the king than all four of them risk their lives and be killed freeing her.

"Tell him I have a plan," Astrid said, standing. She hoped Ewan might be more cautious and patient. "Wait until tomorrow at noon before doing anything, okay?"

Maury dipped his head again. Astrid hoped it was the finch's version of a nod. Enough was already at stake without Ewan trying to be a hero. Either Astrid would take care of herself or she would die trying.

Maury flitted away, taking Astrid's heart with him.

THIRTY

For better or worse, Ewan didn't try to free Astrid.

Neither did Margu, which Astrid hadn't expected, but found herself hoping for. Did the Greater Spirit have a hand in this? Perhaps. Since Margu hadn't visited her, she might be a lost cause.

Or destined to win.

The latter seemed less probable than Astrid and Maera growing wings and flying away from Drakby. She didn't know how involved the Greater Spirits were with the lives of humans but Astrid doubted it would take anything short of a miracle for them to escape with their lives.

Only a few minutes after Oskar left, four of his berzars appeared. They stood at each corner of her cage and hefted it out of the barn and into the arena. The jostling movement sent shocks through her body. Maera protested with low growls, but Astrid's calm voice kept her from lunging at the bars and harming herself.

Without a word, the berzars deposited them in the middle of the arena, and left. The warm, fresh air roused Astrid. She closed her eyes, drawing in deep lungfuls.

Rosamund had sent them food, but Astrid had given Maera the majority of it. She felt the full extent of her weakness. True to Navi's statement, her arm had continued to heal, but still felt tender. Oskar's ferocious grip didn't help matters, either. Blood welled in massive lined bruises where he'd gripped her. She stood, stretching what she could, and tried to think through her strategy.

How could an undersized Skolvarg girl and a half-grown wolf defeat a monstrous bear?

It didn't take long for Thyrlings to enter the arena. Noise bounced around through the stands in growing strains as they gathered on the benches. Some booed or jeered. Others threw bread crusts and rotted food at the cage, but Astrid and Maera were too far away to reach.

Unwilling to be a spectacle, Astrid sat with her arms on her knees in the back corner of the cage, as close to Maera as she could get. About an hour later, a horn sounded. Cheers rose from those already seated in the stands and along the walls. A spectacle of color near the gate doors could only mean one thing.

The king had arrived.

Maera growled, low and steady. "We'll get our chance," Astrid said. "Soon enough we'll get our chance, girl."

Astrid swallowed away all the other frightened thoughts that rose with such a declaration. She couldn't focus on those now.

A moment later, the king's retinue passed through the gate and into the sandy arena. Aside from Oskar and his berzars, Rosamund, Captain Jormund, and a line of jaegars followed, all on horseback.

The procession dismounted at the gates and reins were handed to a host of stable boys and girls. Three jaegars were dressed in their finest. Sapphire gems, inlaid in silver settings, sparkled in the sunlight. Emeralds. Topaz. Golden rings. The finery gave a dazzling impression on such a beautiful afternoon. The woman and the other male jaegar wore the unadorned garb of the warriors.

"On your feet, Skolvarg," an approaching guard called. He reached into the cage to poke Astrid with the butt of his spear. "The king approaches."

Faster than a wolverine, she grabbed the spear haft and yanked. A shout of alarm escaped the man as he crashed into the bars headfirst. Astrid released it and he hurriedly yanked the weapon back out.

Smiling, Astrid bowed to him. Nose bloodied, the guard spat as one of his fellows helped him to his feet.

"I can't wait to see that bear tear out your guts, you filthy wench!"

"He'd probably rather chew on the gristle of your empty head."

He made a threatening move toward Maera, but Astrid was faster. She pushed herself against the edge of the cage near him, fingers gripping the bar until her knuckles turned white.

"Touch my wolf and see what happens."

The guard hesitated, then stepped away from Maera. Astrid kept her eyes on him until he was halfway across the arena again.

Maera whined.

Astrid let out a long breath. "We'll be fine," she whispered. "It's going to be fine."

Less than ten minutes later, every seat in the stand had been filled. King Oskar lumbered across the arena toward her. Rosamund followed just behind him on his left, with Captain Jormund at her side. In the distance, Gorm bellowed and rattled his cage.

Oskar stopped at a pace away.

"If you wish to die a painless death," he said brightly,

"Rosamund will execute you right here and now. No need to face the wrath of Gorm today."

"I accept your surrender if you are afraid for your bear," Astrid replied.

Oskar's lips thinned, but they curved into a smile. Anticipation built behind his eyes as he nodded. "Let none say you are a coward. So be it."

Without glancing back, the king left. Rosamund remained behind, her back to Astrid. Jormund and two guards lingered by the cage.

"Good girl," Astrid crooned to Maera. She faced the wall of the arena, her tail tucked. Her nose lifted in the air, already scenting Gorm out. A whine shook Maera's body. "We'll be okay, Maera."

Minutes later, Oskar climbed into the pavilion overlooking the arena. A rolling, creaking sound issued from beneath him. Astrid's gut clenched. Gorm. They were preparing to release him.

With Rosamund in the pit, Astrid still had a few moments. She drew in deep breaths and attempted to feel calm for Maera's sake. The wolf glanced at her every now and then, then back to the guards.

"Give her the weapons," Rosamund commanded.

Astrid's guard passed her sword, scabbard, belt, and knife through the cage. Astrid buckled them on with trembling fingers, grateful to have them in reach again. She gritted her teeth and forced her hands to work, determined not to show her fear in front of the Thyrlings.

Maera needed to see her confidence.

"And the spear," Rosamund said to the guard.

He hesitated. "But princess, the king—"

"I said the spear!"

The guard immediately held out a boar spear, about three hand spans taller than Astrid, with a metal crossguard below the leaf-shaped blade. The spearhead itself was half the length of Astrid's sword.

"Your Majesty," Jormund began, "the king's order was only—"

"If we arm common criminals with a spear to fend off that devil, then we will do the same for her," Rosamund said.

Jormund opened his mouth to say more, but nodded, face impassive.

Astrid took the boar spear in her hand and tested the weight. It was obviously made for bracing the ground and absorbing the impact of a wild boar. The shaft was as thick as her forearm. It would take two hands to use and Astrid didn't like her chances of setting the butt in slippery sand, but Rosamund's gift would be far better than facing Gorm with just her sword.

Rosamund glanced back to Astrid and caught her gaze. "You will probably not believe me, but I am sorry it had to end this way." She tipped her head toward the spearhead. "Mind the blade."

With that, she strode away from the cages. Jormund followed. When Rosamund was safe in the pavilion, Oskar screamed, "Raise the gate!"

The two guards shoved keys in Astrid and Maera's cages, flung the doors open, and ran as fast as they could the opposite way from Gorm, toward ladders propped against the arena wall. Other guards waited to let them up.

Astrid stepped out of the cage and braced herself. Maera followed.

The creak of rope sounded like a war horn as the background chatter of hundreds of spectators died. The hush fell like a blanket on the arena. Astrid turned to the wooden gate as it lifted upward.

Maera hid behind Astrid's legs. Kneeling down with one knee in the sand, and using the boar spear to support her,

Astrid patted Maera on the side. She whimpered. Across the arena, above the gates where Gorm lurked in the shadows, King Oskar stepped into the light. He raised his hands.

"Today has been long coming," the king shouted. "Since we ended our war with the Skolvarg all those seasons ago, they have continued to fester, like a blight upon these rich lands."

The cheering grew wild at this. The king waited a long moment before he continued, no doubt so Astrid could hear him over the din. She let the fire of anger and hate build inside her.

She'd need it.

Astrid turned aside thoughts of fear or losing or pain and focused instead on Gorm. He remained a shadow as the gate that held him continued to rise, slowly. Didn't matter what Oskar said.

Only her opponent mattered now.

Oskar's voice continued in the background.

"Today, a Skolvarg wolf woman will show us once and for all that her people are nothing compared to the might of Thyrden!"

Once more, he had to pause for the applause to subside.

"She will face the great Gorm the Grizzled in combat. When her blood stains the sands of this arena, we will know for certain that Tyraz favors us! Now is a time for warriors. For bloodshed and glory. After the long winter of peace, it is a spring for spears! Release the bear!"

For an instant, Astrid floundered. She wasn't in the sand, waiting for Gorm. She found herself back in the king's pavilion, watching as the monstrous bear destroyed and then consumed two men. Fear rose inside her again, hot and welling. Astrid swallowed back the urge to vomit.

The bloodthirsty chants of the Thyrlings continued.

"Gorm! Gorm! Gorm! Gorm!"

The last of the gate disappeared. Legs like tree trunks and

paws the size of shields appeared from the darkness. Astrid didn't know if it was her own legs or Maera's that quaked.

"Gorm! Gorm! Gorm! Gorm!"

With a final yank, the gate raised to full height. Gorm the Grizzled stomped into the arena. He paused as the gate slammed shut behind him, raised himself up on two legs, and let out a roar like breaking thunder.

Astrid braced herself.

Gorm had arrived.

Astrid momentarily forgot everything she'd learned about fighting as she stared in dumbstruck terror at Gorm.

Standing upright, the bear cut an imposing figure, even across the short arena. His roar split the air. When he came down hard on the ground, a spray of sand blasted around his claws. The ground shivered beneath Astrid's feet. Spirits help her, the earth actually *quaked*, like they'd trodden on an angry earth spirit. Out of the corner of her eye, she saw Oskar above his bear. The king raised a fist and slammed it on the railing.

Gorm charged.

Astrid's instinct snapped back into place. She ignored Gorm and thrust the butt of the spear into the sand with all her might. As suspected, the sand proved poor ground to set the spear, but there wasn't time to worry about it. She'd barely braced her foot against the end of the spear before Gorm had arrived.

In the last instant before he struck, she dipped the spear in a hasty aim for the bear's chest.

An avalanche of fur and rage barreled into the tip. The great bear crashed into the spearhead, the force of the charge sending Astrid flying back. She stumbled over herself or

Maerea—she didn't know which—and slammed onto her back.

Without waiting to see where anything landed, she scrambled to her feet and ran.

"Maera!" she screamed. "Run!"

Maera darted ahead of her, tail tucked. The screams of the crowd faded in Astrid's ears as she spun, a safer distance away.

Gorm reared up on his hind legs and shook his whole body. The spear had impaled Gorm's shoulder, all the way to the crossguard. Astrid's heart sank. The strike was too high. She'd missed his heart and anything else vital. The massive boar spear was more like a thorn to the bear.

And now, he was *really* angry.

While Gorm attempted to swipe at the spear in his shoulder, Astrid advanced. A few paces away, Gorm spun her direction, still on his hind legs. The spear dragged along the sand as she approached.

Astrid skidded across the ground, grabbed the end of the pole, and drove it deeper with all her might. It felt like a twig to stop a river, but the spear remained set.

Gorm bellowed.

Spittle flew into the air as he screamed, yellowed teeth sharp against the pale blue sky. Astrid thought Maera approached behind her. A growl came near Astrid's left ear, but she ignored it to focus on the thick streak of blood running down Gorm's shoulder. If she could pull it free, she might be able to set up another strike.

The boar spear was the longest Astrid had ever used—twice the length of the spears the Skolvarg used—but the proximity to Gorm stifled her chance to use it well. A stench rolled off him that made it hard to breathe. When he roared again, a blast of hot air reeking of rot and rancid meat struck her full in the face. Gorm attempted to drop to all fours and charge, but

Astrid wrenched the spear to the side. Gorm growled and flailed his arm around the pole.

This time, he struck it with his good paw. The shaft shattered into kindling and Astrid stumbled forward, half the broken spear in her hands. A moment later, the bear closed the distance.

With a shout of surprise, Astrid swung the remnant of the spear high at the same moment his head appeared over her. The broken pole bounced off his jaw like she'd struck a shield.

This is how I die, Astrid thought.

A flash of auburn appeared with a snap and a snarl.

Maera.

The wolf buried her teeth in Gorm's neck. Although far too small on her own for real damage, the distraction gave Astrid just enough time to find her sword in the sand. The notched Nistlefolk steel sang as she swung, striking Gorm on the side of the head. He twisted, trying to pull Maera away with his mouth.

Astrid drove hard again. Her sword struck off an ear, then glanced off his skull. Finally, a solid strike slashed open Gorm's cheek and drew his attention back to Astrid.

Gorm shook Maera free. The young wolf hit the ground in a spray of sand, scrambled to her feet, and made a wide pass away from him. Yellow fangs the size of knives bared as Gorm roared again. He shook his head, droplets of blood spattering the granules at his feet, and turned to face her.

Astrid snarled back.

She rushed away, toward one of the poles driven into the ground of the arena. The blows she'd landed were little more than insect bites, but dark blood ran from the bear's head and the spot where the head of the boar spear was still buried in his shoulder. Nothing fatal, but she'd hampered his ability to charge, which gave her a little working room for now.

Unfortunately, Gorm was nowhere close to death.

He let out a fearsome roar and pawed again at the spear-head. Out of the corner of her eye, Astrid sensed movement in the crowd. Sparing the briefest glance, she saw people fleeing the stands. Her gaze narrowed on scurrying movement.

Were those . . . mountain lions?

Maera lifted her snout, turned toward the stands now. Astrid's gaze narrowed on dark figures dotting the benches as Thyrlings scampered away. Their raucous cries had turned to terrified screams.

Smaller bears and other previously caged animals rushed through the benches now. Amongst them were thin coyotes, boars, and smaller predators, like lynx and wolverines. They charged across the benches, frightening Thyrlings away.

Astrid fought off a smile.

Ewan, she thought.

It had to be. He'd set all the other caged animals free. A sign of hope? A distraction? Whatever it was, Astrid *felt* hope. She wasn't alone—and perhaps that is all he wanted her to know.

But Ewan would be no good to her here.

Gorm snarled again, his small dark eyes full of hate. He took a staggering step forward, holding his injured leg off the ground. The massive animal stumbled to the side with a painful growl.

Astrid risked another glance at the king. Oblivious to the animals running wild through the crowd, he glared at Astrid.

"Get up!" she thought he shrieked. "*Kill her*!"

Rising, the bear released another moan. Pity for him welled up inside her, enslaved as he was to Oskar's will. New strength seemed to flood Gorm right then, and all thoughts of pity vanished.

On three legs and injured, Gorm still moved fast as ever across the short distance. In a blink, he was almost upon her. Astrid swung her sword at his raking claws. He landed a glancing blow on her shoulder, tearing the sword from her grip. Maera leaped at Gorm's forearm, her claws digging and teeth tearing into his injured shoulder.

Gorm slammed his good paw into Maera. She crumpled with a yelp. Astrid dove forward, heedless of the danger to herself. A great weight struck her, followed by piercing pain in her back. She rolled across the sand, gasping for air through the agony.

When the stars faded from her eyes, she saw Gorm, stomping toward her on shaking legs. Astrid reached for her knife, but it was gone. The bear closed in.

Time slowed.

Out of the corner of her eye, Astrid saw Maera shake herself and charge.

She's got spirit, came the weak thought.

Maera grabbed Gorm's throat and gave him all her weight. Though small, the unexpected jerk to his injured side made the bear stumble. Astrid struggled to stand, but the pain in her back flared. She cast around for her sword and spotted it a few paces away, the metal glimmering in the sand.

The stands lay almost empty now, but shouts and screams still filled the air. Desperate, with sand in her mouth and eyelashes, Astrid half crawled toward the sword. Another, sharper yelp came from Maera behind her, but Astrid had no time to look. Her hand stretched out for her sword, hoping Maera hadn't sacrificed herself.

Not close enough.

With a heave, she shoved herself closer. Her back spasmed, but she shouted through it. Sand met her fingertips, ground into her bloody back. She combed through the grains with her fingers again, grunting through the pain.

Sand.

Sand.

Metal.

A blast of rancid air hit the back of her neck as her fingers closed around her mother's snarling wolf hilt.

Astrid flipped onto her back and shoved the sword up.

Gorm's mouth, opened wide to crush her head, absorbed the sword. Tears in her eyes, Astrid shouted and shoved harder. The Nistlefolk steel grated through bone, thrusting into his brain. Her back had turned to fire. Her body a mass of pain.

Blood leaked to the sand beneath her as Gorm sagged forward, his injured shoulder slanting toward Astrid. She reached up to shove him off and felt the edge of the spear shaft nick her thumb. The world became a whirlwind of pain, blood, and bear.

Gorm swayed again.

"Up!" Oskar bellowed in the distance. "Up, you beast!"

Gorm's matted, stinking fur pressed down on Astrid, threatening to smother her. Something hot and sticky ran down her arm. Gorm's labored breaths caressed her wrist, her fingers. She blinked, wide eyed, into his dark black gaze. They stared at each other.

"I'm sorry for what he did to you. I'm sorry for the pain I caused you. Go to your freedom again."

Gorm's eyelids weakened. Astrid shoved the sword farther with a final shriek, and the Nistlefolk steel snapped in half from the force.

The bear fell.

Astrid rolled to the left as he crashed to the right, landing with a heavy *thud* into the sand. She pushed an arm into her face to block the granules from her eyes, then hesitated. A glance confirmed it.

Gorm lay dead.

The world turned around her. Astrid felt swamped by sickness. Although she lay on her back, the world tilted. A tongue licked her face, accompanied by a concerned whine. Astrid reached up, arm bloodied. Maera nudged her palm.

"Good girl," Astrid murmured, voice thick with tears. Her hand had turned numb. It tingled, prickling all the way to her arm.

Why?

Pink foam bubbled from Gorm's mouth around the hilt of her sword. His heavy chest had stilled forever.

Away from the spinning sky, Astrid looked up to King Oskar. He'd collapsed, hanging on the edge of the pavilion. He appeared pale, sickly, a shade from death. His mouth hung open as he sucked in great gasps of air. Oskar raised a shaking hand toward her, then disappeared as he collapsed.

The jaegars rushed toward him.

Rosamund looked at Astrid.

Astrid turned away and stared up at the blue spring sky. So light. So warm. Where was Ewan? Would he find her? A flutter of feathers appeared overhead, then hurried away. Had she imagined Maury? Wished him there? Maera rested her chin on Astrid's chest and whined.

Everything disappeared.

THIRTY-ONE

Astrid moved in and out of foggy dreams.

Maera whining at her side, licking her arm. Heat on her back—like open fire. Uzell appearing. Something foul and thick in her mouth. More pain, a gut-twisting stomach sensation, like tumbling head-first down a hill. Navi tending to her again, brow furrowed as he leaned over her, waving his hands and muttering in a strange tongue.

And then nothing.

What felt like eternities later, Astrid's eyes fluttered open.

Darkness met her. She blinked to clear it, but it remained. A blurry something lay overhead. The inside of the barn? No, the stable. At her back, she thought she felt something soft.

Hay, perhaps?

In the distance came the gentle rasp of breath. Maera? The lack of tension in their connection made Astrid think that she must be alive, at least. She opened her fingers, flexing them. The stiffness in her joints, her easy breath, reassured her.

Alive.

Astrid swallowed, her throat as dry as sand. Snatches of her fight with Gorm replayed back through her mind. The hazy bits of consciousness that followed. Had she imagined all of it? Uzell standing over her with a foul liquid. The priest had placed a hand on her shoulder, the ice of his palm a shock. He'd muttered strangled, guttural words.

Then, he was gone and her pain with him.

She licked her lips, remnants of the bitter flavor acting as a vague reminder of the strange dreams.

No, not dreams.

Astrid continued to lie unmoving before she realized she felt better. The whirling sensation had ebbed. She coughed and her back protested, but the pain had dulled.

Next to her, Maera stirred awake.

Through the vague shadows, Maera blinked her yellowed eyes at Astrid, then tucked her nose under Astrid's hand.

"Hey. You saved my life."

Maera straightened, ears alert.

"You okay?"

Maera ducked her face back into Astrid's side. A low whimper replied. Through their connection, Astrid thought she felt relief. Still some fear. Maera was upset about the stable, but relieved it wasn't a cage.

Astrid ran her hand across Maera's fur. Blood matted parts of it, making it sticky. Astrid didn't care, she kept stroking her anyway. For better or worse, Maera didn't seem on death's door. Only time would tell what kind of recovery they'd both need, however.

Once the motion soothed both of them, Astrid pushed to a sitting position. The world only tilted a little. Upright, she had a better grip on her surroundings.

She moved her arms, then knees. Nothing felt broken, but the skin on her back cracked slightly as she moved. Claw marks from Gorm trickled blood down her back and over her hip. A dark purple welt with angry black lines marked the spot on her thumb where she'd nicked it on the spearhead.

Rosamund's words of caution before the fight returned to Astrid.

Mind the blade.

Astrid's sluggish thoughts struggled to catch up. *Mind the blade.* Had Rosamund poisoned it? Footsteps approached the entry door to this part of the stable. Murmured voices next. Astrid strained to hear the sound.

The clank of a key turning followed.

"Easy," she whispered when Maera's hackles rose.

Slowly, Astrid got her feet underneath her. With one hand braced on the wall of the stall, she rose. Her legs had more strength than she'd expected. A bit wobbly from stiffness, but not deathly weak. She could support her own weight for now

A second later, a cloaked figure entered through the doorway. Astrid blinked. Based on the slender build, it wasn't Ewan, Lara, Liss or Auley. The hood lifted away and sharp green eyes stared out at her.

Rosamund.

"Come with me, Astrid. I suggest you hurry. While you have the official pardon of Thyrden behind you thanks to my father's oath, you are by no means safe in Drakby. I suggest you leave well before the sun rises."

"You're here to save me?"

Rosamund said nothing. Astrid winced and held more tightly to the wall. "How do I know you're not capturing me to experiment on us?"

"I already have saved you," Rosamund said. "Twice. Come. My father swore an oath in front of a witness. Though he may tempt Tyraz, I will not. You earned your freedom."

Rosamund led her past the empty stalls and to the left, where the stable led back into further empty chambers. Storage, mostly. Old crates, unused tools. At the back of the stable was a small door large enough for Maera to easily slip through.

The structures on either side indicated it may have been a chicken coop at one time.

Rosamund pushed through the door and out the other side. Astrid gingerly followed, with Maera coming up behind her. Once the cool wind whispered across her cheeks, Astrid closed her eyes in relief.

Freedom.

Rosamund lifted a bag over her shoulder, then produced what remained of Astrid's sword, knife, and belt. Astrid accepted them without taking her eyes off her.

Maera growled.

"Why are you doing this?" Astrid asked as she buckled her belt and slid half her Mother's sword inside. Her knife followed next.

Rosamund sighed. "You were a fool to challenge Gorm, Astrid, and I would have gladly harmed you myself because my frustration had been so great, but . . . it worked out to my advantage in the end."

"You poisoned the spear head, didn't you?"

Rosamund nodded once, pale and lovely in the moonlight. Her hair gleamed like strands of silver and yellow, braided together on her shoulder and loose, untied by ribbons. The princess appeared weary, but resolute.

"Then Uzell gave me an antidote," Astrid said. "It wasn't a dream."

"Would have been a nightmare, if he was in it," Rosamund quipped, but gave no smile. Astrid pulled in a deep breath.

Shine, but the princess *had* saved her.

Twice.

"Why bother saving me?"

"The wraith bear turned my father into a rabid animal. Daily, he grew worse. Less . . . in control. Like any beast, both of them had to be put down," Rosamund said coldly. "I could not be the person to do that."

"So this was all a set up? You used me to kill the king?"

"No. We gave you the opportunity to bond with a wolf and hoped to learn exactly how to harness magic and create that bond ourselves. In the meantime, you proved to be something of a troublemaker, and in the end, it worked to our advantage. As Uzell and I suspected, my father had given too much of himself over to that cursed bear. He drew his last breath not long after Gorm died. You speak with the Queen of Thyrden."

Shock filled Astrid.

How could this chilly, rote person be the same woman who'd spoken for her, treated her like a friend, even saved her life? How many facets of Rosamund existed? This revelation felt like a greater betrayal than when Astrid had been captured in the forest.

"I did what had to be done," Rosamund replied, her words firm and certain. "He would have driven Thyrden to ruins. I have spent years enduring his disrespect and abuse only to have him marry me off for his own benefit. That would have given the throne to one of my younger brothers. I was not about to let that happen."

Rosamund drew her shoulders back. "Be warned, Astrid. I have already told the jaegars that you were sent to assassinate my father and that your dark Skolvarg magic struck him down through Gorm. Those fools will believe anything in these uncertain times. However, my father's oath has been fulfilled. I'm allowing you to go free out of respect for the agreement he made. After this, you are on your own."

"Why?" Astrid asked, her voice a dark rasp. "I thought you wanted peace with the Skolvarg?"

"What I wanted was to be queen," Rosamund said. "I merely took a different path than I first intended to make it so. Kerys is a powerful ally and Thyrden's alliance with them will bring us even greater wealth and power. The peace treaty was only ever a delay, though I admit I had thought it would be a year or two before I had to break it."

"You'll do all this for wealth and power? Haven't your people taken enough?"

"If the Skolvarg are strong enough to protect their lands, then you shall keep them," Rosamund said. "Perhaps I will be merciful and leave your people the northern Wolfmoors once we have established a route and defenses through the south moors into Ochland."

Astrid's hand strayed to her sword. She should kill Rosamund—or at least try—but she couldn't draw her weapon. Livid tears filled her eyes, but Astrid blinked them back. The part of her that had, stupidly, seen Rosamund as a friend hoped this had all been a misunderstanding. That Rosamund was someone she could trust. Astrid had been the soft-hearted fool all along.

Now, her people would go back to war.

"For your part in this, I give you your life," Rosamund said. "Your bard friends are waiting for you in the forest, unless they thought it a trap and fled when Uzell sent word. Consider our debts paid and oaths fulfilled to one another."

"What about your studies of me and Maera? I have a hard time believing you'll just give that up."

"I must for bigger matters now."

Rosamund's steady expression gave nothing away, but Astrid didn't believe it for a minute. Uzell would try again, if he could. Maybe with someone else.

Astrid studied Rosamund for a long moment, but didn't know what to say. She whistled and Maera appeared at her side. One last lingering glance at Rosamund forced Astrid to nod once.

An unsteady acknowledgment.

"For honoring your father's vow, thank you."

She turned to go, but Rosamund's melodic voice stopped her. "One last thing, Astrid."

Astrid paused, foot halfway off the ground. Maera had started to trot ahead, but stopped and looked back.

"After this night," Rosamund continued, "consider us enemies. Should our paths cross again, I will not be so merciful."

"And the same to you," Astrid whispered, then disappeared into the deepening darkness.

"Well that's a sight for sore eyes," Auley breathed. "Muses love you, lass. I can't believe you survived."

Astrid slowed, a few steps away from the bards. She'd only walked for fifteen minutes outside Drakby as she headed south. The swollen river still poured water not far away, but no one would expect her to head south to cross the Auroran this time of year. It would add days to the trip while they found a safe place to cross, but would be their only guarantee for safety.

Maera settled at Astrid's side, her tongue lolling over her teeth.

"Hello," Astrid said.

"You're alive!" Liss cried.

Astrid's fatigue felt suddenly heavy, overwhelming. The farther she paced herself from Drakby, the more her body trembled. Hearing the kindness in Auley's voice kept her from collapsing.

Darkness bathed most of their figures, except the moonlight that showed their faces. The four of them stood in a semicircle in the trees, in a spot illuminated by the rising moon. The emotion lodged deep in Astrid's chest began to rise. No matter how hard she tried to press it back, it wouldn't go.

The image of Ewan's relieved, haggard expression pushed her over the edge.

"My friends," she whispered, her voice thick.

Ewan reached out as Astrid stumbled. He caught her arms, holding her upright. She tried to apologize, but the words stopped in her throat. The emotion lodged there was too great to speak around.

"We've got you, Astrid," he whispered.

Auley's hand came on her shoulder.

Liss on her forearm.

Lara's on her other arm.

Maeara tucked herself into the middle of them, pressed against Astrid. The rush of anxiety Astrid had felt ebbed the moment Maera touched her. She ducked her head, safe at last, and cried.

Several minutes passed before the current of emotion ebbed. Astrid wiped her cheeks with trembling hands.

"I'm sorry. I—"

"No." Ewan put a hand under her jaw. "No apologies. We saw the whole fight with Gorm, Astrid. It was . . . there are no words for what you went through. I'm sorry we couldn't help you. There was no way—"

"No, it was my fight."

"You make the Skolvarg proud, Astrid," Auley whispered. "Wolf or not, we'll make sure they know it."

Astrid gave a small smile.

"We've been waiting in fear for your life," Liss whispered. "We're so glad you're all right."

Lara stepped forward, a thin-stemmed flower between her fingers. The leaves were too small to distinguish—it was little more than an early bud—but it warmed Astrid's heart all the way through. Her soulful eyes seemed to say everything when Lara pressed it into Astrid's palm.

"Thank you."

"How are you?" Ewan asked, his hand a heavy, comforting touch on her shoulder. "Your back. I saw Gorm . . . it looked pretty painful when he slashed you."

"It will be fine. It's already on the way to healing, I think. We need to cover ground tonight. Rosamund . . . I have a lot to tell you about what I found out. But we need to move as we do it."

Auley offered a bag, "First, food." He lifted a second one. "For the wolf."

Astrid's heart melted.

"Thank you, Auley. For both. We'll gladly eat and then, we move. I will tell you everything on the way."

Epilogue

The bards and Astrid stood atop a sweeping hill that overlooked a grass-filled valley. A meandering creek divided it in half, cleaving the dancing green meadow in two.

A fresh breeze drifted through the warm summer day, bringing a hint of blossoms with it. Skolvarg yurts populated the valley below, and the sound of children laughing carried up the hill. Across the valley, a pair of Ulfsarks spotted their small group.

Maera trotted at Astrid's side, content from a fresh-caught fish out of the stream. Her legs moved quickly to keep up with Vald, the slender, all-white Amarok wolf that strolled just out of sight behind them.

Vald's Ulfsar, Tine, sat on top of Vald. Despite their differences in size, Maera had taken to the Amarok immediately, and daily drew greater confidence from the grace of the Amarok.

A week after leaving Drakby, the traveling bards, Astrid, and Maera had crossed the Auroran. Another grueling week passed of wandering in the Wolfmoors before they found

Tine's tribe. With only two horses left, most of them were forced to walk, which slowed their progress.

Fortunately, no Thyrlings followed.

Tine hosted them for a week of safe respite, sleeping, and familiar healing elixirs. The safety gave all of them a chance to recover their health. Fortunately, Astrid's instincts on *where* Tine's tribe would be located in the spring to summer transition had been correct.

When they prepared to leave, Tine had volunteered to help them locate Odda's tribe. Odda would keep them to the southeast area of the Wolfmoors in the summer, but Vald's keen nose made it easier to hunt and find the Skolvarg.

Even so, a fortnight had passed since they'd left Tine's tribe.

"You will stay for a few days to rest and recover, won't you?" Astrid asked Tine. Vald panted and looked straight ahead, giant nose in the air.

"No," Tine said, "we'll stay the night. I'd like to see Odda and discuss a few things, but then leave in the morning. If the Thyrlings are preparing for war, we will be among the first in their path."

"Thank you," Astrid said again.

Tine smiled and nodded, her dark red hair glimmering.

Up on the hill, the Ulfsark Astrid knew so well—had once deeply envied—turned their Amarok wolves toward them. A huge smile broke across Astrid's face when she recognized one of the giant wolves by his red coat. Syrhan, with Freydis on his back.

She lifted a hand.

"Freydis!" Astrid called, waving. "Freydis!"

Syrhan started toward them. Astrid ran down the hill, her back healed. Maera pranced at her side, eager to follow. Normal-sized wolves usually avoided the Amarok in the wild, but Maera showed no restraint for the approaching wolves.

Perhaps Astrid's ease, or her lightness of heart, taught the wolf not to fear.

Freydis's shout of recognition brought a laugh out of Astrid as she ran. Still several paces away, Freydis leaped from Syrhan's back and raced toward her. She bowled into Astrid, knocking them both in the grass.

"It is you!" Freydis cried.

Astrid groaned and shoved Freydis off her. The wounds caused by Gorm's claws—by some miracle, probably Uzell's concoctions and Navi's powers—hadn't become infected, but they were occasionally tender.

Maera growled, placing herself between Freydis and Astrid in the grass. Astrid reached up, laughing.

"It's okay, Maera," Astrid murmured, a hand on her neck. "Freydis is our friend."

Freydis popped out of the grass and brightened, noticing the wolf for the first time. Her eyebrows rose as she studied Maera, then Astrid. "Something in you is . . . different. Seems like you've got some tales to tell?"

"So many. How is Rolf?"

"Like a man half his age he's so excited to see you." Freydis nodded to Tine, then waved. Tine returned the greeting from farther back. "Other Ulfsarks came ahead of you with news and wild stories of bears and betrayals. We've been waiting for you to come home and tell us the truth of it. Is it true the Thyrlings are going to break their oath of peace?"

Astrid nodded, sober now. "Yes."

"But—"

Astrid put a hand on Freydis' arm. "I'll tell you everything I know, I promise. But first, my uncle. I've missed him so much."

By the time they reached the camp, the entire tribe waited to greet them, with Rolf and Odda in the front. When she saw her uncle, Astrid broke away from Freydis with a cry and ran to meet him.

They met in a fierce embrace. Rolf let out a sob as he pulled her into her arms, holding her so tight she thought the wounds in her back had reopened. She didn't care. She buried her face in his shoulder, his familiar smell of sage a welcome sign she was home at last.

"My niece," Rolf said, voice cracking. "My daughter. I did not know if I would see you again."

When Astrid pulled back, Maera, who stood a few steps away, studied all the new people. She whined and licked her lips. Through their bond, Astrid tried to soothe her, but Maera appeared too agitated to notice.

The crowd of Skolvarg parted, allowing a wide body to step through. Atka pushed his way through the crowd, nose ahead of him. He padded over to Astrid, sniffed, then licked her ear. His not-so-gentle nudge on her shoulder nearly sent her to the ground. She laughed, touching his muzzle.

"Good to see you again, Atka."

Atka peered past her, to Maera. Maera regarded him, mouth open. The whine had exited her voice. As if commanded, Maera stood, padding closer to Atka. Breathless, Astrid watched the two wolves approach each other. After what felt like a short eternity, a burst of emotion flowed to Astrid from their connection. Maera touched noses with Atka, then bowed down in submission to the bigger wolf. Her ears laid back. She pressed her belly to the ground and rolled.

Atka sniffed Maera, then glanced at Astrid. After a light huff, he turned and strode away.

"It appears that Atka has chosen your wolf to be part of the pack," Odda said with a warm smile. She pulled Astrid into her arms far more gently than Rolf and embraced her. Astrid soaked up the feeling of security.

"The Wolf Song?" Odda asked with a nod to Maera.

"Maybe? There's much to tell."

"Most unusual," Odda replied, then laughed. "But I should have expected nothing less from you, Astrid. You are not the same girl who left us a season ago." She held Astrid at arms length. "And I thought I told you not to start a war?"

Odda's gaze moved past Astrid, to Tine and the bards, who stood a few paces away from the tribe now.

"My thanks to you, bard, for returning Astrid to us," Odda called. "You are welcome among my tribe as long as you wish."

"We are grateful, mighty chieftain, but Astrid doesn't need much looking after. Although that you already know, I think." Ewan winked at Astrid. "We have a few tales we'd like to tell over the fire tonight. Tales of a mighty Skolvarg girl that defeated the king of the Thyrlings and the biggest bear in all of Vigard . . . but then we'll be on our way in the morning."

"Our fire is happy to have you." Odda turned to the entire tribe and called, "Our Astrid is home!"

A resounding cry broke through the Wolfmoors, rippling in all directions.

Astrid crouched in the tall grass and crept forward on all fours.

She sensed Maera off to her right, but the golden stalks swaying in the late summer breeze hid her from sight. Together, they crawled toward Atka on top of the hill, facing away from them.

A rustle to her right told her that Maera had attacked. Springing to her feet, Astrid sprinted up the hill, wooden staff in hand. In a single bound, Atka jumped right over Maera and landed in front of Astrid with a snarl.

Astrid swung the wooden stave, but Atka caught the blow on his shoulder, and knocked her over. Quick as summer lightning, Atka whirled just as Maera leaped for his back.

Astrid stood and watched as the two wolves grappled until, at last, Atka pinned Maera to the ground. When he released her, Maera gave a playful bark and nipped at Atka's mouth. Atka growled in warning, then sat down on all fours. Maera stopped tumbling around him and settled in the grass, tongue lolling to the side in happy pants.

Astrid laughed.

In the past few months, Atka had found new life with Maera. The young wolf had nearly doubled in size since Astrid had first seen her. Maera appeared to be the average size of any other adult gray wolf, now. Far too small to ride but Astrid didn't care.

She had her wolf.

Astrid climbed the top of the hill where she'd left their supplies for the day. She took a long drink from her water skin then opened another, which she poured in Atka and Maera's mouths. Both wolves lapped up the water. The last golden days of summer lingered on the horizon, but the weather remained hot, dry and dusty.

While Atka and Maera wandered down the ridge, Astrid remained behind. She gazed out over the vast expanse of the Wolfmoors.

Where was Ewan now?

Odda had sent them east with an Ulfsark escort to meet with the Matrons on the edge of the Wolfwood. Odda believed the Matrons would be interested in an alliance with the Ochlands.

"After all, you are the only neighbors we have left that have not declared war on us," Odda muttered with a grim smile.

The bards' escort had returned only a few days before, with news that the Matrons would discuss an alliance with the Ochlands during the coming winter, when all the Skolvarg tribes gathered together beneath the Wolfwood.

In the meantime, Ewan and the bards were allowed to pass through the Wolfwood, a shorter and safer journey home than if they'd gone through the Stallofells.

As Rosamund had promised, the Thyrlings had already crossed the Auroran. They'd begun to build a series of defenses called hill forts that stretched out from the river. In their previous wars, the Thyrlings relied on large camps that were often the target of Skolvarg raiders.

She couldn't explain it, but Astrid felt a strangeness in the air as autumn approached. A sense, perhaps, or an almost-animal instinct stirred across the north. A feeling that life would never be the same again.

"Brooding isn't a good look on you, my dear."

Astrid reached for her knife, then stopped. One glance to her right confirmed her suspicion. Margu sat beside her, blue robes fluttering in the sunlight. She flashed a wolf-like smile.

"I didn't mean to startle you," Margu said. "Tell me, what is there to worry about? You've got everything a Skolvarg heart might desire. A wolf and a war. I should think you were the happiest woman in the Wolfmoors!"

Astrid glanced at her from the corner of her eye, but said nothing for several moments. At last, she decided she had to know.

"Uzell told me it was his power that bound Maera and me together. Is. . . is that true?"

"That isn't an easy question to answer," Margu said. "I did not know of Uzell before you went Drakby. His presence was shrouded from me which is concerning in and of itself. I confess I *nudged* a few things here and there, hoping you and Maera would find one another. Your fylga would have awakened on its own, though I did not expect it to be so powerful."

Astrid frowned. "You didn't answer the question."

"Well, I'm not *all-knowing*," Margu said with what might have been the trace of a pout. "What I can tell you is this: the bond you have with Maera couldn't exist without both of you *wanting* it to. You may not realize this yet, but you've got other strengths you've only begun to use."

A weight lifted from Astrid that she didn't know she'd been carrying. She didn't know if she could trust Margu about everything, but the Greater Spirit's assurance about this just felt right.

The Spirit of Winter looked at Maera, who was rolling in the dry grass nearby. "Both of you have some growing still to do, in more ways than one. You're a work-in-progress, but we've made a good start."

"Am I an experiment for you, too?"

"Don't be flippant, Astrid, dear. I don't just appear to anyone. I've already told you—I've got *plans* for you."

Astrid didn't like the sound of that.

Margu gazed out over the hills of the Wolfmoors. "Deeds turn to song, song turns to legend and one day, legends are forgotten. Such is fate."

"Sounds ominous," Astrid said, only half-joking,

The Greater Spirit laughed. Echoes of throaty ravens mixed with the sound. A shiver sprinted down Astrid's back. Nothing funny about that.

"Don't concern yourself, Astrid. You'll know my plans when you're ready. Until then, it's a surprise. That's half the fun!"

In a blink, Margu was gone. Astrid sighed and turned back to the horizon. Next summer wouldn't be so calm.

She could already feel the building storm.

NOTE FROM THE AUTHORS

Hey there!

Thanks for reading *Spring for Spears*. Astrid is a work-in-progress that we've been muddling through together for years. I'm so excited to bring it to you now.

More epic medieval-esque fights, wild magic from the stars, and Skolvarg-loving-wolves the size of bears coming your way.

Stick around.

The adventure is pretty sweet around here.

—Katie Cross

Astrid's story has been a long time coming.

It started out as an idea I was going to write alone and grew into something greater, thanks to Katie.

Years later, here we are and the epic journey is only beginning. It's a testament to how much we loved and believed in this book that it survived multiple delays, a global pandemic, and major life events from both of us to get to you.

We think this is a special story and hope you did too.

—Derek Alan Siddoway

Also by Katie Cross

All books are available in ebook, paperback, and audiobook at www. katiecrossbooks.com and on all online ebook, audiobook, and paperback retailers.

The Dragonmaster Trilogy

FLAME

Chronicles of the Dragonmasters (short story collection)

FLIGHT

The Ronan Scrolls (novella)

FREEDOM

The Dragonmaster Trilogy Collection

The Sisterwitches Series

The Sisterwitches Book 1

The Sisterwitches Book 2

The Network Series

Mildred's Resistance (prequel)

Miss Mabel's School for Girls

Alkarra Awakening

The High Priest's Daughter

War of the Networks

The Network Series Complete Collection

The Isadora Interviews (novella)

Short Stories from Miss Mabel's

Short Stories from the Network Series

Hazel (short story)

Alkarra (short story collection)

The Network Saga Suggested Reading Order

The Historical Collection

The High Priestess

The Swordmaker

The Advocate

The Reader Request Series

The Gods

The Plummet

The North

The Wander

The Return

Viveet Forged

Also by Derek Alan Siddoway

All books are available in ebook, paperback, and audiobook at https://store.derekalansiddoway.com/.

Gryphon Riders Trilogy

Windsworn (Gryphon Riders Book 1)

Windswept (Gryphon Riders Book 2)

Windbreak (Gryphon Riders Book 3)

Djinn Tamer

Djinn Tamer: Starter (Bronze League Book 1)

Djinn Tamer: Rivals (Bronze League Book 2)

Djinn Tamer: Evolution (Bronze League Book 3)

MythRune Online

God Mode (MythRune Online Book 1)

Glitch King (MythRune Online Book 2)

Mana Beasts

Beast Mage (Mana Beasts Book 1)

Storm Totem (Mana Beasts Book 2)

ABOUT KATIE CROSS

Katie Cross is ALL ABOUT writing epic magic and wild places. Creating new fantasy worlds is her jam.

When she's not hiking or chasing her two littles through the Montana mountains, you can find her curled up reading a book or arguing with her husband over the best kind of sushi.

Visit her at www.katiecrossbooks.com for free short stories, extra savings on all her books (and some you can't buy on the retailers), and so much more.

ABOUT DEREK ALAN SIDDOWAY

DEREK ALAN SIDDOWAY writes fast-paced fantasy with heart. Most of his tales feature mythical critters of some variety. As a journeyman storyteller, he has over a dozen books under his belt, including the internationally bestselling *Gryphon Riders Trilogy*, *Djinn Tamer*, and *Mana Beasts*. Derek spends his free time wandering through the tall grass, working on a small, fourth-generation farm, adventuring with his wife, and celebrating small victories. He's also a loyal but often disappointed fan of the University of Utah Utes and Minnesota Vikings.